In a remote corner of Zangaro, a small republic in Africa, lies Crystal Mountain.

At certain times of day the mountain emits a strange glow.

Only Sir James Manson knows why.

The mountain contains ten billion dollars worth of the world's most valuable mineral, platinum.

Now, the only question is, how to get hold of it.

Sir James knows how.

Unleash . . .

THE DOGS OF WAR

You are crouching in the darkness of an African night, cradling a Schmeisser machine pistol in your arms, grenades and bazooka components heavy on your back, sweaty fingers gripping a good luck charm.

The starlight flare bursts overhead—and it's time, time to unleash . . .

THE DOGS OF WAR

Frederick Forsyth's third great novel is set in the savage world of mercenary soldiers, the dogs of war, the twentieth century's last free men.

Here is all the famous authenticity that has gripped millions of readers all over the world, making them ask:

IS THIS REALLY A NOVEL, OR A BRILLIANTLY REAL AND EXCITING RECREATION OF FACT?

The Dogs of War

Frederick Forsyth

THE DOGS OF WAR
A Bantam Book / published by arrangement with
The Viking Press, Inc.

PRINTING HISTORY
Viking edition published July 1974
2nd printing ...... July 1974
Literary Guild edition published July 1974
2nd printing .... October 1974
PLAYBOY *Book Club edition published November 1974*
A condensation appeared in READER'S DIGEST *October 1974*
Bantam edition / August 1975

Acknowledgment is made to St. Martin's Press, Inc. for the
quotation from Poems *by Thomas Hardy. Reprinted by*
permission of St. Martin's Press, Inc., and
Macmillan & Co., Ltd.

For Giorgio, and Christian and Schlee,
And Big Marc and Black Johnny,
And the others in the unmarked graves.
At least we tried.

Cry "Havoc!" and let slip the dogs of war.
—William Shakespeare, *Julius Caesar*

That . . . be not told of my death,
Or made to grieve on account of me,
And that I be not buried in consecrated ground,
And that no sexton be asked to toll the bell,
And that nobody is wished to see my dead body,
And that no mourners walk behind me at my funeral,
And that no flowers be planted on my grave,
And that no man remember me,
To this I put my name.
—Thomas Hardy

Contents

PART ONE

The Crystal Mountain

1

There were no stars that night on the bush airstrip, nor any moon; just the West African darkness wrapping round the scattered groups like warm, wet velvet. The cloud cover was lying hardly off the tops of the iroko trees, and the waiting men prayed it would stay a while longer to shield them from the bombers.

At the end of the runway the battered old DC-4, which had just slipped in for a landing by runway lights that stayed alight for just the last fifteen seconds of final approach, turned and coughed its way blindly toward the palm-thatch huts.

Between two of them, five white men sat crouched in a Land Rover and stared toward the incoming aircraft. They said nothing, but the same thought was in each man's mind. If they did not get out of the battered and crumbling enclave before the forces of the central government overran the last few square miles, they would not get out alive. Each man had a price on his head and intended to see that no man collected it. They were the last of the mercenaries who had fought on contract for the side that had lost. Now it was time to go. So they watched the incoming and un-expected cargo plane with silent attention.

A Federal MIG-17 night fighter, probably flown by one of the six East German pilots sent down over the

3

past three months to replace the Egyptians, who had a horror of flying at night, moaned across the sky to the west. It was out of sight above the cloud layers.

The pilot of the taxiing DC-4, unable to hear the scream of the jet above him, flicked on his own lights to see where he was going, and from the darkness a voice cried uselessly, "Kill de lights!" When the pilot had got his bearings, he turned them off anyway, and the fighter above was miles away. To the south there was a rumble of artillery where the front had finally crumbled as men who had had neither food nor bullets for two months threw down their guns and headed for the protecting bush forest.

The pilot of the DC-4 brought his plane to a halt twenty yards from the Superconstellation already parked on the apron, killed the engines, and climbed down to the concrete. An African ran over to him and there was a muttered conversation. The two men walked through the dark toward one of the larger groups of men, a blob of black against the darkness of the palm forest. The group parted as the two from the tarmac approached, until the white man who had flown in the DC-4 was face to face with the one who stood in the center. The white man had never seen him before, but he knew of him, and, even in the darkness dimly illumined by a few cigarettes, he could recognize the man he had come to see.

The pilot wore no cap, so instead of saluting he inclined his head slightly. He had never done that before, not to a black, and could not have explained why he did it.

"My name is Captain Van Cleef," he said in English accented in the Afrikaner manner.

The African nodded his acknowledgment, his bushy black beard brushing the front of his striped camouflage uniform as he did so.

"It's a hazardous night for flying, Captain Van Cleef," he remarked dryly, "and a little late for more supplies."

His voice was deep and slow, the accent more like

that of an English public-school man, which he was, than like an African. Van Cleef felt uncomfortable and again, as a hundred times during his run through the cloudbanks from the coast, asked himself why he had come.

"I didn't bring any supplies, sir. There weren't any more to bring."

Another precedent set. He had sworn he would not call the man "sir." Not a kaffir. It had just slipped out. But they were right, the other mercenary pilots in the hotel bar in Libreville, the ones who had met him. This one was different.

"Then why have you come?" asked the general softly. "The children perhaps? There are a number here the nuns would like to fly out to safety, but no more Caritas planes will come in tonight."

Van Cleef shook his head, then realized no one could see the gesture. He was embarrassed, and thankful that the darkness hid it. Around him the bodyguards clutched their submachine carbines and stared at him.

"No. I came to collect you. If you want to come, that is."

There was a long silence. He could feel the African staring at him through the gloom, occasionally caught a flash of eye-white as one of the attendants raised his cigarette.

"I see. Did your government instruct you to come in here tonight?"

"No," said Van Cleef. "It was my idea."

There was another long pause. The bearded head was nodding slowly in what could have been comprehension or bewilderment.

"I am very grateful," said the voice. "It must have been quite a trip. Actually I have my own transport. The Constellation. Which I hope will be able to take me away to exile."

Van Cleef felt relieved. He had no idea what the political repercussions would have been if he had flown back to Libreville with the general.

"I'll wait till you're off the ground and gone," he said and nodded again. He felt like holding out his hand to shake, but did not know whether he ought. If he had but known it, the African general was in the same quandary. So he turned and walked back to his aircraft.

There was silence for a while in the group of black men after he had left.

"Why does a South African, and an Afrikaner, do a thing like that, General?" one of them asked.

There was a flash of teeth as the general smiled briefly. "I don't think we shall ever understand that," he said.

A match spluttered as another cigarette was lit, the glow setting for a parting instant into sharp relief the faces of the men in the group. At the center was the general, taller than all but two of the guards, heavily built with burly chest and shoulders, distinguishable from others at several hundred yards by the bushy black beard that half the world had come to recognize.

In defeat, on the threshold of an exile he knew would be lonely and humiliating, he still commanded. Surrounded by his aides and several ministers, he was as always slightly aloof, withdrawn. To be alone is one of the prices of leadership; with him it was also a state of reflex.

For two and a half years, sometimes by sheer force of personality when there was nothing else to employ, he had kept his millions of people together and fighting against the central Federal Government. All the experts had told the world they would have to collapse in a few weeks, two months at most. The odds were insuperable against them. Somehow they had kept fighting, surrounded, besieged, starving but defiant.

His enemies had refuted his leadership of his people, but few who had been there had any doubts. Even in defeat, as his car passed through the last village before the airstrip, the villagers had lined the mud road to chant their loyalty. Hours earlier, at the last meeting of the cabinet, the vote had asked him to leave.

There would be reprisals in defeat, the spokesman for the caucus said, but a hundred times worse if he remained. So he was leaving, the man the Federal Government wanted dead by sunrise.

By his side stood one of his confidants, one of those whose loyalty had not been changed. A small, graying professor, he was called Dr. Okoye. He had decided to remain behind, to hide in the bush until he could return quietly to his home when the first wave of reprisals had ended. The two men had agreed to wait six months before making the first steps to contact each other.

Farther up the apron, the five mercenaries sat and watched the dim figure of the pilot return to his plane. The leader sat beside the African driver, and all five were smoking steadily.

"It must be the South African plane," said the leader and turned to one of the four other whites crouched in the Land Rover behind him. "Janni, go and ask the skipper if he'll make room for us."

A tall, rawboned, angular man climbed out of the rear of the vehicle. Like the others, he was dressed from head to foot in predominantly green jungle camouflage uniform, slashed with streaks of brown. He wore green canvas jackboots on his feet, the trousers tucked into them. From his belt hung a water bottle and a Bowie knife, three empty pouches for magazines for the FAL carbine over his shoulder. As he came round to the front of the Land Rover the leader called him again.

"Leave the FAL," he said, stretching out an arm to take the carbine, "and, Janni, make it good, huh? Because if we don't get out of here in that crate, we could get chopped up in a few days."

The man called Janni nodded, adjusted the beret on his head, and ambled toward the DC-4. Captain Van Cleef did not hear the rubber soles moving up behind him.

"*Naand, meneer.*"

Van Cleef spun round at the sound of the Afrikaans

and took in the shape and size of the man beside him. Even in the darkness he could pick out the black and white skull-and-crossbones motif on the man's left shoulder. He nodded warily.

"Naand. Jy Afrikaans?"

The man nodded. "Jan Dupree," he said and held out his hand.

"Kobus Van Cleef," said the airman and shook.

"Waar gaan-jy nou?" asked Dupree.

"To Libreville. As soon as they finish loading. And you?"

Janni Dupree grinned. "I'm a bit stuck, me and my mates. We'll get the chop for sure if the Federals find us. Can you help us out?"

"How many of you?" asked Van Cleef.

"Five in all."

As a fellow mercenary, Van Cleef did not hesitate. Outlaws sometimes need each other.

"All right, get aboard. But hurry up. As soon as that Connie is off, so are we."

Dupree nodded his thanks and jog-trotted back to the Land Rover. The four other whites were standing in a group round the hood.

"It's okay, but we have to get aboard," the South African told them.

"Right, dump the hardware in the back and let's get moving," said the group leader. As the rifles and ammunition pouches thumped into the back of the vehicle, he leaned over to the black officer with second lieutenant's tabs who sat at the wheel.

"We have to go now," he said. "Take the Land Rover and dump it. Bury the guns and mark the spot. Leave your uniform and go for bush. Understand?"

The lieutenant, who had been in his last term of high school when he volunteered to fight and had been with the mercenary-led commando unit for the past year, nodded somberly, taking in the instructions.

"G'by, Patrick," the mercenary said. "I'm afraid it's over now."

The African looked up. "Perhaps," he said. "Perhaps it is over."

"Don't go on fighting," urged the white man. "There's no point."

"Not now," the lieutenant agreed. He nodded toward the steps of the Constellation, where the leader and his group were saying good-by. "But he is leaving for safety. That is good. He is still the leader. While he lives, we will not forget. We will say nothing, do nothing, but we will remember."

He started the engine of the Land Rover and swung the vehicle into a turn. "Good-by," he called.

The four other mercenaries called good-by and walked toward the DC-4.

The leader was about to follow them when two nuns fluttered up to him from the darkness of the bush behind the parking apron.

"Major."

The mercenary turned and recognized the first of them as the sister he had met months earlier, when fighting had raged in the zone where she ran a hospital and he had been forced to evacuate the whole complex.

"Sister Mary Joseph! What are you doing here?"

The elderly Irish nun began talking earnestly, holding the stained uniform sleeve of his jacket.

He nodded. "I'll try, I can do no more than that," he said when she had finished.

He walked across the apron to where the South African pilot was standing under the wing of his DC-4, and the two of them talked for several minutes. Finally the man in uniform came back to the waiting nuns.

"He says yes, but you must hurry, Sister. He wants to get this crate off the ground as soon as he can."

"God bless you," said the figure in the white habit and gave hurried orders to her companion. The latter ran to the rear of the aircraft and began to climb the short ladder to the passenger door. The other scurried back to the shade of a patch of palms behind the parking apron, from which a file of men soon emerged. Each carried a bundle in his arms. At the DC-4 the bundles were passed up to the waiting nun at the top of the steps. Behind her the co-pilot watched her lay the first three side by side in the beginning of a row down the aircraft's hull, then began gruffly to help, taking the bundles from the stretching hands beneath the aircraft's tail and passing them inside.

"God bless you," whispered the Irish nun.

One of the bundles deposited a few ounces of liquid green excrement onto the co-pilot's sleeve. "Bloody hell," he muttered and went on working.

Left alone, the leader of the group of mercenaries glanced toward the Superconstellation. A file of refugees, mainly the relations of the leaders of the defeated people, was climbing up the rear steps. In the dim light from the airplane's door he caught sight of the man he wanted to see. As he approached, the man was about to mount the steps while others waited to pull them away. One of them called to him.

"Sah. Major Shannon come."

The general turned as Shannon approached, and even at this hour he managed a grin.

"So, Shannon, do you want to come along?"

Shannon stepped in front of him and brought up a salute. The general acknowledged it.

"No thank you, sir. We have transport to Libreville. I just wanted to say good-by."

"Yes. It was a long fight. Now it's over, I'm afraid. For some years, at any rate. I find it hard to believe my people will continue to live in servitude forever. By the way, have you and your colleagues been paid up to the contract?"

"Yes, thank you, sir. We're all up to date," replied the mercenary. The African nodded somberly.

"Well, good-by, then. And thank you for all you were able to do." He held out his hand, and the two men shook.

"There's one more thing, sir," said Shannon. "Me and the boys, we were talking things over, sitting in the jeep. If there's ever any time— Well, if you should ever need us, you only have to let us know. We'll all come. You only have to call. The boys want you to know that."

The general stared at him for several seconds. "This night is full of surprises," he said slowly. "You may not know it yet, but half my senior advisers and all of the wealthy ones are crossing the lines tonight to ingratiate themselves with the enemy. Most of the others will follow suit within a month. Thank you for your offer, Mr. Shannon. I will remember it. But how about yourselves? What do the mercenaries do now?"

"We'll have to look around for more work."

"Another fight, Major Shannon?"

"Another fight, sir."

"But always somebody else's."

"That's our way of life," said Shannon.

"And you think you will fight again, you and your men?"

"Yes. We'll fight again."

The general laughed softly. " 'Cry "Havoc!" and let slip the dogs of war,' " he murmured.

"Sir?"

"Shakespeare, Mr. Shannon, just a bit of Shakespeare. Well, now, I must go. The pilot is waiting. Good-by again, and good luck."

He turned and walked up the steps into the dimly lit interior of the Superconstellation just as the first of the four engines coughed into life. Shannon stepped back and gave the man who had employed his services for a year and a half a last salute.

"Good luck to you," he said, half to himself. "You'll need it."

He turned and walked back to the waiting DC-4. When the door had closed, Van Cleef kept the aircraft on the apron, engines turning, as he watched the dim droop-nosed shape of the Super Connie rumble down the runway through the gloom past his nose, and finally lift off. Neither plane carried any lights, but from the cockpit of the Douglas the Afrikaner could

make out the three fins of the Constellation vanishing
over the palm trees to the south and into the welcom-
ing clouds. Only then did he ease the DC-4 forward
to the take-off point.

It was close to an hour before Van Cleef ordered
his co-pilot to switch on the cabin lights, an hour of
jinking from cloudbank to cloudbank, breaking cover
and scooting across low racks of altostratus to find
cover again with another, denser bank, always seeking to avoid being caught out in the moonlit white
plains by a roving MIG. Only when he knew he was
far out over the gulf, with the coast many miles astern,
did he allow the lights on.

Behind him they lit up a weird spectacle which could
have been drawn by Doré in one of his blacker moods.
The floor of the aircraft was carpeted with sodden
and fouled blankets. Their previous contents lay writhing in rows down both sides of the cargo space, forty
small children, shrunken, wizened, deformed by malnutrition. Sister Mary Joseph rose from her crouch behind the cabin door and began to move among the
starvelings, each of whom had a piece of sticking
plaster stuck to his or her forehead, just below the line
of the hair long since turned to an ocher red by anemia.
The plaster bore in ball-point letters the relevant information for the orphanage outside Libreville. Just
name and number; they don't give rank to losers.

In the tail of the plane the five mercenaries blinked
in the light and glanced at their fellow passengers. They
had seen it all before, many times, over the past
months. Each man felt some disgust, but none showed
it. You can get used to anything eventually. In the
Congo, Yemen, Katanga, Sudan. Always the same
story, always the kids. And always nothing you can do
about it. So they reasoned, and pulled out their cigarettes.

The cabin lights allowed them to see one another
properly for the first time since sundown the previous
evening. The uniforms were stained with sweat and
the red earth, and the faces drawn with fatigue. The

leader sat with his back to the washroom door, feet straight out, facing up the fuselage toward the pilot's cabin. Carlo Alfred Thomas Shannon, thirty-three, blond hair cropped to a ragged crew-cut. Very short hair is more convenient in the tropics because the sweat runs out easier and the bugs can't get in. Nick-named Cat Shannon, he came originally from County Tyrone in the province of Ulster. Sent by his father to be educated at a minor English public school, he no longer carried the distinctive accent of Northern Ireland. After five years in the Royal Marines, he had left to try his hand at civilian life and six years ago had found himself working for a London-based trading company in Uganda. One sunny morning he quietly closed his accounts ledgers, climbed into his Land Rover and drove westward to the Congolese border. A week later he signed on as a mercenary in Mike Hoare's Fifth Commando at Stanleyville.

He had seen Hoare depart and John-John Peters take over, had quarreled with Peters and driven north to join Denard at Paulis, had been in the Stanleyville mutiny two years later and, after the Frenchman's evac-uation to Rhodesia with head wounds, had joined Black Jacques Schramme, the Belgian planter-turned-mercenary, on the long march to Bukavu and thence to Kigali. After repatriation by the Red Cross, he had promptly volunteered for another African war and had finally taken command of his own battalion. But too late to win, always too late to win.

He lay with his back against the washroom door as the DC-4 droned on toward Libreville and let his mind range back over the past year and a half. Thinking of the future was harder, for his claim to the general that he and his men would go to another war was based more on optimism than on foreknowledge. In fact he had no idea where the next job would come from. But although he could not know it that night in the plane, he and his men would fight again and would shake some mighty citadels before they finally went down.

To his immediate left sat the man who was arguably the best mortarman north of the Zambesi. Big Jan Dupree was twenty-eight and came from Paarl in Cape Province, a descendant of impoverished Huguenots whose ancestors had fled to the Cape of Good Hope from the wrath of Mazarin more than three hundred years ago. His hatchet face, dominated by a curved beak of a nose above a thin-lipped mouth, looked even more haggard than usual, his exhaustion furrowing deep lines down each cheek. The eyelids were down over the pale blue eyes, the sandy eyebrows and hair were smudged with dirt. He glanced down at the children lying along the aisle of the plane, muttered "*Bliksems*" (bastards) at the world of possession and privilege he held responsible for the ills of this planet, and tried to get to sleep.

By his side sprawled Marc Vlaminck, Tiny Marc, so called because of his vast bulk. A Fleming from Ostend, he stood 6 feet 3 inches in his socks, when he wore any, and weighed 250 pounds. Some people thought he might be fat. He was not. He was regarded with trepidation by the police of Ostend, for the most part peaceable men who would rather avoid problems than seek them out, and was viewed with kindly appreciation by the glaziers and carpenters of that city for the work he provided them. They said you could tell a bar where Tiny Marc had become playful by the number of artisans it needed to put it back together again.

An orphan, he had been brought up in an institution run by priests, who had tried to beat some sense of respect into the overgrown boy, and so repeatedly that even Marc had finally lost patience and, at the age of thirteen, laid one of the cane-wielding holy fathers cold along the flagstones with a single punch.

After that it had been a series of reformatories, then approved school, a dose of juvenile prison, and an almost communal sigh of relief when he enlisted in the paratroops. He had been one of the five hundred men who dropped onto Stanleyville with Colonel Laurent to rescue the missionaries whom the local Simba chief, Christophe Gbenye, threatened to roast alive in the main square.

Within forty minutes of hitting the airfield, Tiny Marc had found his vocation in life. After a week he went AWOL to avoid being repatriated to barracks in Belgium, and joined the mercenaries. Apart from his fists and shoulders, Tiny Marc was extremely useful with a bazooka, his favorite weapon, which he handled with the easy nonchalance of a boy with a peashooter.

The night he flew out of the enclave toward Libreville he was just thirty.

Across the fuselage from the Belgian sat Jean-Baptiste Langarotti, thirty-one. Short, compact, lean, and olive-skinned, he was a Corsican, born and raised in the town of Calvi. At the age of eighteen he had been called up by France to go and fight as one of the hundred thousand "appelés" in the Algerian war. Halfway through his eighteen months he had signed on as a regular and later had transferred to the 10th Colonial Paratroops, the dreaded red berets commanded by General Massu and known simply as *les paras*. He was twenty-one when the crunch came and some units of the professional French colonial army rallied to the cause of an eternally French Algeria, a cause embodied for the moment in the organization of the OAS. Langarotti went with the OAS, deserted, and, after the failure of the April 1961 putsch, went underground. He was caught in France three years later, living under a false name, and spent four years in prison, eating his heart out in the dark and sunless cells of first the Santé in Paris, then Tours, and finally the Ile de Ré. He was a bad prisoner, and two guards would carry the marks to prove it until they died.

Beaten half to death several times for attacks on guards, he had served his full time without remission, and emerged in 1968 with only one fear in the world, the fear of small enclosed spaces, cells and holes. He had long since vowed never to return to one, even if staying out cost him his life, and to take half a dozen men with him if "they" ever came for him again. Within three months of release he had flown down to Africa by paying his own way, talked himself into a war, and joined Shannon as a professional mercenary. Since being released from prison he had practiced steadily with the weapon he had learned to use first as a boy in Corsica and with which he had later made himself a reputation in the back streets of Algiers. Round his left wrist he wore a broad leather razor strop, which was held in place by two press-studs. In moments of idleness he would take it off, turn it over to the side unmarked by the studs, and wrap it round his left fist. That was where it was as he whiled away the time to Libreville. In his right hand was the knife, the six-inch-bladed bone-handled weapon that he could use so fast it was back in its sleeve-sheath before the victim knew he'd been cut. In steady rhythm the blade, already razor-sharp, moved backward and forward across the tense leather of the strop, becoming with each stroke a mite sharper. The movement soothed his nerves. It also annoyed everybody else, but no one ever complained. Nor did those who knew him ever quarrel with the soft voice or the sad half-smile of the little man.

Sandwiched between Langarotti and Shannon was the oldest man in the party, a German. Kurt Semmler was forty, and it was he who, in the early days back in the enclave, had devised the skull-and-crossbones motif that the mercenaries and their African trainees wore. It was also he who had cleared a five-mile sector of Federal soldiers by marking out the front line with stakes, each bearing the head of one of the previous day's Federal casualties. For a month after that, his was the quietest sector of the campaign. Born in 1930, he had been brought up in Hitler's Germany, the son of a Munich engineer who had later died on the Russian front with the Todt Organisation.

At the age of fifteen, a fervent Hitler Youth graduate, as indeed was almost the entire youth of the country after twelve years of Hitler, he had commanded a small unit of children younger than himself and old men over seventy. His mission, armed with one Panzerfaust and three bolt-action rifles, had been to stop the columns of General George Patton's tanks. Not surprisingly, he had failed, and spent his adolescence in Bavaria under American occupation, which he hated. He had little time for his mother, a religious fanatic who wanted him to become a priest. At seventeen he ran away, crossed the French frontier at Strasbourg, and signed on in the Foreign Legion at the recruiting office sited in Strasbourg for the purpose of picking up runaway Germans and Belgians. After a year in Sidi-bel-Abbès, he went with the expeditionary force to Indochina. Eight years and Dien Bien Phu later, with a lung removed by surgeons at Tourane (Danang), fortunately unable to watch the final humiliation in Hanoi, he was flown back to France. After recuperation he was sent to Algeria in 1958 as a top sergeant in the elite of the elite of the French colonial army, the 1er Régiment Etranger Parachutiste. He was one of a handful who had already survived the utter destruction of the 1er REP twice in Indochina, when it was at battalion size and later at regiment size. He revered only two men, Colonel Roger Faulques, who had been in the original Compagnie Etrangère Parachutiste when, at company strength, it had been wiped out the first time, and Commandant le Bras, another veteran, who now commanded the Garde Républicaine of the Republic of Gabon and kept that uranium-rich state safe for France. Even Colonel Marc Rodin, who had once commanded him, had lost his respect when the OAS finally crumbled.

Semmler had been in the 1er REP when it marched to a man into perdition in the putsch of Algiers and was later disbanded permanently by Charles de Gaulle. He had followed where his French officers had led, and later, picked up just after Algerian independence in Marseilles in September 1962, had served two years in prison. His four rows of campaign ribbons had saved him from worse. A civilian for the first time in

twenty years in 1964, he had been contacted by a
former cellmate with a proposition—to join him in a
smuggling operation in the Mediterranean. For three
years, apart from one spent in an Italian jail, he had
run spirits, gold, and occasionally arms from one end
of the Mediterranean to the other. He had been making
a fortune on the Italy-Yugoslavia cigarette run when
his partner had double-crossed the buyers and the sellers at the same time, pointed the finger at Semmler,
and vanished with the money. Wanted by a lot of bel-
ligerent gentlemen, Semmler had hitched a lift by sea
to Spain, ridden a series of buses to Lisbon, contacted
an arms-dealer friend, and taken passage to the African
war, about which he had read in the papers. Shannon
had taken him like a shot, for with sixteen years of
combat he was more experienced than all of them in
jungle warfare. He too dozed on the flight to Libreville.

It was two hours before dawn when the DC-4 began
to circle the airport. Above the mewling of the children, another sound could be made out, the sound of
a man whistling. It was Shannon. His colleagues knew
he always whistled when he was going into action or
coming out of it. They also knew from Shannon that
the tune was called "Spanish Harlem."

The DC-4 circled the airport at Libreville twice
while Van Cleef talked to ground control. As the old
cargo plane rolled to a halt at the end of a runway, a
military jeep carrying two French officers swerved up
in front of the nose; they beckoned Van Cleef to follow them round the taxi track.

They led him away from the main airport buildings
to a cluster of huts on the far side of the airport, and
it was here that the DC-4 was signaled to halt but
keep its engines running. Within seconds a set of steps
was up against the rear of the airplane, and from the
inside the co-pilot heaved open the door. A *képi* poked
inside and surveyed the interior, the nose beneath it
wrinkling in distaste at the smell. The French officer's
eyes came to rest on the five mercenaries, and he beck-

oned them to follow him down the tarmac. When they were on the ground the officer gestured to the co-pilot to close the door, and without more ado the DC-4 moved forward again to roll around the airport to the main buildings, where a team of French Red Cross nurses and doctors was waiting to receive the children. As the aircraft swung past them, the five mercenaries waved their thanks to Van Cleef up in his flight deck and turned to follow the French officer.

They had to wait an hour in one of the huts, perched uncomfortably on upright wooden chairs, while several other young French servicemen peeked in through the door to take a look at *les affreux,* the terrible ones. Finally a jeep squealed to a halt outside and there was the smack of feet coming to attention in the corridor. When the door opened it was to admit a tanned, hard-faced senior officer in tropical fawn uniform and a *képi* with gold braid ringing the peak. Shannon took in the keen, darting eyes, the iron-gray hair cropped short beneath the *képi,* the parachutist's wings pinned above the five rows of campaign ribbons, and the sight of Semmler leaping to ramrod attention, chin up, five fingers pointing straight down what had once been the seams of his combat trousers. Shannon needed no more to tell him who the visitor was—the legendary Le Bras.

The Indochina/Algeria veteran shook hands with each, pausing in front of Semmler longer.

"Alors, Semmler?" he said softly, with a slow smile. "Still fighting. But not an adjutant any more. A captain now, I see."

Semmler was embarrassed. *"Oui, mon commandant —pardon, mon colonel.* Just temporary."

Le Bras nodded pensively several times. Then he addressed them all. "I will have you quartered comfortably. No doubt you will appreciate a bath, a shave, and some food. Apparently you have no other clothes; some will be provided. I am afraid for the time being you will have to remain confined to your quarters. This is solely a precaution. There are a lot of newspapermen in town, and all forms of contact with them must be avoided. As soon as it is feasible, we will arrange to fly you back to Europe."

He had said all he came to say. Raising his right hand to his *képi* brim, he left.

An hour later, after a journey in a closed truck and entrance by the back door, the men were in their quarters, the five bedrooms of the top floor of the Gamba Hotel, a new construction situated only five hundred yards from the airport building across the road, and therefore miles from the center of town. The young officer who accompanied them told them they would have to take their meals in their rooms and remain there until further notice. He provided them with towels, razors, toothpaste and brushes, soap, and sponges. A tray of coffee had already arrived, and each man sank gratefully into a deep, steaming, soap-smelling bath, the first in more than six months.

At noon an army barber came, and a corporal with piles of slacks and shirts, underwear and socks, pajamas and canvas shoes. They tried them on and selected the ones they wanted, and the corporal retired with the surplus. The officer was back at one with four waiters bearing lunch, and told them they must stay away from the balconies. If they wanted to exercise in their confinement they would have to do it in their rooms. He would return that evening with a selection of books and magazines, though he could not promise English or Afrikaans.

After eating as they never had in the previous six months, since their last leave period from the fighting, the five men rolled into bed and slept. While they snored on unaccustomed mattresses between unbelievable sheets, Van Cleef lifted his DC-4 off the tarmac in the dusk, flew a mile away past the windows of the Gamba Hotel, and headed south for Caprivi and Johannesburg. His job was done.

The five mercenaries spent four weeks on the top floor of the hotel, while press interest in them died down and the reporters were all called back to their head offices by editors who saw no point in keeping men in a city where there was no news to be had. One evening, without warning, a captain on the staff of Commandant le Bras came to see the men. He grinned broadly.

"Messieurs, I have news for you. You are flying out tonight. To Paris. You are all booked on the Air Afrique flight at twenty-three-thirty hours."

The five men, bored to distraction by their prolonged confinement, cheered.

The flight to Paris took ten hours, with stops at Douala and Nice. Just before ten the following day they emerged into the blustery cold of Le Bourget airport on a mid-February morning. In the airport coffee lounge they said their good-bys. Dupree elected to take the transit coach to Orly and buy himself a single ticket on the next SAA flight to Johannesburg and Cape Town. Semmler opted to go too, but first he would return to Munich for a visit. Vlaminck said he would head for the Gare du Nord and take the first express to Brussels and connect for Ostend. Langarotti was going to the Gare de Lyon to take the train to Marseilles.

They agreed to stay in touch and looked to Shannon. He was their leader; it would be up to him to look for work, another contract, another war. Similarly, if any of them heard of anything that involved a group, he would want to contact one of the group, and Shannon was the obvious one.

"I'll stay in Paris for a while," said Shannon. "There's more chance of an interim job here than in London."

So they exchanged addresses—*poste restante* addresses, or cafés where the barman would pass on a message or keep a letter until the addressee dropped in for a drink. And then they parted and went their separate ways.

The security surrounding their flight back from Africa had been tight, and there were no waiting newspaperman at Le Bourget. But someone had heard of their arrival, for he was waiting for Shannon when, after the others had left, the group's leader came out of the terminal building.

"Shannon." The voice pronounced the name in the French way, and the tone was not friendly. Shannon turned, and his eyes narrowed fractionally as he saw the figure standing ten yards from him. The man was burly, with a down-turned mustache. He wore a heavy coat against the winter cold and walked forward until the two men faced each other at two feet. To judge by the way they surveyed each other, there was no love lost between them.

"Roux," said Shannon.

"So, you're back," snarled the Frenchman.

"Yes. We're back."

The man called Roux sneered. "And you lost."

"We didn't have much choice," said Shannon.

"A word of advice, my friend," snapped Roux. "Go back to your own country. Do not stay here. It would be unwise. This is my city. If there is any contract to be found here, I will hear first news of it, I will conclude it. And I will select those who share in it."

For answer Shannon walked to the first taxi waiting at the curb and humped his bag into the back. Roux walked after him, his face mottling with anger.

"Listen to me, Shannon. I'm warning you—"

The Irishman turned to face him again. "No, you listen to me, Roux. I'll stay in Paris just as long as I want. I was never impressed by you in the Congo, and I'm not now. So get stuffed."

As the taxi moved away, Roux stared after it angrily. He was muttering to himself as he strode toward the parking lot and his own automobile.

He switched on the engine, slipped into gear, and sat for a few moments staring through the windscreen. "One day I'll kill that bastard," he murmured to himself. But the thought hardly put him in a better mood.

2

Jack Mulrooney shifted his bulk on the canvas-and-frame cot beneath the mosquito netting and watched the slow lightening of the darkness above the trees to the east. A faint paling, enough to make out the trees towering over the clearing. He drew on his cigarette and cursed the primeval jungle which surrounded him, and, like all old Africa hands, asked himself once again why he ever returned to the pestiferous continent.

If he had really tried to analyze himself, he would have admitted he could not live anywhere else, certainly not in London or even Britain. He couldn't take the cities, the rules and regulations, the taxes, the cold. Like all old hands, he alternately loved and hated Africa but conceded it had got into his blood over the past quarter-century, along with the malaria, the whisky, and the million insect stings and bites.

He had come out from England in 1945 at the age of twenty-five, after five years as a fitter in the Royal Air Force, part of them at Takoradi, where he had assembled crated Spitfires for onward flight to East Africa and the Middle East the long way around. That had been his first sight of Africa, and on demobilization he had taken his discharge pay, bidden good-by to frozen, rationed London in December 1945, and taken ship for West Africa. Someone had told him there were fortunes to be made in Africa.

He had found no fortunes but after wandering the continent had got himself a small tin concession in the Benue Plateau, eighty miles from Jos in Nigeria. Prices had been good while the Malay emergency was on. He had worked alongside his Tiv laborers, and at the English club where the colonial ladies gossiped away the last days of the empire they said he had "gone native" and it was a damned bad show. The truth was, Mulrooney really preferred the African way of life. He liked the bush; he liked the Africans, who did not seem to mind that he swore and roared and cuffed them to get more work done. He also sat and took palm wine with them and observed the tribal taboos. He did not patronize them. His tin concession ran out in 1960, around the time of independence, and he went to work as a charge hand for a company running a larger and more efficient concession nearby. It was called Manson Consolidated, and when that concession also was exhausted, in 1962, he was signed on the staff.

At fifty he was still a big, powerful man, large-boned and strong as an ox. His hands were enormous, chipped and scarred by years in the mines. He ran one of them through his wild, crinkly gray hair and with the other stubbed out the cigarette in the damp red earth beneath the cot. It was lighter now; soon it would be dawn. He could hear his cook blowing on the beginnings of a fire on the other side of the clearing.

Mulrooney called himself a mining engineer, although he had no degree in mining or engineering. He had taken a course in both and added what no university could ever teach—twenty-five years of hard experience. He had burrowed for gold on the Rand and copper outside Ndola; drilled for precious water in Somaliland, grubbed for diamonds in Sierra Leone. He could tell an unsafe mineshaft by instinct, and the presence of an ore deposit by the smell. At least that was his claim, and after he had drunk his habitual twenty bottles of beer in the shanty town of an evening, no one was going to argue with him. In reality, he was one of the last of the old prospectors. He knew ManCon gave him the little jobs, the ones in the deep bush, the wild country that was miles from civilization and still had to be checked out, but he liked it that way. He preferred to work alone; it was his way of life.

The latest job had certainly fulfilled these conditions. For three months he had been prospecting in the foothills of the range called the Crystal Mountains in the hinterland of the republic of Zangaro, a tiny enclave on the coast of West Africa.

He had been told where to concentrate his survey, around the Crystal Mountain itself. The chain of large hills, curved hummocks rising to two or three thousand feet, ran in a line from one side of the republic to the other, parallel to the coast and forty miles from it. The range divided the coastal plain from the hinterland. There was only one gap in the chain, and through it ran the only access to the interior, a narrow dirt road, baked like concrete in summer, a quagmire in winter. Beyond the mountains, the natives were the Vindu, a tribe of almost Iron Age development, except that their implements were of wood. He had been in some wild places but vowed he had never seen anything as backward as the hinterland of Zangaro.

Set on the farther side of the range of hills was the single mountain that gave its name to the rest. It was not even the biggest of them. Forty years earlier a lone missionary, penetrating the hills into the interior, branched to the south after following the gap in the range and after twenty miles glimpsed a hill set aside from the rest. It had rained the previous night, a torrential downpour, one of the many that gave the area its annual rainfall of three hundred inches during five soaking months. As the priest looked, he saw that the mountain seemed to be glittering in the morning sun, and he called it the Crystal Mountain. He noted this in his diary. Two days later he was clubbed and eaten.

The diary was found by a patrol of colonial soldiers a year later, being used as a juju by a local village. The soldiers did their duty and wiped out the village, then returned to the coast and handed the diary to the mission society. Thus the name the priest had given to the mountain lived on, even if nothing else he did for an ungrateful world was remembered. Later the same name was given to the entire range of hills.

What the man had seen in the morning light was not crystal but a myriad of streams caused by the water of the night's rain cascading off the mountain. Rain was also cascading off all the other mountains, but the sight of it was hidden by the dense jungle vegetation that covered them all, like a chunky green blanket when seen from afar, which proved to be a steaming hell when penetrated. The one that glittered with a thousand rivulets did so because the vegetation was substantially thinner on the flanks of this hill. It never occurred to the missionary, or to any of the other dozen white men who had ever seen it, to wonder why.

After three months living in the steaming hell of the jungles that surrounded Crystal Mountain, Mulrooney knew why.

He had started by circling the entire mountain and had discovered that there was effectively a gap between the seaward flank and the rest of the chain. This set the Crystal Mountain eastward of the main chain, standing on its own. Because it was lower than the highest peaks to seaward, it was invisible from the other side. Nor was it particularly noticeable in any other way, except that it had more streams running off it per mile of hillside than ran off the other hills, to north and south.

Mulrooney counted them all, both on the Crystal Mountain and on its companions. There was no doubt of it. The water ran off the other mountains after rain, but a lot of water was soaked up in the soil. The other mountains had twenty feet of topsoil over the basic rock structure beneath, the Crystal Mountain hardly any. He had his native workers, locally recruited

Vindu, bore a series of holes with the augur he had with him, and confirmed the difference in depth of the topsoil in twenty places. From these he would work out why.

Over millions of years the earth had been formed by the decomposition of the rock and by dust carried on the wind, and although each rainfall had eroded some of it down the slopes into the streams, and from the streams to the rivers and thence to the shallow, silted estuary, some earth had also remained, lodged in little crannies, left alone by the running water, which had bored its own holes in the soft rock. And these holes had become drains, so that part of the rainfall ran off the mountain, finding its own channels and wearing them deeper and deeper, and some had sunk into the mountain, both having the effect of leaving part of the topsoil intact. Thus the earth layer had built up and up, a little thicker each century or millennium. The birds and the wind had brought seeds, which had found the niches of earth and flourished there, their roots contributing to the process of retaining the earth on the hill slopes. When Mulrooney saw the hills, there was enough rich earth to sustain mighty trees and tangled vines which covered the slopes and the summits of all the hills. All except one.

On this one the water could not burrow channels that became streams, nor could it sink into the rock face, especially on the steepest face, which was to the east, toward the hinterland. Here the earth had collected in pockets, and the pockets had produced clumps of bush, grass, and fern. From niche to niche the vegetation had reached out to itself, linking vines and tendrils in a thin screen across bare patches of rock regularly washed clean by the falling water of the rain season. It was these patches of glistening wet amid the green that the missionary had seen before he died. The reason for the change was simple: the separate hill was of a different rock from the main range, an ancient rock, hard as granite as compared to the soft, more recent rock of the main chain of hills.

Mulrooney had completed his circuit of the mountain and established this beyond a doubt. It took him a fortnight to do it and to establish that no less than seventy streams ran off the Crystal Mountain. Most of them joined up into three main streams that flowed away eastward out of the foothills into the deeper valley. He noticed something else. Along the banks of the streams that came off this mountain, the soil color and the vegetation were different. Some plants appeared unaffected; others were stunted or nonexistent, although they flourished on the other mountains and beside the other streams.

Mulrooney set about charting the seventy streams, drawing his map as he went. He also took samples of the sand and gravel along the beds of the streams, starting with the surface gravel, then working down to bedrock.

In each case he took two buckets full of gravel, poured them out onto a tarpaulin, and coned and quartered. This is a process of sample-taking. He piled the gravel into a cone, then quartered it with a shovel blade, took the two opposite quarters of his choice, remixed them, and made another cone. Then he quartered that one, working down till he had a cross-section of the sample weighing two to three pounds. Then this went into a polyethylene-lined canvas bag after drying; the bag was sealed and carefully labeled. In a month he had fifteen hundred pounds of sand and gravel in six hundred bags from the beds of the seventy streams. Then he started on the mountain itself.

He already believed his sacks of gravel would prove to contain, under laboratory examination, quantities of alluvial tin, minute particles washed down from the mountain over tens of thousands of years, showing that there was cassiterite, or tin ore, buried in the Crystal Mountain.

He divided the mountain faces into sections, seeking to identify the birthplaces of the streams and the rock faces that fed them in the wet season. By the end of the week he knew there was no mother lode of tin inside the rock, but suspected what geologists called a disseminated deposit. The signs of mineralization were everywhere. Beneath the trailing tendrils of vegetation he found faces of rock shot through with stringers, half-inch-wide veins like the capillaries in a drinker's nose, of milky-white quartz, lacing yard after yard of bare rock face.

Everything he saw about him said "tin." He went right around the mountain again three times, and his observations confirmed the disseminated deposit, the ever-present stringers of white in the dark gray rock. With hammer and chisel he smashed holes deep in the rock, and the picture was still the same. Sometimes he thought he saw dark blurs in the quartz, confirming the presence of tin.

Then he began chipping in earnest, marking his progress as he went. He took samples of the pure white stringers of quartz, and to be on the safe side he also took samples of the country rock, the rock between the veins. Three months after he had entered the primeval forest east of the mountains, he was finished. He had another fifteen hundred pounds of rock to carry back to the coast with him. The whole ton and a half of rock and alluvial samples had been carried in portions every three days back from his working camp to the main camp, where he now lay waiting for dawn, and stacked in cones under tarpaulins.

After coffee and breakfast the bearers, whose terms he had negotiated the previous day, would come from the village and carry his trophies back to the track that called itself a road and linked the hinterland with the coast. There, in a roadside village, lay his two-ton truck, immobilized by the absence of the key and distributor rotor that lay in his knapsack. It should still work, if the natives had not hacked it to bits. He had paid the village chief enough to look after it. With his samples aboard the truck and twenty porters walking ahead to pull the lurching vehicle up the gradients and out of the ditches, he would be back in the capital in three days. After a cable to London, he would have to wait several days for the company's chartered ship to come and take him off. He would have preferred to turn north at the coast highway and drive the extra hundred miles into the neighboring republic, where there was a good airport, and freight his samples home. But the agreement between ManCon and the Zangaran government specified that he would take them back to the capital.

Jack Mulrooney heaved himself out of his cot, swung aside the netting, and roared at his cook, "Hey, Dingaling, where's my bloody coffee?"

The Vindu cook, who did not understand a word except "coffee," grinned from beside the fire and waved happily. Mulrooney strode across the clearing toward his canvas washbucket and began scratching as the mosquitoes descended on his sweating torso.

"Bloody Africa," he muttered as he doused his face. But he was content that morning. He was convinced he had found both alluvial tin and tin-bearing rock. The only question was how much tin per rock-ton. With tin standing at about $3300 per ton, it would be up to the analysts and mining economists to work out if the quantity of tin per ton of rock merited establishing a mining camp with its complex machinery and teams of workers, not to mention improved access to the coast by a narrow-gauge railway that would have to be built from scratch. And it was certainly a godforsaken and inaccessible place. As usual, everything would be worked out, taken up or thrown away, on the basis of pounds, shillings, and pence. That was the way of the world. He slapped another mosquito off his upper arm and pulled on his T-shirt.

Six days later Jack Mulrooney leaned over the rail of a small coaster chartered by his company and spat over the side as the coast of Zangaro slid away.

"Bloody bastards," he muttered savagely. He carried a series of livid bruises about his chest and back, and a raw graze down one cheek, the outcome of swinging rifle butts when the troops had raided the hotel.

It had taken him two days to bring his samples from the deep bush to the track, and another grunting, sweating day and night to haul the truck along the pitted and rutted earth road from the interior to the coast. In the wet he would never have made it, and in the dry season, which had another month to run, the concrete-hard mud ridges had nearly smashed the Mercedes to pieces. Three days earlier he had paid and dismissed his Vindu workers and trundled the creaking truck down the last stretch to the blacktop road which started only fourteen miles from the capital. From there it had been an hour to the city and the hotel.

Not that "hotel" was the right word. Since independence, the town's main hostelry had degenerated into a flophouse, but it had a parking lot, and here he had parked and locked the truck, then sent his cable. He had only just been in time. Six hours after he sent it, all hell broke loose, and the port, airport, and all other communications had been closed by order of the President.

The first he had known about it was when a group of soldiers, dressed like tramps and wielding rifles by the barrels, had burst into the hotel and started to ransack the rooms. There was no point in asking what they wanted, for they only screamed back in a lingo that meant nothing to him, though he thought he recognized the Vindu dialect he had heard his workers using over the past three months.

Being Mulrooney, he had taken two clubbings from rifle butts, then swung a fist. The blow carried the nearest soldier halfway down the hotel corridor on his back, and the rest of the pack had gone wild. It was only by the grace of God no shots were fired, and also owing to the fact that the soldiers preferred to use their guns as clubs rather than search for complicated mechanisms like triggers and safety catches.

He had been dragged to the nearest police barracks and had been alternately screamed at and ignored in a subterranean cell for two days. He had been lucky. A Swiss businessman, one of the rare foreign visitors to the republic, had witnessed his departure and feared for his life. The man had looked through Mulrooney's belongings and contacted the Swiss embassy, one of the only six European and North American embassies in the town, and it had contacted ManCon.

Two days later the called-for coaster had arrived from farther up the coast, and the Swiss consul had negotiated Mulrooney's release. No doubt a bribe had been paid, and no doubt ManCon would foot the bill. Jack Mulrooney was still aggrieved. On release he had found his truck broken open and his samples strewn all over the parking lot. The rocks had all been marked and could be reassembled, but the sand, gravel, and chippings were mixed up. Fortunately each of the split bags, about fifty in all, had half its contents intact, so he had resealed them and taken them to the boat. Even here the customs men, police, and soldiers had searched the boat from stem to stern, screamed and shouted at the crew, and all without saying what they were looking for.

The terrified official from the Swiss consulate who had taken Mulrooney back from the barracks to his hotel had told him there had been rumors of an attempt on the President's life and the troops were looking for a missing senior officer who was presumed to be responsible.

Four days after leaving the port of Clarence, Jack Mulrooney, still nursemaiding his rock samples, arrived back at Luton, England, aboard a chartered aircraft. A truck took his samples away for analysis at Watford, and after a checkout by the company doctor he was allowed to start his three weeks' leave. He went to spend it with his sister in Dulwich and within a week was thoroughly bored.

Exactly three weeks later to the day, Sir James Manson, Knight of the British Empire, chairman and managing director of Manson Consolidated Mining Company Limited, leaned back in his leather armchair in the penthouse office suite on the tenth floor of his company's London headquarters, glanced once more at the report in front of him and breathed, "Jesus Christ."

He rose from behind the broad desk, crossed the room to the picture windows on the south face, and gazed down at the sprawl of the City of London, the inner square mile of the ancient capital and heart of a financial empire that was still worldwide, despite what its detractors said. To some of the scuttling beetles in somber gray, topped by black bowler hats, it was perhaps a place of employment only, boring, wearisome, exacting its toll of a man, his youth, his manhood, his middle age, until final retirement. For others, young and hopeful, it was a palace of opportunity, where merit and hard work were rewarded with the prizes of advancement and security. To romantics it was no doubt the home of the houses of the great merchant-adventurers, to a pragmatist the biggest market in the world, and to a left-wing trade unionist a place where the idle and worthless rich, born to wealth and privilege, lolled at ease in luxury. James Manson was a cynic and a realist. He knew what the City was; it was a jungle pure and simple, and in it he was one of the panthers.

A born predator, he had nevertheless realized early that there were certain rules that needed to be publicly revered and privately ripped to shreds; that, as in politics, there was only one commandment, the eleventh, "Thou shalt not be found out." It was by obeying the first requirement that he had acquired his knighthood in the New Year's Honours List a month before. This had been proposed by the Conservative Party (ostensibly for services to industry, but in reality for secret contributions to party funds for the general election), and accepted by the Wilson government because of his support for its policy on Nigeria. And it was by fulfilling the second requirement that he had made his fortune and now, holding twenty-five per cent of the stock of his own mining corporation and occupying the penthouse floor, was a millionaire several times over.

He was sixty-one, short, aggressive, built like a tank, with a thrusting vigor and a piratical ruthlessness that women found attractive and competitors feared. He had enough cunning to pretend to show respect for the establishments of both the City and the realm, of commercial and political life, even though he was aware that both organs were rife with men of almost complete moral unscrupulousness behind the public image. He had collected a few on his board of directors, including two former ministers in Conservative administrations. Neither was averse to a fat supplementary fee over and above director's salary, payable in the Cayman Islands or Grand Bahama—and one, to Manson's knowledge, enjoyed the private diversion of waiting at table upon three or four leather-clad tarts, himself dressed in a maid's cap, a pinafore, and a bright smile. Manson regarded both men as useful, possessing the advantage of considerable influence and superb connections without the inconvenience of integrity. The rest of the public knew both men as distinguished public servants. So James Manson was respectable within the set of rules of the City, a set of rules that had nothing whatever to do with the rest of humanity.

It had not always been so, which was why inquirers into his background found themselves up against one blank wall after another. Very little was known of his start in life, and he knew enough to keep it that way. He would let it be known that he was the son of a Rhodesian train-driver, brought up not far from the sprawling copper mines of Ndola, Northern Rhodesia, now Zambia. He would even let it be known that he had started work at the minehead as a boy and later had made his first fortune in copper. But never how he had made it.

In fact he had quit the mines quite early, before he was twenty, and had realized that the men who risked their lives below ground amid roaring machinery would never make money, not big money. That lay above ground, and not even in mine management. As a teenager he had studied finance, the using and manipulating of money, and his nightly studies had taught him that more was made in shares in copper in a week than a miner made in his whole life.

He had started as a share-pusher on the Rand, had peddled a few illicit diamonds in his time, started a few rumors that sent the punters reaching into their pockets, and sold a few worked-out claims to the gullible. That was where the first fortune came from. Just after the Second World War, at thirty-five, he was in London with the right connections for a copper-hungry Britain trying to get its industries back to work, and in 1948 had founded his own mining company. It had gone public in the mid-fifties and in fifteen years had developed worldwide interests. He was one of the first to see Harold Macmillan's wind of change blowing through Africa as independence for the black republics approached, and he took the trouble to meet and know most of the new power-hungry African politicians while most City businessmen were still deploring independence in the former colonies.

When he met the new men, it was a good match. They could see through his success story, and he could see through their professed concern for their fellow blacks. They knew what he wanted, and he knew what they wanted. So he fed their Swiss bank accounts, and they gave Manson Consolidated mining concessions at prices below par for the course. ManCon prospered.

James Manson had also made several fortunes on the side. His latest was in the shares of the nickel-mining company in Australia called Poseidon. When Poseidon shares in late summer 1969 had been standing at four shillings, he had got a whisper that a survey team in central Australia might have found something on a stretch of land whose mining rights were owned by Poseidon. He had taken a gamble and paid out a very hefty sum to have a sneak preview of the first reports coming out of the interior. Those reports said nickel, and lots of it. In fact nickel was not in shortage on the world market, but that never deterred the punters, and it was they who sent share prices spiraling, not investors.

He contacted his Swiss bank, an establishment so discreet that its only way of announcing its presence in the world was a small gold plate no larger than a visiting card, set into the wall beside a solid oak door in a small street in Zurich. Switzerland has no stockbrokers; the banks do all the investments. Manson instructed Dr. Martin Steinhofer, the head of the investments section of the Zwingli Bank, to buy on his behalf five thousand Poseidon shares. The Swiss banker contacted the prestigious London firm of Joseph Sebag & Co., in the name of Zwingli, and placed the order. Poseidon stood at five shillings a share when the deal was concluded.

The storm broke in late September when the size of the Australian nickel deposit became known. The shares began to rise, and, assisted by helpful rumors, the rising spiral became a rush. Sir James Manson had intended to start to sell when they reached £50 a share, but so vast was the rise that he held on. Finally he estimated that the peak would be £115 and ordered Dr. Steinhofer to start selling at £100 a share. This the discreet Swiss banker did and cleared the lot at an average of £103 for each share. In fact the peak was reached at £120 a share, before common sense began to prevail and the shares slid back to £10. Manson did not mind the extra £20, for he knew the time to sell was just before the peak, when buyers are still plentiful. With all fees paid, he netted a cool £500,-000, which was still stashed in the Zwingli Bank.

It happens to be illegal for a British citizen and resident to have a foreign bank account without informing the Treasury, and also to make half a million sterling profit in sixty days without paying capital gains tax on it. But Dr. Steinhofer was a Swiss resident, and

Dr. Steinhofer would keep his mouth shut. That was what Swiss banks were for.

On that mid-February afternoon Sir James Manson strolled back to his desk, sat back in the lush leather chair behind it, and glanced again at the report that lay on the blotter. It had arrived in a large envelope, sealed with wax and marked for his eyes only. It was signed at the bottom by Dr. Gordon Chalmers, the head of ManCon's Department of Study, Research, Geo-Mapping, and Sample Analysis, situated outside London. It was the analyst's report on tests conducted on the samples a man called Mulrooney had apparently brought back from a place called Zangaro three weeks earlier.

Dr. Chalmers did not waste words. The summary of the report was brief and to the point. Mulrooney had found a mountain, or a hill, some 1800 feet high above ground level and close to 1000 yards across the base. It was set slightly apart from a range of such mountains in the hinterland of Zangaro. The hill contained a widely disseminated deposit of mineral in apparently evenly consistent presence throughout the rock, which was of igneous type and millions of years older than the sandstone and ragstone of the mountains that surrounded it.

Mulrooney had found numerous and ubiquitous stringers of quartz and had predicated the presence of tin. He had returned with samples of the quartz, the country rock surrounding it, and shingle from the beds of the streams surrounding the hill. The quartz stringers did indeed contain small quantities of tin. But it was the country rock that was interesting. Repeated and varied tests showed that this country rock, and the gravel samples, contained minor quantities of low-grade nickel. They also contained remarkable quantities of platinum. It was present in all the samples and was fairly evenly distributed. The richest rock in platinum known in this world was in the Rustenberg mines in South Africa, where concentrations or "grades" ran as high as Point Two Five of a Troy ounce per rock ton. The average concentration in the Mulrooney samples was Point Eight One. I have the honour to remain, Sir, Yours, etc. . . .

Sir James Manson knew as well as anyone in mining that platinum was the third most precious metal in the world, and stood at a market price of $130 a Troy ounce as he sat in his chair. He was also aware that, with the growing world hunger for the stuff, it had to rise to at least $150 an ounce over the next three years, probably to $200 within five years. It would be unlikely to rise to the 1968 peak price of $300 again, because that was ridiculous.

He did some calculations on a scratch pad. Two hundred and fifty million cubic yards of rock at two tons per cubic yard was five hundred million tons. At even half an ounce per rock ton, that was two hundred and fifty million ounces. If the revelation of a new world source dragged the price down to ninety dollars an ounce, and even if the inaccessibility of the place meant a cost of fifty dollars an ounce to get it out and refined, that still meant . . .

Sir James Manson leaned back in his chair again and whistled softly.

"Jesus Christ. A ten-billion-dollar mountain."

3

Platinum is a metal and, like all metals, it has its price. The price is basically controlled by two factors. These are the indispensability of the metal in certain processes that the industries of the world would like to complete, and the rarity of the metal. Platinum is very rare. Total world production each year, apart from stockpiled production, which is kept secret by the producers, is a shade over one and a half million Troy ounces.

The overwhelming majority of it, probably more than ninety-five per cent, comes from three sources: South Africa, Canada, and Russia. Russia, as usual, is the uncooperative member of the group. The producers would like to keep the world price fairly steady so as to be able to make long-term plans for investment in new mining equipment and development of new mines in the confidence that the bottom will not suddenly drop out of the market should a large quantity of stockpiled platinum suddenly be released. The Russians, by stockpiling unknown quantities and being able to release large quantities any time they feel like it, keep tremors running through the market whenever they can.

Russia releases on the world each year about 350,000 Troy ounces out of the 1,500,000 that reach the same market. This gives her between 23 and 24 per cent of the market, enough to ensure her a considerable degree of influence. Her supplies are marketed through Soyuss Prom Export. Canada puts on the market some 200,000 ounces a year, the whole production coming from the nickel mines of International Nickel, and just about the whole of this supply is bought up each year by the Engelhard Industries of the United States. But should the United States need for platinum suddenly rise sharply, Canada might well not be able to furnish the extra quantity.

The third source is South Africa, turning out close to 950,000 ounces a year and dominating the market. Apart from the Impala mines, which were just opening when Sir James Manson sat considering the world position of platinum, and have since become very important, the giants of platinum are the Rustenberg mines, which account for well over half the world's production. These are controlled by Johannesburg Consolidated, which had a big enough slice of the stock to be sole manager of the mines. The world refiner and marketer of Rustenberg's supply was and is the London-based firm of Johnson-Matthey.

James Manson knew this as well as anyone else. Although he was not into platinum when Chalmers' report hit his desk, he knew the position as well as a brain surgeon knows how a heart works. He also knew why, even at that time, the boss of Engelhard Industries of America, the colorful Charlie Engelhard, better known to the populace as the owner of the fabulous racehorse Nijinsky, was buying into South African platinum. It was because America would need much more than Canada could supply for the mid-seventies. Manson was certain of it.

And the particular reason why American consumption of platinum was almost certain to rise, even triple, by the mid- to late seventies, lay in that simple piece of metal the car exhaust pipe and in those dire words "air pollution."

With legislation already passed in the United States projecting ever more stringent controls, and with little likelihood that any nonprecious-metal car exhaust-control device would be marketed before 1980, there was a strong probability that every American car would soon require one-tenth of an ounce of pure platinum. This meant that the Americans would need one and a half million ounces of platinum every year, an amount equal to the present world production, and they would not know where to get it.

James Manson thought he had an idea where. They could always buy it from him. And with the absolute indispensability of a platinum-based anti-pollutant catalyst in every fume-control device established for a decade, and world demand far outstripping supply, the price would be nice, very nice indeed.

There was only one problem. He had to be absolutely certain that he, and no one else, would control all mining rights to the Crystal Mountain. The question was, how?

The normal way would be to visit the republic where the mountain was situated, seek an interview with the President, show him the survey report, and propose to him a deal whereby ManCon secured the mining rights, the government secured a profit-participation clause that would fill the coffers of its treasury, and the President would secure a fat and regular payment into his Swiss account. That would be the normal way.

But apart from the fact that any other mining company in the world, if advised of what lay inside the Crystal Mountain, would counterbid for the same mining rights, sending the government's share up and Manson's down, there were three groups who more than any other would want to take control, either to begin production or to stop it forever. These were the South Africans, the Canadians, and most of all the Russians. For the advent on the world market of a massive new supply source would cut the Soviet slice of the market back to the level of the unnecessary, removing from the Russians their power, influence, and money-making capacity in the platinum field.

Manson had a vague recollection of having heard the name of Zangaro, but it was such an obscure place he realized he knew nothing about it. The first requirement was evidently to learn more. He leaned forward and depressed the intercom switch.

"Miss Cooke, would you come in, please?"

He had called her Miss Cooke throughout the seven years she had been his personal and private secretary, and even in the ten years before that, when she had been an ordinary company secretary, rising from the typing pool to the tenth floor, no one had ever suggested she might have a first name. In fact she had. It was Marjory. But she just did not seem the sort of person one called Marjory.

Certainly men had once called her Marjory, long ago, before the war, when she was a young girl. Perhaps they had even tried to flirt with her, pinch her bottom, those long thirty-five years ago. But that was then. Five years of war, hauling an ambulance through burning rubble-strewn streets, trying to forget a Guardsman who never came back from Dunkirk, and twenty years of nursing a crippled and whining mother, a bedridden tyrant who used tears for weapons, had taken away the youth and the pinchable qualities of Miss Marjory Cooke. At fifty-four, she was tailored, efficient, and severe; her work at ManCon was almost all her life, the tenth floor her fulfillment, and the terrier who shared her neat apartment in suburban Chigwell and slept on her bed, her child and lover.

So no one ever called her Marjory. The young executives called her a shriveled apple, and the secretary birds "that old bat." The others, including her employer, Sir James Manson, about whom she knew more than she would ever tell him or anyone else, called her Miss Cooke.

She entered through the door set in the beech-paneled wall which, when closed, looked like part of the wall.

"Miss Cooke, it has come to my attention that we

have had, during the past few months, a small survey —one man, I believe—in the republic of Zangaro."

"Yes, Sir James. That's right."

"Oh, you know about it."

Of course she knew about it. Miss Cooke never forgot anything that had crossed her desk.

"Yes, Sir James."

"Good. Then please find out for me who secured that government's permission for us to conduct the survey."

"It will be on file, Sir James. I'll go and look."

She was back in ten minutes, having first checked in her daily diary appointment books, which were cross-indexed into two indices, one under personal names and the other under subject headings, and then confirmed with Personnel.

"It was Mr. Bryant, Sir James." She consulted a card in her hand. "Richard Bryant, of Overseas Contracts."

"He submitted a report, I suppose?" asked Sir James.

"He must have done, under normal company procedure."

"Send me in his report, would you, Miss Cooke?"

She was gone again, and the head of ManCon stared out through the plate-glass windows across the room from his desk at the mid-afternoon dusk settling over the City of London. The lights were coming on in the middle-level floors—they had been on all day in the lowest ones—but at skyline level there was still enough winter daylight to see by. But not to read by. Sir James Manson flicked on the reading lamp on his desk as Miss Cooke returned, laid the report he wanted on his blotter, and receded back into the wall.

The report Richard Bryant had submitted was dated six months earlier and was written in the terse style favored by the company. It recorded that, according to instructions from the head of Overseas Contracts, he had flown to Clarence, the capital of Zangaro, and there, after a frustrating week in a hotel, had secured an interview with the Minister of Natural Resources. There were three separate interviews, spaced over six

days, and at length an agreement had been reached that
a single representative of ManCon might enter the
republic to conduct a survey for minerals in the hinterland beyond the Crystal Mountains. The area to be
surveyed was deliberately left vague by the company,
so that the survey team could travel more or less
where it wished. After further haggling, during which
it was made plain to the Minister that he could forget
any idea that the company was prepared to pay the sort
of fee he seemed to expect, and that there were no in-
dications of mineral presence to work on, a sum had
been agreed on between Bryant and the Minister. Inevitably, the sum on the contract was just over half the
total that changed hands, the balance being paid into
the Minister's private account.

That was all. The only indication of the character
of the place was in the reference to a corrupt minister.
So what? thought Sir James Manson. Nowadays Bryant
might have been in Washington. Only the going rate was
different.

He leaned forward to the intercom again. "Tell Mr.
Bryant of Overseas Contracts to come up and see me,
would you, Miss Cooke?"

He lifted the switch and pressed another one. "Martin, come in a minute, please."

It took Martin Thorpe two minutes to come from his
office on the ninth floor. He did not look the part of
a financial whiz-kid and protégé of one of the most
ruthless go-getters in a traditionally ruthless and go-
getting industry. He looked more like the captain of
the Rugby team from a good public school—charming,
boyish, clean-cut, with dark wavy hair and deep blue
eyes. The secretaries called him dishy, and the directors, who had seen stock options they were certain of
whisked out from under their noses or found their companies slipping into control of a series of nominee shareholders fronting for Martin Thorpe, called him something not quite so nice.

Despite the looks, Thorpe had never been either a
public-school man or an athlete. He could not differenti-

ate between a batting average and the ambient air temperature, but he could retain the hourly movement of share prices across the range of ManCon's subsidiary companies in his head throughout the day. At twenty-nine he had ambitions and the intent to carry them out. ManCon and Sir James might provide the means, so far as he was concerned, and his loyalty depended on his exceptionally high salary, the contracts throughout the City that his job under Manson could bring him, and the knowledge that where he was constituted a good vantage point for spotting what he called "the big one."

By the time he entered, Sir James had slipped the Zangaro report into a drawer, and the Bryant report alone lay on his blotter. He gave his protégé a friendly smile.

"Martin, I've got a job I need done with some discretion. I need it done in a hurry, and it may take half the night."

It was not Sir James's way to ask if Thorpe had any engagements that evening. Thorpe knew that; it went with the salary.

"That's okay, Sir James. I had nothing on that a phone call can't kill."

"Good. Look, I've been going over some old reports and came across this one. Six months ago one of our men from Overseas Contracts was sent out to a place called Zangaro. I don't know why, but I'd like to. The man secured that government's go-ahead for a small team from here to conduct a survey for any possible mineral deposits in unchartered land beyond the mountain range called the Crystal Mountains. Now, what I want to know is this: Was it ever mentioned in advance or at the time, or since that visit six months ago, to the board?"

"To the board?"

"That's right. Was it ever mentioned to the board of directors that we were doing any such survey? That's what I want to know. It may not necessarily be on the agenda. You'll have to look at the minutes. And in case

it got a passing mention under 'any other business,'
check through the documents of all board meetings
over the past twelve months. Secondly, find out who
authorized the visit by Bryant six months ago and why,
and who sent the survey engineer down there and why.
The man who did the survey is called Mulrooney. I
also want to know something about him, which you
can get from his file in Personnel. Got it?"

Thorpe was surprised. This was way out of his line of
country.

"Yes, Sir James, but Miss Cooke could do that in half
the time, or get somebody to do it—"

"Yes, she could. But I want you to do it. If you look
at a file from Personnel, or boardroom documents, it
will be assumed it has something to do with finance.
Therefore it will remain discreet."

The light began to dawn on Martin Thorpe. "You
mean . . . they found something down there, Sir
James?"

Manson stared out at the now inky sky and the blaz-
ing lights below him as the brokers and traders, clerks
and merchants, bankers and assessors, insurers and
jobbers, buyers and sellers, lawyers and, in some offices no doubt, lawbreakers, worked on through the
winter afternoon toward the witching hour of five-
thirty.

"Never mind," he said gruffly to the young man behind him. "Just do it."

Martin Thorpe was grinning as he slipped through
the back entrance of the office and down the stairs
to his own premises. "Cunning bastard," he said to
himself on the stairs.

"Mr. Bryant is here, Sir James."

Manson crossed the room and switched on the main
lights. Returning to his desk, he depressed the intercom
button. "Send him in, Miss Cooke."

There were three reasons why middle-level executives had occasion to be summoned to the sanctum
on the tenth floor. One was to hear instructions or deliver a report that Sir James wanted to issue or hear

personally, which was business. One was to be chewed
into a sweat-soaked rag, which was hell. The third was
that the chief executive had decided he wanted to play
favorite uncle to his cherished employees, which was
reassuring.

On the threshold Richard Bryant, at thirty-nine a
middle-level executive who did his work competently
and well but needed his job, was plainly aware that
the first reason of the three could not be the one that
brought him here. He suspected the second and was
immensely relieved to see it had to be the third.

From the center of the office Sir James walked toward him with a smile of welcome. "Ah, come in,
Bryant. Come in."

As Bryant entered, Miss Cooke closed the door behind him and retired to her desk.

Sir James Manson gestured to his employee to take
one of the easy chairs set well away from the desk in
the conference area of the spacious office. Bryant, still
wondering what it was all about, took the indicated
chair and sank into its brushed suede cushions. Manson
advanced toward the wall and opened two doors, revealing a well-stocked bar cabinet.

"Take a drink, Bryant? Sun's well down, I think."

"Thank you, sir—er—scotch, please."

"Good man. My own favorite poison. I'll join you."

Bryant glanced at his watch. It was quarter to five,
and the tropical maxim about taking a drink after the
sun has gone down was hardly coined for London
winter afternoons. But he recalled an office party at
which Sir James had snorted his derision of sherry-
drinkers and the like and spent the evening on scotch.
It pays to watch things like that, Bryant reflected, as
his chief poured his special Glenlivet into two fine old
crystal glasses. Of course he left the ice bucket strictly
alone.

"Water? Dash of soda?" he called from the bar.

Bryant craned around and spotted the bottle. "Is that
a single malt, Sir James? No, thank you, straight as it
comes."

Manson nodded several times in approval and brought the glasses over. They "Cheers"ed each other and savored the whisky. Bryant was still waiting for the conversation to start. Manson noted this and gave him the gruff-uncle look.

"No need to worry about me having you up here like this," he began. "I was just going through a sheaf of old reports in my desk drawers and came across yours, or one of them. Must have read it at the time and forgotten to give it back to Miss Cooke for filing."

"My report?" queried Bryant.

"Eh? Yes, yes, the one you filed after your return from that place—what's it called again? Zangaro? Was that it?"

"Oh, yes, sir. Zangaro. That was six months ago."

"Yes, quite so. Six months, of course. Noticed as I reread it that you'd had a bit of a rough time with that Minister fellow."

Bryant began to relax. The room was warm, the chair extremely comfortable, and the whisky like an old friend. He smiled at the memory. "But I got the contract for survey permission."

"Damn right you did," congratulated Sir James. He smiled as if at fond memories. "I used to do that in the old days, y'know. Went on some rough missions to bring home the bacon. Never went to West Africa, though. Not in those days. Went later, of course. But after all this started."

To indicate "all this" he waved his hand at the luxurious office.

"So nowadays I spend too much time up here, buried in paperwork," Sir James continued. "I even envy you younger chaps going off to clinch deals in the old way. So tell me about your Zangaro trip."

"Well, that really was doing things the old way. One look, and I half expected to find people running around with bones through their noses," said Bryant.

"Really? Good Lord. Rough place is it, this Zangaro?" Sir James Manson's head had tilted back into the shadows, and Bryant was sufficiently comfortable not to catch the gleam of concentration in the eye that belied the encouraging tone of voice.

"Too right, Sir James. It's a bloody shambles of a place, moving steadily backward into the Middle Ages since independence five years ago." He recalled something else he had heard his chief say once in an aside remark to a group of executives. "It's a classic example of the concept that most of the African republics today have thrown up power groups whose performance in power simply cannot justify their entitlement to leadership of a town dump. As a result, of course, it's the ordinary people who suffer."

Sir James, who was as capable as the next man of recognizing his own words when he heard them played back at him, smiled quietly, rose, and walked to the window to look down at the teeming streets below.

"So who does run the show out there?" he asked quietly.

"The President. Or rather the dicator," said Bryant from his chair. His glass was empty. "A man called Jean Kimba. He won the first and only election, just before independence five years ago, against the wishes of the colonial power—some said by the use of terrorism and voodoo on the voters. They're pretty backward, you know. Most of them didn't know what a vote was. Now they don't need to know."

"Tough guy, is he, this Kimba?" asked Sir James.

"It's not that he's tough, sir. He's just downright mad. A raving megalomaniac, and probably a paranoid to boot. He rules completely alone, surrounded by a small coterie of political yes-men. If they fall out with him, or arouse his suspicions in any way, they go into the cells of the old colonial police barracks. Rumor has it Kimba goes down there himself to supervise the torture sessions. No one has ever come out alive."

"Hm, what a world we live in, Bryant. And they've got the same vote in the UN General Assembly as Britain or America. Whose advice does he listen to in government?"

"No one of his own people. Of course, he has his

voices—so the few local whites say, those who've stuck it out by staying on."

"Voices?" queried Sir James.

"Yes, sir. He claims to the people he is guided by divine voices. He says he talks to God. He's told the people and the assembled diplomatic corps that in so many words."

"Oh dear, not another," mused Manson, still gazing down at the streets below. "I sometimes think it was a mistake to introduce the Africans to God. Half their leaders now seem to be on first-name terms with Him."

"Apart from that, he rules by a sort of mesmeric fear. The people think he has a powerful juju, or voodoo, or magic or whatever. He holds them in the most abject terror."

"What about the foreign embassies?" queried the man by the window.

"Well, sir, they keep themselves to themselves. It seems they are just as terrified of the excesses of this maniac as the natives. He's a bit like a cross between Sheikh Abeid Karume in Zanzibar, Papa Doc Duvalier in Haiti, and Sékou Touré in Guinea."

Sir James turned smoothly from the window and asked with deceptive softness, "Why Sékou Touré?"

"Well, Kimba's next best thing to a Communist, Sir James. The man he really worshiped all his political life was Lumumba. That's why the Russians are so strong. They have an enormous embassy, for the size of the place. To earn foreign currency, now that the plantations have all failed through maladministration, Zangaro sells most of its produce to the Russian trawlers that call. Of course the trawlers are electronic spy ships or supply ships for submarines. Again, the money they get from the sale doesn't go to the people; it goes into Kimba's bank account."

"It doesn't sound like Marxism to me," joked Manson.

Bryant grinned widely. "Money and bribes are where the Marxism stops," he replied. "As usual."

"But the Russians are strong, are they? Influential? Another whisky, Bryant?"

While Bryant replied, the head of ManCon poured two more glasses of Glenlivet.

"Yes, Sir James. Kimba has virtually no understanding of matters outside his immediate experience, which has been exclusively inside his own country and maybe a couple of visits to other African states nearby. So he sometimes consults on matters when dealing with outside concerns. Then he uses any one of three advisers, black ones, who come from his own tribe. Two Moscow-trained, and one Peking-trained. Or he contacts the Russians direct. I spoke to a trader in the bar of the hotel one night, a Frenchman. He said the Russian ambassador or one of his counselors was at the palace almost every day."

Bryant stayed for another ten minutes, but Manson had learned most of what he needed to know. At five-twenty he ushered Bryant out as smoothly as he had welcomed him. As the younger man left, Manson beckoned Miss Cooke in.

"We employ an engineer in mineral exploration work called Jack Mulrooney," he said. "He returned from a three-month sortie into Africa, living in rough bush conditions, three months ago, so he may be on leave still. Try and get him at home. I'd like to see him at ten tomorrow morning. Secondly, Dr. Gordon Chalmers, the chief survey analyst. You may catch him at Watford before he leaves the laboratory. If not, reach him at home. I'd like him here at twelve tomorrow. Cancel any other morning appointments and leave me time to take Chalmers out for a spot of lunch. And you'd better book me a table at Wilton's in Bury Street. That's all, thank you. I'll be on my way in a few minutes. Have the car round at the front in ten minutes."

When Miss Cooke withdrew, Manson pressed one of the switches on his intercom and murmured, "Come up for a minute, would you, Simon?"

Simon Endean was as deceptive as Martin Thorpe

but in a different way. He came from an impeccable background and, behind the veneer, had the morals of an East End thug. Going with the polish and the ruthlessness was a certain cleverness. He needed a James Manson to serve, just as James Manson, sooner or later on his way to the top or his struggle to stay there in big-time capitalism, needed the services of a Simon Endean.

Endean was the sort to be found by the score in the very smartest and smoothest of London's West End gambling clubs—beautifully spoken hatchet men who never leave a millionaire unbowed to or a showgirl unbruised. The difference was that Endean's intelligence had brought him to an executive position as aide to the chief of a very superior gambling club.

Unlike Thorpe, he had no ambitions to become a multimillionaire. He thought one million would do, and until then the shadow of Manson would suffice. It paid for the six-room pad, the Corvette, the girls.

He too came from the floor below and entered from the interior stairwell through the beech-paneled door across the office from the one Miss Cooke came and left by. "Sir James?"

"Simon, tomorrow I'm having lunch with a fellow called Gordon Chalmers. One of the back-room boys. The chief scientist and head of the laboratory out at Watford. He'll be here at twelve. Before then I want a rundown on him. The Personnel file, of course, but anything else you can find. The private man, what his home life is like, any failings; above all, if he has any pressing need for money over and above his salary. His politics, if any. Most of these scientific people are Left. Not all, though. You might have a chat with Errington in Personnel tonight before he leaves. Go through the file tonight and leave it for me to look at in the morning. Sharp tomorrow, start on his home environment. Phone me not later than eleven-forty-five. Got it? I know it's a short-notice job, but it could be important."

Endean took in the instructions without moving a

muscle, filing the lot. He knew the score; Sir James Manson often needed information, for he never faced any man, friend or foe, without a personal rundown on the man, including the private life. Several times he had beaten opponents into submission by being better prepared. Endean nodded and left, making his way straight to Personnel.

As the chauffeur-driven Rolls-Royce slid away from the front of ManCon House, taking its occupant back to his third-floor apartment in Arlington House behind the Ritz, a long, hot bath, and a dinner sent up from the Caprice, Sir James Manson leaned back and lit his first cigar of the evening. The chauffeur handed him a late *Evening Standard,* and they were abreast of Charing Cross Station when a small paragraph in the "Stop Press" caught his eye. It was in among the racing results. He glanced back at it, then read it several times. He stared out at the swirling traffic and huddled pedestrians shuffling toward the station or plodding to the buses through the February drizzle, bound for their homes in Edenbridge and Sevenoaks after another exciting day in the City.

As he stared, a small germ of an idea began to form in his mind. Another man would have laughed and dismissed it out of hand. Sir James Manson was not another man. He was a twentieth-century pirate and proud of it. The nine-point-type headline above the obscure paragraph in the evening paper referred to an African republic. It was not Zangaro, but another one. He had hardly heard of the other one either. It had no known mineral wealth. The headline said:

NEW COUP D'ETAT IN AFRICAN STATE

4

Martin Thorpe was waiting in his chief's outer office when Sir James arrived at five past nine, and followed him straight in.

"What have you got?" demanded Sir James Manson, even while he was taking off his vicuña topcoat and hanging it in the closet. Thorpe flicked open a note-book he had pulled from his pocket and recited the result of his investigations of the night before.

"One year ago we had a survey team in the republic lying to the north and east of Zangaro. It was accompanied by an aerial reconnaissance unit hired from a French firm. The area to be surveyed was close to, and partly on the border with, Zangaro. Unfortunately there are few topographical maps of that area, and no aerial maps at all. Without Decca or any other form of beacon to give him cross-bearings, the pilot used speed and time of flight to assess the ground he had covered.

"One day when there was a following wind stronger than forecast, he flew several times up and down the entire strip to be covered by aerial survey, to his own satisfaction, and returned to base. What he did not know was that on each downwind leg he had flown over the border and forty miles into Zangaro. When the aerial film was developed, it showed that he had overshot the survey area by a large margin."

"Who first realized it? The French company?" asked Manson.

"No, sir. They developed the film and passed it to us without comment, as per our contract with them. It was up to the men in our own aerial-survey department to identify the areas on the ground represented by the pictures they had. Then they realized that at the end of each run was a stretch of territory not in the survey area. So they discarded the pictures, or at any rate put them on one side. They had realized that in one section of pictures a range of hills was featured that could not be in our survey area because there were no hills in that part of the area.

"Then one bright spark had a second look at the surplus photographs and noticed a part of the hilly area, slightly to the east of the main range, had a variation in the density and type of the plant life. The sort of thing you can't see down on the ground, but an aerial picture from three miles up will show it up like a beer-mat on a billiard table."

"I know how it's done," growled Sir James. "Go on."

"Sorry, sir, I didn't know this. It was new to me. So, anyway, half a dozen photos were passed to someone in the Photo-Geology section, and he confirmed from a blow-up that the plant life was different over quite a small area involving a small hill about eighteen hundred feet high and roughly conical in shape. Both sections prepared a report, and that went to the head of Topographic section. He identified the range as the Crystal Mountains and the hill as probably the original Crystal Mountain. He sent the file to Overseas Contracts, and Willoughby, the head of O.C., sent Bryant down there to get permission to survey."

"He didn't tell me," said Manson, now seated behind his desk.

"He sent a memo, Sir James. I have it here. You were in Canada at the time and were not due back for a month. He makes plain he felt the survey of that area was only an off-chance, but since a free aerial survey had been presented to us, and since Photo-Geology felt there had to be some reason for the different vegetation, the expense could be justified. Willoughby also suggested it might serve to give his man Bryant a bit of experience to go it alone for the first time. Up till then he had always accompanied Willoughby."

"Is that it?"

"Almost. Bryant got visa-ed up and went in six months ago. He got permission and arrived back after three weeks. Four months ago Ground Survey agreed to detach an unqualified prospector-cum-surveyor called Jack Mulrooney from the diggings in Ghana and send him to look over the Crystal Mountains, provided that the cost would be kept low. It was. He got back three weeks ago with a ton and a half of samples, which have been at the Watford laboratory ever since."

"Fair enough," said Sir James Manson after a pause. "Now, did the board ever hear about all this?"

"No, sir." Thorpe was adamant. "It would have been considered much too small. I've been through every board meeting for twelve months, and every document presented, including every memo and letter sent to the board members over the same period. Not a mention of it. The budget for the whole thing would simply have been lost in the petty cash anyway. And it didn't originate with Projects, because the aerial photos were a gift from the French firm and their ropy old navigator. It was just an *ad hoc* affair throughout and never reached board level."

James Manson nodded in evident satisfaction. "Right. Now, Mulrooney. How bright is he?"

For answer, Thorpe tended Jack Mulrooney's file from Personnel. "No qualifications, but a lot of practical experience, sir. An old sweat. A good African hand."

Manson flicked through the file on Jack Mulrooney, scanned the biography notes and the career sheet since the man had joined the company. "He's experienced all right," he grunted. "Don't underestimate the old

Africa hands. I started out in the Rand, on a mining camp. Mulrooney just stayed at that level. But never condescend; such people are very useful. And they can be perceptive."

He dismissed Martin Thorpe and muttered to himself, "Now let's see how perceptive Mr. Mulrooney can be."

He depressed the intercom switch and spoke to Miss Cooke. "Is Mr. Mulrooney there yet, Miss Cooke?"

"Yes, Sir James, he's here waiting."

"Show him in, please."

Manson was halfway to the door when his employee was ushered in. He greeted him warmly and led him to the chairs where he had sat with Bryant the previous evening. Before she left, Miss Cooke was asked to produce coffee for them both. Mulrooney's coffee habit was in his file.

Jack Mulrooney in the penthouse suite of a London office building looked as out of place as Thorpe would have in the dense bush. His hands hung way out of his coat sleeves, and he did not seem to know where to put them. His gray hair was plastered down with water, and he had cut himself shaving. It was the first time he had ever met the man he called the gaffer. Sir James used all his efforts to put him at ease.

When Miss Cooke entered with a tray of porcelain cups, matching coffee pot, cream jug and sugar bowl, and an array of Fortnum and Mason biscuits, she heard her employer telling the Irishman, ". . . that's just the point, man. You've got what I or anyone else can't teach these boys fresh out of college, twenty-five years' hard-won experience getting the bloody stuff out of the ground and into the skips."

It is always nice to be appreciated, and Jack Mulrooney was no exception. He beamed and nodded. When Miss Cooke had gone, Sir James Manson gestured at the cups.

"Look at these poofy things. Used to drink out of a good mug. Now they give me thimbles. I remember back on the Rand in the late thirties, and that would be before your time, even . . ."

Mulrooney stayed for an hour. When he left he felt the gaffer was a damn good man despite all they said about him. Sir James Manson thought Mulrooney was a damn good man—at his job, at any rate, and that was and would always be chipping bits of rock off hills and asking no questions.

Just before he left, Mulrooney had reiterated his view. "There's tin down there, Sir James. Stake my life on it. The only thing is, whether it can be got out at an economical figure."

Sir James had slapped him on the shoulder. "Don't you worry about that. We'll know as soon as the report comes through from Watford. And don't worry, if there's an ounce of it that I can get to the coast below market value, we'll have the stuff. Now how about you? What's your next adventure?"

"I don't know, sir. I have three more days' leave yet; then I report back to the office."

"Like to go abroad again?" said Sir James expansively.

"Yes, sir. Frankly, I can't take this city and the weather and all."

"Back to the sun, eh? You like the wild places, I hear."

"Yes, I do. You can be your own man out there."

"You can indeed." Manson smiled. "You can indeed. I almost envy you. No, dammit, I *do* envy you. Anyway, we'll see what we can do."

Two minutes later Jack Mulrooney was gone. Manson ordered Miss Cooke to send his file back to Personnel, rang Accounts and instructed them to send Mulrooney a £1000 merit bonus and make sure he got it before the following Monday, and rang the head of Ground Survey.

"What surveys have you got pending in the next few days or just started?" he asked without preamble.

There were three, one of them in a remote stretch of the extreme north of Kenya, close to the Somaliland border, where the midday sun fries the brain like an egg in a pan, the nights freeze the bone marrow like

Blackpool rock, and the shifta bandits prowl. It would be a long job, close to a year. The head of Ground Survey had nearly had two resignations trying to get a man to go there for so long.

"Send Mulrooney," said Sir James and hung up.

He glanced at the clock. It was eleven. He picked up the Personnel report on Dr. Gordon Chalmers, which Endean had left on his desk the previous evening.

Chalmers was a graduate with honors from the London School of Mining, which is probably the best of its kind in the world, even if Witwatersrand liked to dispute that claim. He had taken his degree in geology and later chemistry and gone on to a doctorate in his mid-twenties. After five years of fellowship work at the college he had joined Rio Tinto Zinc in its scientific section, and six years earlier ManCon had evidently stolen him from RTZ for a better salary. For the last four years he had been head of the company's Scientific Department situated on the outskirts of Watford in Hertfordshire, one of the counties abutting London to the north. The ID photograph in the file showed a man in his late thirties glowering at the camera over a bushy ginger beard. He wore a tweed jacket and a purple shirt. The tie was of knitted wool and askew.

At eleven-thirty-five the private phone rang and Sir James Manson heard the regular pips of a public coin box at the other end of the line. A coin clunked into the slot, and Endean's voice came on the line. He spoke concisely for two minutes from Watford station. When he had finished, Manson grunted his approval.

"That's useful to know," he said. "Now get back to London. There's another job I want you to do. I want a complete rundown on the republic of Zangaro. I want the lot. Yes, Zangaro." He spelled it out.

"Start back in the days when it was discovered, and work forward. I want the history, geography, lie of the land, economy, crops, mineralogy if any, politics, and state of development. Concentrate on the ten years prior to independence, and especially the period since. I want to know everything there is to know about the President, his cabinet, parliament if any, administration, executive, judiciary, and political parties. There are three things that are more important than all else. One is the question of Russian or Chinese involvement and influence, or local Communist influence, on the President. The second is that no one remotely connected with the place is to know any questions are being asked, so don't go there yourself. And thirdly, under no circumstances are you to announce you come from ManCon. So use a different name. Got it? Good. Well, report back as soon as you can, and not later than twenty days. Draw cash from Accounts on my signature alone, and be discreet. For the record, consider yourself on leave; I'll let you make it up later."

Manson hung up and called down to Thorpe to give further instructions. Within three minutes Thorpe came up to the tenth floor and laid the piece of paper his chief wanted on the desk. It was the carbon copy of a letter.

Ten floors down, Dr. Gordon Chalmers stepped out of his taxi at the corner of Moorgate and paid it off. He felt uncomfortable in a dark suit and topcoat, but Peggy had told him they were necessary for an interview and lunch with the Chairman of the Board.

As he walked the last few yards toward the steps and doorway of ManCon House, his eye caught a poster fronting the kiosk of a seller of the *Evening News* and *Evening Standard:* THALIDOMIDE PARENTS URGE SETTLEMENT. He curled his lip in a bitter sneer, but he bought both papers.

The stories backed up the headline in greater detail, though they were not long. They recorded that after another marathon round of talks between representatives of the parents of the four-hundred-odd children in Britain who had been born deformed because of the thalidomide drug ten years earlier, and the company that had marketed the drug, a further impasse had been reached. So talks would be resumed "at a later date."

Gordon Chalmers' thoughts went back to the house

outside Watford that he had left earlier that same morning, to Peggy, his wife, just turned thirty and looking forty, and to Margaret, legless, one-armed Margaret, coming up to nine years, who needed a special pair of legs and a specially built house, which they now lived in at long last, the mortgage on which was costing him a fortune.

"At a later date," he snapped to no one in particular and stuffed the newspapers into a trash basket. He seldom read the evening papers anyway. He preferred the *Guardian, Private Eye,* and the left-wing *Tribune.* After nearly ten years of watching a group of almost unmoneyed parents try to face down the giant distillers for their compensation, Gordon Chalmers harbored bitter thoughts about big-time capitalists. Ten minutes later he was facing one of the biggest.

Sir James Manson could not put Chalmers off his guard as he had Bryant and Mulrooney. The scientist clutched his glass of beer firmly and stared right back. Manson grasped the situation quickly and, when Miss Cooke had handed him his whisky and retired, he came to the point.

"I suppose you can guess what I asked you to come and see me about, Dr. Chalmers."

"I can guess, Sir James. The report on Crystal Mountain."

"That's it. Incidentally, you were quite right to send it to me personally in a sealed envelope. Quite right."

Chalmers shrugged. He had done it because he realized that all important analysis results had to go direct to the Chairman, according to company policy. It was routine, as soon as he had realized what the samples contained.

"Let me ask you two things, and I need specific answers," said Sir James. "Are you absolutely certain of these results? There could be no other possible explanation of the tests of the samples?"

Chalmers was neither shocked nor affronted. He knew the work of scientists was seldom accepted by laymen as being far removed from black magic, and that they therefore considered it imprecise. He had long since ceased trying to explain the precision of his craft.

"Absolutely certain. For one thing, there are a variety of tests to establish the presence of platinum, and these samples passed them all with unvarying regularity. For another, I not only did all the known tests on every one of the samples, I did the whole thing twice. Theoretically it is possible someone could have interfered with the alluvial samples, but not with the internal structures of the rocks themselves. The summary of my report is accurate beyond scientific dispute."

Sir James Manson listened to the lecture with head-bowed respect, and nodded in admiration. "And the second thing is, how many other people in your laboratory know of the results of the analysis of the Crystal Mountain samples?"

"No one," said Chalmers with finality.

"No one?" echoed Manson. "Come now, surely one of your assistants . . ."

Chalmers downed a swig of his beer and shook his head. "Sir James, when the samples came in they were crated as usual and put in store. Mulrooney's accompanying report predicated the presence of tin in unknown quantities. As it was a very minor survey, I put a junior assistant onto it. Being inexperienced, he assumed tin or nothing and did the appropriate tests. When they failed to show up positive, he called me over and pointed this out. I offered to show him how, and again the tests were negative. So I gave him a lecture on not being mesmerized by the prospector's opinion and showed him some more tests. These too were negative. The laboratory closed for the night, but I stayed on late, so I was alone in the place when the first tests came up positive. By midnight I knew the shingle sample from the stream bed, of which I was using less than half a pound, contained small quantities of platinum. After that I locked up for the night.

"The next day I took the junior off that assignment

and put him on another. Then I went on with it myself. There were six hundred bags of shingle and gravel, and fifteen hundred pounds' weight of rocks—over three hundred separate rocks taken from different places on the mountain. From Mulrooney's photographs I could picture the mountain. The disseminated deposit is present in all parts of the formation. As I said in my report." With a touch of defiance he drained his beer.

Sir James Manson continued nodding, staring at the scientist with well-feigned awe.

"It's incredible," he said at length. "I know you scientists like to remain detached, impartial, but I think even you must have become excited. This could form a whole new world source of platinum. You know how often that happens with a rare metal? Once in a decade, maybe once in a lifetime."

In fact Chalmers had been excited by his discovery and had worked late into the night for three weeks to cover every single bag and rock from the Crystal Mountain, but he would not admit it. Instead he shrugged and said, "Well, it'll certainly be very profitable for ManCon."

"Not necessarily," said James Manson quietly. This was the first time he shook Chalmers.

"Not?" queried the analyst. "But surely it's a fortune?"

"A fortune in the ground, yes," replied Sir James, rising and walking to the window. "But it depends very much who gets it, if anyone at all. You see, there is a danger it could be kept unmined for years, or mined and stockpiled. Let me put you in the picture, my dear Doctor . . ."

He put Dr. Chalmers in the picture for thirty minutes, talking finance and politics, neither of which was the analyst's forte.

"So there you are," he finished. "The chances are it will be handed on a plate to the Russian government if we announce it immediately."

Dr. Chalmers, who had nothing in particular against the Russian government, shrugged slightly. "I can't change the facts, Sir James."

Manson's eyebrows shot up in horror. "Good gracious, Doctor, of course you can't." He glanced at his watch in surprise. "Close to one," he exclaimed. "You must be hungry. I know I am. Let's go and have a spot of lunch."

He had thought of taking the Rolls, but after Endean's phone call from Watford that morning and the information from the local news agent about the regular subscription to the *Tribune,* he opted for an ordinary taxi.

A spot of lunch proved to be pâté, truffled omelet, jugged hare in red-wine sauce, and trifle. As Manson had suspected, Chalmers disapproved of such indulgence but at the same time had a healthy appetite. And even he could not reverse the simple laws of nature, which are that a good meal produces a sense of repletion, contentment, euphoria, and a lowering of moral resistance. Manson had also counted on a beer-drinker's being unused to the fuller red wines, and two bottles of Côte du Rhône had encouraged Chalmers to talk about the subjects that interested him: his work, his family, and his views on the world.

It was when he touched on his family and their new house that Sir James Manson, looking suitably sorrowful, mentioned that he recalled having seen Chalmers in a television interview in the street a year back.

"Do forgive me," he said, "I hadn't realized before— I mean, about your little girl. What a tragedy."

Chalmers nodded and gazed at the tablecloth. Slowly at first, and then with more confidence, he began to tell his superior about Margaret.

"You wouldn't understand," he said at one point.

"I can try," replied Sir James quietly. "I have a daughter myself, you know. Of course, she's older."

Ten minutes later there was a pause in the talking. Sir James Manson drew a folded piece of paper from his inside pocket. "I don't really know how to put this," he said with some embarrassment, "but—well, I am as aware as any man how much time and trouble you put in for the company. I am aware you work long hours, and the strain of this personal matter must have its effect on you, and no doubt on Mrs. Chalmers. So I issued this instruction to my personal bank this morning."

He passed the carbon copy of the letter across to Chalmers, who read it. It was brief and to the point. It instructed the manager of Coutts Bank to remit by registered mail each month on the first day fifteen bank-notes, each of value £10, to Dr. Gordon Chalmers at his home address. The remittances were to run for ten years unless further instructions were received.

Chalmers looked up. His employer's face was all concern, tinged with embarrassment.

"Thank you," said Chalmers softly.

Sir James's hand rested on his forearm and shook it. "Now come on, that's enough of this matter. Have a brandy."

In the taxi on the way back to the office, Manson suggested he drop Chalmers off at the station where he could take his train for Watford.

"I have to get back to the office and get on with this Zangaro business and your report," he said.

Chalmers was staring out of the cab window at the traffic moving out of London that Friday afternoon. "What *are* you going to do about it?" he asked.

"Don't know, really. Of course, I'd like not to send it. Pity to see all that going into foreign hands, which is what must happen when your report gets to Zangaro. But I've got to send them something, sooner or later."

There was another long pause as the taxi swung into the station forecourt.

"Is there anything I can do?" asked the scientist.

Sir James Manson breathed a long sigh. "Yes," he said in measured tones. "Junk the Mulrooney samples in the same way as you would junk any other rocks and bags of sand. Destroy your analysis notes completely. Take your copy of the report and make an exact copy, with one difference—let it show the tests prove conclusively that there exist marginal quantities of low-grade tin which could not be economically mined. Burn your own copy of the original report. And then never mention a word of it."

The taxi came to a halt, and as neither of his passengers moved, the cabbie poked his nose through the screen into the rear compartment. "This is it, guv."

"You have my solemn word," murmured Sir James Manson. "Sooner or later the political situation may well change, and when that happens, ManCon will put in a tender for the mining concession exactly as usual and in accordance with normal business procedures."

Dr. Chalmers climbed out of the taxi and looked back at his employer in the corner seat. "I'm not sure I can do that, sir," he said. "I'll have to think it over."

Manson nodded. "Of course you will. I know it's asking a lot. Look, why don't you talk it over with your wife? I'm sure she'll understand."

Then he pulled the door to and told the cabbie to take him to the City.

Sir James dined with an official of the Foreign Office that evening and took him to his club. It was not one of the very uppercrust clubs of London, for Manson had no intention of putting up for one of the bastions of the old Establishment and finding himself blackballed. Besides, he had no time for social climbing and little patience with the posturing idiots one found at the top when one got there. He left the social side of things to his wife. The knighthood was useful, but that was an end to it.

He despised Adrian Goole, whom he reckoned for a pedantic fool. That was why he had invited him to dinner. That, and the fact that the man was in the Economic Intelligence section of the FO.

Years ago, when his company's activities in Ghana and Nigeria had reached a certain level, he had accepted a place on the inner circle of the City's West Africa Committee. This organ was and still is a sort of trade union of all major firms based in London and carrying on operations in West Africa. Concerned far more with trade, and therefore money, than, for example, the East Africa Committee, the WAC periodically reviewed events of both commercial and political interest in West Africa—and usually the two were bound to become connected in the long term—and tendered advice to the Foreign and Commonwealth Office on what would in its view constitute an advisable policy for British interests.

Sir James Manson would not have put it that way. He would have said the WAC was in existence to suggest to the government what to do in that part of the world to improve profits. He would have been right, too. He had been on the committee during the Nigerian civil war and heard the various representatives of banks, mines, oil, and trade advocate a quick end to the war, which seemed to be synonymous with a Federal victory in double time.

Predictably, the committee had proposed to the government that the Federal side be supported, provided it could show it was going to win and win quickly, and provided corroborative evidence from British sources on the spot confirmed this. The committee then sat back and watched the government, on Foreign Office advice, make another monumental African cockup. Instead of lasting six months, the war had lasted thirty. But the businessmen were sick to their teeth at the whole mess and would, with hindsight, have preferred a negotiated peace at month three rather than thirty months of war. But Harold Wilson, once committed to a policy, was no more going to concede that his minions might have made a mistake on his behalf than fly to the moon.

Manson had lost a lot in revenue from his disrupted mining interests and because of the impossibility of shipping the stuff to the coast on crazily running railways throughout the period, but MacFazdean of Shell-BP had lost a lot more in oil production.

Adrian Goole had been the FO's liaison officer on the committee for most of the time. Now he sat opposite James Manson in the alcove dining recess, his cuffs shot the right inch and a quarter, his face register-ing earnest intent.

Manson told him some of the truth but kept the reference to platinum out of it. He stuck to a tale of tin but increased the quantities. It would have been viable to mine it, of course, but quite frankly he'd been scared off by the close dependence of the President on the Russian advisers. The profit-participation of the Zangaran government could well have made it a tidy sum, and since the despot was almost a puppet of the Russkies, who wanted to increase the republic's power and influence through wealth? Goole took it all in. His face wore a solemn expression of deep concern.

"Damnably difficult decision," he said with sym-pathy. "Mind you, I have to admire your political sense. At the moment Zangaro is bankrupt and obscure. But if it became rich— Yes, you're quite right. A real dilemma. When do you have to send them the survey report and analysis?"

"Sooner or later," grunted Manson. "The question is, what do I do about it? If they show it to the Russians at the embassy, the trade counselor is bound to realize the tin deposits are viable. Then it will go out for tender. So someone else will get it, still help to make the dictator rich, and then who knows what problems he'll make for the West? One is back to square one."

Goole thought it over for a while.

"I just thought I ought to let you chaps know," said Manson.

"Yes, yes, thank you." Goole was absorbed. "Tell me," he said at length, "what would happen if you halved the figures showing the quantity of tin per rock-ton in the report?"

"Halved them?"

"Yes. Halved the figures, showing a purity figure of tin per rock-ton of fifty per cent the figures shown by your rock samples?"

"Well, the quantity of tin present would be shown to be economically unviable."

"And the rock samples could have come from another area, a mile away, for example?" asked Goole.

"Yes, I suppose they could. But my surveyor found the richest rock samples."

"But if he had not done so," pursued Goole. "If he had taken his samples from a mile from where he actually operated. The content could be down by fifty per cent?"

"Yes, it could. They probably would, probably would show even less than fifty per cent. But he operated where he did."

"Under supervision?" asked Goole.

"No. Alone."

"And there are no real traces of where he worked?"

"No," replied Manson. "Just a few rock chippings, long since overgrown. Besides, no one goes up there. It's miles from anywhere."

He paused for a few instants to light a cigar. "You know, Goole, you're a damnably clever fellow. Steward, another brandy, if you please."

They parted with mutual jocularity on the steps of the club. The doorman hailed a taxi for Goole to go back to Mrs. Goole in Holland Park.

"One last thing," said the FO man by the taxi door. "Not a word to anyone else about this. I'll have to file it, well classified, at the department, but otherwise it remains just between you and us at the FO."

"Of course," said Manson.

"I'm very grateful you saw fit to tell me áll this. You have no idea how much easier it makes our job on the economic side to know what's going on. I'll keep a quiet eye on Zangaro, and if there should be any change in the political scene there, you'll be the first to know. Good night."

Sir James Manson watched the taxi head down the road and signaled to his Rolls-Royce waiting up the street.

"You'll be the first to know," he mimicked. "Too

bloody right I will, boy. 'Cause I'm going to start it."

He leaned through the passenger-side window and observed to Craddock, his chauffeur, "If pisswilly little buggers like that had been in charge of building our empire, Craddock, we might by now just about have colonized the Isle of Wight."

"You're absolutely right, Sir James," said Craddock.

When his employer had climbed into the rear, the chauffeur slid open the communicating panel. "Gloucestershire, Sir James?"

"Gloucestershire, Craddock."

It was starting to drizzle again as the sleek limousine swished down Piccadilly and up Park Lane, heading for the A40 and the West Country, carrying Sir James Manson toward his ten-bedroom mansion bought three years earlier for him by a grateful company for £250,000. It also contained his wife and nineteen-year-old daughter, but these he had won himself.

An hour later Gordon Chalmers lay beside his wife, tired and angry from the row they had had for the past two hours. Peggy Chalmers lay on her back, looking up at the ceiling.

"I can't do it," Chalmers said for the umpteenth time. "I can't just go and falsify a mining report to help James Bloody Manson make more money."

There was a long silence. They had been over it all a score of times since Peggy had read Manson's letter to his banker and heard from her husband the conditions of future financial security.

"What does it matter?" she said in a low voice from the darkness beside him. "When all's said and done, what does it matter? Whether he gets the concession, or the Russians, or no one. Whether the price rises or falls. What does it matter? It's all pieces of rock and grains of metal."

Peggy Chalmers swung herself across her husband's torso and stared at the dim outline of his face. Outside, the night wind rattled the branches of the old elm close to which they had built the new house with the special fittings for their crippled daughter.

When Peggy Chalmers spoke again it was with passionate urgency. "But Margaret is not a piece of rock, and I am not a few grains of metal. We need that money, Gordon, we need it now and for the next ten years. Please, darling, please just one time forget the idea of a nice letter to *Tribune* or *Private Eye* and do what he wants."

Gordon Chalmers continued to stare at the slit of window between the curtains, which was half open to let in a breath of air.

"All right," he said at length.

"You'll do it?" she asked.

"Yes, I'll bloody do it."

"You swear it, darling? You give me your word?"

There was another long pause. "You have my word," said the low voice from the face above her.

She pillowed her head in the hair of his chest. "Thank you, darling. Don't worry about it. Please don't worry. You'll forget it in a month. You'll see."

Ten minutes later she was asleep, exhausted by the nightly struggle to get Margaret bathed and into bed, and by the unaccustomed quarrel with her husband.

Gordon Chalmers continued to stare into the darkness. "They always win," he said softly and bitterly after a while. "The bastards, they always bloody win."

The following day, Saturday, he drove the five miles to the laboratory and wrote out a completely new report for the republic of Zangaro. Then he burned his notes and the original report and trundled the core samples over to the scrap heap, where a local builder would remove them for concrete and garden paths. He mailed the fresh report, registered, to Sir James Manson at the head office, went home, and tried to forget it.

On Monday the report was received in London, and the instructions to the bankers in Chalmers' favor were mailed. The report was sent down to Overseas Contracts for Willoughby and Bryant to read, and Bryant was told to leave the next day and take it to the Minister of Natural Resources in Clarence. A letter from the company would be attached, expressing the appropriate regret.

On Tuesday evening Richard Bryant found himself in Number One Building at London's Heathrow Airport, waiting for a BEA flight to Paris, where he could get the appropriate visa and make a connecting flight by Air Afrique. Five hundred yards away, in Three Building, Jack Mulrooney humped his bag through Passport Control to catch the BOAC overnight Jumbo to Nairobi. He was not unhappy. He had had enough of London. Ahead lay Kenya, sun, bush, and the chance of a lion.

By the end of the week only two men had in their heads the knowledge of what really lay inside the Crystal Mountain. One had given his word to his wife to remain silent forever, and the other was plotting his next move.

5

Simon Endean entered Sir James Manson's office with a bulky file containing his hundred-page report on the republic of Zangaro, a dossier of large photographs, and several maps. He told his chief what he had brought.

Manson nodded his approval. "No one learned while you were putting all this together who you were or who you worked for?" he asked.

"No, Sir James. I used a pseudonym, and no one questioned it."

"And no one in Zangaro could have learned that a file of data could have been put together about them?"

"No. I used existing archives, sparse though they are, some university libraries here and in Europe, standard works of reference, and the one tourist guide published by Zangaro itself, although in fact this is a leftover from colonial days and five years out of date. I always claimed I was simply seeking information for a graduate thesis on the entire African colonial and postcolonial situation. There will be no comebacks."

"All right," said Manson. "I'll read the report later. Give me the main facts."

For answer Endean took one of the maps from the file and spread it across the desk. It showed a section of the African coastline, with Zangaro marked.

"As you see, Sir James, it's stuck like an enclave on

the coast here, bordered on the north and east by this republic and on the short southern border by this one. The fourth side is the sea, here.

"It's shaped like a matchbox, the short edge along the seacoast, the longer sides stretching inland. The borders were completely arbitrarily drawn in the old colonial days during the scramble for Africa, and merely represent lines on a map. On the ground there are no effective borders, and due to the almost complete nonexistence of roads there is only one border-crossing point—here, on the road leading north to the neighbor country, Manandi. All land traffic enters and leaves by this road."

Sir James Manson studied the enclave on the map and grunted. "What about the eastern and southern borders?"

"No road, sir. No way in or out at all, unless you cut straight through the jungle, and in most places it is impenetrable bush.

"Now, in size it has seven thousand square miles, being seventy miles along the coast and a hundred miles deep into the hinterland. The capital, Clarence, named after the sea captain who first put in there for fresh water two hundred years ago, is here, in the center of the coast, thirty-five miles from the northern and southern borders.

"Behind the capital lies a narrow coastal plain which is the only cultivated area in the country, apart from the bush natives' tiny clearings in the jungle. Behind the plain lies the river Zangaro, then the foothills of the Crystal Mountains, the mountains themselves, and beyond that, miles and miles of jungle up to the eastern border."

"How about other communications?" asked Manson.

"There are virtually no roads at all," said Endean. "The river Zangaro flows from the northern border fairly close to the coast across most of the republic until it reaches the sea just short of the southern border. On the estuary there are a few jetties and a shanty or two which constitute a small port for the exporting of timber. But there are no wharves, and the timber businesses have virtually ceased since independence. The fact that the Zangaro River flows almost parallel to the coast, slanting in toward it, for sixty miles, in effect cuts the republic in two; there is this strip of coastal plain to the seaward side of the river, ending in mangrove swamps which make the whole coast unapproachable by shipping or small boats, and the hinterland beyond the river. East of the river are the mountains, and beyond them the hinterland. The river could be used for barge traffic, but no one is interested. Manandi has a modern capital on the coast with a deep-water harbor, and the Zangaro River itself ends in a silted-up estuary."

"What about the timber-exporting operations? How were they carried out?"

Endean took a larger-scale map of the republic out of the file and laid it on the table. With a pencil he tapped the Zangaro estuary in the south of Zangaro.

"The timber used to be cut upcountry, either along the banks or in the western foothills of the mountains. There's still quite good timber there, but since independence no one is interested. The logs were floated downriver to the estuary and parked there. When the ships came they would anchor offshore and the log rafts were towed out to them by power boats. Then they hoisted the logs aboard by using their own derricks. It always was a tiny operation."

Manson stared intently at the large-scale map taking in the seventy miles of coast, the river running almost parallel to it twenty miles inland, the strip of impenetrable mangrove swamp between the river and the sea, and the mountains behind the river. He could identify the Crystal Mountain but made no mention of it.

"What about the main roads? There must be some."

Endean warmed to his explanation. "The capital is stuck on the seaward end of a short, stubby peninsula here, midway down the coast. It faces toward the open sea. There's a small port, the only real one in the country, and behind the town the peninsula runs back to join the main landmass. There is one road which runs down the spine of the peninsula and six miles inland, going straight east. Then there is the junction—here. A road runs to the right, heading south. It is laterite for seven miles, then becomes an earth road for the next twenty. Then it peters out on the banks of the Zangaro estuary.

"The other branch turns left and runs north, through the plain west of the river and onward to the northern border. Here there is a crossing point manned by a dozen sleepy and corrupt soldiers. A couple of travelers told me they can't read a passport anyway, so they don't know whether there is a visa in it or not. You just bribe them a couple of quid to get through."

"What about the road into the hinterland?" asked Sir James.

Endean pointed with his finger. "It's not even marked, it's so small. Actually, if you follow the north-running road after the junction, go along it for ten miles, there is a turn-off to the right, toward the hinterland. It's an earth road. It crosses the remainder of the plain and then the Zangaro River, on a rickety wooden bridge—"

"So that bridge is the only communication between the two parts of the country on either side of the river?" asked Manson in wonderment.

Endean shrugged. "It's the only crossing for wheeled traffic. But there is hardly any wheeled traffic. The natives cross the Zangaro by canoe."

Manson changed the subject, though his eyes never left the map. "What about the tribes who live there?"

"There are two," said Endean. "East of the river and right back to the end of the hinterland is the country of the Vindu. For that matter, more Vindu live over the eastern border. I said the borders were arbitrary. The Vindu are practically in the Stone Age. They seldom, if ever, cross the river and leave their bush country. The plain to the west of the river and down to the sea, including the peninsula on which the capital stands, is the country of the Caja. They hate the Vindu, and vice versa."

"Population?"

"Almost uncountable in the interior. Officially put at two hundred and twenty thousand in the entire country. That is, thirty thousand Caja and an estimated one hundred and ninety thousand Vindu. But the numbers are a total guess—except probably the Caja can be counted accurately."

"Then how the hell did they ever hold an election?" asked Manson.

"That remains one of the mysteries of creation," said Endean. "It was a shambles, anyway. Half of them didn't know what a vote was or what they were voting for."

"What about the economy?"

"There is hardly any left," replied Endean. "The Vindu country produces nothing. The lot of them just about subsist on what they can grow in yam and cassava plots cut out of the bush by the women, who do any work there is to be done, which is precious little— unless you pay them well; then they will carry things. The men hunt. The children are a mass of malaria, trachoma, bilharzia, and malnutrition.

"In the coastal plain there were in colonial days plantations of low-grade cocoa, coffee, cotton, and bananas. These were run and owned by whites, who used native labor. It wasn't high-quality stuff, but it made enough, with a guaranteed European buyer, the colonial power, to make a bit of hard currency and pay for the minimal imports. Since independence, these have been nationalized by the President, who expelled the whites, and given to his party hacks. Now they're about finished, overgrown with weeds."

"Got any figures?"

"Yes, sir. In the last year before independence total cocoa output, that was the main crop, was thirty thousand tons. Last year it was one thousand tons, and there were no buyers. It's still rotting on the ground."

"And the others—coffee, cotton, bananas?"

"Bananas and coffee virtually ground to a halt through lack of attention. Cotton got hit by a blight, and there were no insecticides."

"What's the economic situation now?"

"Total disaster. Bankrupt, money worthless paper, exports down to almost nothing, and nobody letting them have any imports. There have been gifts from the UN, the Russians, and the colonial powers, but as the government always sells the stuff elsewhere and pockets the cash, even these three have given up."

"A cheap tinhorn dictatorship, eh?" murmured Sir James.

"In every sense. Corrupt, vicious, brutal. They have seas off the coast rich in fish, but they can't fish. The two fishing boats they had were skippered by whites. One got beaten up by the army thugs, and both quit. Then the engines rusted up, and the boats were abandoned. So the locals have protein deficiency. There aren't even goats and chickens to go around."

"What about medicines?"

"There's one hospital in Clarence, which is run by the United Nations. That's the only one in the country."

"Doctors?"

"There were two Zangarans who were qualified doctors. One was arrested and died in prison. The other fled into exile. The missionaries were expelled by the President as imperialist influences. They were mainly medical missionaries as well as preachers and priests. The nuns used to train nurses, but they got expelled as well."

"How many Europeans?"

"In the hinterlands, probably none. In the coastal plain, a couple of agronomists, technicians sent by the United Nations. In the capital, about forty diplomats, twenty of them in the Russian embassy, the rest spread among the French, Swiss, American, West German, East German, Czech, and Chinese embassies, if you call the Chinese white. Apart from that, about five United Nations hospital staff, another five technicians manning the electrical generator, the airport control tower, the waterworks, and so on. Then there must be fifty others, traders, managers, businessmen who have hung on hoping for an improvement.

"Actually, there was a ruckus six weeks ago and one of the UN men was beaten half to death. The five nonmedical technicians threatened to quit and sought refuge in their respective embassies. They may be gone by now, in which case the water, electricity, and airport will soon be out of commission."

"Where is the airport?"

"Here, on the base of the peninsula behind the capital. It's not of international standards, so if you want to fly in you have to take Air Afrique to here, in Manandi, and take a connecting flight by a small two-engined plane that goes down to Clarence three times a week. It's a French firm that has the concession, though nowadays it's hardly economic."

"Who are the country's friends, diplomatically speaking?"

Endean shook his head. "They don't have any. No one is interested, it's such a shambles. Even the Organization of African Unity is embarrassed by the whole place. It's so obscure no one ever mentions it. No newsmen ever go, so it never gets publicized. The government is rabidly anti-white, so no one wants to send staff men down there to run anything. No one invests anything, because nothing is safe from confiscation by any Tom, Dick, or Harry wearing a party badge. There's a party youth organization that beats up anyone it wants to, and everyone lives in terror."

"What about the Russians?"

"They have the biggest mission and probably a bit of say over the President in matters of foreign policy, about which he knows nothing. His advisers are mainly Moscow-trained Zangarans, though he wasn't schooled in Moscow personally."

"Is there any potential at all down there?" asked Sir James.

Endean nodded slowly. "I suppose there is enough

potential, well managed and worked, to sustain the population at a reasonable degree of prosperity. The population is small, the needs few; they could be self-sufficient in clothing, food, the basics of a good local economy, with a little hard currency for the necessary extras. It could be done, but in any case, the needs are so few the relief and charitable agencies could provide the total necessary, if it wasn't that their staffs are always molested, their equipment smashed or looted, and their gifts stolen and sold for the government's private profit."

"You say the Vindu won't work hard. What about the Caja?"

"Nor they either," said Endean. "They just sit about all day, or fade into the bush if anyone looks threatening. Their fertile plain has always grown enough to sustain them, so they are happy the way they are."

"Then who worked the estates in the colonial days?"

"Ah, the colonial power brought in about twenty thousand black workers from elsewhere. They settled and live there still. With their families, they are about fifty thousand. But they were never enfranchised by the colonial power, so they never voted in the election at independence. If there is any work done, they still do it."

"Where do they live?" asked Manson.

"About fifteen thousand still live in their huts on the estates, even though there is no more work worth doing, with all the machinery broken down. The rest have drifted toward Clarence and grub a living as best they can. They live in a series of shanty towns scattered down the road at the back of the capital, on the road to the airport."

For five minutes Sir James Manson stared at the map in front of him, thinking deeply about a mountain, a mad President, a coterie of Moscow-trained advisers, and a Russian embassy. Finally he sighed. "What a bloody shambles of a place."

"That's putting it mildly," said Endean. "They still have ritual public executions before the assembled populace in the main square. Death by being chopped to pieces with a machete. Quite a bunch."

"And who precisely has produced this paradise on earth?"

For answer, Endean produced a photograph and placed it on the map.

Sir James Manson found himself looking at a middle-aged African in a silk top hat, black frock coat, and checked trousers. It was evidently inauguration day, for several colonial officials stood in the background, by the steps of a large mansion. The face beneath the shining black silk was not round, but long and gaunt, with deep lines on each side of the nose. The mouth was twisted downward at each corner, so that the effect was of deep disapproval of something.

But the eyes held the attention. There was a glazed fixity about them, as one sees in the eyes of fanatics.

"That's the man," said Endean. "Mad as a hatter, and nasty as a rattlesnake. West Africa's own Papa Doc. Visionary, communicant with spirits, liberator from the white man's yoke, redeemer of his people, swindler, robber, police chief and torturer of the suspicious, extractor of confessions, hearer of voices from the Almighty, seer of visions, Lord High Everything Else, His Excellency, President Jean Kimba."

Sir James Manson stared longer at the face of the man who, unbeknownst to himself, was sitting in control of ten billion dollars' worth of platinum. I wonder, he thought to himself, if the world would really notice his passing on.

He said nothing, but, after he had listened to Endean, that event was what he had decided to arrange.

Six years earlier the colonial power ruling the enclave now called Zangaro, increasingly conscious of world opinion, had decided to grant independence. Overhasty preparations were made among a population wholly inexperienced in self-government, and a general election and independence were fixed for the following year.

In the confusion, five political parties came into be-

ing. Two were wholly tribal, one claiming to look
after the interests of the Vindu, the other of the Caja.
The other three parties devised their own political
platforms and pretended to make appeal through the
tribal division of the people. One of these parties was
the conservative group, led by a man holding office under the colonialists and heavily favored by them. He
pledged he would continue the close links with the
mother country, which, apart from anything else,
guaranteed the local paper money and bought the ex-
portable produce. The second party was centrist, small
and weak, led by an intellectual, a professor who had
studied in Europe. The third was radical and led by a
man who had served several prison terms under a
security classification. This was Jean Kimba.

Long before the elections, two of his aides, men who
during their time as students in Europe had been
contacted by the Russians (who had noticed their
presence in anti-colonial street demonstrations) and
who had accepted scholarships to finish their schooling
at the Patrice Lumumba University outside Moscow,
left Zangaro secretly and flew to Europe. There they
met emissaries from Moscow and, as a result of their
conversations, received a sum of money and considerable advice of a very practical nature.

Using the money, Kimba and his men formed squads
of political thugs from among the Vindu and completely ignored the small minority of Caja. In the
unpoliced hinterland the political squads went to work.
Several agents of the rival parties came to very sticky
ends, and the squads visited all the clan chiefs of the
Vindu.

After several public burnings and eye-gougings, the
clan chiefs got the message. When the elections came,
acting on the simple and effective logic that you do
what the man with the power to extract painful retribu-
tion tells you, and ignore or mock the weak and the
powerless, the chiefs ordered their people to vote for
Kimba. He won the Vindu by a clear majority, and
the total votes cast for him swamped the combined

opposition and the Caja votes. He was aided by the fact that the number of the Vindu votes had been almost doubled by the persuasion of every village chief to increase the number of people he claimed lived in his village. The rudimentary census taken by the colonial officials was based on affidavits from each village chief as to the population of his village.

The colonial power had made a mess of it. Instead of taking a leaf from the French book and ensuring that the colonial protégé won the first, vital election and then signed a mutual defense treaty to ensure that a company of white paratroops kept the pro-Western president in power in perpetuity, the colonials had allowed their worst enemy to win. A month after the election, Jean Kimba was inaugurated as first President of Zangaro.

What followed was along traditional lines. The four other parties were banned as "divisive influences," and later the four party leaders were arrested on trumped-up charges. They died under torture in prison, after making over the party funds to the liberator, Kimba. The colonial army and police officers were dismissed as soon as a semblance of an exclusively Vindu army had been brought into being. The Caja soldiers, who had constituted most of the gendarmerie under the colonists, were dismissed at the same time, and trucks were provided to take them home. After leaving the capital, the six trucks headed for a quiet spot on the Zangaro River, and here the machine guns opened up. That was the end of the trained Caja.

In the capital, the police and customs men, mainly Caja, were allowed to stay on, but their guns were emptied and all their ammunition was taken away. Power passed to the Vindu army, and the reign of terror started. It had taken eighteen months to achieve this. The confiscation of the estates, assets, and businesses of the colonists began, and the economy ran steadily down. There were no Vindu trained to take over who could run the republic's few enterprises with even moderate efficiency, and the estates were in any case given to Kimba's party supporters. As the colonists left, a few UN technicians came in to run the basic essentials, but the excesses they witnessed caused most sooner or later to write home to their governments insisting they be removed.

After a few short, sharp examples of terror, the timorous Caja were subdued into absolute submission, and even across the river in Vindu country several savage examples were made of chiefs who mumbled something about the pre-election promises. After that the Vindu simply shrugged and went back to their bush. What happened in the capital had never affected them anyway in living memory, so they could afford to shrug. Kimba and his group of supporters, backed by the Vindu army and the unstable and highly dangerous teenagers who made up the party's youth movement, continued to rule from Clarence entirely for their own benefit and profit.

Some of the methods used to obtain the latter were mind-boggling. Simon Endean's report contained documentation of an instance where Kimba, frustrated over the nonarrival of his share of a business deal, arrested the European businessman involved and imprisoned him, sending an emissary to his wife with the pledge that she would receive her husband's toes, fingers, and ears by post unless a ransom were paid. A letter from her imprisoned husband confirmed this, and the woman raised the necessary half-million dollars from his business partners and paid. The man was released, but his government, terrified of black African opinion at the United Nations, urged him to remain silent. The press never heard about it. On another occasion two nationals of the colonial power were arrested and beaten in the former colonial police barracks, since converted into the army barracks. They were released after a handsome bribe was paid to the Minister of Justice, of which a part evidently went to Kimba. Their offense was failing to bow as Kimba's car drove past.

In the previous five years since independence, all

conceivable opposition to Kimba had been wiped out or driven into exile, and those who suffered the latter were the lucky ones. As a result there were no doctors, engineers, or other qualified people left in the republic. There had been few enough in the first place, and Kimba suspected all educated men as possible opponents.

Over the years he had developed a psychotic fear of assassination and never left the country. He seldom left the palace, and, when he did, it was under a massive escort. Firearms of every kind and description had been rounded up and impounded, including hunting rifles and shotguns, so that the scarcity of protein food increased. Import of cartridges and black powder was halted, so eventually the Vindu hunters of the interior, coming to the coast to buy the powder they needed to hunt game, were sent back empty-handed and hung up their useless dane guns in their huts. Even the carrying of machetes within the city limits was forbidden. The carrying of any of these items was punishable by death.

When he had finally digested the lengthy report, studied the photographs of the capital, the palace, and Kimba, and pored over the maps, Sir James Manson sent again for Simon Endean.

The latter was becoming highly curious about his chief's interest in this obscure republic and had asked Martin Thorpe in the adjoining office on the ninth floor what it was about. Thorpe had just grinned and tapped the side of his nose with a rigid forefinger. Thorpe was not completely certain either, but he suspected he knew. Both men knew enough not to ask questions when their employer had got an idea in his head and needed information.

When Endean reported to Manson the following morning, the latter was standing in his favorite position by the plate-glass windows of his penthouse, looking down into the street, where pygmies hurried about their business.

"There are two things I need to know more about,

Simon," Sir James Manson said without preamble and walked back to his desk, where the Endean report was lying. "You mention here a ruckus in the capital about six to seven weeks ago. I heard another report about the same upset from a man who was there. He mentioned a rumor of an attempted assassination of Kimba. What was it all about?"

Endean was relieved. He had heard the same story from his own sources but had thought it too small to include in the report.

"Every time the President has a bad dream there are arrests and rumors of an attempt on his life," said Endean. "Normally it just means he wants justification to arrest and execute somebody. In this case, in late January, it was the commander of the army, Colonel Bobi. I was told, on the quiet, the quarrel between the two men was really about Kimba's not getting a big enough cut in the rake-off from a deal Bobi put through. A shipment of drugs and medicines had arrived for the UN hospital. The army impounded them at the quayside and stole half. Bobi was responsible, and the stolen portion of the cargo was sold elsewhere on the black market. The proceeds of the sale should have passed to Kimba. Anyway, the head of the UN hospital, when making his protest to Kimba and tendering his resignation, mentioned the true value of the missing stuff. It was a lot more than Bobi had admitted to Kimba.

"The President went mad and sent some of his own guards out looking for Bobi. They ransacked the town, arresting anyone who got in the way or took their fancy."

"What happened to Bobi?" asked Manson.

"He fled. He got away in a jeep and made for the border. He got across by abandoning his jeep and walking through the bush round the border control point."

"What tribe is he?"

"Oddly enough, a halfbreed. Half Vindu and half

Caja, probably the outcome of a Vindu raid on a Caja village forty years ago."

"Was he one of Kimba's new army, or the old colonial one?" asked Manson.

"He was corporal in the colonial gendarmerie, so presumably he had some form of rudimentary training. Then he was busted, before independence, for drunkenness and insubordination while drunk. When Kimba came to power he took him back in the early days because he needed at least one man who could tell one end of a gun from the other. In the colonial days Bobi styled himself a Caja, but as soon as Kimba came to power he swore he was a true Vindu."

"Why did Kimba keep him on? Was he one of his original supporters?"

"From the time Bobi saw which way the wind was blowing, he went to Kimba and swore loyalty to him. Which was smarter than the colonial governor, who couldn't believe Kimba had won the election until the figures proved it. Kimba kept Bobi on and even promoted him to command the army, because it looked better for a half-Caja to carry out the reprisals against the Caja opponents of Kimba."

"What's he like?" asked Manson pensively.

"A big thug," said Simon. "A human gorilla. No brains as such, but a certain low animal cunning. The quarrel between the two men was only a question of thieves falling out."

"But Western-trained? Not Communist?" insisted Manson.

"No, sir. Not a Communist. Not anything politically."

"Bribable? Cooperate for money?"

"Certainly. He must be living pretty humbly now. He couldn't have stashed much away outside Zangaro. Only the President could get the big money."

"Where is he now?" asked Manson.

"I don't know, sir. Living somewhere in exile."

"Right," said Manson. "Find him, wherever he is."

Endean nodded. "Am I to visit him?"

"Not yet," said Manson. "There was one other matter. The report is fine, very comprehensive, except in
one detail. The military side. I want to have a complete
breakdown of the military security situation in and
around the President's palace and the capital. How
many troops, police, any special presidential bodyguards, where they are quartered, how good they are,
level of training and experience, the amount of fight
they would put up if under attack, what weapons they
carry, can they use them, what reserves are there,
where the arsenal is situated, whether they have guards
posted overall, if there are armored cars or artillery, if
the Russians train the army, if there are strike-force
camps away from Clarence—in fact, the whole lot."

Endean stared at his chief in amazement. The phrase
"if under attack" stuck in his mind. What on earth was
the old man up to? he wondered, but his face remained
impassive.

"That would mean a personal visit, Sir James."

"Yes, I concede that. Do you have a passport in another name?"

"No, sir. In any case, I couldn't furnish that information. It requires a sound judgment of military matters,
and a knowledge of African troops as well. I was too
late for National Service. I don't know a thing about
armies or weapons."

Manson was back at the window, staring across the
City. "I know," he said softly. "It would need a soldier
to produce that report."

"Well, Sir James, you would hardly get an army man
to go and do that sort of mission. Not for any money.
Besides, a soldier's passport would have his profession
on it. Where could I find a military man who would
go down to Clarence and find that sort of information?"

"There is a kind," said Manson. "The mercenaries.
They fight for whoever pays them and pays them well.
I'm prepared to do that. So go and find me a mercenary
with initiative and brains. The best in Europe."

Cat Shannon lay on his bed in the small hotel in Montmartre and watched the smoke from his cigarette drifting up toward the ceiling. He was bored. In the weeks that had passed since his return from Africa he had spent most of his saved pay traveling around Europe trying to set up another job.

In Rome he had seen an order of Catholic priests he knew, with a view to going to South Sudan on their behalf to set up in the interior an airstrip into which medical supplies and food could be ferried. He knew there were three separate groups of mercenaries operating in South Sudan, helping the Christian blacks in their civil war against the Arab North. In Bahr-el-Gazar two other British mercenaries, Ron Gregory and Rip Kirby, were leading a small operation of Dinka tribesmen, laying mines along the roads used by the Sudanese army in an attempt to knock out their British Saladin armored cars. In the south, in Equatoria Province, Rolf Steiner had a camp that was supposed to be training the locals in the arts of war, but nothing had been heard of him for months. In Upper Nile, to the east, there was a much more efficient camp, where four Israelis were training the tribesmen and equipping them with Soviet weaponry from the vast stocks the Israelis had taken from the Egyptians in 1967. The warfare in the three provinces of South Sudan kept the bulk of the Sudanese army and air force pinned down there, so that five squadrons of Egyptian fighters were based around Khartoum and thus not available to confront the Israelis on the Suez Canal.

Shannon had visited the Israeli embassy in Paris and talked for forty minutes to the military attaché. The latter had listened politely, thanked him politely, and just as politely ushered him out. The only thing the officer would say was that there were no Israeli advisers on the rebel side in South Sudan, and therefore he could not help. Shannon had no doubts the conversation had been tape-recorded and sent to Tel Aviv, but doubted he would hear any more. He conceded the

Israelis were first rate as fighters and good at intelligence, but he thought they knew nothing about black Africa and were heading for a fall in Uganda and probably elsewhere.

Apart from Sudan, there was little else being offered. Rumors abounded that the CIA was hiring mercenaries for training anti-Communist Meos in Cambodia, and that some Persian Gulf sheiks were getting fed up with their dependence on British military advisers and were looking for mercenaries who would be entirely their own dependents. The story was that there were jobs going for men prepared to fight for the sheiks in the hinterland or take charge of palace security. Shannon doubted all these stories; for one thing he wouldn't trust the CIA as far as he could spit, and the Arabs were not much better when it came to making up their minds.

Outside of the Gulf, Cambodia, and Sudan, there was little scope and there were no good wars. In fact he foresaw in the offing a very nasty outbreak of peace. That left the chance of working as a bodyguard for a European arms dealer, and he had had one approach from such a man in Paris who felt himself threatened and needed someone good to give him cover.

Hearing Shannon was in town and knowing his skill and speed, the arms dealer had sent an emissary with the proposition. Without actually turning it down, the Cat was not keen. The dealer was in trouble through his own stupidity: a small matter of sending a shipment of arms to the Provisional IRA and then tipping off the British as to where it would be landed. There had been a number of arrests, and the Provos were furious. Having Shannon giving gun-cover would send most professionals back home while still alive, but the Provos were mad dogs and probably did not know enough to stay clear. So there would be a gunfight, and the French police would take a dim view of one of their streets littered with bleeding Fenians. Moreover, as he was an Ulster Protestant, they would never believe Shannon had just been doing his job. Still, the offer was open.

The month of March had opened and was ten days through, but the weather remained dank and chill, with daily drizzle and rain, and Paris was unwelcoming. Outdoors meant fine weather in Paris, and indoors cost a lot of money. Shannon was husbanding his remaining resources of dollars as best he could. So he left his telephone number with the dozen or so people he thought might hear something to interest him and read several paperback novels in his hotel room.

He lay staring at the ceiling and thinking of home. Not that he really had a home any more, but for want of a better word he still thought of the wild sweep of turf and stunted trees that sprawls across the border of Tyrone and Donegal as the place that he came from.

He had been born and brought up close to the small village of Castlederg, situated inside County Tyrone but lying on the border with Donegal. His parents' house had been set a mile from the village on a slope looking out to the west across Donegal.

They called Donegal the county God forgot to finish, and the few trees were bent toward the east, curved over by the constant beating of the winds from the North Atlantic.

His father had owned a flax mill that turned out fine Irish linen and had been in a small way the squire of the area. He was Protestant, and almost all the workers and local farmers were Catholic, and in Ulster never the twain shall meet, so the young Carlo had had no other boys to play with. He made his friends among the horses instead, and this was horse country. He could ride before he could mount a bicycle, and had a pony of his own when he was five, and he could still remember riding the pony into the village to buy a halfpennyworth of sherbet powder from the sweetshop of old Mr. Sam Gailey.

At eight he had been sent to boarding school in England at the urging of his mother, who was English and came from moneyed people. So for the next ten years he had learned to be an Englishman and had to all intents and purposes lost the stamp of Ulster in both speech and attitudes. During the holidays he had gone home to the moors and the horses, but he knew no contemporaries near Castlederg, so the vacations were lonely if healthy, consisting of long, fast gallops in the wind.

It was while he was a sergeant in the Royal Marines at twenty-two that his parents had died in a car crash on the Belfast Road. He had returned for the funeral, smart in his black belt and gaiters, topped by the green beret of the Commandos. Then he had accepted an offer for the run-down, nearly bankrupt mill, closed up the house, and returned to Portsmouth.

That was eleven years ago. He had served the remainder of his five-year contract in the Marines, and on returning to civilian life had pottered from job to job until taken on as a clerk by a London merchant house with widespread African interests. Working his probationary year in London, he had learned the intricacies of company structure, trading and banking the profits, setting up holding companies, and the value of a discreet Swiss account. After a year in London he had been posted as assistant manager of the Uganda branch office, from which he had walked out without a word and driven into the Congo. So for the last six years he had lived as a mercenary, often as outlaw, at best regarded as a soldier for hire, at worst as a paid killer. The trouble was, once he was known as a mercenary, there was no going back. It was not a question of being unable to get a job in a business house; that could be done at a pinch, or even by giving a different name. Even without going to these lengths, one could always get hired as a truck-driver, as a security guard, or for some manual job if the worst came to the worst. The real problem was being able to stick it out, to sit in an office under the orders of a wee man in a dark gray suit and look out of the window and recall the bush country, the waving palms, the smell of sweat and cordite, the grunts of the men hauling the jeeps over the river crossings, the copper-tasting fears just before the attack, and the wild, cruel joy of being alive afterward. To remember, and then to go back to the ledgers and the commuter train, that was what was impossible. He knew he would eat his heart out if it ever came to that. For Africa bites like a tse-tse fly, and once the drug is in the blood it can never be wholly exorcised.

So he lay on his bed and smoked some more and wondered where the next job was coming from.

6

Simon Endean was aware that somewhere in London there had to exist the wherewithal to discover just about any piece of knowledge known to man, including the name and address of a first-class mercenary. The only problem sometimes is to know where to start looking and whom to start asking.

After a reflective hour drinking coffee in his office, he left and took a taxi down to Fleet Street. Through a friend on the city desk of one of London's biggest daily papers, he got access to that paper's morgue and to virtually every newspaper clipping in Britain over the previous ten years concerning mercenaries. There were articles about Katanga, the Congo, Yemen, Vietnam, Cambodia, Laos, Sudan, Nigeria, and Rwanda; news items, commentaries, editorial feature articles, and photographs. He read them all and paid special attention to the names of the writers.

At this stage he was not looking for the name of a mercenary. There were in any case too many names—pseudonyms, noms de guerre, nicknames—and he had little doubt some of them were false. He was looking for the name of an expert on mercenaries, a writer or reporter whose articles seemed to be authoritative enough to indicate that the journalist knew his subject well, who could find his way around the bewildering labyrinth of rival claims and alleged exploits and give a balanced judgment. At the end of two hours he had secured the name he was looking for, although he had never heard of the man before.

There were three articles over the previous three years carrying the same byline, apparently that of an Englishman or American. The writer seemed to know what he was talking about, and he mentioned mercenaries from half a dozen different nationalities, neither overpraising them nor sensationalizing their careers to set spines atingling. Endean noted the name and the three newspapers in which the articles had appeared, a fact which seemed to indicate that the writer was freelancing. A second phone call to his newspaper friend eventually produced the writer's address. It was a small flat in North London.

Darkness had already fallen when Endean left Man-Con House, and, having taken his Corvette from the underground parking lot, he drove northward to find the journalist's flat. The lights were off when he got there, and there was no answer to the doorbell. Endean hoped the man was not abroad, and the woman in the basement flat confirmed that he was not. He was glad to see the house was not large or smart and hoped the reporter might be hard up for a little extra cash, as freelances usually are. He decided to come back in the morning.

Simon Endean pressed the bell next to the writer's name just after eight the following morning, and half a minute later a voice tinkled "Yes" at him from the metal grill set in the woodwork.

"Good morning," said Endean into the grill. "My name is Harris. Walter Harris. I'm a businessman. I wonder if I might have a word with you?"

The door opened, and he mounted to the fourth floor, where a door stood open onto the landing. Framed in it was the man he had come to see. When they were seated in the sitting room, Endean came straight to the point.

"I am a businessman in the City," he lied smoothly. "I am here, in a sense, representing a consortium of friends, all of whom have this in common: that we all have business interests in a state in West Africa."

The writer nodded warily and sipped his coffee.

"Recently there have been increasing reports of the possibility of a coup d'état. The President is a moderate and reasonably good man, as things go down there, and very popular with his people. One of my business friends was told by one of his workers that the coup, if and when it came, could well be Communist-backed. Do you follow me?"

"Yes. Go on."

"Well now, it is felt that no more than a small portion of the army would support a coup unless the speed of it threw them into confusion and left them leaderless. In other words, if it were a *fait accompli,* the bulk of the army might agree to go along in any case, once they realized the coup had succeeded. But if it came and half failed, the bulk of the army would, we all feel sure, support the President. As you may know, experience shows the twenty hours following the strike are the vital ones."

"What has this to do with me?" asked the writer.

"I'm coming to that," said Endean. "The general feeling is that, for the coup to succeed, it would be necessary for the plotters first to assassinate the President. If he remained alive, the coup would fail, or might not even be tried, and all would be well. Therefore the question of palace security is vital and becoming more so. We have been in touch with some friends in the Foreign Office, and they feel it is out of the question to send a professional British officer to advise on security in and around the palace."

"So?" The writer sipped more coffee and lit a cigarette. He reckoned his visitor was too smooth, too smooth by half.

"So the President would be prepared to accept the services of a professional soldier to advise, on the basis of a contract, on all security matters regarding the person of the President. What he is seeking is a man who could go down there, make a complete and thorough survey of the palace and all its security arrangements, and plug any loopholes in the existing security measures surrounding the President."

The freelance nodded several times. He had few doubts that the story of the man who called himself Harris was some way from true. For one thing, if palace security was really what was sought, the British government would not be against providing the expert to advise on its improvement. For another, there was a perfectly capable firm at 22 Sloane Street, London, called Watchguard International, whose specialty was precisely that. In a few sentences he pointed this out to Harris.

Endean was not fazed in the slightest. "Ah," he said, "evidently I have to be a little more candid."

"It would help," said the writer.

"The point is, you see, that HMG might agree to send an expert merely to advise, but if the advice was that the palace security troops needed extensive further training—and a crash course, at that—politically speaking a Britisher sent by the government could not do that. And if the President wished to offer the man a longer-term post on his staff, the same would apply. As for Watchguard, one of their ex-Special Air Service men would be fine, but if he were on the staff of the palace guard and a coup were tried despite his presence, there might be a question of combat. Now you know what the rest of Africa would think about a staff man from Watchguard, which most of these blacks regard as being linked to the Foreign Office in some way, doing that. But a pure outsider, although not respectable, would at least be understandable, without exposing the President to the sneer of being a tool of the dirty old imperialists."

"So what do you want?" asked the writer.

"The name of a good mercenary soldier," said Endean. "One with brains and initiative, who'll do a workmanlike job for his money."

"Why come to me?"

"Your name was recalled by one of our group from an article you wrote several months ago. It seemed very authoritative."

"I write for my living," said the freelance.

Endean gently withdrew £200 in £10 notes from his pocket and laid them on the table. "Then write for me."

"What? An article?"

"No, a memorandum. A list of names and track records. Or you can talk if you like."

"I'll write," said the freelance. He walked to a corner, where his desk, a typewriter, and a stack of white paper comprised the working area of the open-plan flat. Having run a sheet into his machine, he wrote steadily for fifty minutes, consulting occasionally from a set of files beside his desk. When he rose, he walked over to the waiting Endean with three sheets of quarto paper and held them out.

"These are the best around today, the older generation of the Congo six years ago and the new up-and-comers. I haven't bothered with men who couldn't command a platoon well. Mere heavies would be no use to you."

Endean took the sheets and studied them intently. The contents were:

COLONEL LAMOULINE. Belgian, probably government man. Came into Congo in 1964 under Moïse Tshombe. Probably with full approval of Belgian government. First-class soldier, not really a mercenary in full sense of the word. Set up Sixth Commando (French-speaking) and commanded until 1965, when he handed over command to Denard and left.

ROBERT DENARD. Frenchman. Police background, not army. Was in Katanga secession in 1961–62, probably as gendarmerie adviser. Left after failure of secession and exile of Tshombe. Commanded French mercenary operation in Yemen for Jacques Foccart. Returned Congo 1964, joined Lamouline. Commanded Sixth after Lamouline and up till 1967. Took part, halfheartedly, in second Stanleyville revolt (the mercenaries' mutiny) in 1967. Wounded badly in head by ricocheting bullet from own side. Flown out of Rhodesia for treatment. Tried to return by mounting November 1967 mercenary invasion of Congo from the south at Dilolo. Operation delayed, some said as a result of CIA bribes, was a fiasco when it happened. Since lived in Paris.

JACQUES SCHRAMME. Belgian. Planter-turned-mercenary. Nicknamed Black Jacques. Formed own unit of Katangese early in 1961 and was prominent in Katangese secession attempt. One of the last to flee into Angola on defeat of the secession. Took his Katangese with him. Waited in Angola until return of Tshombe, then marched back into Katanga. Through the 1964–65 war against the Simba rebels, his 10th Codo was more or less independent. Sat out the first Stanleyville revolt of 1966 (the Katangese mutiny), and his mixed mercenary/Katangese force was left intact. Launched 1967 Stanleyville mutiny, in which Denard later joined. Took joint command after wounding of Denard and led the march to Bukavu. Repatriated 1968, no further mercenary work since.

ROGER FAULQUES. Much-decorated French professional officer. Sent, probably by French govt., into Katanga during secession. Later commanded Denard, who ran the French operation in the Yemen. Was not involved in Congolese mercenary operations. Mounted small operation at French behest in Nigerian civil war. Ferociously brave but now nearly crippled by combat wounds.

MIKE HOARE. British-turned-South African. Acted as mercenary adviser in Katanga secession, became close personal friend of Tshombe. Invited back to Congo in 1964, when Tshombe returned to power, and formed English-speaking Fifth Commando. Commanded through bulk of anti-Simba war, retired in December 1965 and handed over to Peters. Well off and semi-retired.

JOHN PETERS. Joined Hoare in 1964 in first mercenary war. Rose to become deputy commander. Fearless and totally ruthless. Several officers under Hoare refused to serve under Peters and transferred or left 5th Codo. Retired wealthy late 1966.

N.B. The above six count as "the older generation," inasmuch as they were the originals who came to prominence in the Katanga and Congolese wars. The following five are younger in age, except Roux, who is now in his mid-forties, but may be considered the "younger" generation because they had junior commands in the Congo or came to prominence since the Congo.

ROLF STEINER. German. Began first mercenary operation under Faulques-organized group that went into Nigerian civil war. Stayed on and led the remnants of the group for nine months. Dismissed. Signed on for South Sudan.

GEORGE SCHROEDER. South African. Served under Hoare and Peters in 5th Codo in the Congo. Prominent in the South African contingent in that unit. Their choice as leader after Peters. Peters conceded and gave him the command. 5th Codo disbanded and sent home a few months later. Not heard of since. Living in South Africa.

CHARLES ROUX. French. Very junior in Katangese secession. Quit early and went to South Africa via Angola. Stayed there and returned with South Africans to fight under Hoare in 1964. Quarreled with Hoare and went to join Denard. Promoted and transferred to 6th Codo subsidiary unit, the 14th Codo, as second-in-command. Took part in 1966 Katangese revolt in Stanleyville, in which his unit was nearly wiped out. Was smuggled out of the Congo by Peters. Returned by air with several South Africans and joined Schramme, May 1967. Took part in 1967 Stanleyville revolt as well. After wounding of Denard, proposed for overall command of 10th and 6th Commandos, now merged. Failed. Wounded at Bukavu in a shoot-out, quit, and returned home via Kigali. Not in action since. Lives in Paris.

CARLO SHANNON. British. Served under Hoare in 5th, 1964. Declined to serve under Peters. Transferred to Denard 1966, joined the 6th. Served under Schramme on march to Bukavu. Fought throughout siege. Repatriated among the last in April 1968. Volunteered for Nigerian civil war, served under Steiner. Took over remnants after Steiner's dismissal, November 1968. Commanded till the end. Believed staying in Paris.

LUCIEN BRUN. Alias Paul Leroy. French, speaks fluent English. Served as enlisted officer French Army, Algerian war. Normal discharge. Was in South Africa 1964, volunteered for Congo. Arrived 1964 with South African unit, joined Hoare's 5th Commando. Fought well, wounded late 1964. Returned 1965. Refused to serve under Peters, transferred to Denard and the 6th in early 1966. Left Congo May 1966, sensing forthcoming revolt. Served under Faulques in Nigerian civil war. Wounded and repatriated. Returned and tried for his own command. Failed. Repatriated 1968. Lives in Paris. Highly intelligent, also very politically minded.

When he had finished, Endean looked up. "These men would all be available for such a job?" he asked.

The writer shook his head. "I doubt it," he said. "I included all those who could do such a job. Whether they would want to is another matter. It would depend on the size of the job, the number of men they would command. For the older ones there is a question of the prestige involved. There is also the question of how much they need the work. Some of the older ones are more or less retired and comfortably off."

"Point them out to me," invited Endean.

The writer leaned over and ran his finger down the list. "First the older generation. Lamouline you'll never get. He was always virtually an extension of Belgian government policy, a tough veteran and revered by his men. He's retired now. The other Belgian, Black Jacques Schramme, is now retired and runs a chicken farm in Portugal. Of the French, Roger Faulques is perhaps the most decorated ex-officer of the French Army. He also is revered by the men who fought under him, in and out of the Foreign Legion, and regarded as a gentleman by others. But he's also crippled with wounds, and the last contract he got was a failure because he delegated the command to a subordinate who failed.

"Denard was good in the Congo but got a very bad head wound at Stanleyville. Now he's past it. The French mercenaries still stay in contact with him, looking for a bite, but he hasn't been given a command or a project to set up since the fiasco at Dilolo. And little wonder.

"Of the Anglo-Saxons, Mike Hoare is retired and comfortably off. He might be tempted by a million-pound project, but even that's not certain. His last foray was into Nigeria, where he proposed a project to each side, costed at half a million pounds. They both turned him down. John Peters is also retired and runs a factory in Singapore. All six made a lot of money in the heyday, but none has adapted to the smaller, more technical mission that might be called for nowadays, some because they don't wish to, or because they can't!"

"What about the other five?" asked Endean.

"Steiner was good once, but deteriorated. The press publicity got to him, and that's always bad for a mercenary. They begin to believe they are as fearsome as the Sunday papers say they are. Roux became bitter when he failed to get the Stanleyville command after Denard's wounding and claims leadership over all French mercenaries, but he hasn't been employed since Bukavu. The last two are better; both in their thirties, intelligent, educated, and with enough guts in combat to be able to command other mercs. Incidentally, mercs only fight under a leader they choose themselves. So hiring a bad mercenary to recruit others serves no purpose, because no one else wants to know about serving under a guy who once ran out. So the combat record is important.

"Lucien Brun, alias Paul Leroy, could do this job. Trouble is, you would never be quite sure if he was not passing stuff to French intelligence, the SDECE. Does that matter?"

"Yes, very much," said Endean shortly. "You left out Schroeder, the South African. What about him? You say he commanded Fifth Commando in the Congo?"

"Yes," said the writer. "At the end, the very end. It also broke up under his command. He's a first-class soldier, within his limitations. For example, he would command a battalion of mercenaries excellently, providing it were within the framework of a brigade with a good staff. He's a good combat man, but conventional. Very little imagination, not the sort who could set up his own operation starting from scratch. He'd need staff officers to take care of the admin."

"And Shannon? He's British?"

"Anglo-Irish. He's new; he got his first command only a year ago, but he did well. He can think unconventionally and has a lot of audacity. He can also organize down to the last detail."

Endean rose to go. "Tell me something," he said at the door. "If you were mounting an—seeking a man to go on a mission and assess the situation, which would you choose?"

The writer picked up the notes on the breakfast table. "Cat Shannon," he said without hesitation. "If I were doing that, or mounting an operation, I'd pick the Cat."

"Where is he?" asked Endean.

The writer mentioned a hotel and a bar in Paris. "You could try either of those," he said.

"And if this man Shannon was not available, or for

some other reason could not be employed, who would be second on the list?"

The writer thought for a while. "If not Lucien Brun, then the only other who would almost certainly be available and has the experience would be Roux," he said.

"You have his address?" asked Endean.

The writer flicked through a small notebook that he took from a drawer in his desk.

"Roux has a flat in Paris," he said and gave Endean the address. A few seconds later he heard the clump of Endean's feet descending the stairs. He picked up the phone and dialed a number. "Carrie? Hi, it's me. We're going out tonight. Somewhere expensive. I just got paid for a feature article."

Cat Shannon walked slowly and pensively up the rue Blanche toward the Place Clichy. The little bars were already open on both sides of the street, and from the doorways the hustlers tried to persuade him to step inside and see the most beautiful girls in Paris. The latter, who, whatever else they were, most certainly were not that, peered through the lace curtains at the darkened street. It was just after five o'clock on a mid-March evening, with a cold wind blowing. The weather matched Shannon's mood.

He crossed the square and ducked up another side street toward his hotel, which had few advantages but a fine view from its top floors, since it was close to the summit of Montmartre. He was thinking about Dr. Dunois, whom he had visited for a general checkup a week earlier. A former paratrooper and army doctor, Dunois had become a mountaineer and gone on two French expeditions to the Himalayas and the Andes as the team medico.

He had later volunteered for several tough medical missions in Africa, on a temporary basis and for the duration of the emergency, working for the French Red Cross. There he had met the mercenaries and had patched up several of them after combat. He had become known as the mercenaries' doctor, even in Paris, and had sewn up a lot of bullet holes, removed many splinters of mortar casing from their bodies. If they had a medical problem or needed a checkup, they usually went to him at his Paris surgery. If they were well off, flush with money, they paid on the nail in dollars. If not, he forgot to send his bill, which is unusual in French doctors.

Shannon turned into the door of his hotel and crossed to the desk for his key. The old man was on duty behind the desk.

"Ah, monsieur, one has been calling you from London. All day. He left a message."

The old man handed Shannon the slip of paper in the key aperture. It was written in the old man's scrawl, evidently dictated letter by letter. It said simply "Careful Harris," and was signed with the name of a freelance writer he knew from his African wars and who he knew lived in London.

"There is another, m'sieur. He is waiting in the salon."

The old man gestured toward the small room set aside from the lobby, and through the archway Shannon could see a man about his own age, dressed in the sober gray of a London businessman, watching him as he stood by the desk. There was little of the London businessman in the ease with which the visitor came to his feet as Shannon entered the salon, or about the build of the shoulders. Shannon had seen men like him before. They always represented older, richer men.

"Mr. Shannon?"

"Yes."

"My name is Harris, Walter Harris."

"You wanted to see me?"

"I've been waiting a couple of hours for just that. Can we talk here, or in your room?"

"Here will do. The old man understands no English."

The two men seated themselves facing each other.

Harris relaxed and crossed his legs. He reached for a pack of cigarettes and gestured to Shannon with the pack. Shannon shook his head and reached for his own brand in his jacket pocket.

"I understand you are a mercenary, Mr. Shannon?"

"Yes."

"In fact you have been recommended to me. I represent a group of London businessmen. We need a job done. A sort of mission. It needs a man who has some knowledge of military matters, and who can travel to a foreign country without exciting any suspicions. Also a man who can make an intelligent report on what he saw there, analyze a military situation, and then keep his mouth shut."

"I don't kill on contract," said Shannon briefly.

"We don't want you to," said Harris.

"All right, what's the mission? And what's the fee?" asked Shannon. He saw no sense in wasting words. The man in front of him was unlikely to be shocked by a spade being called a spade.

Harris smiled briefly. "First, you would have to come to London for briefing. We would pay for your trip and expenses, even if you decided not to accept."

"Why London? Why not here?" asked Shannon.

Harris exhaled a long stream of smoke. "There are some maps and other papers involved," he said. "I didn't want to bring them with me. Also, I have to consult my partners, report to them that you have accepted or not, as the case may be."

There was silence as Harris drew a wad of French 100-franc notes from his pocket.

"Fifteen hundred francs," he said. "About a hundred and twenty pounds. That's for your air ticket to London, single or return, whichever you wish to buy. And your overnight stay. If you decline the proposition after hearing it, you get another hundred for your trouble in coming. If you accept, we discuss the further salary."

Shannon nodded. "All right. I'll listen—in London. When?"

"Tomorrow," said Harris and rose to leave. "Arrive any time during the course of the day, and stay at the Post House Hotel on Haverstock Hill. I'll book your room when I get back tonight. At nine the day after tomorrow I'll phone you in your room and make a rendezvous for later that morning. Clear?"

Shannon nodded and picked up the francs. "Book the room in the name of Brown, Keith Brown," he said.

The man who called himself Harris left the hotel and headed downhill, looking for a taxi. He had not seen any reason to mention to Shannon that he had spent three hours earlier that afternoon talking with another mercenary, a man by the name of Charles Roux. Nor did he mention that he had decided, despite the Frenchman's evident eagerness, that Roux was not the man for the job; he had left the man's flat with a vague promise to get in touch again, with his decision.

Twenty-four hours later Shannon stood at his bedroom window in the Post House Hotel and stared out at the rain and the commuter traffic swishing up Haverstock Hill from Camden Town toward Hampstead and the commuter suburbs.

He had arrived that morning on the first plane, using his passport in the name of Keith Brown. Long since, he had had to acquire a false passport by the normal method used in mercenary circles. At the end of 1967 he had been with Black Jacques Schramme at Bukavu, surrounded and besieged for months by the Congolese army. Finally, undefeated but running out of ammunition, the mercenaries had vacated the Congolese lakeside city, walked across the bridge into neighboring Rwanda, and allowed themselves, with Red Cross guarantees which the Red Cross could not possibly fulfill, to be disarmed.

From then on, for nearly six months, they had sat idle in an internment camp at Kigali while the Red Cross and the Rwanda government hassled over their repatriation to Europe. President Mobutu of the Congo wanted them sent back to him for execution, but the mercenaries had threatened if that was the decision they would take the Rwandan army barehanded, recover their guns and find their own way home. The Rwandan government had believed, rightly, that they might do it.

When finally the decision was made to fly them back to Europe, the British consul had visited the camp and soberly told the six British mercenaries present that he would have to impound their passports. They had soberly told him they had lost everything across the lake in Bukavu. On being flown home to London, Shannon and the others had been told by the Foreign Office that each man owed £350 for the air fare and would receive no new passport ever again.

Before leaving the camp, the men had been photographed and fingerprinted and had had their names taken. They also had to sign documents pledging never to set foot on the continent of Africa. These documents would be sent in copy to every African government.

The reaction of the mercenaries was predictable. Every one had a lush beard and mustache and hair left uncut after months in the camp, where no scissors were allowed in case they went on the warpath with them. The photographs were therefore unrecognizable. Each man then submitted his own fingerprints for another man's prints, and they all exchanged names. The result was that every identity document contained one man's name, another man's fingerprints, and a third man's photograph. Finally, they signed the pledge to leave Africa forever with names like Sebastian Weetabix and Neddy Seagoon.

Shannon's reaction to the Foreign Office demand was no less unhelpful. As he still had his "lost" passport, he kept it and traveled where he wished until it expired. Then he took the necessary steps to secure another one, issued by the Passport Office but based on a birth certificate, secured from the Registry of Births in Somerset House for the standard fee of five shillings, which referred to a baby who had died of meningitis in Yarmouth about the time Shannon was born.*

On arrival in London that morning, he had contacted the writer he had first met in Africa and learned how Walter Harris had found him. He thanked the man for recommending him and asked if he knew the name of a good agency of private inquirers. Later that afternoon he visited the agency and paid a deposit of £20, promising to phone the next morning with further instructions.

Harris called, as he had promised, on the dot of nine the following morning and was put through to Mr. Brown's room.

"There's a block of flats in Sloane Avenue called Chelsea Cloisters," he said without preamble. "I have booked flat three-seventeen for us to talk. Please be there at eleven sharp. Wait in the lobby until I arrive, as I have the key." Then he hung up.

Shannon checked the address in the telephone book under the bedside table and called the detective agency. "I want your man in the lobby of Chelsea Cloisters in Sloane Avenue at ten-fifteen," he said. "He had better have his own transport."

"He'll have a scooter," said the head of the agency.

An hour later Shannon met the man from the agency in the lobby of the apartment house. Rather to his surprise, the man was a youth in his late teens, with long hair.

Shannon surveyed him suspiciously. "Do you know your job?" he asked.

The boy nodded. He seemed full of enthusiasm, and Shannon only hoped it was matched by a bit of skill.

"Well, park that crash helmet outside on the scooter," he said. "People who come in here don't carry crash helmets. Sit over there and read a newspaper."

---

*For a more detailed explanation of this procedure, which was used by a would-be assassin of General de Gaulle, see *The Day of the Jackal* (New York: The Viking Press, 1971; Bantam Books, Inc., 1972).

The youth did not have one, so Shannon gave him his own. "I'll sit on the other side of the lobby. At about eleven a man will come in, nod to me, and we'll go into the lift together. Note that man, so you will recognize him again. He should come out about an hour later. By then you must be across the road, astride the scooter, with the helmet on and pretending to be busy with a breakdown. Got it?"

"Yes. I've got it."

"The man will either take his own car from nearby, in which case grab the number of it. Or he'll take a taxi. In either case, follow him and note where he goes. Keep on his tail until he arrives at what looks like his final destination."

The youth drank in the instructions and took his place in the far corner of the lobby behind his newspaper.

The lobby porter frowned but left him alone. He had seen quite a few meetings take place in front of his reception desk.

Forty minutes later Simon Endean walked in. Shannon noticed that he dismissed a taxi at the door, and hoped the youth had noticed it as well. He stood up and nodded to the newcomer, but Endean strolled past him and pressed the summons button for the lift. Shannon joined him and remarked the youth peering over his newspaper.

For God's sake, thought Shannon and mentioned something about the foul weather lest the man who called himself Harris should glance round the lobby.

Settled into an easy chair in flat 317, Harris opened his briefcase and took out a map. Spreading it out on the bed, he told Shannon to look at it. Shannon gave it three minutes and had taken in all the details the map had to give. Then Harris began his briefing.

It was a judicious mixture of fact and fiction. He still claimed he represented a consortium of British businessmen, all of whom did some form of business with Zangaro and all of whose businesses, including some which were virtually out of business, had suffered as a result of President Kimba.

Then he went into the background of the republic from independence onward, and what he said was truthful, most of it out of his own report to Sir James Manson. The punch line came at the end.

"A group of officers in the army has got in touch with a group of local businessmen—who are, incidentally, a dying breed. They have mentioned that they are considering toppling Kimba in a coup. One of the local businessmen mentioned it to one of my group, and put their problem to us. It is basically that they are virtually untrained in military terms, despite their officer status, and do not know how to topple the man, because he spends too much time hidden inside the walls of his palace, surrounded by his guards.

"Frankly, we would not be sorry to see this Kimba go, and neither would his people. A new government would be good for the economy of the place and good for the country. We need a man to go down there and make a complete assessment of the military and security situation in and around the palace and the important institutions. We want a complete report on Kimba's military strength."

"So you can pass it on to your officers?" asked Shannon.

"They are not our officers. They are Zangaran officers. The fact is, if they are going to strike at all, they had better know what they are doing."

Shannon believed half of the briefing, but not the second half. If the officers, who were on the spot, could not assess the situation, they would be incompetent to carry out a coup. But he did not say so.

"I'd have to go in as a tourist," he said. "There's no other cover that would work."

"That's right."

"There must be precious few tourists that go there. Why cannot I go in as a company visitor to one of your friends' business houses?"

"That will not be possible," said Harris. "If anything went wrong, there would be all hell to pay."

If I get caught, you mean, thought Shannon, but kept silent. He was being paid, so he would take risks. That, and his knowledge, was what he was being paid for.

"There's the question of pay," he said shortly.

"Then you'll do it?"

"If the money's right, yes."

Harris nodded approvingly. "Tomorrow morning a round-trip ticket from London to the capital of the neighboring republic will be at your hotel," he said. "You have to fly back to Paris and get a visa for this republic. Zangaro is so poor there is only one embassy in Europe, and that's in Paris also. But getting a Zangaran visa there takes a month. In the next-door republic's capital there is a Zangaran consulate. There you can get a visa for cash, and within an hour if you tip the consul. You understand the procedure."

Shannon nodded. He understood it very well.

"So get visa-ed up in Paris, then fly down by Air Afrique. Get your Zangaran visa on the spot and take the connecting plane service from there to Clarence, paying cash. With the tickets at your hotel tomorrow will be three hundred pounds in French francs as expenses."

"I'll need five," said Shannon. "It'll be ten days at least, possibly more, depending on connections and how long the visas take to get. Three hundred leaves no margin for the occasional bribe or any delay."

"All right, five hundred in French francs. Plus five hundred for yourself," said Harris.

"A thousand," said Shannon.

"Dollars? I understand you people deal in U.S. dollars."

"Pounds," said Shannon. "That's twenty-five hundred dollars, or two months at flat salary if I were on a normal contract."

"But you'll only be away ten days," protested Harris.

"Ten days of high risk," countered Shannon. "If this place is half what you say it is, anyone getting caught on this kind of job is going to be very dead, and very painfully. You want me to take the risks rather than go yourself, you pay."

"Okay, a thousand pounds. Five hundred down and five hundred when you return."

"How do I know you'll contact me when I return?" said Shannon.

"How do I know you'll even go there at all?" countered Harris.

Shannon considered the point. Then he nodded. "All right, half now, half later."

Ten minutes later Harris was gone, after instructing Shannon to wait five minutes before leaving himself.

At three that afternoon the head of the detective agency was back from his lunch. Shannon called at three-fifteen.

"Ah, yes, Mr. Brown," said the voice on the phone. "I have spoken to my man. He waited as you instructed, and when the subject left the building he recognized him and followed. The subject hailed a taxi from the curb, and my man followed him to the City. There he dismissed the taxi and entered a building."

"What building?"

"ManCon House. That's the headquarters of Manson Consolidated Mining."

"Do you know if he works there?" asked Shannon.

"It would seem he does," said the agency chief. "My man could not follow him into the building, but he noticed the commissionaire touched his cap to the subject and held the door open for him. He did not do that for a stream of secretaries and evidently junior executives who were emerging for lunch."

"He's brighter than he looks," conceded Shannon. The youth had done a good job. Shannon gave several further instructions and that afternoon mailed £50 by registered mail to the detective agency. He also opened a bank account and put down £10 deposit in it. The following morning he banked a further £500 and that evening flew to Paris.

Dr. Gordon Chalmers was not a drinking man. He seldom touched anything stronger than beer, and when he did he became talkative, as his employer, Sir James Manson, had found out for himself over their luncheon at Wilton's. The evening that Cat Shannon was changing planes at Le Bourget to catch the Air Afrique DC-8 to West Africa, Dr. Chalmers was having dinner with an old college friend, now also a scientist and working in industrial research.

There was nothing special about their meal. He had run into his former classmate in one of those coincidental meetings on the street a few days earlier, and they had agreed to have dinner together.

Fifteen years earlier they had been young undergraduates, single and working hard on their respective degrees, earnest and concerned as so many young scientists feel obliged to be. In the mid-1950s the concern had been the bomb and colonialism, and they had joined thousands of others marching for the Campaign for Nuclear Disarmament and the various movements that sought an instant end to empire, and world freedom now. Both had been indignant, serious, committed, and both had changed nothing. But in their indignation over the state of the world they had dabbled with the Young Communist movement. Chalmers had grown out of it, married, started his family, secured a mortgage for his house, and slowly merged into the salaried middle class.

The combination of worries that had come his way over the previous two weeks caused him to take more than his usual single glass of wine with dinner, considerably more. His friend, a kindly man with soft brown eyes, noticed his worry and asked if he could help.

It was over the brandy that Dr. Chalmers felt he had to confide his worries to someone, someone who, unlike his wife, was a fellow scientist and would understand the problem. Of course it was highly confidential, and his friend was solicitous and sympathetic.

When he heard about the crippled daughter and the need for the money to pay for her expensive equipment, the man's eyes clouded over with sympathy, and he reached across the table to grip Dr. Chalmers' forearm.

"Don't worry about it, Gordon. It's completely understandable. Anyone else would have done the same thing," he told him. Chalmers felt better when they left the restaurant and made their separate ways home. He was easier in his mind, his problem somehow shared.

Though he had asked his old friend how he had fared in the intervening years since their undergraduate days together, the man had been slightly evasive. Chalmers, bowed under his own worries and his observation blunted by wine, had not pressed for detail. Even had he done so, it was unlikely the friend would have told him that, far from merging into the bourgeoisie, he had remained a fully committed member of the Communist party.

7

The Convair 440 that ran the connecting air service into Clarence banked steeply over the bay and began its descent toward the airfield. Being intentionally on the left side of the plane, Shannon could look down toward the town as the aircraft overflew it. From a thousand feet he could see the capital of Zangaro occupying the end of the peninsula, surrounded on three sides by the palm-fringed waters of the gulf, and on the fourth side by the land, where the stubby peninsula, just eight miles long, ran back to join the main coastline.

The spit of land was three miles wide at its base, set in the mangrove swamps on the coastline, and a mile wide at the tip, where the town was situated. The flanks along each side were also composed of mangrove, and only at the end did the mangroves give way to some shingly beaches.

The town spanned the end of the peninsula from side to side and stretched about a mile back down the length of it. Beyond the fringes of the town at this end, a single road ran between cultivated patches the remaining seven miles to the main coast.

Evidently all the best buildings were set toward the seaward tip of the land, where the breezes would blow, for the aerial view showed the buildings to be set in their own plots of land, one to an acre. The landward side of the town was evidently the poorer section, where thousands of tin-roofed shanties intersected with narrow muddy alleys. He concentrated on the richer section of Clarence, where the colonial masters had once lived, for here would be the important buildings, and he would only have a few seconds to see them from this angle.

At the very end was a small port, formed where, for no geological reason, two long curving spits of shingle ran out into the sea like the antlers of a stag beetle or the pincers of an earwig. The port was set along the landward side of this bay. Outside the arms of the bay, Shannon could see the water ruffled by the breeze, while inside the three-quarter-circle enclosed within the arms, the water was a flat calm. No doubt it was this anchorage, tacked onto the end of the peninsula in one of nature's afterthoughts, which had attracted the first mariners.

The center of the port, directly opposite the opening to the high seas, was dominated by a single concrete quay without any ship tied up to it, and a warehouse of sorts. To the left of the concrete quay was evidently the natives' fishing area, a shingly beach littered with long canoes and nets laid out to dry, and to the right of the quay was the old port, a series of decrepit wooden jetties pointing toward the water.

Behind the warehouse there were perhaps two hundred yards of rough grass, ending with a road along the shore, and behind the road the buildings started. Shannon caught a glimpse of a white colonial-style church and what could have been the governor's palace in bygone days, surrounded by a wall. Inside the wall, apart from the main buildings, was a large courtyard surrounded by lean-to hutments of evidently recent addition.

At this point the Convair straightened up, the town disappeared from view, and they were on final approach.

Shannon had already had his first experience of Zan-

garo the previous day when he had applied for his visa
for a tourist visit. The consul in the neighboring capital had received him with some surprise, being unused
to such applications. He had to fill out a five-page form
giving his parents' first names (as he had no idea of
Keith Brown's parents' names, he invented them) and
every other conceivable piece of information.

His passport, when he handed it over, had a handsome banknote idly lying between the first and second
pages. This went into the consul's pocket. The man then
examined the passport from every angle, read every
page, held it up to the light, turned it over, checked
the currency allowances at the back. After five minutes of this, Shannon began to wonder if there was
something wrong. Had the British Foreign Office made
an error in this particular passport?

Then the consul looked at him and said, "You are an
American."

With a sense of relief Shannon realized the man was
illiterate. He had his visa in five minutes more. But at
Clarence airport the fun stopped.

He had no luggage in the aircraft hold, just a hand
grip. Inside the main (and only) passenger building
the heat was overpowering, and the place buzzed with
flies. About a dozen soldiers lounged about, and ten
policemen. They were evidently of different tribes. The
policemen were self-effacing, hardly speaking even to
each other, leaning against the walls. It was the soldiers
who attracted Shannon's attention. He kept half an eye
on them as he filled in another immensely long form
(the same one he had filled the previous day at the
consulate) and penetrated Health and Passport Control, both manned by officials whom he took to be
Caja, like the policemen.

It was when he got to customs that the trouble
started. A civilian was waiting for him and instructed
him with a curt gesture to go into a side room. As he
did so, taking his bag with him, four soldiers swag-
gered in after him. Then he realized what it was about
them that rang a bell in his memory.

Long ago in the Congo he had seen the same attitude, the blank-eyed sense of menace conveyed by an African of almost primeval cultural level, armed with a weapon, in a state of power—wholly unpredictable, with reactions to a situation that were utterly illogical, ticking away like a moving time bomb. Just before the worst of the massacres he had seen launched by Congolese on Katangese, Simbas on missionaries, and Congolese army on Simbas, he had noticed this same menacing mindlessness, the sense of power without reason, that can suddenly and for no recollected explanation turn to frenetic violence. The Vindu soldiers of President Kimba had it.

The civilian customs officer ordered Shannon to put his bag on the rickety table and then began to go through it. The search looked thorough, as if for concealed weapons, until he spotted the electric shaver, took it from its case, examined it, tried the "on" switch. Being a Remington Lektronic and fully charged, it buzzed furiously. Without a trace of expression, the customs man put it in his pocket.

Finishing with the bag, he gestured to Shannon to empty his pockets onto the table. Out came the keys, handkerchief, coins, wallet, and passport. The customs man went for the wallet, extracted the travelers' checks, looked at them, grunted, and handed them back. The coins he swept into his hand and pocketed them. Of the banknotes, there were two 5000-French-African-franc notes and several 100s. The soldiers had crowded nearer, still making no sound but for their breathing in the roasting atmosphere, gripping guns like clubs, but overcome with curiosity. The civilian behind the table pocketed the two 5000-franc notes, and one of the soldiers picked up the smaller denominations.

Shannon looked at the customs man. The man looked back. Then he lifted his singlet and showed the butt of a Browning 9-mm. short, or perhaps an 875, jammed into his trouser band. He tapped it.

"Police," he said, and kept staring. Shannon's fingers itched to smash the man in the face. Inside his head he kept telling himself: Keep cool, baby, absolutely cool.

He gestured slowly, very slowly, to what remained of his belongings on the table and raised his eyebrows. The civilian nodded, and Shannon began to pick them up and put them back. Behind him he felt the soldiers back off, though they still gripped their rifles with both hands, able to swing or butt-jab as the mood took them.

It seemed an age before the civilian nodded toward the door and Shannon left. He could feel the sweat running in a stream down the spine toward the waistband of his pants.

Outside in the main hall, the only other white tourist on the flight, an American girl, had been met by a Catholic priest, who, with his voluble explanations to the soldiers in coast pidgin, was having less trouble. He looked up and caught Shannon's eye. Shannon raised an eyebrow slightly. The father looked beyond Shannon at the room he had come from and nodded imperceptibly.

Outside, in the heat of the small square before the airport building, there was no transport. Shannon waited. Five minutes later he heard a soft Irish-American voice behind him.

"Can I give you a lift into town, my son?"

They traveled in the priest's car, a Volkswagen beetle, which he had hidden for safety in the shade of a palm grove several yards outside the gate. The American girl was shrill and outraged; someone had opened her handbag and gone through it. Shannon was silent, knowing how close they could all have come to a beating. The priest was with the UN hospital, combining the roles of chaplain, almoner, and doctor of medicine. He glanced across at Shannon with understanding.

"They shook you down."

"The lot," said Shannon. The loss of £15 was nothing but both men had recognized the mood of the soldiery.

"One has to be very careful here, very careful indeed," said the priest softly. "Have you a hotel?"

When Shannon told him he had not, the priest drove

him to the Independence, the only hotel in Clarence where Europeans were permitted to stay.

"Gomez is the manager, he's a good enough sort," said the priest.

Usually when a new face arrives in an African city there are invitations from the other Europeans to visit the club, come back to the bungalow, have a drink, come to a party that evening. The priest, for all his helpfulness, issued no such offers. That was another thing Shannon learned quickly about Zangaro. The mood affected the whites as well. He would learn more in the days to come, much of it from Gomez.

It was that same evening that he came to know Jules Gomez, formerly proprietor and latterly manager of the Independence Hotel. Gomez was fifty and a *pied noir,* a Frenchman from Algeria. In the last days of French Algeria, almost ten years earlier, he had sold his flourishing business in agricultural machinery just before the final collapse, when one could not give a business away. With what he had made, he returned to France, but after a year found he could not live in the atmosphere of Europe any longer and looked around for another place to go. He had settled on Zangaro, five years before independence and before it was even in the offing. Taking his savings, he had bought the hotel and steadily improved it over the years.

After independence, things had changed. Three years before Shannon arrived, Gomez had been brusquely informed that the hotel was to be nationalized and he would be paid in local currency. He never was, and it was worthless paper in any case. But he hung on as manager, hoping against hope that one day things might improve again and something would be left of his only asset on this planet to secure him in his old age. As manager, he ran the reception desk and the bar. Shannon found him at the bar.

It would have been easy to win Gomez' friendship by mentioning the friends and contacts Shannon had who were former OAS men, fighters in the Legion and the paras, who had turned up in the Congo. But that

would have blown his cover as a simple English tourist who, with five days to kill, had flown down from
the north, impelled only by curiosity to see the obscure republic of Zangaro. So he stuck to his role of
tourist.

But later, after the bar closed, he suggested Gomez
join him for a drink in his room. For no explicable reason, the soldiers at the airport had left him a bottle of
whisky he had been carrying in his case. Gomez' eyes
opened wide at the sight of it. Whisky was another
import the country could not afford. Shannon made
sure Gomez drank more than he. When he mentioned
that he had come to Zangaro out of curiosity, Gomez
snorted.

"Curiosity? Huh, it's curious, all right. It's bloody
weird."

Although they were talking French, and alone in
the room, Gomez lowered his voice and leaned forward
as he said it. Once again Shannon got an impression
of the extraordinary sense of fear present in everyone
he had seen, except the bully-boy army thugs and the
secret policeman who posed as a customs officer at the
airport. By the time Gomez had sunk half the bottle, he
had become slightly garrulous, and Shannon probed
gently for information. Gomez confirmed much of the
briefing Shannon had been given by the man he knew
as Walter Harris, and added more anecdotal details of
his own, some of them highly gruesome.

He confirmed that President Kimba was in town,
that he hardly ever left it these days, except for the occasional trip to his home village across the river in
Vindu country, and that he was in his presidential
palace, the large, walled building Shannon had seen
from the air.

By the time Gomez bade him good night and wove
his way back to his own room at two in the morning,
further nuggets of information had been culled. The
three units known as the civilian police force, the gendarmerie, and the customs force, although all carried
sidearms, had, Gomez swore, no ammunition in their

weapons. Being Caja, they were not trusted to have any, and Kimba, with his paranoia about an uprising, kept them without one round of ammunition between the lot of them. He knew they would never fight for him and must not have the opportunity of fighting against him. The sidearms were just for show.

Gomez had also vouchsafed that the power in the city was exclusively in the hands of Kimba's Vindu. The dreaded secret police usually wore civilian clothes and carried automatics, the soldiers of the army had bolt-action rifles such as Shannon had seen at the airport, and the President's own Praetorian Guards had submachine guns. The latter lived exclusively in the palace grounds and were ultra-loyal to Kimba, and he never moved without at least a squad of them hemming him in.

The next morning Shannon went out for a walk. Within seconds he found a small boy of ten or eleven scampering by his side, sent after him by Gomez. Only later did he learn why. He thought Gomez must have sent the boy as a guide, though, as they could not exchange a word, there was not much point in that. The real purpose was different, a service Gomez offered to all his guests, whether they asked or not. If the tourist was arrested for whatever reason, and carted off, the small boy would speed away through the bushes and tell Gomez, who would slip the information to the Swiss or West German embassy so that someone could begin to negotiate the tourist's release before he was beaten half dead. The boy's name was Boniface.

Shannon spent the morning walking, mile after mile, while the small boy trotted at his heels. As he expected, they were stopped by no one. Shannon knew that the sheer inefficiency of the place meant that no one would seriously question why a foreigner should spend a week as a tourist. Such countries even advertise for tourism in the waiting rooms of their embassies in Europe. Moreover, in the case of Zangaro there was a community of about a hundred whites in the capital, and no soldier was going to know that the white walking

down the street was not a local one, or care, provided
he was given a dollar for beer.

There was hardly a vehicle to be seen, and the streets
in the residential area were mainly deserted. From Gomez, Shannon had obtained a small map of the town,
a leftover from colonial days, and with this he tracked
down the main buildings of Clarence. At the only bank,
the only post office, half a dozen ministries, the port,
and the UN hospital there were groups of six or seven
soldiers lounging about the steps. Inside the bank, where
he went to cash a travelers' check, he noticed bedrolls
in the lobby, and in the lunch hour he twice saw pots of
food being carried by a soldier to his colleagues. Shannon judged that the guard details lived on the premises
of each building. Gomez confirmed this later the same
evening.

He noticed a soldier in front of each of six embassies he passed, three of them asleep in the dust. By
the lunch hour he estimated there were about a hundred
soldiers scattered in twelve groups around the main
area of the town. He noted what they were armed with.
Each carried an old Mauser 7.92 bolt-action rifle, most
of them looking rusted and dirty. The soldiers wore
drab green trousers and shirts, canvas boots, webbing
belts, and peaked caps rather like American baseball
caps. Without exception they were shabby, unpressed,
unwashed, and unprepossessing. He estimated their
level of training, weapons familiarization, leadership,
and fighting capacity at nil. They were a rabble, undis-
ciplined thugs who could terrify the timorous Caja by
their arms and their brutishness, but had probably never
fired a shot in anger and certainly had never been fired
at by people who knew what they were doing. Their
purpose on guard duty seemed to be to prevent a civilian riot, but he estimated that in a real firefight
they would quit and run.

The most interesting thing about them was the state
of their ammunition pouches. They were pressed flat,
empty of magazines. Each Mauser had its fixed magazine, of course, but Mausers hold only five shells.

That afternoon Shannon patrolled the port. Seen from the ground, it looked different. The two spits of sand running out across the water and forming the natural harbor were about twenty feet high at the base and six feet above the water at the tip. He walked down both until he reached the end. Each one was covered in knee-to-waist-high scrub vegetation, burned brown at the end of the long dry season, and invisible from the air. Each spit was about forty feet wide at the tip, forty yards wide at the base, where it left the shoreline. From the tip of each, looking back toward the port area, one had a panoramic view of the waterfront.

The concreted area was at dead center, backed by the warehouse. To the north of this stood the old wooden jetties, some long crumbled away, their supports sticking up like broken teeth above or below the water. To the south of the warehouse was the shingly beach where the fishing canoes lay. From the tip of one sandspit the President's palace was invisible, hidden behind the warehouse, but from the other spit the uppermost story of the palace was plainly visible. Shannon walked back to the port and examined the fishing beach. It was a good place for a landing, he thought idly, a gentle slope to the water's edge.

Behind the warehouse the concrete ended and a sloping bank of waist-high scrub, dissected by numerous footpaths and one laterite road for trucks, ran back toward the palace. Shannon took the road. As he breasted the top of the rise the full façade of the old colonial governor's mansion came into view, two hundred yards away. He continued another hundred yards and reached the lateral road running along the seashore. At the junction a group of soldiers waited, four in all, smarter, better dressed than the army, armed with Kalashnikov AK 47 assault rifles. They watched him in silence as he turned right along the road toward his hotel. He nodded, but they just stared back. The palace guards.

He glanced to his left as he walked and took in the

details of the palace. Thirty yards wide, its ground-floor windows now bricked up and painted over the same off-white wash as the rest of the building, it was dominated at ground level by a tall, wide, bolt-studded timber door, almost certainly another new addition. In front of the bricked-up windows ran a terrace, now useless because there was no access from the building to it. On the second floor a row of seven windows ran from side to side of the façade, three left, three right, and one above the main entrance. The topmost floor had ten windows, all much smaller. Above these were the gutter and the red-tiled roof sloping away toward the apex.

He noticed more guards lounging around the front door, and that the second-floor windows had shutters which might have been of steel (he was too far away to tell) and were drawn down. Evidently no closer access to the front of the building than the road junction was permitted, except on official business.

He completed the afternoon just before the sun went down by making a tour of the palace from afar. At each side he saw that a new wall eight feet high ran from the main mansion toward the land for a distance of eighty yards, and the fourth wall joined them together at the rear. Interestingly, there were no other gates to the entire compound. The wall was uniformly eight feet high—he could tell by the height of a guard he saw walking near the wall—and topped by broken bottles. He knew he would never see inside, but he could retain the image from the air. It almost made him laugh.

He grinned at Boniface. "You know, kid, that bloody fool thinks he has protected himself with a big wall topped with glass and only one entrance. All he has really done is pin himself inside a brick trap, a great big closed-in killing ground."

The boy grinned widely, not understanding a word, and indicated he wanted to go home and eat. Shannon nodded, and they went back to the hotel, feet burning and legs aching.

Shannon made no notes or maps but retained every detail in his head. He returned Gomez' map and after dinner joined the Frenchman at the bar.

Two Chinese from the embassy sat quietly drinking beer at the back tables, so conversation between the Europeans was minimal. Besides, the windows were open. Later, however, Gomez, longing for company, took a dozen bottles of beer and invited Shannon up to his room on the top floor, where they sat on the balcony and looked out through the night at the sleeping town, mainly in darkness because of an electricity breakdown.

Shannon was of two minds whether to take Gomez into his confidence, but decided not to. He mentioned that he had found the bank and it had not been easy to change a £50 check.

Gomez snorted. "It never is," he said. "They don't see travelers' checks here, or much foreign currency for very long."

"They must see it at the bank, surely."

"Not for long. The entire treasure of the republic Kimba keeps locked up inside the palace."

Shannon was at once interested. It took two hours to learn, in dribs and drabs, that Kimba kept not only the national armory of ammunition in the old wine cellar of the governor's palace, under his own lock and key, but also the national radio-broadcasting station so that he could broadcast direct from his communications room to the nation and the world and no one else could take control of it from outside the palace. National radio stations always play a vital role in coups d'état. Shannon also learned he had no armored cars and no artillery, and that apart from the hundred soldiers scattered around the capital there were another hundred outside the town, a score in the native township on the airport road, and the rest dotted in the Caja villages beyond the peninsula toward the Zangaro River bridge. These two hundred were half the army. The other half were in the army barracks, which were not barracks in truth but the old colonial police lines four hundred

yards from the palace—rows of low tin shanties inside
a reed fence enclosure. The four hundred men constituted the entire army, and the personal palace guards
numbered from forty to sixty, living in the lean-to sheds
inside the palace courtyard walls.

On his third day in Zangaro, Shannon checked out
the police lines, where the two hundred army men not
on guard duty lived. They were, as Gomez had said,
surrounded by a reed fence, but a visit to the nearby
church enabled Shannon to slip unnoticed into the bell-
tower, run up the circular brick staircase, and sneak a
view from the belfry. The lines were two rows of shanties, adorned with some clothes hung out to dry. At one
end was a row of low brick kilns, over which pots
of stew bubbled. Twoscore men lounged around in various stages of boredom, and all were unarmed. Their
guns might be in the hutments, but Shannon guessed
they were more probably in the armory, a small stone
pillbox set aside from the huts. The other facilities of
the camp were primitive in the extreme.

It was that evening, when he had gone out without
Boniface, that he met his soldier. He spent an hour
circling the darkened streets, which fortunately for him
had never seen lamplighting, trying to get close to the
palace.

He had managed a good look at the back and sides
and had assured himself there were no patrolling guards
on these sides. Trying the front of the palace, he had
been intercepted by two of the palace guards, who had
brusquely ordered him on his way home. He had established that there were three of them sitting at the
road junction halfway between the top of the rise from
the port and the front gate of the palace. More impor-
tantly, he had also established that they could not see
the harbor from where they stood. From that road junction the soldiers' eyeline, passing over the top of the
rise, would meet the sea beyond the tips of the arms of
the harbor, and without a brilliant moon they would
not even see the water five hundred yards away, though

undoubtedly they would see a light out there, if there were one.

In the darkness on the road junction, Shannon could not see the front gate of the palace a hundred yards inland, but assumed there were two other guards there as usual. He offered packets of cigarettes to the soldiers who had accosted him, and left.

On the road back to the Independence he passed several bars, lit inside by kerosene lamps, and then moved on down the darkened street. A hundred yards farther on, the soldier stopped him. The man was evidently drunk and had been urinating in a rain ditch by the roadside. He swayed up to Shannon, gripping his Mauser two-handed by the butt and barrel. In the moonlight Shannon could see him quite clearly as he moved toward him. The soldier grunted something Shannon failed to understand, though he assumed it was a demand for money.

He heard the soldier mutter, "Beer," several times and add some more indistinguishable words. Then, before Shannon could reach for money or pass on, the man snarled and jabbed the barrel of the gun toward him. From then on it was quick and silent. Shannon took the barrel in one hand and moved it away from his stomach, jerking hard and pulling the soldier off balance. The man was evidently surprised at the reaction, which was not what he was accustomed to. Recovering, he squealed with rage, reversed the gun, gripped it by the barrel, and swung it clubwise. Shannon stepped in close, blocked the swing by gripping the soldier by both biceps, and brought up his knee.

It was too late to go back after that. As the gun dropped he brought up his right hand, crooked into a ninety-degree angle, stiff-armed, and slammed the base of the hand under the soldier's jawbone. A stab of pain went up his arm and shoulder as he heard the neck crack, and he later found he had torn a shoulder muscle with the effort. The Zangaran went down like a sack.

Shannon looked up and down the road, but no one was coming. He rolled the body into the rain ditch and examined the rifle. One by one, he pumped the cartridges out of the magazine. At three they stopped coming. There had been nothing in the breech. He removed the bolt and held the gun to the moon, looking down the barrel. Several months' accumulation of grit, dirt, dust, grime, rust, and earth particles met his eye. He slipped the bolt back home, replaced the three cartridges where they had been, tossed the rifle onto the corpse, and walked home.

"Better and better," he murmured as he slipped into the darkened hotel and went to bed. He had few doubts there would be no effective police inquiry. The broken neck would be put down to a fall into the rain ditch, and tests for fingerprints were, he was sure, unheard of.

Nevertheless, the next day he pleaded a headache, stayed in, and talked to Gomez. On the following morning he left for the airport and took the Convair 440 back to the north. As he sat in the plane and watched the republic disappear beneath the port wing, something Gomez had mentioned in passing ran like a current through his head.

There were not, and never had been, any mining operations in Zangaro.

Forty hours later he was back in London.

Ambassador Leonid Dobrovolsky always felt slightly uneasy when he had his weekly interview with President Kimba. Like others who had met the dictator, he had few doubts about the man's insanity. Unlike most of the others, Leonid Dobrovolsky had orders from his superiors in Moscow to make his utmost efforts to establish a working relationship with the unpredictable African. He stood in front of the broad mahogany desk in the President's study on the second floor of the palace and waited for Kimba to show some sort of reaction.

Seen close to, President Kimba was neither as large

nor as handsome as his official portraits indicated. Behind the enormous desk he seemed almost dwarfish, the more so as he held himself hunched in his chair in a state of total immobility. Dobrovolsky waited for the period of immobility to end. He knew it could end one of two ways. Either the man who ruled Zangaro would speak carefully and lucidly, in every sense like a perfectly sane man, or the almost catatonic stillness would give way to a screaming rage, during which the man would rant like someone possessed, which was in any case what he believed himself to be.

Kimba nodded slowly. "Please proceed," he said.

Dobrovolsky breathed a sigh of relief. Evidently the President was prepared to listen. But he knew the bad news was yet to come, and he had to give it. That could change things.

"I am informed by my government, Mr. President, that it has received information that a mining survey report recently sent to Zangaro by a British company may not be accurate. I am referring to the survey carried out several weeks ago by a firm called Manson Consolidated of London."

The President's eyes, slightly bulging, still stared at the Russian Ambassador without a flicker of expression. Nor was there any word from Kimba to indicate that he recalled the subject that had brought Dobrovolsky to his palace.

The Ambassador continued to describe the mining survey that had been delivered by a certain Mr. Bryant into the hands of the Minister for Natural Resources.

"In essence, then, Your Excellency, I am instructed to inform you that my government believes the report was not a true representation of what was really discovered in the area that was then under survey, specifically, the Crystal Mountain range."

He waited, aware that he could say little more. When Kimba finally spoke, it was calmly and cogently, and Dobrovolsky breathed again.

"In what way was this survey report inaccurate?" whispered Kimba.

"We are not sure of the details, Your Excellency, but it is fair to assume that since the British company has apparently not made any effort to secure from you a mining concession, the report it submitted must have indicated that there were no mineral deposits worth exploiting in that region. If the report was inaccurate, then it was probably in this respect. In other words, whatever the mining engineer's samples contained, it would appear there was more than the British were prepared to inform you."

There was another long silence, during which the Ambassador waited for the explosion of rage. It did not come.

"They cheated me," whispered Kimba.

"Of course, Your Excellency," cut in Dobrovolsky hurriedly, "the only way of being completely sure is for another survey party to examine the same area and take further samples of the rocks and the soil. To this end I am instructed by my government most humbly to ask Your Excellency to grant permission for a survey team from the Institute of Mining of Sverdlovsk to come to Zangaro and examine the same area as that covered by the British engineer."

Kimba took a long time digesting the proposal. Finally he nodded. "Granted," he said.

Dobrovolsky bowed. By his side Volkov, ostensibly Second Secretary at the embassy but more pertinently the resident of the KGB detachment, shot him a glance.

"The second matter is that of your personal security," said Dobrovolsky. At last he secured some reaction from the dictator. It was a subject that Kimba took extremely seriously. His head jerked up, and he shot suspicious glances around the room. Three Zangaran aides standing behind the two Russians quaked.

"My security?" said Kimba in his usual whisper.

"We would respectfully seek once again to reiterate the Soviet government's view of the paramount importance of Your Excellency's being able to continue to lead Zangaro on the path of peace and progress that

Your Excellency has already so magnificently established," said the Russian. The flow of flattery caused no incongruous note; it was Kimba's habitual due and a regular part of any words addressed to him.

"To guarantee the continued security of the invaluable person of Your Excellency and in view of the recent and most dangerous treason by one of your army officers, we would respectfully once again propose that a member of my embassy staff be permitted to reside inside the palace and lend his assistance to Your Excellency's own personal security corps."

The reference to the "treason" of Colonel Bobi brought Kimba out of his trance. He trembled violently, though whether from rage or fear the Russians could not make out. Then he began to talk, slowly at first, in his usual whisper, then faster, his voice rising as he glared at the Zangarans across the room. After a few sentences he lapsed back into the Vindu dialect, which only the Zangarans understood, but the Russians already knew the gist: the everpresent danger of treason and treachery that Kimba knew himself to be in, the warnings he had received from the spirits telling him of plots in all corners, his complete awareness of the identity of all those who were not loyal and who harbored evil thoughts in their minds, his intention to root them out, all of them, and what would happen to them when he did. He went on for half an hour in this vein, before calming down and reverting to a European language the Russians could understand.

When they emerged into the sunlight and climbed into the embassy car, both men were sweating, partly from the heat, for the air-conditioning in the palace was broken yet again, partly because that was the effect Kimba usually had on them.

"I'm glad that's over," muttered Volkov to his colleague as they drove back toward the embassy. "Anyway, we got permission. I'll install my man tomorrow."

"And I'll get the mining engineers sent in as soon as possible," said Dobrovolsky. "Let's hope there really is something fishy about that British survey report. If there isn't, I don't know how I'll explain that to the President."

Volkov grunted. "Rather you than me," he said.

Shannon checked into the Lowndes Hotel off Knightsbridge, as he had agreed with Walter Harris to do before he left London. The agreement was that he would be away about ten days, and each morning at nine Harris would phone that hotel and ask for Mr. Keith Brown. Shannon arrived at noon to find the first call for him had been three hours earlier that morning. The news meant he had till the next day to himself.

One of his first calls after a long bath, a change, and lunch, was to the detective agency. The head of it recognized the name of Keith Brown after a few moments' thought, and Shannon heard him sorting out some files on his desk. Eventually he found the right one.

"Yes, Mr. Brown, I have it here. Would you like me to mail it to you?"

"Rather not," said Shannon. "Is it long?"

"No, about a page. Shall I read it over the phone?"

"Yes, please."

The man cleared his throat and began. "On the morning following the client's request, my operative waited close to the entrance of the underground parking lot beneath ManCon House. He was lucky, in that the subject, whom he had noted the day before arriving back there by taxi from his interview at Sloane Avenue with our client, arrived by car. The operative got a clear view of him as he swung into the parking lot tunnel entrance. It was beyond doubt the subject. He was at the wheel of a Chevrolet Corvette. The operative took the number as the car went down the ramp. Inquiries were later made with a contact at the Licensing Department at County Hall. The vehicle is registered in the name of one Simon John Endean, resident in South Kensington." The man paused. "Do you want the address, Mr. Brown?"

"Not necessarily," said Shannon. "Do you know what this man Endean does at ManCon House?"

"Yes," said the private agent. "I checked up with a friend who's a City journalist. He is the personal aide and right hand man of Sir James Manson, chairman and managing director of Manson Consolidated."

"Thank you," said Shannon and put the phone down.

"Curiouser and curiouser," he murmured as he left the hotel lobby and strolled down to Jermyn Street to cash a check and buy some shirts. It was the first of April, April Fool's Day; the sun was shining and daffodils covered the grass around Hyde Park Corner.

Simon Endean had also been busy while Shannon was away. The results of his labors he imparted to Sir James Manson that afternoon in the penthouse over Moorgate.

"Colonel Bobi," he told his chief as he entered the office.

The mining boss furrowed his brow. "Who?"

"Colonel Bobi. The former commander of the army of Zangaro. Now in exile, banished forever by President Jean Kimba. Who, incidentally, has sentenced him to death by presidential decree for high treason. You wanted to know where he was."

Manson was at his desk by this time, nodding in recollection. "All right, where is he?" he asked.

"In exile in Dahomey," said Endean. "It took a hell of a job to trace him without being too obvious about it. But he's taken up residence in the capital of Dahomey. Place called Cotonou. He must have a little money, but probably not much, or he'd be in a walled villa outside Geneva with all the other rich exiles. He has a small rented villa and lives very quietly, probably because it is the safest way of ensuring the Dahomey government doesn't ask him to leave. It's believed Kimba has asked for his extradition back home, but no one has done anything about it. Besides, he's far enough away from Kimba to assume he'll never present a threat."

"And Shannon, the mercenary?" asked Manson.

"Due back sometime today or tomorrow," said Endean. "I booked him into the Lowndes from yesterday onward to be on the safe side. He hadn't arrived this morning at nine. I'm due to try again tomorrow at the same time."

"Try now," said Manson.

The hotel confirmed to Endean that Mr. Brown had indeed arrived, but that he was out. Sir James Manson listened on the extension.

"Leave a message," he growled at Endean. "Ring him tonight at seven."

Endean left the message, and the two men put the phones down.

"I want his report as soon as possible," said Manson. "He should finish it at noon tomorrow. You meet him first and read the report. Make sure it covers every point I told you I wanted answered. Then bring it to me. Put Shannon on ice for two days to give me time to digest it."

Shannon got Endean's message just after five and was in his room to take the call at seven. He spent the rest of the evening between supper and bed making up his notes and the memorabilia he had brought back from Zangaro—a series of sketches done freehand on a pad of cartridge paper he had bought in the airport in Paris to while away the time, some scale-drawings done from measurements between fixed points in Clarence that he had paced out stride by stride, a local guidebook showing "points of interest," of which the only interesting one was titled "the residence of His Excellency the Governor of the Colony" and dated from 1959, and an official and highly flattering portrait of Kimba, one of the few items not in short supply in the republic.

The next day he strolled down Knightsbridge just as the shops opened, bought himself a typewriter and a pad of paper, and spent the morning writing his report. It covered three subjects: a straight narrative of his visit, including the episode of the soldier he had killed; a detailed description of the capital, building by building, accompanied by the diagrams; and an equally detailed description of the military situation. He mentioned the fact that he had seen no signs of either an air force or a navy, and Gomez' confirmation that neither existed. He did not mention his stroll down the peninsula to the native shanty towns, where he had seen the clustered shacks of the poorer Caja and beyond them the shanties of the thousands of immigrant workers and their families, who chattered to one another in their native tongue, brought with them from many miles away.

He finished the report with a summary:

The essence of the problem of toppling Kimba has been simplified by the man himself. In all respects the majority of the republic's land area, the Vindu country beyond the river, is of nil political or economic value. If Kimba should ever lose control of the coastal plain producing the bulk of the nation's few resources, he must lose the country. To go one step further, he and his men could not hold this plain in the face of the hostility and hatred of the entire Caja population, which, although muted by fear, exists beneath the surface, if he had once lost the peninsula. Again, the peninsula is untenable by Vindu forces if once the town of Clarence is lost. And lastly, he has no strength within the town of Clarence if he and his forces have lost the palace. In short, his policy of total centralization has reduced the number of targets necessary to be subdued for a take-over of the state to one—his palace complex, containing himself, his guards, the armory, treasury and radio station.

As to means of taking and reducing this palace and compound, they have been reduced to one, by virtue of the wall surrounding the entire place. It has to be stormed.

The main gate could perhaps be rammed down by a

very heavy truck or bulldozer driven straight at it by a man prepared to die in the attempt. I saw no evidence of any such spirit among the citizenry or the army, nor signs of a suitable truck. Alternatively, self-sacrificing courage by hundreds of men with scaling ladders could overwhelm the palace walls and take the place. I saw no signs of such spirit either. More realistically, the palace and grounds could be taken with little life loss after being first pulverized with mortar fire. Against a weapon like this the encircling wall, far from being a protection, becomes a death-trap to those inside. The door could be taken apart by a bazooka rocket. I saw no signs of either of these weapons, nor any sign of one single person capable of using them. The unavoidable conclusion reached from the above has to be as follows:

Any section or faction within the republic seeking to topple Kimba and take over must destroy him and his Praetorian Guards inside the palace compound. To achieve this they would require expert assistance at a technical level they have not reached, and such assistance would have to arrive, complete with all necessary equipment, from outside the country. With these conditions fulfilled, Kimba could be destroyed and toppled in a firefight lasting no longer than one hour.

"Is Shannon aware that there is no faction inside Zangaro that has indicated it wants to topple Kimba?" asked Sir James Manson the following morning when he read the report.

"I haven't told him so," said Endean. "I briefed him as you told me. Just said there was an army faction inside, and that the group I represented, as interested businessmen, were prepared to pay for a military assessment of their chances of success. But he's no fool. He must have seen for himself there's no one there capable of doing the job anyway."

"I like the sound of this Shannon," said Manson,

closing the military report. "He's obviously got nerve, to judge by the way he dealt with the soldier. He writes quite well; he's short and to the point. Question is, could he do the whole of this job himself?"

"He did mention something significant," interjected Endean. "He said when I was questioning him that the caliber of the Zangaran army was so low that any assisting force of technicians would have to do practically the whole job anyway, then hand over to the new men when it was done."

"Did he now? Did he?" Manson said musingly. "Then he suspects already the reason for his going down there was not the stated one."

He was still musing when Endean asked, "May I put a question, Sir James?"

"What is it?" asked Manson.

"Just this: What did he go down there for? Why do you need a military report on how Kimba could be toppled and killed?"

Sir James Manson stared out of the window for some time. Finally he said, "Get Martin Thorpe up here." While Thorpe was being summoned, Manson walked to the window and gazed down, as he usually did when he wanted to think hard.

He knew he had personally taken Endean and Thorpe as young men and promoted them to salaries and positions beyond their years. It was not simply because of their intelligence, although they had plenty of it. It was because he recognized an unscrupulousness in each of them that matched his own, a preparedness to ignore so-called moral principles in pursuit of the goal success. He had made them his team, his hatchet-men, paid by the company but serving him personally in all things. The problem was: Could he trust them with this one, the big one? As Thorpe entered the office, he decided he had to. He thought he knew how to guarantee their loyalty.

He bade them sit down and, remaining standing with his back to the window, he told them, "I want you two to think this one over very carefully, then give me your reply. How far would you be prepared to go to be assured of a personal fortune in a Swiss bank of five million pounds each?"

The hum of the traffic ten floors down was like a buzzing bee, accentuating the silence in the room.

Endean stared back at his chief and nodded slowly. "A very, very long way," he said softly.

Thorpe made no reply. He knew this was what he had come to the City for, joined Manson for, absorbed his encyclopedic knowledge of company business for. The big one, the once-in-a-decade grand slam. He nodded assent.

"How?" whispered Endean. For answer Manson walked to his wall safe and extracted two reports. The third, Shannon's, lay on his desk as he seated himself behind it.

Manson talked steadily for an hour. He started at the beginning and soon read the final six paragraphs of Dr. Chalmers' report on the samples from the Crystal Mountain.

Thorpe whistled softly and muttered, "Jesus."

Endean required a ten-minute lecture on platinum to catch the point; then he too breathed a long sigh.

Manson went on to relate the exiling of Mulrooney to northern Kenya, the suborning of Chalmers, the second visit of Bryant to Clarence, the acceptance of the dummy report by Kimba's Minister. He stressed the Russian influence on Kimba and the recent exiling of Colonel Bobi, who, given the right circumstances, could return as a plausible alternative in the seat of power.

For Thorpe's benefit he read much of Endean's general report on Zangaro and finished with the conclusion of Shannon's report.

"If it is to work at all, it must be a question of mounting two parallel, highly secret operations," Manson said finally. "In one, Shannon, stage-managed throughout by Simon, mounts a project to take and destroy that palace and all its contents, and for Bobi, accompanied by Simon, to take over the powers of state the following morning and become the new president. In the other, Martin would have to buy a shell company without revealing who had gained control or why."

Endean furrowed his brow. "I can see the first operation, but why the second?" he asked.

"Tell him, Martin," said Manson.

Thorpe was grinning, for his astute mind had caught Manson's drift. "A shell company, Simon, is a company, usually very old and without assets worth talking about, which has virtually ceased trading and whose shares are very cheap—say, a shilling each."

"So why buy one?" asked Endean, still puzzled.

"Say Sir James has control of a company, bought secretly through unnamed nominees, hiding behind a Swiss bank, all nice and legal, and the company has a million shares valued at one shilling each. Unknown to the other shareholders or the board of directors or the Stock Exchange, Sir James, via the Swiss bank, owns six hundred thousand of these million shares. Then Colonel—beg his pardon—President Bobi sells that company an exclusive ten-year mining franchise for an area of land in the hinterland of Zangaro. A new mining survey team from a highly reputable company specializing in mining goes out and discovers the Crystal Mountain. What happens to the shares of Company X when the news hits the stock market?"

Endean got the message. "They go up," he said with a grin.

"Right up," said Thorpe. "With a bit of help they go from a shilling to well over a hundred pounds a share. Now do your arithmetic. Six hundred thousand shares at a shilling each cost thirty thousand pounds to buy. Sell six hundred thousand shares at a hundred pounds each—and that's the minimum you'd get—and what do you bring home? A cool sixty million pounds, in a Swiss bank. Right, Sir James?"

"That's right." Manson nodded grimly. "Of course, if you sold half the shares in small packets to a wide variety of people, the control of the company owning the concession would stay in the same hands as before. But a bigger company might put in a bid for the whole block of six hundred thousand shares in one flat deal."

Thorpe nodded thoughtfully. "Yes, control of such a company bought at sixty million pounds would be a good market deal. But whose bid would you accept?"

"My own," said Manson.

Thorpe's mouth opened. "Your own?"

"ManCon's bid would be the only acceptable one. That way the concession would remain firmly British, and ManCon would have gained a fine asset."

"But," queried Endean, "surely you would be paying yourself sixty million quid?"

"No," said Thorpe quietly. "ManCon's shareholders would be paying Sir James sixty million quid, without knowing it."

"What's that called—in financial terms, of course?" asked Endean.

"There is a word for it on the Stock Exchange," Thorpe admitted.

Sir James Manson tendered them each a glass of whisky. He reached round and took his own. "Are you on, gentlemen?" he asked quietly.

Both younger men looked at each other and nodded.

"Then here's to the Crystal Mountain."

They drank.

"Report to me here tomorrow morning at nine sharp," Manson told them, and they rose to go.

At the door to the back stairs Thorpe turned. "You know, Sir James, it's going to be bloody dangerous. If one word gets out . . ."

Sir James Manson stood again with his back to the window, the westering sun slanting onto the carpet by his side. His legs were apart, his fists on his hips.

"Knocking off a bank or an armored truck," he said, "is merely crude. Knocking off an entire republic has, I feel, a certain style."

8

"What you are saying in effect is that there is no dissatisfied faction within the army that, so far as you know, has ever thought of toppling President Kimba?"

Cat Shannon and Simon Endean were sitting in Shannon's room at the hotel, taking midmorning coffee. Endean had phoned Shannon by agreement at nine and told him to wait for a second call. He had been briefed by Sir James Manson and had called Shannon back to make the eleven-o'clock appointment.

Endean nodded. "That's right. The information has changed in that one detail. I can't see what difference it makes. You yourself said the caliber of the army was so low that the technical assistants would have to do all the work themselves in any case."

"It makes a hell of a difference," said Shannon. "Attacking the palace and capturing it is one thing. Keeping it is quite another. Destroying the palace and Kimba simply creates a vacuum at the seat of power. Someone has to step in and take over that power. The mercenaries must not even be seen by daylight. So who takes over?"

Endean nodded again. He had not expected a mercenary to have any political sense at all.

"We have a man in view," he said cautiously.

"He's in the republic now, or in exile?"

"In exile."

"Well, he would have to be installed in the palace and broadcasting on the radio that he has conducted an internal coup d'état and taken over the country, by midday of the day following the night attack on the palace."

"That could be arranged."

"There's one more thing."

"What's that?" asked Endean.

"There must be troops loyal to the new regime, the same troops who ostensibly carried out the coup of the night before, visibly present and mounting the guard by sunrise of the day after the attack. If they don't show up, we would be stuck—a group of white mercenaries holed up inside the palace, unable to show themselves for political reasons, and cut off from retreat in the event of a counterattack. Now your man, the exile, does he have such a back-up force he could bring in with him when he comes? Or could he assemble them quickly once inside the capital?"

"I think you have to let us take care of that," said Endean stiffly. "What we are asking you for is a plan in military terms to mount the attack and carry it through."

"That I can do," said Shannon without hesitation. "But what about the preparations, the organization of the plan, getting the men, the arms, the ammo?"

"You must include that as well. Start from scratch and go right through to the capture of the palace and the death of Kimba."

"Kimba has to get the chop?"

"Of course," said Endean. "Fortunately he has long since destroyed anyone with enough initiative or brains to become a rival. Consequently, he is the only man who might regroup his forces and counterattack. With him dead, his ability to mesmerize the people into submission will also end."

"Yeah. The juju dies with the man."

"The what?"

"Nothing. You wouldn't understand."

"Try me," said Endean coldly.

"The man has a juju," said Shannon, "or at least the people believe he has. That's a powerful protection given him by the spirits, protecting him against his enemies, guaranteeing him invincibility, guarding him from attack, ensuring him against death. In the Congo the Simbas believed their leader, Pierre Mulele, had a similar juju. He told them he could pass it on to his supporters and make them immortal. They believed him. They thought bullets would run off them like water. So they came at us in waves, bombed out of their minds on dagga and whisky, died like flies, and still kept coming. It's the same with Kimba. So long as they think he's immortal, he is. Because they'll never lift a finger against him. Once they see his corpse, the man who killed him becomes the leader. He has the stronger juju."

Endean stared in surprise. "It's really that backward?"

"It's not so backward. We do the same with lucky charms, holy relics, the assumption of divine protection for our own particular cause. But we call it religion in us, savage superstition in them."

"Never mind," snapped Endean. "All the more reason why Kimba has to die."

"Which means he must be in that palace when we strike. If he's upcountry it's no good. No one will support your man if Kimba is still alive."

"He usually is in the palace, so I'm told."

"Yes," said Shannon, "but we have to guarantee it. There's one day he never misses. Independence Day. On the eve of Independence Day he will be sleeping in the palace, sure as eggs is eggs."

"When's that?"

"Three and a half months away."

"Could a project be mounted in that time?" asked Endean.

"Yes, with a bit of luck. I'd like at least a couple of weeks longer."

"The project has not been accepted yet," observed Endean.

"No, but if you want to install a new man in that palace, an attack from outside is the only way of doing it. Do you want me to prepare the whole project from start to finish, with estimated costings and time schedule?"

"Yes. The costing is very important. My—er—associates will want to know how much they are letting themselves in for."

"All right," said Shannon. "The report will cost you five hundred pounds."

"You've already been paid," said Endean coldly.

"I've been paid for a mission into Zangaro and a report on the military situation there," replied Shannon. "What you're asking for is a new report right outside the original briefing you gave me."

"Five hundred is a bit steep for a few sheets of paper with writing on them."

"Rubbish. You know perfectly well if your firm consults a lawyer, architect, accountant, or any other technical expert you pay him a fee. I'm a technical expert in war. What you pay for is the knowledge and the experience—where to get the best men, the best arms, how to ship them, et cetera. That's what costs five hundred pounds, and the same knowledge would cost you double if you tried to research it yourself in twelve months, which you couldn't anyway because you haven't the contacts."

Endean rose. "All right. It will be here this afternoon by special messenger. Tomorrow is Friday. My partners would like to read your report over the weekend. Please have it prepared by tomorrow afternoon at three. I'll collect it here."

He left, and as the door closed behind him Shannon raised his coffee cup in mock toast. "Be seeing you, Mr. Walter Harris oblique stroke Simon Endean," he said softly.

Not for the first time he thanked his stars for the amiable and garrulous hotelkeeper Gomez. During one of their long nightly conversations Gomez had mentioned the affair of Colonel Bobi, now in exile. He had also mentioned that, without Kimba, Bobi was nothing, being hated by the Caja for his army's cruelties against them on the orders of Kimba, and not able to command Vindu troops either. Which left Shannon with the problem of a back-up force with black faces to take over on the morning after.

Endean's brown manila envelope containing fifty £10 notes arrived just after three in a taxicab and was delivered to the reception desk of the Lowndes Hotel. Shannon counted the notes, stuffed them into the inside pocket of his jacket, and began work. It took him the rest of the afternoon and most of the night.

He worked at the writing desk in his room, poring over his own diagrams and maps of the city of Clarence, its harbor, port area, and the residential section that included the presidential palace and the army lines.

The classical military approach would have been to land a force on the side of the peninsula near the base with the main coastline, march the short distance inland, and take the road from Clarence to the interior, with guns covering the T-junction. That would have sealed off the peninsula and the capital from reinforcement. It would also have lost the element of surprise.

Shannon's talent was that he understood Africa and the African soldier, and his thinking was unconventional. Tactics suited to African terrain and opposition are almost the exact opposite of those that will work in a European situation.

Had Shannon's plans ever been considered by a European military mind thinking in conventional terms, they would have been styled as reckless and without hope of success. He was banking on Sir James Manson's not having been in the British army—there was no reference in *Who's Who* to indicate that he had—and accepting the plan. Shannon knew it was workable and the only one that was.

He based his plan on three facts about war in Africa

that he had learned the hard way. One is that the European soldier fights well and with precision in the dark, provided he has been well briefed on the terrain he can expect, while the African soldier, even on his own terrain, is sometimes reduced to near helplessness by his fear of the hidden enemy in the surrounding darkness. The second is that the speed of recovery of the disoriented African soldier—his ability to regroup and counterattack—is slower than the European soldier's, exaggerating the normal effects of surprise. The third is that firepower and hence noise can bring African soldiers to fear, panic, and headlong flight, without consideration of the smallness of the actual numbers of their opponents.

So Shannon based his plan on a night attack of total surprise in conditions of deafening noise and concentrated firepower.

He worked slowly and methodically and, being a poor typist, tapped out the words with two forefingers. At two in the morning the occupant of the bedroom next door could stand no more and banged on the wall to ask plaintively for a bit of peace so that he could get to sleep. Shannon concluded what he was doing five minutes later and packed up for the night. There was one other sound that disturbed the man next door, apart from the clacking of the typewriter. As he worked, and later as he lay in bed, the writer kept whistling a plaintive little tune. Had the insomniac next door known more of music, he would have recognized "Spanish Harlem."

Martin Thorpe was also lying awake that night. He knew he had a long weekend ahead, two and a half days of monotonous and time-consuming poring over cards, each bearing the basic details of one of the forty-five hundred public companies registered at Companies House in the City of London.

There are two agencies in London which provide their subscribers with such an information service about British companies. These are Moodies and the

Exchange Telegraph, known as Extel. In his office in ManCon House, Thorpe had the set of cards provided by Extel, the agency whose service ManCon took as a necessary part of its commercial activities. But for the business of searching for a shell company, Thorpe had decided to buy the Moodies service and have it sent to his home, partly because he thought Moodies did a better information job on the smaller companies registered in the United Kingdom, and partly for security reasons.

After his briefing from Sir James Manson on Thursday, he had gone straight to a firm of lawyers. Acting for him, and keeping his name to themselves, they had ordered a complete set of Moodies cards. He had paid the lawyer £260 for the cards, plus £50 for the three gray filing cabinets in which they would arrive, plus the lawyer's fee. He had also engaged a small moving firm to send a van around to Moodies, after being told the set of cards would be ready for pickup on Friday afternoon.

As he lay in bed in his elegant detached house in Hampstead Garden Suburb, he too was planning his campaign—not in detail like Shannon, for he had too little information, but in general terms, using nominee shareholders and parcels of voting stock as Shannon used submachine guns and mortars. He had never met the mercenary and never would. But he would have understood him.

Shannon handed his completed project to Endean at three on Friday afternoon. It contained fourteen pages, four of them diagrams and two of them lists of equipment. He had finished it after breakfast and had enclosed it in a brown folder. He was tempted to put "For Sir James Manson's Eyes Only" on the cover, but had resisted. There was no need to blow the affair wantonly, and he could sniff a good contract in the offing if the mining baron offered the job to him.

So he continued to call Endean Harris and to refer to "your associates" instead of "your boss." After taking the folder, Endean told him to stay in town over the weekend and to be available from Sunday midnight onward.

Shannon went shopping during the rest of the afternoon, but his mind was on the references he had already seen in *Who's Who* to the man he now knew employed him, Sir James Manson, self-made millionaire and tycoon.

He had an urge, partly from curiosity, partly from the feeling that one day he might need the information, to learn more about Sir James Manson, about the man himself and about why he had hired a mercenary to make war in Zangaro on his behalf.

The reference from *Who's Who* that stuck in his mind was the mention of a daughter Manson had, a girl who would now be in her late teens or just turned twenty. In the middle of the afternoon he stepped into a phone booth off Jermyn Street and called the private inquiry agents who had traced Endean from their first meeting in Chelsea and identified him as Manson's aide.

The head of the agency was cordial when he heard his former client on the phone. Previously, he knew, Mr. Brown had paid promptly and in cash. Such customers were valuable. If he wished to remain on the end of a telephone, that was his affair.

"Do you have access to a fairly comprehensive newspaper cuttings library?" Shannon asked.

"I could have," the agency chief admitted.

"I wish to get a brief description of a young lady to whom there has probably at one time been a reference in society gossip columns somewhere in the London press. I need very little, simply what she does and where she lives. But I need it quickly."

There was a pause on the other end. "If there are such references, I could probably do it by phone," said the inquiry agent. "What is the name?"

"Miss Julia Manson, daughter of Sir James Manson."

The inquiry agent thought it over. He recalled that this client's previous assignment had concerned a man who turned out to be Sir James Manson's aide. He also knew he could find out what Mr. Brown wanted to know within an hour.

The two men agreed on the fee, a modest one, and Shannon promised to mail it in cash by registered mail within the hour. The inquiry agent decided to accept the promise and asked his client to call him back just before five.

Shannon completed his shopping and called back on the dot of five. Within a few seconds he had what he wanted. He was deep in thought as he walked back to his hotel and phoned the writer who had originally introduced him to "Mr. Harris."

"Hi," he said gruffly, "it's me, Cat Shannon."

"Oh, hello, Cat," came the surprised reply. "Where have you been?"

"Around," said Shannon. "I just wanted to say thanks for recommending me to that fellow Harris."

"Not at all. Did he offer you a job?"

Shannon was cautious. "Yeah, a few days' worth. It's over now. But I'm in funds. How about a spot of dinner?"

"Why not?" said the writer.

"Tell me," said Shannon, "are you still going out with that girl you used to be with when we met last?"

"Yeah. The same one. Why?"

"She's a model, isn't she?"

"Yes."

"Look," said Shannon, "you may think this crazy, but I very much want to meet a girl who's also a model but I can't get an introduction to. Name of Julie Manson. Could you ask your girl if she ever met her in the modeling world?"

The writer thought it over. "Sure. I'll call Carrie and ask her. Where are you now?"

"In a call box. I'll call you back in half an hour."

Shannon was lucky. The two girls had been at modeling school together. They were also handled by the same agency. It took another hour before Shannon, by then speaking directly to the writer's girlfriend, learned that Julia Manson had agreed to a dinner date, providing it was a foursome with Carrie and her boyfriend. They agreed to meet at Carrie's flat just after eight, and she would have Julie Manson there.

Shannon and the writer turned up within a few minutes of each other at Carrie's flat off Maida Vale, and the four of them went off to dinner. The writer had reserved a table at a small cellar restaurant called the Baker and Oven in Marylebone, and the meal was the kind Shannon liked, enormous portions of English roast meats and vegetables, washed down with two bottles of Piat de Beaujolais. He liked the food, and he liked Julie.

She was quite short, a little over five feet, and to give the impression of more height she wore high heels and carried herself well. She said she was nineteen, and she had a pert, round face that could be innocently angelic when she wanted, or extremely sexy when she thought no one else was looking.

She was evidently spoiled and too accustomed to getting things her own way—probably, Shannon estimated, the result of an overindulgent upbringing. But she was amusing and pretty, and Shannon had never asked more of a girl. She wore her dark brown hair loose so that it fell to her waist, and beneath her dress she evidently had a very curved figure. She also seemed to be intrigued by her blind date.

Although Shannon had asked his friend not to mention what he did for a living, Carrie had nevertheless let it slip that he was a mercenary. But the conversation managed to avoid the question during dinner. As usual Shannon did less talking than anyone, which was not difficult because Julie and the tall auburn-haired Carrie did enough for four between them.

As they left the restaurant and climbed back into the cool night air of the streets, the writer mentioned that he and his girlfriend were taking the car back to his flat. He hailed a taxi for Shannon, asking him if he would take Julie home before going on to his hotel.

As the mercenary climbed in, the writer gave him a slow wink. "I think you're on," he whispered. Shannon grunted.

Outside her Mayfair flat Julie suggested he might like to come in for coffee, so he paid off the taxi and accompanied her up to the evidently expensive apartment. Only when they were seated on the settee drinking the appalling coffee Julie had prepared did she refer to the way he earned his living.

He was leaning back in the corner of the settee; she was perched on the edge of the seat, turned toward him.

"Have you killed people?" she asked.

"Yes."

"In battle?"

"Sometimes. Mostly."

"How many?"

"I don't know. I never counted."

She savored the information and swallowed several times. "I've never known a man who had killed people."

"You don't know that," countered Shannon. "Anyone who has been in a war has probably killed people."

"Have you got any scars from wounds?"

It was another of the usual questions. In fact Shannon carried over a score of marks on his back and chest, legacies of bullets, fragments of mortar, and shards of grenade. He nodded. "Some."

"Show me," she said.

"No."

"Go on, show me. Prove it." She stood up.

He grinned up at her. "I'll show you mine if you'll show me yours," he taunted, mimicking the old kindergarten challenge.

"I haven't got any," Julie said indignantly.

"Prove it," said Shannon shortly and turned to place his empty coffee cup on the table behind the sofa. He heard a rustle of cloth. When he turned back he nearly choked on the last mouthful of coffee. It had taken her less than a second to unzip her dress at the back and let it slip to a pool of crumpled cloth around her ankles. Beneath it she wore a thin gold waist-chain.

"See," she said softly, "not a mark anywhere."

She was right. Her small nubile teenager's body was an unblemished milky white from the floor to the mane of dark hair that hung round her shoulders and almost touched the waist-chain.

Shannon swallowed. "I thought you were supposed to be Daddy's sweet little girl," he said.

She giggled. "That's what they all think, especially Daddy," she said. "Now it's your turn."

Sir James Manson sat at the same hour in the library of his country mansion not far from the village of Notgrove in the rolling Gloucestershire countryside, Shannon's file on his knee and a brandy and soda at his elbow. It was close to midnight, and Lady Manson had long since gone up to bed. He had saved the Shannon project to read alone in his library, resisting the temptation to open it in the car on the way down or to slip away early from dinner. When he wanted to concentrate hard he preferred the night hours, and on this document he wanted to concentrate hard.

He flicked the cover open and set on one side the maps and sketches. Then he started on the narrative. It read:

Preamble. The following plan has been prepared on the basis of the report on the republic of Zangaro prepared by Mr. Walter Harris, my own visit to Zangaro and my own report on that visit, and the briefing given by Mr. Harris on what it is desired to achieve. It cannot take into account elements known to Mr. Harris but undisclosed by him to me. Notable among these must be the aftermath of the attack and the installation of the successor government. Nevertheless, this aftermath may well require preparations built in to the planning of the attack, and these I have obviously not been able to make.

Object of the Exercise. To prepare, launch, and carry out an attack on the presidential palace at Clarence, capital of Zangaro, to storm and capture that palace, and to liquidate the President and his personal guards living inside. Also, to take possession of the bulk of the weapons and armory of the republic, its national treasury and broadcasting radio station, also inside the palace. Lastly, to create such conditions that any armed survivors of the guard unit or the army are scattered outside the town and in no position to mount a viable counterattack.

Method of Attack. After studying the military situation of Clarence, there is no doubt the attack must be from the sea, and launched directly from the sea at the palace itself. I have studied the idea of an airborne landing at the airport. It is not feasible. Firstly, the authorities at the airport of take-off would not permit the necessary quantity of arms and men to board a charter aircraft without suspecting the nature of the flight. Any authorities, even if they permitted such a take-off, would constitute a serious risk of arrest, or a breach of security.

Secondly, a land attack offers no extra advantages and many disadvantages. To arrive in an armed column over the northern border would only mean the men and arms would have to be smuggled into the neighboring republic, which has an efficient police and security system. The risk of premature discovery and arrest would be extremely high, unacceptably so. To land elsewhere on the coast of Zangaro and march to Clarence would be no more realistic. For one thing, most of the coast is of tangled mangrove swamp impenetrable by boats, and such tiny coves as there are would be unfindable in darkness. For another, being without motor transport, the attack force would have a long march to the capital, and the defenders would be forewarned. For a third, the paucity of the numbers of the attacking force would be visible in daylight, and would hearten the defenders to put up a stiff resistance.

Lastly, the idea was examined to smuggle the arms and the men into the republic clandestinely and hide them out until the night of the attack. This too is unrealistic, partly because the quantity of weapons would be too great in weight terms, partly because such quantities and so many unaccustomed visitors would inevitably be spotted and betrayed, and partly because such a plan would require an assisting organization on the ground inside Zangaro, which does not exist.

In consequence it is felt the only realistic plan must be for an attack by light boats, departing from a larger vessel moored out at sea, straight into the harbor of Clarence, and an attack on the palace immediately on landing.

Requirements for the Attack. The force should be not less than a dozen men, armed with mortars, bazookas, and grenades, and all carrying as well submachine carbines for close-quarters use. The men should come off the sea between two and three in the morning, giving ample time for all in Clarence to be asleep, but sufficiently before dawn for no visible traces of white mercenaries to be available by sunrise of the same day.

The report continued for six more pages to describe exactly how Shannon proposed to plan the project and engage the necessary personnel; the arms and ammunition he would need, the ancillary equipment of radio sets, assault craft, outboard engines, flares, uniforms, webbing, food and supplies; how each item could be costed; and how he would destroy the palace and scatter the army.

On the question of the ship to carry the attacking force he said:

Apart from the arms, the acquisition of the ship will prove the most difficult part. On reflection I would be against chartering a vessel, since this involves crew who may turn out to be unreliable, a captain who could at any time change his mind, and the security hazard that vessels of a kind likely to undertake such a charter are probably notorious to the authorities of the countries bordering on the Mediterranean. I advocate spending more money to buy outright a small freighter, crew it with men paid by and loyal to the patrons and with a legal reputation in shipping circles. Such a boat would in any case be a returnable asset and might work out cheaper in the long run.

Shannon had also stressed the necessity of security at all times. He pointed out:

Since I am unaware of the identity of the patrons, with the exception of Mr. Harris, it is recommended that, in the event of the project being accepted, Mr. Harris remain the sole link between the patrons and me. Payments of the necessary money should be made to me by Mr. Harris, and my accounting of expenditure returned the same way. Similarly, although I would need four subordinate operatives, none would know the nature of the project, and certainly not the destination, until all are well out to sea. Even the coastal charts should be handed over to the captain only after sailing. The above plan takes in the security angle, since wherever possible the purchases may be made legally on the open market, and only the arms an illegal purchase. At each stage there is a cut-out at which any investigator comes up against a blank wall, and also at each stage the equipment is being bought separately in different countries by different operatives. Only myself, Mr. Harris, and the patrons would know the whole plan, and in the worst event I could not identify the patrons, nor, probably, Mr. Harris.

Sir James Manson nodded and grunted in approval several times as he read. At one in the morning he poured himself another brandy and turned to the costings and timings, which were on separate sheets. These read:

COMPLETED

Reconnaissance visit to Zangaro. Two reports	£	2,500
Project commander's fee	£	10,000
Engagement all other personnel and their salaries	£	10,000
Total administrative costs, traveling, hotels, etc., for CO and all subordinates	£	10,000
Purchase of arms	£	25,000
Purchase of vessel	£	30,000
Purchase of ancillary equipment	£	5,000
Reserve	£	2,500
TOTAL	£	100,000

The second sheet bore the estimated timings.

Preparatory Stage: Recruitment and assembly of personnel. Setting up of bank account. Setting up of foreign-based company to cover purchases.   20 days

Purchasing Stage: Period to cover purchase of all items in sections.   40 days

Assembly Stage: Assembly of equipment and personnel onto the vessel, culminating in sailing day.   20 days

Shipment Stage: Transporting entire project by sea from embarkation port to point off coast of Clarence.   20 days

Strike day would take place on Zangaran Independence Day, which in the above calendar, if set in motion not later than next Wednesday, would be Day 100.

Sir James Manson read the report twice and slowly smoked one of his Upmann Coronas while he stared at the rich paneling and Morocco-bound books that lined his walls. Finally he locked the project file in his wall safe and went upstairs to bed.

Cat Shannon lay on his back in the darkened bedroom and ran his hand idly over the girl's body that lay half across his own. It was a small but highly erotic body, as he had discovered during the previous hour, and whatever Julie had spent her time learning in the two years since she left school, it had not had much to do with shorthand and typing. Her appetite and taste for sexual variety were equaled only by her energy and almost constant stream of chatter between meals.

As he stroked her she stirred and began to play with him.

"Funny," he said reflectively, "it must be a sign of the times. We've been screwing half the night, and I don't know a thing about you."

She paused for a second, said, "Like what?" and resumed.

"Where your home is," he said. "Apart from this pad."

"Gloucestershire," she mumbled.

"What does your old man do?" he asked softly. There was no answer. He took a handful of her hair and pulled her face around to him.

"Ow, you're hurting. He's in the City. Why?"

"Stockbroker?"

"No, he runs some company to do with mining. That's his specialty, and this is mine. Now, watch."

Half an hour later she rolled off him and asked, "Did you like that, darling?"

Shannon laughed, and she caught a flash of teeth in the darkness as he grinned.

"Oh yes," he said softly, "I enjoyed that enormously. Tell me about your old man."

"Daddy? Oh he's a boring old businessman. Spends all his day in a stuffy office in the City."

"Some businessmen interest me. So tell me, what's he like?"

Sir James Manson was enjoying his midmorning coffee in the sun lounge on the south side of his country mansion that Saturday morning when the call came through from Adrian Goole. The Foreign Office official was speaking from his own home in Kent.

"I hope you won't mind my calling you over the weekend," he said.

"Not at all, my dear fellow," said Manson quite untruthfully. "Any time."

"I would have called at the office last night, but I got held up at a meeting. Recalling our conversation some time ago about the results of your mining survey down in that African place. You remember?"

Manson supposed Goole felt obliged to go through the security rigmarole on an open line.

"Yes indeed," he said. "I took up your suggestion made at that dinner. The figures concerned were slightly changed, so that the quantities revealed were quite unviable from a business standpoint. The report went off, was received, and I've heard no more about it."

Goole's next words jerked Sir James Manson out of his weekend relaxation.

"Actually, we have," said the voice on the phone. "Nothing really disturbing, but odd all the same. Our Ambassador in the area, although accredited to that country and three other small republics, doesn't live there, as you know. But he sends in regular reports, gleaned from a variety of sources, including normal liaison with other friendly diplomats. A copy of a section of his latest report, concerned with the economic side of things out there, landed on my desk yesterday at the office. It seems there's a rumor out there that the Soviet government has secured permission to send in a mining survey team of their own. Of course, they may not be concerned with the same area as your chaps. . . ."

Sir James Manson stared at the telephone as Goole's voice twittered on. In his head a pulse began to hammer, close to his left temple.

"I was only thinking, Sir James, that if these Russian chaps go over the same area your man went over, their findings might be somewhat different. Fortunately, it's only a question of minor quantities of tin. Still, I thought you ought to know. Hello? Hello? Are you there?"

Manson jerked himself out of his reverie. With a massive effort he made his voice appear normal.

"Yes indeed. Sorry, I was just thinking. Very good of you to call me, Goole. I don't suppose they'll be in the same area as my man. But damn useful to know, all the same."

He went through the usual pleasantries before hanging up, and walked slowly back to the sun terrace, his mind racing. Coincidence? Could be, it just could be. If the Soviet survey team was going to cover an area miles away from the Crystal Mountain range, it would be purely a coincidence. On the other hand, if it went straight toward the Crystal Mountain without having done any aerial survey work to notice the differences in vegetation in that area, then that would be no coincidence. That would be bloody sabotage. And there was no way he could find out, no way of being absolutely certain, without betraying his own continuing interest. And that would be fatal.

He thought of Chalmers, the man he was convinced he had silenced with money. His teeth ground. Had he talked? Wittingly? Unwittingly? He had half a mind to let Endean take care of Dr. Chalmers, or one of Endean's friends. But that would change nothing. And there was no proof of a security leak.

He could shelve his plans at once and think no more of them. He considered this, then considered again the pot of pure gold at the end of this particular rainbow. James Manson was not where he was because he had the habit of backing down on account of risk.

He sat down in his deck chair next to the now cold coffeepot and thought hard. He intended to go forward as planned, but he had to assume the Russian mining team would touch on the area Mulrooney had visited, and he had to assume that it too would notice the vegetation changes. Therefore there was now a new element, a time limit. He did some mental calculation and came up with the figure of three months. If the Russians learned the content of the Crystal Mountain, there would be a "technical aid" team in there like a dose of salts. A big one at that, and half the members would be hard men from KGB.

Shannon's shortest schedule had been a hundred days, but he had originally told Endean that another fortnight added to the timetable would make the whole project that much more feasible. Now they did not have that fortnight. In fact, if the Russians moved faster than usual, they might not even have a hundred days.

He returned to the telephone and called Simon Endean. His own weekend had been disturbed; there was no reason why Endean should not start doing a bit of work.

Endean called Shannon at the hotel on Monday morning and set up a rendezvous for two that afternoon at a small apartment house in St. John's Wood. He had hired the flat on the instructions of Sir James Manson, after having had a long briefing at the country mansion on Sunday afternoon. He had taken the flat for a month in the name of Harris, paying cash and giving a fictitious reference which no one checked. The reason for the hiring was simple: the flat had a telephone that did not go through a switchboard.

Shannon was there on time and found the man he still called Harris already installed. The telephone was hung in a desk microphone set that would enable a telephone conference to be held between one or more people in the room and the person on the other end of the line.

"The chief of the consortium has read your report," he told Shannon, "and wants to have a word with you."

At two-thirty the phone rang. Endean threw the "speak" switch on the machine, and Sir James Manson's voice came on the line. Shannon already knew who it would be but gave no sign.

"Are you there, Mr. Shannon?" asked the voice.

"Yes, sir."

"Now, I have read your report, and I approve your judgment and conclusions. If offered this contract, would you be prepared to go through with it?"

"Yes, sir, I would," said Shannon.

"There are a couple of points I want to discuss. I notice in the budget you award yourself the sum of ten thousand pounds."

"Yes, sir. Frankly, I don't think anyone would do the job for less, and most would ask more. Even if a budget were prepared by another person which quoted a lower sum, I think that person would still pass a minimum of ten per cent to himself, simply by hiding the sum in the prices of purchases that could not be checked out."

There was a pause; then the voice said, "All right. I accept that. What does this salary buy me?"

"It buys you my knowledge, my contacts, my acquaintanceship with the world of arms dealers, smugglers, gun-runners, and mercenaries. It also buys my silence in the event of anything's going wrong. It pays me for three months' damned hard work, and the constant risk of arrest and imprisonment. Lastly, it buys the risk of my getting killed in the attack."

There was a grunt. "Fair enough. Now as regards financing. The sum of one hundred thousand pounds will be transferred into a Swiss account which Mr. Harris will open this week. He will pay you the necessary money in slices, as and when you need it over the forthcoming two months. For that purpose you will have to set up your own communications system with him. When the money is spent, he will either have to be present or to receive receipts."

"That will not always be possible, sir. There are no receipts in the arms business, least of all in black-market deals, and most of the men I shall be dealing with would not have Mr. Harris present. He is not in their world. I would suggest the extensive use of travelers' checks and credit transfers by banks. At the same time, if Mr. Harris has to be present to countersign every banker's draft or check for a thousand pounds, he must either follow me around everywhere, which I would not accept on grounds of my own security, or we could never do it all inside a hundred days."

There was another long pause. "What do you mean by your own security?" asked the voice.

"I mean, sir, that I don't know Mr. Harris. I could not accept that he be in a position to know enough to get me arrested in a European city. You have taken your security precautions. I have to take mine. These are that I travel and work alone and unsupervised."

"You're a cautious man, Mr. Shannon."

"I have to be. I'm still alive."

There was a grim chuckle. "And how do I know you can be trusted with large sums of money to handle on your own?"

"You don't, sir. Up to a point Mr. Harris can keep the sums low at each stage. But the payments for the arms have to be made in cash and by the buyer alone. The only alternatives are to ask Mr. Harris to mount the operation personally, or to hire another professional. And you would not know if you could trust him either."

"Fair enough, Mr. Shannon. Mr. Harris."

"Sir?" answered Endean immediately.

"Please return to see me at once after leaving where you are now. Mr. Shannon, you have the job. You have one hundred days, Mr. Shannon, to steal a republic. One hundred days."

PART TWO

The Hundred Days

9

For several minutes after Sir James Manson had hung up, Simon Endean and Cat Shannon sat and stared at each other. It was Shannon who recovered first.

"Since we're going to have to work together," he told Endean, "let's get this clear. If anyone, anyone at all, gets to hear about this project, it will eventually get back to one or another of the secret services of one of the main powers. Probably the CIA, or at least the British SIS or maybe the French SDECE. And they will screw, but good. There'll be nothing you or I could do to prevent them ending the affair stone dead. So we keep security absolute."

"Speak for yourself," snapped Endean. "I've got a lot more tied up in this than you."

"Okay. First thing has to be money. I'll fly to Brussels tomorrow and open a new bank account somewhere in Belgium. I'll be back by tomorrow night. Contact me then, and I'll tell you where, in which bank and in what name. Then I shall need a transfer of credit to the tune of at least ten thousand pounds. By tomorrow night I'll have a complete list of where it has to be spent. Mainly, it will be in salary checks for my assistants, deposits, and so on."

"Where do I contact you?" asked Endean.

"That's point number two," said Shannon. "I'm going to need a permanent base, secure for telephone calls and letters. What about this flat? Is it traceable to you?"

Endean had not thought of that. He considered the problem. "It's hired in my name. Cash in advance for one month," he said.

"Does it matter if the name Harris is on the tenancy agreement?" asked Shannon.

"No."

"Then I'll take it over. That gives me a month's tenancy—seems a pity to waste it—and I'll take up the payments at the end of that time. Do you have a key?"

"Yes, of course. I let myself in by it."

"How many keys are there?"

For answer Endean reached into his pocket and brought out a ring with four keys on it. Two were evidently for the front door of the house and two for the flat door. Shannon took them from his hand.

"Now for communications," he said. "You can contact me by phoning here any time. I may be in, I may not. I may be away abroad. Since I assume you will not want to give me your phone number, set up a *poste restante* mailing address in London somewhere convenient to either your home or office, and check twice daily for telegrams. If I need you urgently, I'll telegraph the phone number of where I am, and a time to phone. Understood?"

"Yes. I'll have it by tomorrow night. Anything else?"

"Only that I'll be using the name of Keith Brown throughout the operation. Anything signed as coming from Keith is from me. When calling a hotel, ask for me as Keith Brown. If ever I reply by saying 'This is Mr. Brown,' get off the line fast. It means trouble. Explain that you have the wrong number, or the wrong Brown. That's all for the moment. You'd better get back to the office. Call me here at eight tonight, and I'll give you the progress to date."

A few minutes later Endean found himself on the pavements of St. John's Wood, looking for a taxi.

Luckily Shannon had not banked the £500 he had received from Endean before the weekend for his attack project, and he still had £450 of it left.

He rang BEA and booked an economy-class round trip on the morning flight to Brussels, returning at 1600 hours, which would get him back in his flat by six. Following that, he telephoned four telegrams abroad, one to Paarl, Cape Province, South Africa; one to Ostend; one to Marseilles; and one to Munich. Each said simply, "Urgent you phone me London 507-0041 any midnight over next three days. Shannon." Finally he summoned a taxi and had it take him back to the Lowndes Hotel. He checked out, paid his bill, and left as he had come, anonymously.

At eight Endean rang him as agreed, and Shannon told Manson's aide what he had done so far. They agreed Endean would ring again at ten the following evening.

Shannon spent a couple of hours exploring the block he was now living in, and the surrounding area. He spotted several small restaurants, including a couple not far away in St. John's Wood High Street, and ate a leisurely supper at one of them. He was back home by eleven.

He counted his money—there was more than £400 left—put £300 on one side for the air fare and expenses the following day, and checked over his effects. The clothes were unremarkable, all of them less than three months old, most bought in the last ten days in London. He had no gun to bother about, and for safety destroyed the typewriter ribbon he had used to type his reports, replacing it with one of his spares.

Though it was dark early in London that evening, it was still light on a warm, sunny summer evening in Cape Province as Janni Dupree gunned his car past Seapoint and on toward Cape Town. He too had a Chevrolet, older than Endean's, but bigger and flashier, bought second-hand with some of the dollars with which he had returned from Paris four weeks earlier.

After spending the day swimming and fishing from a friend's boat at Simonstown, he was driving back to his home in Paarl. He always liked to come home to Paarl after a contract, but inevitably it bored him quickly, just as it had when he left it ten years before.

As a boy he had been raised in the Paarl Valley and had spent his preschool years scampering through the thin and poor vineyards owned by people like his parents. He had learned to stalk birds and shoot in the valley with Pieter, his klonkie, the black playmate a white boy is allowed to play with until he grows too old and learns what skin color is all about.

Pieter, with his enormous brown eyes, tangled mass of black curls, and mahogany skin, was two years older than Janni and had been supposed to look after him. In fact they had been the same size, for Janni was physically precocious and had quickly taken the leadership of the pair. On summer days like this one, twenty years ago, the two barefoot boys used to take the bus along the coast to Cape Agulhas, where the Atlantic and the Indian oceans finally meet, and fish for yellowtail, galjoen, and red steenbras off the point.

After Paarl Boys' High, Janni had been a problem —too big, aggressive, restless, getting into fights with those big scything fists and ending up twice in front of the magistrates. He could have taken over his parents' farm and tended with his father the stubby little vines that produced such thin wine. The prospect appalled him—of becoming old and bent trying to make a living from the smallholding, with only four black boys working with him. At eighteen he volunteered for the army, did his basic training at Potchefstroom, and transferred to the paratroops at Bloemfontein. It was here he had found the thing he wanted to do most in life, here and in the counterinsurgency training in the harsh bushveld around Pietersburg. The army had agreed with him about his suitability, except on one point: his propensity for going to war while pointing in the wrong direction. In one fistfight too many, Corporal Dupree had beaten a sergeant senseless, and the commanding officer had busted him to private.

Bitter, he went AWOL, was taken in a bar in East London, battered two MPs before they held him down, and did six months in the stockade. On release he saw an advertisement in an evening newspaper, reported to a small office in Durban, and two days later was flown out of South Africa to Kamina base in Katanga. He had become a mercenary at twenty-two, and that was six years ago.

As he drove along the winding road through Franshoek toward the Paarl Valley, he wondered if there would be a letter from Shannon or one of the boys, with news of a contract. But when he got there, nothing was waiting at the post office. Clouds were blowing up from the sea, and there was a hint of thunder in the air.

It would rain that evening, a nice cooling shower, and he glanced up toward the Paarl Rock, the phenomenon that had given the valley and the town its name long ago when his ancestors first came into the valley. As a boy he had stared in wonderment at the rock, which was a dull gray when dry but after rain glistened like an enormous pearl in the moonlight. Then it became a great glistening, gleaming thing, dominating the tiny town beneath it. Although the town of his boyhood could never offer him the kind of life he wanted, it was still home; and when he saw the Paarl Rock glistening in the light, he always knew he was back home again. That evening he wished he were somewhere else, heading toward another war.

Tiny Marc Vlaminck leaned on the bar counter and downed another foaming schooner of Flemish ale. Outside the front windows of the place his girlfriend managed, the streets of Ostend's red-light district were almost empty. A chill wind was blowing off the sea, and the summer tourists had not started to arrive yet. He was bored already.

For the first month since his return from the tropics, it had been good to be back, good to take hot baths again, to chat with his friends who had dropped in to see him. Even the local press had taken an interest, but he had told them to get lost. The last thing he needed was trouble from the authorities, and he knew they would leave him alone if he did or said nothing to embarrass them with the African embassies in Brussels.

But after weeks the inactivity had palled. A few nights back it had been enlivened when he thumped a seaman who had tried to fondle Anna's bottom, an area he regarded as entirely his own preserve. The memory started a thought running through his mind. He could hear a low thump-thump from upstairs, where Anna was doing the housework in the small flat that they shared above the bar. He heaved himself off his barstool, drained the tankard, and called, "If anyone comes in, serve 'em yourself."

Then he lumbered up the back stairs. As he did so, the door opened and a telegram came in.

It was a clear spring evening with just a touch of chill in the air, and the water of the Old Port of Marseilles was like glass. Across its center, a few months ago a mirror for the surrounding bars and cafés, a single homecoming trawler cut a swathe of ripples that wandered across the harbor and died chuckling under the hulls of the fishing boats already moored. The cars were locked solid along the Canebière, smells of cooking fish emanated from a thousand windows, the old men sipped their anisette, and the heroin-sellers scuttled through the alleys on their lucrative missions. It was an ordinary evening.

In the multinational, multilingual caldron of seething humanity that called itself Le Panier, where only a policeman is illegal, Jean-Baptiste Langarotti sat at a corner table in a small bar and sipped a long, cool Ricard.

He was not as bored as Janni Dupree or Marc Vlaminck. Years in prison had taught him the ability to keep himself interested in even the smallest things, and he could survive long periods of inactivity better than most.

Moreover, he had been able to get himself a job and earn a living, so that his savings were still intact. He saved steadily, the results of his economies mounting up in a bank in Switzerland that no one knew about. One day they would buy him the little bar in Calvi that he wanted.

A month earlier a good friend of his from the Algerian days had been picked up for a small matter of a suitcase containing twelve former French army Colt .45s and from Les Baumettes had sent Jean-Baptiste a message asking him to "mind" the girl on whose earnings the imprisoned friend normally lived. He knew he could trust the Corsican not to cheat him. She was a good girl, a broad-beamed hoyden called Marie-Claire, who went under the name of Lola and did her nightly stint in a bar in the Tubano district. She had taken quite a fancy to Langarotti, perhaps because of his size, and her only complaint was that he did not knock her about the way her boyfriend in prison had done. Being small was no hindrance to being a "minder," because the rest of the underworld, who might have made a claim for Lola, needed no education about Langarotti.

So Lola was happy to be the best-minded girl in town, and Jean-Baptiste was content to while away the days until another contract to fight came up. He was in contact with a few people in the mercenary business but, being new to it, was relying more on Shannon to hear of something first. Shannon was more the sort clients would come to.

Shortly after returning to France, Langarotti had been contacted by Charles Roux in Paris, who had proposed that the Corsican sign on with him exclusively in exchange for first choice if and when a contract turned up. Roux had talked largely of the half-dozen projects he had brewing at the time, and the Corsican had remained noncommittal. Later he had checked up and found Roux was mostly talk, for he had set up no projects of his own since his return from Bukavu in the autumn of '67 with a hole through his arm.

With a sigh Langarotti glanced at his watch, finished his drink, and rose to go. It was time to fetch Lola from their apartment and escort her to the bar for work, and then drop in at the all-night post office to see if there was a telegram from Shannon offering a prospect of a new war.

In Munich it was even colder than in Marc Vlaminck's Ostend, and Kurt Semmler, his blood thinned by years in the Far East, Algeria, and Africa, shivered in his knee-length black leather coat as he headed toward the all-night post office. He made a regular check-call at the counter every morning and evening, and each time hoped for some letter or telegram bearing news or an invitation to meet someone for an interview for possible selection for a mercenary assignment.

The period since his return from Africa had been one of idleness and boredom. Like most army veterans, he disliked civilian life, wore the clothes badly, despised the politics, and longed again for some form of routine combined with action. The return to his birth city had not been encouraging. Everywhere he saw long-haired youths, sloppy and ill-disciplined, waving their banners and screaming their slogans. There seemed to be none of the sense of purpose, of commitment to the ideal of the greatness of the Fatherland and its leader, that had so completely absorbed his own childhood and youth, nor the sense of order that characterized army life.

Even the smuggling life in the Mediterranean, although it had been free and easy, at least could offer the sense of activity, the scent of danger, the feeling of a mission planned, executed, and accomplished. Easing a fast launch in toward the Italian coast with two tons of American cigarettes on board, he had at least been able to imagine himself back on the Mekong, going into action with the Legion against the Xoa Binh river pirates.

Munich offered him nothing. He had drunk too much, smoked too much, whored a bit, and become thoroughly disgruntled.

At the post office there was nothing for him that evening.

At midnight Marc Vlaminck phoned in from Ostend. The Belgian telegram delivery service is excellent and delivers until ten at night. Shannon told Vlaminck simply to meet him in front of Brussels National Airport the following morning with a car, and gave him his flight number.

Belgium has, from the point of view of those wishing to operate a discreet but legal bank account, many advantages that outweigh those offered by the much better-publicized Swiss banking system. Not nearly as rich or powerful as Germany, not neutral like Switzerland, Belgium nevertheless offers the facility of permitting unlimited quantities of money to pass in and out without government control or interference. The banks are also just as discreet as those of Switzerland, which is why they and the banks of Luxembourg and Lichtenstein have been steadily increasing their volume of business at the expense of the Swiss.

It was to the Kredietbank in Brugge, seventy minutes' driving time from the Brussels airport, that Shannon had himself driven by Marc Vlaminck the following morning. The big Belgian was evidently full of curiosity, but he kept it to himself. When they were on the road to Brugge, Shannon mentioned briefly that he had been given a contract and there was room for four helpers. Was Vlaminck interested?

Tiny Marc indicated that of course he was. Shannon told him he could not say what the operation was, other than that it was a job that had to be not merely fought but set up from scratch. He was prepared to offer normal rates of $1250 a month, plus expenses, for the next three months, and the job, although not requiring absence from home until the third month, would require a few hours' risk in Europe. That, of course, was not strictly mercenary work, but it had to be done.

Marc grunted. "I'm not knocking off banks," he said. "Not for that kind of money."

"It's nothing like that. I need some guns taken on board a boat. We have to do it ourselves. After we sail, it's all set for Africa and a nice little firefight."

Marc grinned. "A long campaign, or a quick in-and-out job?"

"An attack," said Shannon. "Mind you, if it works there could be a long contract in the offing. Can't promise, but it looks like that. And a fat success bonus."

"Okay, I'm on," said Marc, and they drove into the main square at Brugge.

The Kredietbank head office is situated at number 25 in the Vlamingstraat, a narrow thoroughfare flanked by house after house in the distinctive style of eighteenth-century Flemish architecture, and all in a perfect state of preservation. Most of the ground floors have been converted into shops, but upward from the ground floors the façades resemble something from a painting by one of the old masters.

Inside the bank, Shannon introduced himself to the head of the foreign accounts' section, Mr. Goossens, and proved his identity as Keith Brown by tendering his passport. Within forty minutes he had opened a current account with a deposit of £100 sterling in cash, informed Mr. Goossens that a sum of £10,000 in the form of a transfer from Switzerland could be expected any day, and left instructions that of this sum £5000 was to be transferred at once to his account in London. He left several examples of his Keith Brown signature and agreed on a method of establishing his identity over the phone by reeling off the twelve numbers of his account in reverse order, followed by the previous day's date. On this basis oral instructions for transfers and withdrawals could be made without his coming to Brugge again. He signed an indemnity form protecting the bank from any risk in using this method of communication, and agreed to write his account number in red ink under his signature on any written instruction to the bank, again to prove authenticity.

By half past twelve he was finished and joined Vlaminck outside. They ate a lunch of solid food accompanied by the inevitable french-fried potatoes at the Café des Arts on the main square before the town hall, and then Vlaminck drove him back to Brussels airport. Before parting from the Fleming, Shannon gave him £50 in cash and told him to take the Ostend-Dover ferry the next day and be at the London flat at six in the evening. He had to wait an hour for his plane and was back in London by teatime.

Simon Endean had also had a busy day. He had caught the earliest flight of the day to Zurich and had landed at Kloten Airport by just after ten. Within an hour he was standing at the counter of the Handelsbank of Zurich's main office, at 58 Talstrasse, and opening a current account in his own name. He too left several specimen signatures and agreed with the bank official who interviewed him on a method of signing all written communications to the bank simply by writing the account number at the bottom of the letter and under the day of the week on which the letter had been written. The day would be written in green ink, while the account number would invariably be in black. He deposited the £500 in cash that he had brought, and informed the bank the sum of £100,000 would be transferred into the account within the week. Last, he instructed the bank that as soon as the credit had been received they were to remit £10,000 to an account in Belgium which he would identify for them later by letter. He signed a long contract which exonerated the bank from anything and everything, including culpable negligence, and left him no protection whatever in law. Not that there was any point in contesting a Swiss bank before a Swiss court, as he well knew.

Taking a taxi from Talstrasse, he dropped a wax-sealed letter through the door of the Zwingli Bank and headed back to the airport.

The letter, which Dr. Martin Steinhofer had in his hand within thirty minutes, was from Sir James Manson. It was signed in the approved manner in which Manson signed all his correspondence with his Zurich bank. It requested Dr. Steinhofer to transfer £100,000 to the account of Mr. Simon Endean at the Handelsbank forthwith, and informed him that Sir James would be calling on him at his office the following day, Wednesday.

Endean was at London airport just before six.

Martin Thorpe was exhausted when he came into the office that Tuesday afternoon. He had spent the two days of the weekend and Monday going methodically through the 4500 cards in the Moodies index of companies quoted on the London Stock Exchange.

He had been concentrating on finding a suitable shell company and had sought out the small companies, preferably founded many years ago, largely run-down and with few assets, companies which over the past three years had traded at a loss, or broken even, or made a profit below £10,000. He also wanted a company with a market capitalization of under £200,000.

He had come up with two dozen companies that fitted the bill, and these names he showed to Sir James Manson. He had listed them provisionally in order from 1 to 24 on the basis of their apparent suitability.

He still had more to do, and by midafternoon he was at Companies House, in City Road, E.C.2.

He sent up to the archivists the list of his first eight companies and paid his statutory fee for each name on the list, giving him, as it would any other member of the public, the right to examine the full company documents. As he waited for the eight bulky folders to come back to the reading room, he glanced through the latest Stock Exchange Official List and noted with satisfaction that none of the eight was quoted at over three shillings a share.

When the files arrived he started with the first on his list and began to pore over the records. He was looking for three things not given in the Moodies cards, which are simply synopses. He wanted to study the distribution of the ownership of the shares, to ensure that the company he sought was not controlled by the combined board of directors, and to be certain there had not been a recent build-up of share holdings by another person or associated group, which would have indicated that another City predator was looking for a meal.

By the time Companies House closed for the evening, he had been through seven of the eight files. He could cover the remaining seventeen the following day. But already he was intrigued by the third on his list and mildly excited. On paper it looked great, from his point of view—even too good, and that was the rub. It looked so good he was surprised no one had snapped it up ages ago. There had to be a flaw somewhere, but Martin Thorpe's ingenuity might even find a way of overcoming it. If there was such a way—it was perfect.

Simon Endean phoned Cat Shannon at the latter's flat at ten that evening. Shannon reported what he had done, and Endean gave a résumé of his own day. He told Shannon the necessary £100,000 should have been transferred to his new Swiss account before closing time that afternoon, and Shannon told Endean to have the first £10,000 sent to him under the name of Keith Brown at the Kredietbank in Brugge, Belgium.

Within a few minutes of hanging up, Endean had written his letter of instruction to the Handelsbank, stressing that the transferred sum should be sent at once but that under no condition was the name of the Swiss account-holder to become known to the Belgian bank. The account number alone should be quoted on the transfer, which should be by Telex. He mailed the letter express rate from the all-night post office in Trafalgar Square just before midnight.

At eleven-forty-five the phone rang again in Shannon's flat. It was Semmler on the line from Munich. Shannon told him he had work for all of them if they wanted it, but that he could not come to Munich. Semmler should take a single ticket by air to London the following day and be there by six. He gave his address and promised to repay the German his expenses in any case, and pay his fare back to Munich if he declined the job. Semmler agreed to come, and Shannon hung up.

The next on the line was Langarotti from Marseilles. He had checked his *poste restante* box and found Shannon's telegram waiting for him. He would be in London by six and would report to the flat.

Janni Dupree's call was late, coming through at half past midnight. He too agreed to pack his bags and fly the eight thousand miles to London, though he could not be there for a day and a half. He would be at Shannon's flat on Thursday evening instead.

With the last call taken, Shannon read *Small Arms of the World* for an hour and switched off the light. It was the end of Day One.

Sir James Manson, first class on the businessman's Trident III to Zurich, ate a hearty breakfast that Wednesday morning. Shortly before noon he was ushered respectfully into the paneled office of Dr. Martin Steinhofer.

The two men had known each other for ten years, and during this time the Zwingli Bank had several times carried out business on Manson's behalf in situations where he had needed a nominee to buy shares which, had it become known that the name of Manson was behind the purchase, would have trebled in value. Dr. Steinhofer valued his client and rose to shake hands and usher the English knight to a comfortable armchair.

The Swiss offered cigars, and coffee was brought, along with small glasses of Kirschwasser. Only when the male secretary had gone did Sir James broach his business.

"Over the forthcoming weeks I shall be seeking to acquire a controlling interest in a small British company, a public company. At the moment I cannot give the name of it, because a suitable vehicle for my particular operation has not yet come to light. I hope to know it fairly soon."

Dr. Steinhofer nodded silently and sipped his coffee.

"At the start it will be quite a small operation, involving relatively little money. Later, I have reason to believe news will hit the Stock Exchange that will have quite an interesting effect on the share value of that company," Sir James went on.

There was no need for him to explain to the Swiss banker the rules that apply in share dealings on the London Stock Exchange, for Steinhofer was as familiar with them as Manson, as he was also with the rules of all the main exchanges and markets throughout the world.

Under British company law, any person acquiring 10 per cent or more of the shares of a public quoted company must identify himself to the directors within fourteen days. The aim of the law is to permit the public to know who owns what, and how much, of any public company.

For this reason, a reputable London stockbrokerage house, buying on behalf of a client, will also abide by the law and inform the directors of their client's name, unless the purchase is less than 10 per cent of the company's stock, in which case the buyer may remain anonymous.

One way around this rule for a tycoon seeking to gain secret control of a company is to use nominee buyers. But again, a reputable firm on the Stock Exchange will soon spot whether the real buyer of a big block of shares is in fact one man operating through nominees, and will obey the law.

But a Swiss bank, not bound by the laws of Britain,

abiding by its own laws of secrecy, simply refuses to answer questions about who stands behind the names it presents as its clients, nor will it reveal anything else, even if it privately suspects that the front men do not exist at all.

Both of the men in Dr. Steinhofer's office that morning were well aware of all the finer points involved.

"In order to make the necessary acquisition of shares," Sir James went on, "I have entered into association with six partners. They will purchase the shares on my behalf. They have all agreed they would wish to open small accounts with the Zwingli Bank and to ask you to be so kind as to make the purchases on their behalf."

Dr. Steinhofer put down his coffee cup and nodded. As a good Swiss, he agreed there was no point in breaking rules where they could be legally bent, with the obvious proviso that they were not Swiss rules, and he could also see the point in not wantonly sending the share price upward, even in a small operation. One started by saving pfennigs, and one became rich after a lifetime of application.

"That presents no problem," he said carefully. "These gentlemen will be coming here to open their accounts?"

Sir James exhaled a stream of aromatic smoke. "It may well be they will find themselves too busy to come personally. I have myself appointed my financial assistant to stand in for me—to save time and trouble, you understand. It may well be the other six partners will wish to avail themselves of the same procedure. You have no objection to that?"

"Of course not," murmured Dr. Steinhofer. "Your financial assistant is who, please?"

"Mr. Martin Thorpe." Sir James Manson drew a slim envelope from his pocket and handed it to the banker. "This is my power of attorney, duly notarized and witnessed, and signed by me. You have my signature for comparison, of course. In here you will find Mr. Thorpe's full name and the number of his passport, by which he will identify himself. He will be visiting Zurich in the next week or ten days to finalize arrangements. From then on he will act in all matters on my behalf, and his signature will be as good as mine. Is that acceptable?"

Dr. Steinhofer scanned the single sheet in the envelope and nodded. "Certainly, Sir James. I see no problems."

Manson rose and stubbed out his cigar. "Then I'll bid you good-by, Dr. Steinhofer, and leave further dealings in the hands of Mr. Thorpe, who of course will consult with me on all steps to be taken."

They shook hands, and Sir James Manson was ushered down to the street. As the solid oak door clicked quietly shut behind him, he pulled up his coat collar against the still chilly air of the north Swiss town, stepped into the waiting hired limousine, and gave instructions for the Baur au Lac for lunch. One ate well there, he reflected, but otherwise Zurich was a dreary place. It did not even have a good brothel.

Assistant Under Secretary Sergei Golon was not in a good humor that morning. The mail had brought a letter to his breakfast table to notify him that his son had failed the entrance examination for the Civil Service Academy, and there had been a general family quarrel. In consequence, his perennial problem of acid indigestion had elected to ensure him a day of unrelenting misery, and his secretary was out sick.

Beyond the windows of his small office in the West Africa section of the Foreign Ministry, the canyons of Moscow's windswept boulevards were still covered with snow slush, a grimy gray in the dim morning light, waiting tiredly for the thaw of spring.

"Neither one thing nor the other," the attendant had remarked as he had berthed his Moskvitch in the parking lot beneath the ministry building.

Golon had grunted agreement and taken the elevator to his eighth-floor office to begin the morning's work. Devoid of a secretary, he had taken the pile of files brought for his attention from various parts of the building and started to go through them, an antacid tablet revolving slowly in his mouth.

The third file had been marked for his attention by the office of the Under Secretary, and the same clerkish hand had written on the cover sheet: "Assess and Instigate Necessary Action." Golon perused it gloomily. He noted that the file had been started on the basis of an interdepartmental memorandum from Foreign Intelligence, that his ministry had, on reflection, given Ambassador Dobrovolsky certain instructions, and that, according to the latest cable from Dobrovolsky, they had been carried out. The request had been granted, the Ambassador reported, and he urged prompt action.

Golon snorted. Passed over for an ambassadorship, he held firmly to the view that men in diplomatic posts abroad were far too prone to believe their own parishes were of consummate importance.

"As if we have nothing else to bother about," he grunted. Already his eye had caught the folder beneath the one he was reading. He knew it concerned the Republic of Guinea, where the constant stream of telegrams from the Soviet Ambassador reported the growth of Chinese influence in Conakry. Now that, he mused, was something of concern. Compared to this, he could not see the importance of whether there was, or was not, tin in commercial quantities in the hinterland of Zangaro. Besides, the Soviet Union had enough tin.

Nevertheless, action had been authorized from above, and, as a good civil servant, he took it. To a secretary borrowed from the typing pool, he dictated a letter to the director of the Sverdlovsk Institute of Mining, requiring him to select a small team of survey geologists and engineers to carry out an examination of a suspected tin deposit in West Africa, and to inform the Assistant Under Secretary in due course that the team and its equipment were ready to depart.

Privately he thought he would have to tackle the question of transportation to West Africa through the appropriate directorate, but pushed the thought to the back of his mind. The painful burning in his throat subsided, and he observed that the scribbling stenographer had rather pretty knees.

Cat Shannon had a quiet day. He rose late and went into the West End to his bank, where he withdrew most of the £1000 his account contained. He was confident the money would be replaced, and more, when the transfer came through from Belgium.

After lunch he rang his friend the writer, who seemed surprised to hear from him. "I thought you'd left town."

"Why should I?" asked Shannon.

"Well, little Julie has been looking for you. You must have made an impression. Carrie says she has not stopped talking. But she rang the Lowndes, and they said you had left, address unknown."

Shannon promised he'd call. He gave his own phone number, but not his address. With the small talk over, he requested the information he wanted.

"I suppose I could," said the friend dubiously. "But honestly, I ought to ring him first and see if it's okay."

"Well, do that," said Shannon. "Tell him it's me, that I need to see him and am prepared to go down there for a few hours with him. Tell him I wouldn't trouble him if it wasn't important, in my opinion."

The writer agreed to put through the call and ring him back with the telephone number and address of the man Shannon wished to talk to, if the man agreed to speak to Shannon.

In the afternoon Shannon wrote a letter to Mr Goossens at the Kredietbank to tell him that he would in the future give two or three business partners the Kredietbank as his mailing address and would keep in contact by phone with the bank to check whether any mail was waiting for collection. He would also be sending some letters to business associates via the Kredietbank, in which case he would mail an envelope to Mr. Goossens from wherever he happened to be. He requested Mr. Goossens to take the envelope which would be enclosed, addressed but not stamped, and forward it from Brugge to its destination. Last, he bade Mr. Goossens deduct all postal and bank charges from his account.

At five that afternoon Endean called him at the flat, and Shannon gave him a progress report, omitting to mention his contact with his writer friend, whom he had never mentioned to Endean. He told him, however, that he expected three of his four chosen associates to be in London for their separate briefings that evening, and the fourth to arrive on Thursday evening at the latest.

Martin Thorpe had his fifth tiring day, but at least his search was over. He had perused the documents of another seventeen companies in the City Road, and had drawn up a second short list, this time of five companies. At the top of the list was the company that had caught his eye the previous day. He finished his reading by midafternoon and, as Sir James Manson had not returned from Zurich, decided to take the rest of the day off. He could brief his chief in the morning and later begin his private inquiries into the set-up of his chosen company, a series of inquiries to determine why such a prize was still available. By the late afternoon he was back in Hampstead Garden Suburb, mowing the lawn.

10

The first of the mercenaries to arrive at London's Heathrow Airport was Kurt Semmler, on the Lufthansa flight from Munich. He tried to reach Shannon by phone soon after clearing customs, but there was no reply. He was early for his check-in call, so he decided to wait at the airport and took a seat by the restaurant window overlooking the apron of Number Two building. He chain-smoked nervously as he sat over coffee and watched the jets leaving for Europe.

Marc Vlaminck phoned to check in with Shannon just after five. The Cat glanced down the list of three hotels in the neighborhood of his apartment and read out the name of one. The Belgian took it down in his Victoria Station phone booth, letter by letter. A few minutes later he hailed a taxi outside the station and showed the paper to the driver.

Semmler was ten minutes after Vlaminck. He too received from Shannon the name of a hotel, wrote it down, and took a minicab from the front of the airport building.

Langarotti was the last, checking in just before six from the air terminal in Cromwell Road. He too hired a taxi to take him to his hotel.

At seven Shannon rang them all, one after the other, and bade them assemble at his flat within thirty minutes.

When they greeted one another, it was the first indication any of them had had that the others had been invited. Their broad grins came partly from the pleasure of meeting friends, partly from the knowledge that Shannon's investment in bringing them all to London with a guarantee of a reimbursed air fare could only mean he had money. If they wondered who the patron might be, they knew better than to ask.

Their first impression was strengthened when Shannon told them that he had instructed Dupree to fly in from South Africa on the same terms. A £500 air ticket meant Shannon was not playing games. They settled down to listen.

"The job I've been given," he told them, "is a project that has to be organized from scratch. It has not been planned, and the only way to set it up is to do it ourselves. The object is to mount an attack, a short, sharp attack, commando-style, on a town on the coast of Africa. We have to shoot the shits out of one building, storm it, capture it, knock off everyone in it, and pull back out again."

The reaction was what he had confidently expected. The men exchanged glances of approval. Vlaminck gave a wide grin and scratched his chest; Semmler muttered, "*Klasse*," and lit a fresh cigarette from the stub of the old one. Langarotti remained deadpan, his eyes on Shannon, the knife blade slipping smoothly across the black leather around his left fist.

Shannon spread a map out on the floor in the center of the circle, and the men eyed it keenly. It was a hand-drawn map depicting a section of seashore and a series of buildings on the landward side. It was not accurate, for it excluded the two curving spits of shingle that were the identifying marks of the harbor of Clarence, but it sufficed to indicate the kind of operation required.

The mercenary leader talked for twenty minutes, outlining the kind of attack he had already proposed to his patron as the only feasible way of taking the objective, and the three men concurred. None of them asked the name of the destination. They knew he would not tell them and that they did not need to know It was not a question of lack of trust, simply of security. If a leak were sprung in the secret, they did not want to be among the possible suspects.

Shannon spoke in strongly accented French, which he had picked up in the Sixth Commando in the Congo He knew Vlaminck had a reasonable grasp of English, as a barman in Ostend must have, and that Semmler commanded a vocabulary of about two hundred words But Langarotti knew very little indeed, so French was the common language, except when Dupree was present, when everything had to be translated

"So that's it," said Shannon as he finished. "The terms are that you all go on a salary of twelve hundred and fifty dollars a month from tomorrow morning, plus expenses for living and traveling while in Europe The budget is ample for the job. Only two of the tasks that have to be done in the preparation stages are illegal, because I've planned to keep the maximum strictly legal Of these tasks, one is a border crossing from Belgium to France, the other a problem of loading some cases onto a ship somewhere in southern Europe. We'll all be involved in both jobs.

"You get three months' guaranteed salary, plus five thousand dollars' bonus each for success. So what do you say?"

The three men looked at each other. Vlaminck nodded. "I'm on," he said. "Like I said yesterday, it looks good."

Langarotti stropped his knife. "Is it against French interests?" he asked. "I don't want to be an exile."

"You have my word it is not against the French in Africa."

"D'accord," said the Corsican simply.

"Kurt?" asked Shannon.

"What about insurance?" asked the German. "It doesn't matter for me, I have no relatives, but what about Marc?"

The Belgian nodded. "Yes, I don't want to leave Anna with nothing," he said.

Mercenaries on contract are usually insured by the contractor for $20,000 for loss of life and $6000 for loss of a major limb.

"You have to take out your own, but it can be as high as you want to go. If anything happens to anyone, the rest swear blind he was lost overboard at sea by accident. If anyone gets badly hurt and survives, we all swear the injury was caused by shifting machinery on board. You all take out insurance for a sea trip from Europe to South Africa as passengers on a small freighter. Okay?"

The three men nodded.

"I'm on," said Semmler.

They shook on it, and that was enough. Then Shannon went into the jobs he wanted each man to do.

"Kurt, you'll get your first salary check and one thousand dollars for expenses on Friday. I want you to go down to the Mediterranean and start looking for a boat. I need a small freighter with a clean record. Get that: it must be clean. Papers in order, ship for sale. One hundred to two hundred tons, coaster or converted trawler, possibly converted navy vessel if need be, but not looking like an MTB. I don't want speed, but reliability. The sort that can pick up a cargo in a Mediterranean port without exciting attention, even an arms cargo. Registered as a general freighter owned by a small company or its own skipper. Price not over twenty-five thousand pounds, including the cost of any work that needs doing on it. Absolute latest sailing date, fully fueled and supplied for a trip to Cape Town, not later than sixty days from now. Got it?"

Semmler nodded and began to think at once of his contacts in the shipping world.

"Jean-Baptiste, which city do you know best in the Mediterranean?"

"Marseilles," said Langarotti without hesitation.

"Okay. You get salary and five hundred pounds on Friday. Get to Marseilles, set up in a small hotel, and start looking. Find me three large inflatable semi-rigid craft of the same kind as Zodiac makes. The sort developed for water sports from the basic design of the Marine Commando assault craft. Buy them from separate suppliers, then book them into the bonded warehouse of a respectable shipping agent for export to Morocco. Purpose, water-skiing and sub-aqua diving at a holiday resort. Color, black. Also three powerful outboard engines, battery-started. The boats should take up to a ton of payload. The engines should move such a craft and that weight at not less than ten knots, with a big reserve. You'll need about sixty horsepower. Very important: make sure they are fitted with underwater exhausts for silent running. If they can't be had in that condition, get a mechanic to make you three exhaust-pipe extensions with the necessary outlet valves, to fit the engines. Store them at the same export agent's bonded warehouse, for the same purpose as the dinghies: water sports in Morocco. You won't have enough money in the five hundred. Open a bank account and send me the name and number, by mail, to this address. I'll send the money by credit transfer. Buy everything separately, and submit me the price lists by mail here. Okay?"

Langarotti nodded and resumed his knife-stropping.

"Marc. You remember you mentioned once that you knew a man in Belgium had knocked off a German store of a thousand brand-new Schmeisser submachine pistols in nineteen-forty-five and still had half of them in store? I want you to go back to Ostend on Friday with your salary and five hundred pounds and locate that man. See if he'll sell. I want a hundred, and in first-class working order. I'll pay a hundred dollars each, which is way over the rate. Write me by letter only, here at this flat, when you have found the man and can set up a meeting between him and me. Got it?"

By nine-thirty they were through, the instructions memorized, noted, and understood.

"Right. What about a spot of dinner?" Shannon asked his colleagues.

He took them around the corner to the Paprika for a meal. They still spoke in French, but no one else took much notice, except to glance over when a loud burst of laughter came from the group of four. Evidently they were excited at something, though none of the diners could have surmised that what elated the group in the corner was the prospect of going once again to war under the leadership of Cat Shannon.

Across the Channel another man was thinking hard about Carlo Alfred Thomas Shannon, and his thoughts were not charitable. He paced the living room of his apartment on one of the residential boulevards near the Place de la Bastille and considered the information he had been gathering for the previous week, and the snippet from Marseilles that had reached him several hours earlier.

If the writer who had originally recommended Charles Roux to Simon Endean as a second possible mercenary for Endean's project had known more about the Frenchman, his description would not have been so complimentary. But he knew only the basic facts of the man's background and little about his character. Nor did he know, and thus was unable to tell Endean, of the vitriolic hatred that Roux bore for the other man he had recommended, Cat Shannon.

After Endean had left Roux, the Frenchman had waited a full fortnight for a second contact to be made. When it never came, he was forced to the conclusion either that the project in the mind of the visitor who had called himself Walter Harris had been abandoned, or that someone else had got the job.

Pursuing the latter line of inquiry, he had looked for anyone among the other possible selections that the English businessman could have made. It was while he was making these inquiries, or having them made for him, that he had learned Cat Shannon had been in Paris, staying under his own name at a small hotel in Montmartre. This had shaken Roux, for he had lost trace of Shannon after their parting at Le Bourget Airport and had thought the man had left Paris.

At this point, more than a week earlier, he had briefed one of the men he knew to be loyal to him to make intensive inquiries about Shannon. The man was called Henri Alain and was a former mercenary.

Alain had reported back within twenty-four hours that Shannon had left his Montmartre hotel and not re-appeared. He had also been able to tell Roux two other things: that Shannon's disappearance had taken place the morning after Roux had received the London businessman in his own apartment, and that Shannon had also received a visitor the same afternoon. The hotel clerk, with a little currency persuasion, had been able to describe Shannon's visitor, and privately Roux had no doubt the visitor in Montmartre had been the same man who came to him.

So Mr. Harris from London had seen two mercenaries in Paris, although he needed only one. As a result, Shannon had disappeared while he, Roux, had been left on the shelf. That it was Shannon of all people who seemed to have got the contract made his rage even worse, for there was no one the man in the flat in the 11th *arrondissement* hated more.

He had had Henri Alain stake out the hotel for four days, but Shannon had not come back. Then he tried another tack. He recalled that newspaper reports had linked Shannon with the Corsican Langarotti in the fighting in the last days of the enclave. Presumably if Shannon was back in circulation, so was Langarotti. So he had sent Henri Alain to Marseilles to find the Corsican and discover where Shannon might be. Alain had just arrived back, bearing the news that Langarotti had left Marseilles that same afternoon. Destination, London.

Roux turned to his informant. *"Bon,* Henri. That's all. I'll contact you when I need you. Meantime, the clerk in the Montmartre place will let you know if Shannon returns?"

"Sure," said Alain as he rose to go.

"Then ring me immediately if you hear."

When Alain had gone, Roux thought things over. For him the disappearance of Langarotti to London of all places meant the Corsican had gone to join Shannon there. That in turn meant Shannon was recruiting, and that could only mean he had got a contract. Roux had no doubt it was Walter Harris's contract, one he felt he personally should have had. It was an impertinence, compounded by the recruiting of a Frenchman, and on French territory, which Roux regarded as being his own exclusive preserve.

There was another reason why he wanted the Harris contract. He had not worked since the Bukavu affair, and his ability to keep his hold over the French mercenary community was likely to slip unless he could produce some form of work for it. If Shannon was unable to continue, if for instance he were to disappear permanently, Mr. Harris would presumably have to come back to Roux and engage him, as he should have done in the first place.

Without further delay he made a local Paris phone call.

Back in London, the dinner was nearing its end. The men had drunk a lot of carafe wine, for, like most mercenaries, they preferred it. Tiny Marc raised his glass and proposed the often-heard toast of the Congo.

> Vive la mort, vive la guerre,
> Vive le sacré mercenaire.

Sitting back in his chair, clear-headed while the rest got drunk, Cat Shannon wondered idly how much havoc would be wreaked when he let slip this group of dogs on Kimba's palace. Silently he raised his own glass and drank to the dogs of war.

Charles Roux was forty-eight, and several parts mad, although the two facts were quite unconnected. He could never have been certified insane, but most psychiatrists would at least have held him to be mentally unstable. The basis for such a diagnosis would have been the presence of a fair degree of megalomania, but this is present in many people outside lunatic asylums and is usually more kindly interpreted, at least when present in the rich and famous, as merely exaggerated egocentricity.

The same psychiatrists would probably have detected a tinge of paranoia, and a severe examiner might have gone so far as to suggest there was a streak of the psychopath in the French mercenary. But as Roux had never been examined by a skilled psychiatrist, and as his instability was usually well camouflaged beneath an exterior of some intelligence and considerable cunning, these questions were never raised.

The only exterior clues to his make-up lay in his capacity to impute a status and importance to himself that was wholly illusory, a self-pity that insisted he had never once been at fault but that all others who disagreed with him were wholly in the wrong, and the capacity for vicious hatred toward those he felt had wronged him.

Often the victims of his hatred had done little or nothing beyond frustrating Roux, but in Shannon's case there were at least grounds for the dislike.

Roux had been a top sergeant in the French army until his late thirties, when he was dismissed after an affair involving certain missing funds. In 1961, at a loose end, he had paid his own fare to Katanga and proposed himself as a well-qualified adviser to the secessionist movement of the then Katangese leader, Moïse Tshombe. That year was the height of the struggle to tear the mineral-rich province of Katanga out of the union with the sprawling, anarchic, and newly independent Congo. Several of the men who later became mercenary chieftains began their freelance careers in the imbroglio in Katanga. Hoare, Denard, and Schramme were among them. Despite his claims to greater things, Roux was permitted only a small role

in the Katangese events, and when the mighty United
Nations finally managed to vanquish the small bands of
freebooting pistoleros—which had to be done politically, since it could not be done militarily—Roux was
among those who got out.

That was in 1962. Two years later, with the Congo
falling like a set of skittles to the Communist-backed
Simbas, Tshombe was recalled from exile to take over
not Katanga but the whole Congo. He in turn sent for
Hoare, and Roux was among those who flew back to
enter service under Hoare. As a Frenchman, he nat-
urally would have been in the French-speaking Sixth
Commando, but as he had been in South Africa at
the time, it was to the Fifth that he went. Here he
was put in charge of a company, and one of his section commanders six months later was a young Anglo-
Irishman called Shannon.

Roux's break with Hoare came three months later.
Already becoming convinced of his own superiority as
a military commander, Roux was entrusted with the
job of knocking out a Simba roadblock. He devised his
own plan of attack, and it was a total disaster. Four
white mercenaries were killed and more than a score
of his Katangese levies. Part of the reason was the
plan of attack, part the fact that Roux had been blind
drunk. Behind the drunkenness was the secret cer-
tainty that, for all his bombast, Roux did not like combat.

Colonel Hoare called for a report from Roux and
got it. Parts of it did not tally with the known facts.
Hoare sent for the only surviving section commander,
Carlo Shannon, and questioned him closely. From
what emerged, he sent for Roux and dismissed him on
the spot.

Roux went north and joined the Sixth Commando
under Denard at Paulis, explaining his defection from
the Fifth as being due to dislike of a superb French
commander by the inferior British, a reason Denard
found little difficulty in believing. He posted Roux as

second-in-command of a smaller commando, nominally dependent on the Sixth but in fact almost independent. This was the Fourteenth Commando at Watsa, ruled by Commandant Tavernier.

By 1966 Hoare had retired and gone home, and Tavernier had left. The Fourteenth was commanded by Commandant Wautier—like Tavernier, a Belgian. Roux was still second-in-command and hated Wautier. Not that the Belgian had done anything; the reason for the loathing was that Roux had expected the command after Tavernier's departure. He had not got it. So he hated Wautier.

The Fourteenth, heavily staffed by Katangese levies, was the spearpoint of the 1966 mutiny against the Congolese government. This had been planned, and well so, by Wautier, and would probably have succeeded. Black Jacques Schramme was holding his own predominantly Katangese Tenth Commando in check only to see how things went. Had Wautier led the revolt, it might well have succeeded; Black Jacques would probably have brought his Tenth into the affair, had it been successful, and the Congolese government might well have fallen. To launch the revolt, Wautier had brought his Fourteenth to Stanleyville, where on the left bank of the Congo River the vast arsenal stood, containing enough munitions to enable anyone holding it to rule the central and eastern Congo for years.

Two hours before the attack, Commandant Wautier was shot dead, and although it was never proved, it was Roux who murdered him with a shot in the back of the head. A wiser man might have called off the attack. Roux insisted on taking command, and the mutiny was a disaster. His forces never got across the river to the left bank, the Congolese army rallied on learning the armory was still in its hands, and Roux's unit was wiped out to the last man. Schramme thanked his stars he had kept his own men out of the fiasco. On the run and terrified, Roux sought refuge with John Peters, new commander of the English-speaking Fifth, which was also not involved. Peters smuggled the desperate Roux, swathed in bandages and masquerading as an Englishman, out of the country.

The only plane out was heading for South Africa, and that was where Roux went. Ten months later, he flew back into the Congo, this time accompanied by five South Africans. He had got wind of the coming July 1967 revolt and came to join Schramme at the headquarters of the Tenth Commando near Kindu. He was in Stanleyville again when mutiny broke out, this time with Schramme and Denard participating. Within hours Denard was out of action, hit in the head by a ricochet bullet loosed off in error by one of his own men. At a crucial point the leader of the joint forces of the Sixth and Tenth was out of the fight. Roux, claiming that as a Frenchman he should take precedence over the Belgian Schramme, maintaining he was the best commander present and the only one who could command the mercenaries, put himself forward for overall command.

The choice fell on Schramme, not because he was the best man to command the whites but because he was the only man who could command the Katangese, and without these levies the small band of Europeans would have been too badly outnumbered.

Roux's claim failed on two fronts. The Katangese loathed and distrusted him, remembering the unit of their own people he had led to annihilation the previous year. And at the mercenaries' council, held the night Denard was flown out on a stretcher to Rhodesia, one of those who spoke against Roux's nomination was one of Denard's company commanders, Shannon, who had left the Fifth eighteen months earlier and joined the Sixth rather than serve under Peters.

A second time the mercenaries failed to take the arsenal, and Schramme opted for the long march from Stanleyville to Bukavu, a resort town on Lake Bukavu, abutting the neighboring republic of Rwanda and offering some form of retreat if things went wrong.

By this time Roux was gunning for Shannon, and to

keep them apart Schramme gave Shannon's company the hazardous job of point unit, breaking trail up front as the column of mercenaries, Katangese, and thousands of camp followers fought their way through the Congolese toward the lake. Roux was given a job at the rear of the convoy, so the two never met on the march.

They finally met in Bukavu town after the mercenaries had settled in and the Congolese had surrounded them on all sides except the lake behind the town. It was September 1967, and Roux was drunk. Over a game of cards he lost through lack of concentration, he accused Shannon of cheating. Shannon replied that Roux made as big a mess of his poker as he had of attacks on Simba roadblocks and for the same reason —he had no nerve. There was dead silence among the group around the table as the other mercenaries edged back toward the walls. But Roux backed down. Glaring at Shannon, he let the younger man get up and walk toward the door. Only when the Irishman had his back turned did Roux reach for the Colt .45 he, like all of them, carried, and take aim.

Shannon, listening, heard the scrape of a chair and reacted first. He turned, pulled his own automatic, and fired down the length of the hall. The slug was a lucky one for a shot from the hip on a half-turn. It took Roux high in the right arm, tore a hole through the biceps, and left his arm hanging limp from his side, the fingers dripping blood onto the useless Colt on the floor by his side.

"There's one other thing I remember," Shannon called down the room. "I remember what happened to Wautier."

Roux was finished after the shoot-out. He evacuated himself across the bridge into Rwanda, had himself driven to Kigali, the capital, and flew back to France. Thus he missed the fall of Bukavu when finally the ammunition ran out in November, and the five months in an internment camp in Kigali. He also missed a chance to settle scores with Shannon.

Being the first back into Paris from Bukavu, Roux

had given several interviews in which he spoke glow-ingly of himself, his battle wound, and his desire to get back and lead his men. The fiasco at Dilolo, when a recuperated Denard tried a badly planned invasion of the Congo from Angola in the south as a diver-sion to take the strain off his men in Bukavu, and the virtual retirement of the former leader of the Sixth, gave Roux the impression he had every right to claim leadership over the French mercenaries. He had made quite a lot of money from looting in the Congo and had salted it away.

With the money, he was able to make a splash among the barflies and streetcorner bums who like to style themselves mercenaries, and from them he still retained a certain degree of loyalty, but of the bought kind.

Henri Alain was one such, and so was Roux's next visitor, who came in answer to his telephoned sum-mons. He was another mercenary, but of a different type.

Raymond Thomard was a killer by instinct and pro-fession. He too had been in the Congo once, when on the run from the police, and Roux had used him as a hatchet man. For a few small handouts and in the mistaken view that Roux was a big shot, Thomard was as loyal as a paid man can ever be.

"I've got a job for you," Roux told him. "A contract worth five thousand dollars. Are you interested?"

Thomard grinned. "Sure, *patron*. Who's the bugger you want knocked off?"

"Cat Shannon."

Thomard's face dropped.

Roux went on before he could reply. "I know he's good. But you're better. Besides, he knows nothing. You'll be given his address when he checks into Paris next time. You just have to wait till he leaves, then take him at your own convenience. Does he know you by sight?"

Thomard shook his head. "We never met," he said.

Roux clapped him on the back. "Then you've got nothing to worry about. Stay in touch. I'll let you know when and where you'll find him."

11

Simon Endean's letter sent on Tuesday night arrived at ten on Thursday morning at the Handelsbank in Zurich. According to the instructions the bank Telexed £10,000 to the account of Mr. Keith Brown at the Kredietbank in Brugge.

By noon Mr. Goossens had seen the Telex and wired £5000 to Mr. Brown's account in the West End of London. Shortly before four that afternoon, Shannon made a check call to his bank and learned the credit was there waiting for him. He asked the manager personally to give him drawing facilities in cash up to £3500 the following morning. He was told it would be available for collection by eleven-thirty.

Shortly after nine the same morning Martin Thorpe presented himself in Sir James Manson's office with his findings. The two men went over the short list together, studying the pages of photostat documents acquired at Companies House on Tuesday and Wednesday. When they finished, Manson sat back in his chair and gazed at the ceiling.

"There's no doubt you are right about Bormac, Martin," he said, "but why the hell hasn't the major stockholder been bought out long ago?"

It was the question Martin Thorpe had been asking himself all the previous night and day.

The Bormac Trading Company Limited had been founded in 1904 to exploit the output of a series of vast rubber plantations that had been created during the last years of the previous century on the basis of slave labor by Chinese coolies.

The founder of the estates had been an enterprising and ruthless Scot by the name of Ian Macallister, later created Sir Ian Macallister in 1921, and the estates were situated in Borneo, hence the name of the company.

More of a builder than a businessman, Macallister had agreed in 1903 to enter into partnership with a group of London businessmen, and the following year Bormac was created and floated with an issue of half a million ordinary shares. Macallister, who had married a seventeen-year-old girl the previous year, received 150,000 shares, a place on the board, and managership during his lifetime of the rubber estates.

Ten years after the company's founding, the London businessmen had clinched a series of lucrative contracts with companies supplying the British war effort with rubber, and the share price had climbed from its issue price of four shillings to more than two pounds. The war profiteers' boom lasted until 1918. There was a slump for the company just after the First World War, until the motor-car craze of the 1920s boosted the need for rubber tires, and again shares rose. This time there was a one-for-one new issue, raising the total amount of the company's shares on the market to 1 million and Sir Ian's block to 300,000. There had been no more share issues after that.

The slump of the Depression sent prices and shares down again, and they were recovering by 1937. In that year one of the Chinese coolies finally ran amok and performed an unpleasantness on the sleeping Sir Ian with a heavy-bladed parang. The under manager took over but lacked the drive of his dead master, and production fell as prices rose. The Second World War could have been a boon to the company, but the Japanese invasion of Borneo in 1941 disrupted supplies.

The death knell of the company was finally sounded by the Indonesian nationalist movement, which wrested control of the Dutch East Indies and Borneo from Holland in 1948. When the border between Indonesian Borneo and British North Borneo was finally drawn, the estates were on the Indonesian side and were promptly nationalized without compensation.

For more than twenty years the company had staggered on, its assets unrecoverable, fruitless lawsuits with President Sukarno's regime eating away at the cash, prices falling. By the time Martin Thorpe went over the company's books, the shares stood at a shilling each, and their highest price over the previous year had been one shilling and threepence.

The board was composed of five directors, and the company rules stipulated that two of them made a quorum for the purposes of passing a resolution. The company office's address was given and turned out to be the premises of an old-established firm of City solicitors, one of whose partners acted as company secretary and was also on the board. The original offices had long since been given up because of rising costs. Board meetings were rare and usually consisted of the chairman, an elderly man living in Sussex, who was the younger brother of Sir Ian's former under manager, who had died in Japanese hands during the war. Sitting with the chairman were the company secretary, the City solicitor, and occasionally one of the other three, who all lived a long way from London. There was seldom any business to discuss, and the company income consisted mainly of the occasional belated compensation payments now being made by the Indonesian government under General Suharto.

The combined five directors controlled no more than 18 per cent of the million shares, and 52 per cent was distributed among 6500 shareholders scattered across the country. There seemed to be a fair proportion of married women and widows. No doubt portfolios of long-forgotten shares sat in deed boxes and banks and solicitors' offices up and down the land and had done so for years.

But these were not what interested Thorpe and Manson. If they tried to acquire a controlling interest by buying through the market, first it would take years, and second, it would become quickly plain to other City-watchers that someone was at work on Bormac. Their interest was held by the one single block of 300,000 shares held by the widowed Lady Macallister.

The puzzle was why someone had not long since bought the entire block from her and taken on the shell of the once-flourishing rubber company. In every other sense it was ideal for the purpose, for its memorandum was widely drawn, permitting the company to operate in any field of exploitation of any country's natural assets outside the United Kingdom.

"She must be eighty-five if she's a day," said Thorpe at last. "Lives in a vast, dreary old block of flats in Kensington, guarded by a long-serving lady companion, or whatever they are called."

"She must have been approached," said Sir James musingly, "so why does she cling to them?"

"Perhaps she just doesn't want to sell," said Thorpe, "or didn't like the people who came to ask her to let them buy. Old people can be funny."

It is not simply old people who are illogical about buying and selling stocks and shares. Most stockbrokers have long since had the experience of seeing a client refuse to do business when proposed a sensible and advantageous offer, solely and simply for the reason that he did not like the stockbroker.

Sir James Manson shot forward in his chair and planted his elbows on the desk. "Martin, find out about the old woman. Find out who she is, where she is, what she thinks, what she likes and hates, what are her tastes, and above all, find out where her weak spot is. She has to have one, some little thing that would be too big a temptation for her and for which she would sell her holding. It may not be money, probably isn't, for she's been offered money before now. But there has to be something. Find it."

Thorpe rose to go. Manson waved him back to his chair. From his desk drawer he drew six printed forms, all identical and all application forms for numbered accounts at the Zwingli Bank in Zurich.

He explained briefly and concisely what he wanted done, and Thorpe nodded.

"Book yourself on the morning flight, and you can be back tomorrow night," said Manson as his aide left.

Simon Endean rang Shannon at his flat just after two and was given an up-to-date report on the arrangements the mercenary was making. Manson's assistant was pleased by the precision of Shannon's reporting, and he noted the details on a scratch pad so that he could later make up his own report for Sir James.

When he had finished, Shannon put forward his next requirements. "I want five thousand pounds Telexed direct from your Swiss bank to my credit as Keith Brown at the head office of the Banque de Luxembourg in Luxembourg by next Monday noon," he told Endean, "and another five thousand Telexed direct to my credit at the head office of the Landesbank in Hamburg by Wednesday morning."

He explained tersely how the bulk of the £5000 he had imported to London was already spoken for and the other £5000 was needed as a reserve in Brugge. The two identical sums required in Luxembourg and Hamburg were mainly so that he could show his contacts there a certified check to prove his credit before entering into purchasing negotiations. Later, most of the money would be remitted to Brugge and the balance fully accounted for.

"In any case, I can write you out a complete accounting of money spent to date or committed for spending," he told Endean, "but I have to have your mailing address."

Endean gave him the name of a professional accommodation address where he had opened a box that morning in the name of Walter Harris, and promised to get the instructions off to Zurich within the hour to have both sums of £5000 awaiting collection by Keith Brown in Luxembourg and Hamburg.

Big Janni Dupree checked in from London airport at five. His had been the longest journey; from Cape Town to Johannesburg the previous day, and then the long SAA flight, through Luanda in Portuguese Angola and the Isla do Sol stopover, which avoided overflying the territory of any black African country. Shannon ordered him to take a taxi straight to the flat.

At six there was a second reunion when the other three mercenaries all came around to greet the South African. When he heard Shannon's terms, Janni's face cracked into a grin.

"We going to go fighting again, Cat? Count me in."

"Good man. So here's what I want from you. Stay here in London, find yourself a small bed-sitting-room flat. I'll help you do that tomorrow. We'll go through the *Evening Standard* and get you fixed up by nightfall.

"I want you to buy all our clothing. We need fifty sets of T-shirts, fifty sets of underpants, fifty pair of light nylon socks. Then a spare set for each man, making a hundred. I'll give you the list later. After that, fifty sets of combat trousers, preferably in jungle camouflage and preferably matching the jackets. Next, fifty combat blouses, zip-fronted and in the same jungle camouflage.

"You can get all these quite openly at camping shops, sports shops, and army surplus stores. Even the hippies are beginning to wear combat jackets about town, and so do people who go shooting in the country.

"You can get all the T-shirts, socks, and underpants at the same stockist, but get the trousers and blouses at different ones. Then fifty green berets and fifty pairs of boots. Get the trousers in the large size, we can shorten them later; get the blouses half in large size, half in medium. Get the boots from a camping-equipment shop. I don't want heavy British army boots, I want the green canvas jackboots with front lacing and waterproofed.

"Now for the webbing. I need fifty webbing belts, ammo pouches, knapsacks, and campers' haversacks, the ones with the light tubular frame to support them. These will carry the bazooka rockets with a bit of reshaping. Lastly, fifty light nylon sleeping bags. Okay? I'll give you the full written list later."

Dupree nodded. "Okay. How much will that lot cost?"

"About a thousand pounds. This is how you buy it. Take the Yellow Pages telephone directory, and under Surplus Stores you'll find over a dozen shops and stockists. Get the jackets, blouses, belts, berets, webbing harnesses, knapsacks, haversacks, and boots at different shops, placing one order at each. Pay cash and take the purchase away with you. Don't give your real name—not that anyone should ask it—and don't leave a real address.

"When you have bought the stuff, store it in a normal storage warehouse, have it crated for export, and contact four separate freight agents accustomed to handling export shipments. Pay them to send it in four separate consignments in bond to a shipping freight agent in Marseilles for collection by Mr. Jean-Baptiste Langarotti."

"Which agent in Marseilles?" asked Dupree.

"We don't know yet," said Shannon. He turned to the Corsican. "Jean, when you have the name of the shipping agent you intend to use for the export of the boats and engines, send the full name and address by mail to London, one copy to me here at the flat, and a second copy to Jan Dupree, Poste Restante, Trafalgar Square Post Office, London. Got it?"

Langarotti noted the address while Shannon translated the instructions for Dupree.

"Janni, go down there in the next few days and get

yourself *poste restante* facilities. Then check in every week or so until Jean's letter arrives. Then instruct the freight agents to send the crates to the Marseilles agent in a bonded shipment for export by sea from Marseilles onward, in the ownership of Langarotti. Now for the question of money. I just heard the credit came through from Brussels."

The three Europeans produced slips of paper from their pockets while Shannon took Dupree's airline ticket stub. From his desk Shannon took four letters, each of them from him to Mr. Goossens at the Kredietbank. Each letter was roughly the same. It required the Kredietbank to transmit a sum of money in United States dollars from Mr. Keith Brown's account to another account for the credit of Mr. X.

In the blanks Shannon filled in the sum equivalent to the round-trip air fare to and from London, starting at Ostend, Marseilles, Munich, and Cape Town. The letters also bade Mr. Goossens transmit $1250 to each of the named men in the named banks on the day of receipt of the letter, and again on May 5 and again on June 5. Each mercenary dictated to Shannon the name of his bank—most were in Switzerland—and Shannon typed it in.

When he had finished, each man read his own letter and Shannon signed them at his desk, sealed them in separate envelopes, and gave each man his own envelope for mailing.

Last, he gave each £50 in cash to cover the forty-eight-hour stay in London and told them to meet him outside the door of his London bank at eleven the following morning.

When they had gone, he sat down and wrote a long letter to a man in Africa. He rang the writer, who, having checked by phone that it was in order to do so, gave him the African's mailing address. That evening Shannon mailed his letter, express rate, and dined alone.

Martin Thorpe got his interview with Dr. Steinhofer at the Zwingli Bank just before lunch. Having been previously announced by Sir James Manson, Thorpe received the same red-carpet treatment.

He presented the banker with the six application forms for numbered accounts. Each had been filled out in the required manner and signed. Separate cards carried the required two specimen signatures of the men seeking to open the accounts. They were in the names of Messrs. Adams, Ball, Carter, Davies, Edwards, and Frost.

Attached to each form were two other letters. One was a signed power of attorney, in which Messrs. Adams, Ball, Carter, Davies, Edwards, and Frost separately gave power of attorney to Mr. Martin Thorpe to operate the accounts in their names. The other was a letter signed by Sir James Manson, requesting Dr. Steinhofer to transfer to the accounts of each of his associates the sum of £50,000 from Sir James's account.

Dr. Steinhofer was neither so gullible nor so new to the business of banking as not to suspect that the fact the names of the six "business associates" began with the first six letters of the alphabet was a remarkable coincidence. But he was quite able to believe that the possible nonexistence of the six nominees was not his business. If a wealthy British businessman chose to get around the tiresome rules of his own Companies Act, that was his own business. Besides, Dr. Steinhofer knew certain things about quite a number of City businessmen that would have created enough Department of Trade inquiries to keep that London ministry occupied for the rest of the century.

There was another good reason why he should stretch out his hand and take the application forms from Thorpe. If the shares of the company Sir James was going to try to buy secretly shot up from their present level to astronomic heights—and Dr. Steinhofer could see no other reason for the operation—there was nothing to prevent the Swiss banker from buying a few of those shares for himself.

"The company we have our eye on is called Bormac Trading Company," Thorpe told him quietly. He out-

lined the position of the company, and the fact that old
Lady Macallister held 300,000 shares, or 30 per cent
of the company.

"We have reason to believe attempts may already
have been made to persuade this old lady to sell her
holding," he went on. "They appear to have been un-
successful. We are going to have another try. Even
should we fail, we will still go ahead and choose another
shell company."

Dr. Steinhofer listened quietly as he smoked his cigar.

"As you know, Dr. Steinhofer, it would not be possible for one purchaser to buy these shares without de-
claring his identity. Therefore the four buyers will be
Mr. Adams, Mr. Ball, Mr. Carter, and Mr. Davies, who
will each acquire seven and a half per cent of the company. We would wish you to act on behalf of all four of
them."

Dr. Steinhofer nodded. It was standard practice. "Of
course, Mr. Thorpe."

"I shall attempt to persuade the old lady to sign the
share-transfer certificates with the name of the buyer
left out. This is simply because some people in England,
especially old ladies, find Swiss banks rather—how shall
I say?—secretive organizations."

"I am sure you mean sinister," said Dr. Steinhofer
smoothly. "I completely understand. Let us leave it like
this, then. When you have had an interview with this
lady, we will see how best it can be arranged. But tell
Sir James to have no fear. The purchase will be by
four separate buyers, and the rules of the Companies
Act will not be affronted."

As Sir James Manson had predicted, Thorpe was
back in London by nightfall to begin his weekend.

The four mercenaries were waiting on the pavement
when Shannon came out of his bank just before twelve.
He had in his hand four brown envelopes.

"Marc, here's yours. There's five hundred pounds in
it. Since you'll be living at home, your expenses will be
the smallest. So within that five hundred you have to

buy a truck and rent a lock-up garage. There are other items to be bought. You'll find the list inside the envelope. Trace the man who has the Schmeissers for sale and set up a meeting between me and him. I'll be in touch with you by phone at your bar in about ten days."

The giant Belgian nodded and hailed a taxi at the curb to take him to Victoria Station and the boat train back to the Ostend ferry.

"Kurt, this is your envelope. There's a thousand inside it, because you'll have to do much more traveling. Find that ship, and inside forty days. Keep in touch by phone and cable, but be very discreet and brief when using either. You can be frank in written letters to my flat. If my mail is on intercept we're finished anyway.

"Jean-Baptiste, here's five hundred for you. It has to keep you for forty days. Stay out of trouble and avoid your old haunts. Find the boats and engines and let me know by letter. Open a bank account and tell me where it is. When I approve the type and price of the stuff, I'll transmit you the money. And don't forget the shipping agent. Keep it nice and legal all down the line."

The Frenchman and the German took their money and instructions and looked for a second taxi to get them to London airport, Semmler bound for Naples and Langarotti for Marseilles.

Shannon took Dupree's arm, and they strolled down Piccadilly together. Shannon passed Dupree his envelope.

"I've put fifteen hundred in there for you, Janni. A thousand should cover all the purchases and the storage, crating, and shipping costs to Marseilles, with something to spare. The five hundred should keep you easily for the next month to six weeks. I want you to get straight into the buying first thing Monday morning. Make your list of shops and warehouses with the Yellow Pages and a map over the weekend. You have to finish the buying in thirty days, because I want the stuff in Marseilles in forty-five."

He stopped and bought the *Evening Standard*,

opened it at the "Properties to Let" page, and showed Dupree the columns of advertisements for flats and flatlets for rent, furnished and unfurnished. There were, as usual, about 300 flats to rent, ranging from £6 a week to £200.

"Find yourself a small flat by tonight and let me know the address tomorrow."

They parted just short of Hyde Park Corner.

Shannon spent the evening writing out a complete statement of accounts for Endean. He pointed out that the total had eaten up the bulk of the £5000 transferred from Brugge and that he would leave the few hundreds left over from that sum in the London account as a reserve.

Last, he pointed out that he had not taken any part of his own £10,000 fee for the job and proposed either that Endean transfer it straight from Endean's Swiss account into Shannon's Swiss account, or remit the money to the Belgian bank for credit to Keith Brown.

He mailed his letter that Friday evening.

The weekend was free, so he called Julie Manson and suggested taking her out to dinner. She had been about to set off for a weekend at her parents' country house, but called and told them she was not coming. As it was late by the time she was ready, she came to collect Shannon, looking pert and spoiled at the wheel of her red MGB.

"Have you booked anywhere?" she asked.

"Yes. Why?"

"Let's go and eat at one of my places," she suggested. "Then I can introduce you to some of my friends."

Shannon shook his head. "Forget it," he said. "That's happened to me before. I am not spending the whole evening being stared at like a zoo animal and asked damnfool questions about killing people. It's sick."

She pouted. "Please, Cat darling."

"Nope."

"Look, I won't say what you are and what you do.

I'll just keep it secret. Come on. No one will know you by your face."

Shannon weakened. "One condition," he said. "My name is Keith Brown. Got it? Keith Brown. That's all. Nothing else do you say about me or where I come from. Nor about what I do. Understood?"

She giggled. "Great," she said. "Great idea. Mystery Man himself. Come on, then, Mr. Keith Brown."

She took him to Tramps, where she was evidently well known. Johnny Gold rose from his doorside table as they entered and greeted her effusively with kisses on both cheeks. He shook hands with Shannon as she introduced him. "Nice to see you, Keith. Have a good time."

They dined at the long row of tables running parallel to the bar, and started by ordering the house lobster cocktail in a hollowed-out pineapple. Seated facing the room, Shannon glanced around at the diners; most, from their long hair and casual dress, could be placed in show business or on its fringes. Others were evidently young-generation businessmen trying to be trendy or make a model or an actress. Among the latter he spotted a face he knew across the room, with a group, out of Julie's vision.

After the lobster Shannon ordered "bangers and mash" and, excusing himself, got up. He strolled slowly out of the door and into the center lobby as if on his way to the men's room. Within seconds a hand fell on his shoulder, and he turned to face Simon Endean.

"Are you out of your mind?" grated the City hard boy.

Shannon looked at him in mock surprise, a wide-eyed innocent. "No. I don't think so. Why?" he asked.

Endean was about to tell him, but checked himself in time. His face was white with anger. He knew his boss well enough to know how Manson doted on his supposedly innocent little girl, and knew roughly what his reaction would be should he ever hear about Shannon taking her out, let alone climbing into bed with her.

But he was checkmated. He assumed Shannon was

still unaware of his own real name, and certainly of Manson's existence. To bawl him out for dining with a girl called Julie Manson would blow both his own concern and Manson's name, together with both their roles as Shannon's employer. Nor could he tell Shannon to leave her alone, for fear Shannon would consult the girl and she would tell him who Endean was. He choked back his anger.

"What are you doing here?" he asked lamely.

"Having dinner," said Shannon, appearing puzzled. "Look, Harris, if I want to go out and have dinner, that's my affair. There's nothing to be done over the weekend. I have to wait till Monday to fly to Luxembourg."

Endean was even angrier. He could not explain that Shannon's slacking on the job was not what concerned him. "Who's the girl?" he asked.

Shannon shrugged. "Name's Julie. Met her in a café two days ago."

"Picked her up?" asked Endean in horror.

"Yes, you might say that. Why?"

"Oh, nothing. But be careful about girls, all girls. It would be better if you left them alone for a while, that's all."

"Harris, don't worry about my security. There won't be any indiscretions, in bed or out. Besides, I told her my name was Keith Brown; I'm on leave in London and I'm in the oil business."

For answer Endean spun round, snapped at Paolo to tell the group he was with that he had been called away, and headed for the stairs to the street before Julie Manson could recognize him.

Shannon watched him leave. "Up yours," he said quietly, "with Sir Bloody James Manson's biggest drill."

On the pavement outside, Endean swore quietly. Apart from that, he could only pray that Shannon had been telling the truth about the Keith Brown business and that Julie Manson would not tell her father about her new boyfriend.

Shannon and his girl danced until shortly before three

and had their first quarrel on the way back to Shannon's flat. He had told her it would be better if she did not tell her father she was going out with a mercenary, or even mention his name. "From what you have already told me about him, he seems to dote on you. He'd probably send you away somewhere, or have you made a ward of court."

Her response had been to start teasing, keeping a straight face and saying she would be able to handle her father, as she always had, and in any case being made a ward of court would be fun and would get her name in all the papers. Besides, she argued, Shannon could always come and get her, fight his way out, and elope with her.

Shannon was not sure how serious she was and thought he might have gone too far in provoking Endean that evening, although he had not planned on meeting him, anyway. They were still arguing when they reached the living room of his flat.

"Anyway, I'm not being told what I'll do and what I won't do," said the girl as she dropped her coat over the armchair.

"You will be by me," growled Shannon. "You'll just keep damn silent about me when you're with your father. And that's flat."

For answer the girl stuck her tongue out at him. "I'll do what I damn well like," she insisted and, to emphasize her words, stamped her foot. Shannon got angry. He picked her up, spun her around, marched her to the armchair, sat down, and pulled her over his knee. For five minutes there were two conflicting sounds in the sitting room, the girl's protesting squeals and the crack of Shannon's hand. When he let her up she scuttled into the bedroom, sobbing loudly, and slammed the door.

Shannon shrugged. The die was cast one way or the other, and there was nothing he could do about it. He went into the kitchen, made coffee, and drank it slowly by the window, looking out at the backs of the houses across the gardens, almost all dark as the respectable folk of St. John's Wood slept.

When he entered the bedroom it was in darkness. In the far corner of the double bed was a small hump, but no sound, as if she were holding her breath. Halfway across the floor his foot scuffed her fallen dress, and two paces farther he kicked one of her discarded shoes. He sat on the edge of the bed and as his eyes grew accustomed to the darkness he made out her face on the pillow, eyes watching him.

"You're rotten," she whispered.

He leaned forward and slipped a hand into the angle of her neck and jaw, stroking slowly and firmly.

"No one's ever hit me before."

"That's why you've turned out the way you have," he murmured.

"How is that?"

"A spoiled little girl."

"I'm not." There was a pause. "Yes, I am."

He continued caressing her.

"Cat."

"Yes."

"Did you really think Daddy might take me away from you if I told him?"

"Yes. I still do."

"And do you think I'd really tell him?"

"I thought you might."

"Is that why you got angry?"

"Yes."

"Then you only smacked me because you love me?"

"I suppose so."

She turned her head, and he felt her tongue busily licking the inside of his palm.

"Get into bed, Cat, darling. I'm so randy I can't wait any more."

He was only half out of his clothes when she threw the bedsheets back and knelt on the mattress, running her hands over his chest and muttering, "Hurry, hurry," between kisses.

"You're a lying bastard, Shannon," he thought as he lay on his back, feeling this avid and infatuated young girl go to work on him.

There was a light gray glow in the east over Camden
Town when they lay still two hours later. Julie was
curled up in the crook of his arm, her varied appetites
for the moment satisfied.

"Tell me something," she said.

"What?"

"Why do you live the way you do? Why be a mercenary and go around making wars on people?"

"I don't make wars. The world we live in makes wars,
led and governed by men who pretend they are crea-
tures of morality and integrity, whereas most of them
are self-seeking bastards. They make the wars, for increased profits or increased power. I just fight the wars
because it's the way I like to live."

"Buy why for money? Mercenaries fight for money,
don't they?"

"Not only the money. The bums do, but when it
comes to a crunch the bums who style themselves mercenaries usually don't fight. They run away. Most of the
best ones fight for the same reason I do; they enjoy the
life, the hard living, the combat."

"But why do there have to be wars? Why can't they
all live in peace?"

He stirred and in the darkness scowled at the ceiling.
"Because there are only two kinds of people in this
world: the predators and the grazers. And the predators
always get to the top, because they're prepared to fight
to get there and consume people and things that get in
their way. The others haven't the nerve, or the courage,
or the hunger or the ruthlessness. So the world is governed by the predators, who become the potentates.
And the potentates are never satisfied. They must go on
and on seeking more of the currency they worship.

"In the Communist world—and don't ever kid yourself into thinking the Communist leaders are peace-lov-
ing—the currency is power. Power, power, and more
power, no matter how many people have to die so they
can get it. In the capitalist world the currency is money.
More and more money. Oil, gold, stocks and shares,
more and more, are the goals, even if they have to lie,

steal, bribe, and cheat to get it. These make the money, and the money buys the power. So really it all comes back to the lust for power. If they think there's enough of it to be taken, and it needs a war to grab it, you get a war. The rest, the so-called idealism, is a load of cock."

"Some people fight for idealism. The Vietcong do. I've read it in the papers."

"Yeah, some people fight for idealism, and ninety-nine out of a hundred of them are being conned. So are the ones back home who cheer for war. We're always right, and they're always wrong. In Washington and Peking, London and Moscow. And you know what? They're being conned. Those GIs in Vietnam, do you think they die for life, liberty, and the pursuit of happiness? They die for the Dow Jones Index in Wall Street, and always have. And the British soldiers who died in Kenya, Cyprus, Aden. You really think they rushed into battle shouting for God, king, and country? They were in those lands because their colonel ordered them there, and he was ordered by the War Office, and that was ordered by the Cabinet, to keep British control over the economies. So what? They went back to the people who owned them in the first place, and who cared about the bodies the British army left behind? It's a big con, Julie Manson, a big con. The difference with me is that no one tells me to go and fight, or where to fight, or which side to fight on. That's why the politicians, the Establishments, hate mercenaries. It's not that we are more lethal than they are; in fact we're a damn sight less so. It's because they can't control us; we don't take their orders. We don't shoot the ones they tell us to shoot, and we don't start when they say, 'Start,' or stop when they say, 'Stop.' That's why we're outlaws; we fight on contract and we pick our own contracts."

Julie sat up and ran her hands over the hard, scarred muscles of his chest and shoulders. She was a conventionally raised girl and, like so many of her generation, could not understand even a tiny fraction of the world she saw about her.

"What about the wars when people fight for what they know is right?" she asked. "I mean, what about fighting against Hitler? That was right, wasn't it?"

Shannon sighed and nodded. "Yes, that was right. He was a bastard all right. Except that they, the big shots in the Western world, sold him steel up to the outbreak of war and then made more fortunes making more steel to crush Hitler's steel. And the Communists were no better. Stalin signed a pact with him and waited for capitalism and Nazism to destroy each other so he could take over the rubble. Only when Hitler struck Russia did the world's so idealistic Communists decide Nazism was naughty. Besides, it cost thirty million lives to kill Hitler. A mercenary could have done it with one bullet costing less than a shilling."

"But we won, didn't we? It was the right thing to do, and we won."

"We won, my little darling, because the Russians, British, and Americans had more guns, tanks, planes, and ships than Adolf. That's why, and that's the only reason why. If he had had more, he'd have won, and you know what? History would have written that he was right and we were wrong. Victors are always right. There's a nice little adage I heard once: 'God is on the side of the big battalions.' It's the gospel of the rich and powerful, the cynical and the gullible. Politicians believe in it, the so-called quality newspapers preach it. The truth is, the Establishment is on the side of the big battalions, because it created and armed them in the first place. It never seems to occur to the millions of readers of that garbage that maybe God, if there is one, has something to do with truth, justice, and compassion rather than sheer brute force, and that truth and justice might possibly be on the side of the little platoons. Not that it matters. The big battalions always win, and the 'serious' press always approves, and the grazers always believe it."

"You're a rebel, Cat," she murmured.

"Sure. Always have been. No, not always. Since I

buried six of my mates in Cyprus. That was when I began to question the wisdom and integrity of all our leaders."

"But, apart from killing people, you could die yourself. You could get killed in one of these futile wars."

"Yes, and I could live on, like a battery hen, in one of these futile cities. Filling in futile forms, paying futile taxes to enable futile politicians and state managers to fritter it away on electorally useful white elephants. I could earn a futile salary in a futile office and commute futilely on a train, morning and evening, until a futile retirement. I prefer to do it my way, live my way and die my way."

"Do you ever think of death?" she asked him.

"Of course. Often. Don't you?"

"Yes. But I don't want to die. I don't want to die."

"Death's not so bad. You get used to the idea when it has come very close and passed by many times. Let me tell you something. The other day I was clearing out the drawers in this place. There was some newspaper, a year old, at the bottom of one. I saw a piece of news and began to read it. It dated from the winter before last. There was this old man, see? He lived alone in a basement. They found him dead one day, a week or so after he died. The coroner was told no one never came to see him and he couldn't get out much. The pathologist said he had been undernourished for at least a year. You know what they found in his throat? Bits of cardboard. He had been nibbling bits of cardboard from a cereal package to try and get nourishment. Well, not me, baby. When I go, I'll go my way. I'd prefer to go with a bullet in my chest and blood in my mouth and a gun in my hand; with defiance in my heart and shouting, 'Sod the lot of you,' than to flicker out in a damp basement with a mouth full of cardboard.

"Now go to sleep, love, it's dawn already."

12

Shannon arrived in Luxembourg just after one on the following Monday and from the airport took a taxi to the Banque de Crédit. He identified himself as Keith Brown by using his passport and asked for the £5000 that should be waiting for collection by him.

After a delay while the Telex room was checked, the credit was discovered. It had just come through from Zurich. Instead of drawing the whole sum in cash, Shannon took the equivalent in Luxembourg francs of £1000 and signed a form making over the balance of £4000 to the bank. In exchange for this he was given a certified bank check for the equivalent of £4000.

He had time for a quick lunch before making his way to the Hougstraat, where he had an appointment with the firm of accountants Lang and Stein.

Luxembourg, like Belgium and Lichtenstein, maintains a system of offering to the investor a highly discreet and even secretive service in banking and the operation of companies, into whose affairs a foreign police force has the greatest difficulty in trying to pry. By and large, unless a company registered in Luxembourg can be shown to have broken the laws of the archduchy or can be proved beyond doubt to have been involved in international illegal activities of a highly unpleasant nature, foreign police inquiries as to who owns or controls such a company will be met with a stoic refusal to cooperate. It was this kind of facility that Shannon sought.

His interview, arranged by phone three days earlier, was with Mr. Emil Stein, one of the partners in the highly respectable firm. For the occasion Shannon wore a newly acquired charcoal-gray suit, white shirt, and school tie. He carried a briefcase and the *Times* under one arm. For some reason, the carrying of this newspaper always seems to impress Europeans with the idea that the bearer is a respectable Englishman.

"Over the forthcoming few months," he told the gray-haired Luxembourger, "a group of British associates, of whom I am one, wish to engage in commercial activities in the Mediterranean area, possibly Spain, France, and Italy. For this purpose we would like to establish a holding company in Luxembourg. As you may imagine, being British citizens and residents and doing business in several European countries with differing financial laws could prove very complicated. From a tax standpoint alone, a holding company in Luxembourg seems to be advisable."

Mr. Stein nodded, for the request was no surprise. Many such holding companies were already registered in his tiny country, and his firm received such requests every day.

"That should present no problem, Mr. Brown," he told his visitor. "You are aware of course that all the procedures required by the Archduchy of Luxembourg must be complied with. Once that is done, the holding company may hold the majority of shares in an array of other companies registered elsewhere, and after that the company affairs remain entirely private from foreign tax investigations."

"That's very kind of you. Perhaps you would outline the essentials of starting such a company in Luxembourg," said Shannon.

The accountant could reel off the requisites in a few seconds. "Unlike the situation in Britain, all limited liability companies in Luxembourg must have a minimum of seven shareholders and a minimum of three directors. However, quite often the accountant asked to help in setting the company up takes the chairmanship of the directors, his junior partners are the other two, and his staff becomes shareholders, each with a purely nominal number of shares. In this manner the person wishing to establish the company is merely the seventh shareholder, although by virtue of his greater number of shares he controls the company.

"Shares will normally be registered, and the names of the shareholders also, but there is the provision for the issue of bearer shares, in which case no registration of the identity of the majority holder is necessary. The snag to that is that the bearer shares are exactly what they mean, and the bearer of the majority controls the company. Should one man lose them, or have them stolen, the new owner would automatically become the controller without needing a vestige of proof as to how he acquired them. Do you follow me, Mr. Brown?"

Shannon nodded. This was the arrangement he hoped to establish, in order to have Semmler buy the boat behind the cover of an uncheckable company.

"A holding company," said Mr. Stein, "as its name implies, may not trade in any form. It may only hold stock in other companies. Does your group of associates hold shares in other companies which it would like to have taken over and held in Luxembourg?"

"No, not yet," said Shannon. "We hope to acquire existing companies in the area of chosen operations, or found other limited-liability companies and transfer the majority shareholdings to Luxembourg for safekeeping."

By the end of an hour the agreement had been reached. Shannon had shown Mr. Stein his £4000 banker's check to prove his solvency, and had paid a deposit of £500 in cash.

Mr. Stein had agreed to proceed at once with the foundation and registration of a holding company to be called Tyrone Holdings SA, after searching through the bulky lists of already registered companies to ensure that no such name existed on the register. The total share capital would be £40,000 of which only £1000 would be issued immediately, and this would be issued in 1000 bearer shares of £1 each. Mr. Stein would accept one share and the chairmanship of the board. One share each would go to his partner, Mr. Lang, and a junior partner in the firm. These three men would form the board. Three other staff members of the firm—they turned out later to be secretaries—would be issued with one bearer share each, and the remaining 994 shares would be held by Mr. Brown, who would thus control the company and whose wishes the board would have to implement.

A general meeting to float the company was fixed for twelve days thence, or any time after that, if Mr. Brown would let them know in writing when he could be in Luxembourg to attend it. On that note Shannon left.

Before closing time he was back at the bank, returned the check, and had the £4000 transferred to the account at Brugge. He checked into the Excelsior and spent the night in Luxembourg. He already had his reservation for Hamburg the next morning, and he had the hotel call to confirm it. It was to Hamburg that he flew the following morning. This time, he was looking for arms.

The trade in lethal weapons is the world's most lucrative, after narcotics, and, not surprisingly, the governments of the world are deeply involved in it. Since 1945 it has become almost a point of national prestige to have one's own native arms industry, and these industries have flourished and multiplied to the point where by the early 1970s it was estimated there existed one military firearm for every man, woman, and child on the face of the planet. Arms manufacture simply cannot be kept down to arms consumption except in case of war, and the logical response has to be either to export the surplus or encourage war, or both. As few governments want to be involved in a war themselves but also do not wish to run down their arms industries just in case, the accent has for years been on the exporting of arms. To this end, all the major powers operate highly paid teams of salesmen to trot the globe persuading any potentate with whom they can secure an interview that he does not have enough weapons, or that what he does possess are not modern enough and should be replaced.

It is of no concern to the sellers that 95 per cent of all the hardware on the face of, for example, Africa is used not to protect the owner-country from external aggression but to keep the populace in subjection to the dictator. Arms sales having logically started as a product of the profits rivalry between competing Western nations, the entry of Russia and China into the arms-manufacturing and -exporting business has equally logically transferred the salesmanship into an extension of the power rivalry.

The interaction of profit desirability and political desirability has produced a tangled web of calculations that continue daily in the capitals of the major world powers. One power will sell arms to republic A, but not to B. At which a rival power will rush to sell weapons to B but not to A. This is called establishing a power balance and therefore keeping the peace. The profit desirability of selling arms is permanent; it is always profitable. The only constraints are imposed by the political desirability of this or that country having certain arms in its possession at all, and from this shifting quicksand of expediency versus profit has evolved the intimate link between Foreign Affairs Departments and Defense Departments all over the world.

To establish an indigenous arms industry is not difficult, providing it is kept basic. It is relatively simple to manufacture rifles and submachine guns and ammunition for both, along with hand grenades and hand guns. The required level of technology is not high industrial development, and the variety of needed raw materials is not large. But the smaller countries usually buy their weaponry ready-made from the larger ones, because their internal requirements are too small to justify the necessary industrialization, and they know their technical level would not put them into the export market with a chance.

Nevertheless, a very large and growing number of medium-sized countries have in the past two decades gone ahead and established their own native, if basic, arms factories. The difficulties increase, and therefore the number of participating nations decreases, with the complexity of the weapon to be made. It is easy to make small arms, harder to make artillery, armored cars and tanks, very difficult to create an entire shipbuilding industry to build modern warships, and hardest of all to turn out modern jet fighters and bombers. The level of development of a local arms industry can be judged by the point at which local weaponry reaches its technical limits, and imports have to be made for anything above those limits.

The main world arms-makers and -exporters are the United States, Canada, Britain, France, Italy, West Germany (with certain banned manufactures under the 1954 Paris treaty), Sweden, Switzerland, Spain, Belgium, Israel, and South Africa in the Western world. Sweden and Switzerland are neutral but still make and export very fine weaponry, while Israel and South Africa built up their arms industries in light of their peculiar situations, because they did not wish to be dependent on anyone in the event of a crisis, and both export very little indeed. The others are all NATO countries and linked by a common defense policy. They also share an ill-defined degree of cooperation on foreign policy as it relates to arms sales, and an application for an arms purchase made to any of them habitually undergoes a close scrutiny before it is granted and the arms are sold. In the same vein, the small buyer country always has to sign a written undertaking not to pass weaponry sold to itself to another party without express written permission from the supplier. In other words, a lot of questions are asked, before a sale is agreed to, by the Foreign Affairs Office rather than the Weapons Sales Office, and sales are almost inevitably deals made government-to-government.

Communist arms are largely standardized and come mainly from Russia and Czechoslovakia. The newcomer, China, now also produces weaponry up to a sufficiently high level of sophistication for Mao's guerrilla-war theory's requirements. For Communists the sales policy is different. Political influence, not money, is the overriding factor, and many Soviet arms shipments are made as gifts to curry favor, not as commercial deals. Being committed to the adage that power grows out of the barrel of a gun, and obsessed with power, the Communist nations will not merely sell weapons to other sovereign governments, but also to "liberation" organizations that they politically favor. In most cases these are not sales, but gifts. Thus a Communist, Marxist, extreme Left-wing, or revolutionary movement almost anywhere in the world can be reasonably assured of not running short of the necessary hardware for guerrilla war.

In the middle, the neutral Swiss and Swedes have their own self-imposed inhibitions on whom they will sell to and thus curtail their arms export by their own volition on moral grounds. No one else does.

With the Russians selling or giving their hardware from governmental source to nongovernmental recipients, and the West being too shy to do so, the private arms dealer enters into the picture. The Russians have no private arms dealers, so this creature fills the gap for the West. He is a businessman who may be used as a source of weaponry by someone seeking to buy, but in order to stay in business he must liaise closely with the defense department of his own country, or the department will see that he goes out of business. It is in his interest to abide by his native country's wishes anyway; that country may be the source of his own purchases, which could be cut off if he causes displeasure, apart from his fear of being put out of business by other, less pleasant means.

Thus the licensed arms dealer, a national and resident usually of his native country, sells arms to buyers after consulting his own government to be sure that the sale is acceptable to them. Such dealers are usually large companies and hold stocks.

This is at the highest level of the private-enterprise arms business. Lower in the pond are more dubious fish. Next down the scale is the licensed dealer who does not hold a stock of weapons in a warehouse but is licensed to hold a franchise by one of the large, often government-owned or -controlled arms-manufacturing companies. He will negotiate a deal on behalf of a client and take his cut. His license depends on his toeing the line with the government whose franchise to operate he holds. This does not prevent some licensed arms dealers from occasionally pulling a fast one, though two well-established arms dealers have been put out of business by their governments when discovered doing it.

Down in the mud at the bottom sit the black-market arms dealers. These are self-styled, since they hold no license. They may not therefore legally hold any stocks of weapons at all. They remain in business by being of value to the secret buyer, a man or organization who, not being a government or representing one, cannot clinch an intergovernmental deal; who would not be tacitly approved of by a Western government as desirable to receive arms; who cannot persuade a Communist government to support his cause on the grounds of political ideology; but who needs arms.

The vital document in an arms deal is called the End User Certificate. This certifies that the weapons purchase is being made by, or on behalf of, the End User, who almost without exception in the Western world has to be a sovereign government. Only in the case of a flat gift by a secret-service organization to an irregular army, or of a pure black-market deal, does the question of an End User Certificate not apply. Examples of the former were the arming, without payment, by the CIA of the anti-Castro forces of the Bay of Pigs, and the arming of the Congo mercenaries, also by the CIA. An example of the latter is the shipment to Ireland from various European and United States private sources of arms for the Provisional IRA.

The End User Certificate, being an international document, has no specific form, shape, or size, or specific wording. It is a written affirmation from a certified representative of a national government that either he, the bearer, or Mr. X, the dealer, is authorized to apply to the supplier government for permission to purchase *and export* a quantity of arms.

The vital point about the End User Certificate is that some countries carry out the most rigorous checks to ensure the authenticity of this document, while others come under the heading of "no questions asked" suppliers. Needless to say, End User Certificates, like anything else, can be forged. It was into this world that Shannon carefully entered when he flew to Hamburg.

He was aware that he could certainly not make a direct application for permission to buy arms to any European government with a chance of success. Nor would any Communist government be kind enough to donate the weapons; indeed, it would be totally opposed to the toppling of Kimba. By the same token, any direct application would surely blow the entire operation.

He was also not in a position, for the same reason, to approach one of the leading government-owned armsmakers, such as Fabrique Nationale of Belgium, for any request put to a government-owned combine in the arms-making and -selling business would be passed on to the government; similarly, he could not approach a large private arms dealer, such as Cogswell and Harrison of London or Parker Hale of Birmingham. In the same category, Bofors of Sweden, Oerlikon of Switzerland, CETME of Spain, Werner and others in Germany, Omnipol of Czechoslovakia, and Fiat of Italy were ruled out.

He also had his own peculiar buying circumstances to consider. The amount he had to spend was too small to interest the big legitimate licensed dealers who habitually dealt in millions. He could not have interested the erstwhile king of the private arms dealers, Sam Cummings of Interarmco, who for two decades after the war ran a private arms empire from his penthouse suite in

Monaco and had retired to enjoy his wealth; nor Dr. Strakaty of Vienna, the licensee franchise holder for Omnipol across the border at Washington Street 11, Prague; nor Dr. Langenstein in Munich; nor Dr. Peretti in Rome; nor M. Cammermundt in Brussels; nor Herr Otto Schlueter in Hamburg.

He had to go farther down the scale, to the men who dealt in smaller sums and quantities. He knew the names of Günther Leinhauser, the German, former associate of Cummings; in Paris, of Pierre Lorez, Maurice Herscu, and Paul Favier. But on consideration he had decided to go and see two men in Hamburg.

The trouble with the packet of arms he sought was that it looked like what it was: a single packet of arms for a single job, and it would not need a keen military mind to realize that job had to be the taking of one building within a short period. There was not enough leeway in the quantities to kid any professional soldier that a Defense Ministry, even a small one, was behind the order.

Shannon had therefore decided to split the packet even smaller, so that at least the items sought from each dealer were consistent. A mixed package would be a giveaway.

From one of the men he was going to see he wanted 400,000 rounds of standard 9mm. ammunition, the kind that fits into automatic pistols and also submachine carbines. Such a consignment was too large and too heavy to be bought on the black market and shipped without a large amount of complicated smuggling to get it on board. But it could well be the kind of consignment needed by the police force of any small country, and was not suspicious in that there were no matching guns in the same packet and it could therefore pass under scrutiny as an order designed simply to replenish stock.

To get it, he needed a licensed arms dealer who could slip such a small order through the procedures among a batch of bigger orders. Although licensed to trade in arms, the dealer must nevertheless be prepared to do a bent deal with a forged End User Certificate. This was where an intimate knowledge of the no-questions-asked countries came in useful.

Ten years earlier there had been vast quantities of superfluous weaponry lying about Europe in private hands, "black," i.e. illegally held, arms, leftovers from colonial wars such as those of the French in Algeria and the Belgians in the Congo.

But a series of small irregular operations and wars throughout the 1960s, notably Yemen and Nigeria, had used them up. So he would have to find a man who would use a bent End User Certificate and present it to a supplier government that asked no or few questions. Only four years earlier the most noted of these was the Czech government, which, although Communist, had continued the old Czech tradition of selling arms to all comers. Four years earlier one could have walked into Prague with a suitcase full of dollars, gone to the Omnipol headquarters, selected one's hardware, and a few hours later have taken off from the airport in one's chartered plane with the stuff on board. It was that simple. But since the Soviet takeover in 1968 the KGB had taken to vetting all such applications, and far too many questions were being asked.

Two other countries had earned a reputation of asking few questions about where the presented End User Certificate really came from. One was Spain, traditionally interested in earning foreign currency, and whose CETME factories produced a wide range of weapons, which were then sold by the Spanish Army Ministry to almost all comers. The other, a newcomer, was Yugoslavia.

Yugoslavia had begun manufacturing her own arms only a few years earlier and inevitably had reached a point where her own armed forces were equipped with domestic arms. The next step was overproduction (because factories cannot be abandoned a few years after they have been most expensively started), and hence the desire to export. Being a newcomer to the arms market, with weapons of unknown quality, and eager for foreign currency, Yugoslavia had adopted the "ask me no questions and I'll tell you no lies" attitude to applicants for weaponry. She produced a good light company mortar and a useful bazooka, the latter based heavily on the Czech RPG-7.

Because the goods were new, Shannon estimated a dealer could persuade Belgrade to sell a tiny quantity of these arms, consisting of two 60mm. mortar tubes and a hundred bombs, plus two bazooka tubes and forty rockets. The excuse could well be that the customer was a new one, wishing to make some tests with the new weaponry and then come back with a far larger order.

For the first of his orders (the 400,000 rounds of 9mm. ammunition), Shannon intended to go to a dealer licensed to trade with CETME in Madrid but known also not to be above putting through a phony End User Certificate. For the second, Shannon had heard the name of another man in Hamburg who had skilfully cultivated the baby Yugoslav arms-makers at an early stage and had established good relationships with them, although he was unlicensed.

Normally there is no point in going to an unlicensed dealer. Unless he can fulfill the order out of illegally held stocks of his own, which means no export license, his only use can be in securing a bent but plausible End User Certificate for those who cannot find their own, and then persuading a licensed dealer to accept this piece of paper. The licensed dealer can then fulfill it, with government approval, from his own legally held stocks and secure an export license—or put the phony certificate to a government, with his name and guarantee backing it up. But occasionally he has one other use which makes him employable: his intimate knowledge of the state of the market and where to go at any given moment with any given requirement to have the best chance of success. It was for this quality that Shannon was visiting the second man on his Hamburg list.

When he arrived in the Hansa city, Shannon stopped by the Landesbank to find his £5000 was there already. He took the whole sum in the form of a banker's check made out to himself and went on to the Atlantic Hotel, where his room was booked. Deciding to give the Reeperbahn a miss, and being tired, he dined early and went to bed.

Johann Schlinker, whom Shannon confronted in his small and modest office the next morning, was short, round, and jovial. His eyes sparkled with bonhomie and welcome, so much so that it took Shannon ten seconds to realize the man could be trusted as far as the door. The pair of them spoke in English but talked of dollars —the twin languages of the arms marketplace.

Shannon thanked the arms dealer for agreeing to see him and offered his passport in the name of Keith Brown as identification.

The German flicked through it and handed it back. "And what brings you here?" he asked.

"You were recommended to me, Herr Schlinker, as a businessman with a high reputation for reliability in the business of military and police hardware."

Schlinker smiled and nodded, but the flattery made no impression. "By whom, may I ask?"

Shannon mentioned the name of a man in Paris, closely associated with African affairs on behalf of a certain French governmental but clandestine service. The two had met during one of Shannon's previous African wars, and a month earlier Shannon had looked him up in Paris for old times' sake. A week ago Shannon had called the man again, and he had indeed recommended Schlinker to Shannon for the kind of merchandise he wanted. Shannon had told the man he would be using the name Brown.

Schlinker raised his eyebrows. "Would you excuse me a minute?" he asked and left the room. In an adjoining booth Shannon could hear the chatter of a Telex.

It was thirty minutes before Schlinker came back. He was smiling. "I had to call a friend of mine in Paris on a business matter," he said brightly. "Please go on."

Shannon knew perfectly well he had Telexed to another arms dealer in Paris, asking the man to contact the French agent and get a confirmation that Keith Brown was all right. Apparently the confirmation had just come back.

"I want to buy a quantity of nine-mm. ammunition," he said bluntly. "I know it is a small order, but I have been approached by a group of people in Africa who need this ammunition for their own affairs, and I believe if those affairs go well there would be further and much larger shipments in the future."

"How much would the order be?" asked the German.

"Four hundred thousand rounds."

Schlinker made a moue. "That is not very much," he said simply.

"Certainly. For the moment the budget is not large. One is hoping a small investment now might lead to greater things later on."

The German nodded. It had happened in the past. The first order is usually a small one. "Why did they come to you? You are not a dealer in arms or ammunition."

"They happened to have retained me as a technical adviser on military matters of all kinds. When the question of seeking a fresh supplier for their needs arose, they asked me to come to Europe for them," said Shannon.

"And you have no End User Certificate?" the German asked.

"No, I'm afraid not. I hoped that sort of thing could be arranged."

"Oh, yes, it can," said Schlinker. "No problem there. It takes longer and costs more. But it can be done. One could supply this order from stocks, but they are held in my Vienna office. That way there would be no requirement for an End User Certificate. Or one could obtain such a document and make the application normally through legal channels."

"I would prefer the latter," said Shannon. "The delivery has to be by ship, and to bring that sort of quantity through Austria and into Italy, then on board a ship, would be hazardous. It enters an area I am not familiar with. Moreover, interception could mean long terms in prison for those found in possession. Apart from that, the cargo might be identified as coming from your stocks."

Schlinker smiled. Privately he knew there would be no danger of that, but Shannon was right about the border controls. The newly emergent menace of the Black September terrorists had made Austria, Germany, and Italy highly nervous about strange cargoes passing through the borders.

Shannon, for his part, did not trust Schlinker not to sell them the ammunition one day and betray them the next. With a phony End User Certificate, the German would have to keep his side of the bargain; it would be he who presented the bent certificate to the authorities.

"I think you are perhaps right," Schlinker said at last. "Very well. I can offer you nine-mm. standard ball at sixty-five dollars per thousand. There would be a surcharge of ten per cent for the certificate, and another ten per cent free on board."

Shannon calculated hastily. Free on board meant a cargo complete with export license, cleared through customs and loaded onto the ship, with the ship itself clearing the harbor mouth. The price would be $26,000 for the ammunition, plus $5200 surcharge.

"How would payment be made?" he asked.

"I would need the fifty-two hundred dollars before starting work," said Schlinker. "That has to cover the certificate, which has to be paid for, plus all personal traveling and administrative costs. The full purchase price would have to be paid here in this office when I am able to show you the certificate, but before purchase. As a licensed dealer I would be buying on behalf of my client, the government named on the certificate. Once the stuff had been bought, the selling government would be extremely unlikely to take it back and repay the money. Therefore I would need total payment in advance. I would also need the name of the exporting vessel, to fill in the application for export permit. The vessel would have to be a scheduled liner or freighter, or a general freighter owned by a registered shipping company."

Shannon nodded. The terms were steep, but beggars cannot be choosers. If he had really represented a sovereign government, he would not be here in the first place.

"How long from the time I give you the money until shipment?" he asked.

"Madrid is quite slow in these matters. About forty days at the outside," said the German.

Shannon rose. He showed Schlinker the banker's check to prove his solvency, and promised to be back in an hour with 5200 United States dollars in cash, or the equivalent in German marks. Schlinker opted for German marks, and when Shannon returned, he gave him a standard receipt for the money.

While Schlinker was writing out the receipt, Shannon glanced through a series of brochures on the coffee table. They covered the items put on sale by another company, which evidently specialized in nonmilitary pyrotechnic goods of the kind that are not covered by the classification of "arms," and a wide variety of items used by security companies, including riot sticks, truncheons, walkie-talkies, riot-gas canisters and launchers, flares, rockets, and the like.

As Schlinker handed him his receipt, Shannon asked, "Are you associated with this company, Herr Schlinker?"

Schlinker smiled broadly. "I own it," he said. "It is what I am best known for to the general public."

And a damn good cover for holding a warehouse full of crates labeled "Danger of Explosion," thought Shannon. But he was interested. Quickly he wrote out a list of items and showed them to Schlinker. "Could you fulfill this order, for export, out of your stocks?" he asked.

Schlinker glanced at the list. It included two rocket-launching tubes of the type used by coast guards to send up distress flares, ten rockets containing magnesium flares of maximum intensity and duration attached to parachutes, two penetrating foghorns powered by compressed-gas canisters, four sets of night binoculars, three fixed-crystal walkie-talkie sets with a range of not less than five miles, and five wrist compasses.

"Certainly," he said. "I stock all these things."

"I'd like to place an order for the list. As they are off the classification of arms, I assume there would be no problems with exporting them?"

"None at all. I can send them anywhere I want, particularly to a ship."

"Good," said Shannon. "How much would that lot cost, with freight in bond to an exporting agent in Marseilles?"

Schlinker went through his catalogue and priced the list, adding on 10 per cent for freight. "Four thousand, eight hundred dollars," he said.

"I'll be in touch with you in twelve days," said Shannon. "Please have the whole lot ready-crated for freighting. I will give you the name of the exporting agent in Marseilles, and mail you a banker's check in your favor for forty-eight hundred dollars. Within thirty days I expect to be able to give you the remaining twenty-six thousand dollars for the ammunition deal, and the name of the ship."

He met his second contact for dinner that night at the Atlantic. Alan Baker was an expatriate, a Canadian who had settled in Germany after the war and married a German girl. A former Royal Engineer during the war, he had got himself involved during the early postwar years in a series of border-crossing operations into and out of the Soviet Zone, running nylons, watches, and refugees. From there, he had drifted into arms-running to the scores of tiny nationalist or anti-Communist bands of *maquis* who, left over from the war, still ran their resistance movements in Central and Eastern Europe—with the sole difference that during the war they had been resisting the Germans, while after it they were resisting the Communists.

Most of them had been paid for by the Americans, but Baker was content to use his knowledge of German and commando tactics to slip quantities of arms to them and take a hefty salary check from the Americans for doing so. When these groups finally petered out, he found himself in Tangier in the early 1950s, using the smuggling talents he had learned in the war and after it to bring cargoes of perfume and cigarettes into Italy and Spain from the then international and free port on the north coast of Morocco. Finally put out of business by the bombing and sinking of his ship in a gangland feud, he had returned to Germany and gone into the business of wheeler-dealing in any commodity that had a buyer and a supplier. His most recent feat had been to negotiate a deal in Yugoslav arms on behalf of the Basques in northern Spain.

He and Shannon had met when Baker was running guns into Ethiopia and Shannon had been at a loose end after returning from Bukavu in April 1968. Baker knew Shannon under his real name.

The short, wiry man listened quietly while Shannon explained what he wanted, his eyes flickering from his food to the other mercenary.

"Yes, it can be done," he said when Shannon had finished. "The Yugoslavs would accept the idea that a new customer wanted a sample set of two mortars and two bazookas for test purposes before placing a larger order if he was satisfied. It's plausible. There's no problem from my side in getting the stuff from them. My relations with the men in Belgrade are excellent. And they are quick. Just at the moment I have to admit I have one other problem, though."

"What's that?"

"End User Certificate," said Baker. "I used to have a man in Bonn, diplomat for a certain East African country, who would sign anything for a price and a few nice big German girls laid on at a party, the sort he liked. He was transferred back to his own country two weeks ago. I'm a bit stuck for a replacement at the moment."

"Are the Yugoslavs particular about End Users?"

Baker shook his head. "Nope. So long as the documentation is in order, they don't check further. But there has to be a certificate, and it must have the right governmental stamp on it. They can't afford to be too slack, after all."

Shannon thought for a moment. He knew of a man in Paris who had once boasted he had a contact in an embassy there who could make out End User Certificates.

"If I could get you one, a good one, from an African country? Would that work?" he asked.

Baker inhaled on his cigar. "No problem at all," he said. "As for the price, a sixty-mm. mortar tube would run you eleven hundred dollars each. Say, twenty-two hundred for the pair. The bombs are twenty-four dollars each. The only problem with your order is that the sums are really too small. Couldn't you up the number of mortar bombs from a hundred to three hundred? It would make things much easier. No one throws off just a hundred bombs, not even for test purposes."

"All right," said Shannon, "I'll take three hundred, but no more. Otherwise I'll go over budget, and that comes off my cut."

It did not come off his cut, for he had allowed a margin for overexpenditure, and his own salary was secure. But he knew Baker would accept the argument as final.

"Good," said Baker. "So that's seventy-two hundred dollars for the bombs. The bazookas cost a thousand dollars each, two thousand for the pair. The rockets are forty-two dollars and fifty cents each. The forty you want come out at ... let's see ..."

"Seventeen hundred dollars," said Shannon. "The whole packet comes out at thirteen thousand, one hundred dollars."

"Plus ten per cent for getting the stuff free on board your ship, Cat. Without the End User Certificate. If I could have got one for you, it would have been twenty per cent. Let's face it, it's a tiny order, but the traveling and out-of-pocket expenses for me are constants. I ought to charge you fifteen per cent for such a small order. So the total is fourteen thousand, four hundred dollars. Let's say fourteen and a half, eh?"

"We'll say fourteen four," said Shannon. "I'll get the certificate and mail it to you, along with a fifty-per-cent deposit. I'll pay another twenty-five per cent when I see the stuff in Yugoslavia crated and ready to go, and twenty-five per cent as the ship leaves the quay. Travelers' checks in dollars, okay?"

Baker would have liked it all in advance, but, not being a licensed dealer, he had no offices, warehouses, or business address as Schlinker had. He would act as broker, using another dealer he knew to make the actual purchase on his behalf. As a black-market man, he had to accept these terms, the lower cut, and less in advance.

One of the oldest tricks in the book is to promise to fulfill an arms order, show plenty of confidence, assure the customer of the broker's absolute integrity, take the maximum in advance, and disappear. Many a black and brown seeker after arms in Europe has had that trick played on him. Baker knew Shannon would never fall for it; besides, 50 per cent of $14,400 was too small a sum to disappear for.

"Okay. The moment I get your End User Certificate I'll get straight onto it."

They rose to leave.

"How long from the time you make your first approach until shipping date?" asked Shannon.

"About thirty to thirty-five days," said Baker. "By the way, have you got a ship?"

"Not yet. You'll need the name, I suppose. I'll let you have it with the certificate."

"If you haven't, I know a very good one for charter. Two thousand German marks a day and all found. Crew, food, the lot. Take you and the cargo anywhere, and discreet as you like."

Shannon thought it over. Twenty days in the Mediterranean, twenty days out to target, and twenty days back.

A hundred and twenty thousand marks, or £15,000. Cheaper than buying one's own ship. Tempting. But he objected to the idea of one man outside the operation controlling part of the arms deal and the ship, and being aware of the target as well. It would involve making Baker, or the man he would have to go to for the charter, virtually a partner.

"Yes," he said cautiously. "What's she called?"

"The *San Andrea*," said Baker.

Shannon froze. He had heard Semmler mention that name. "Registered in Cyprus?" asked Shannon.

"That's right."

"Forget it," he said shortly.

As they left the dining room, Shannon caught a swift glimpse of Johann Schlinker dining in an alcove. For a moment he thought the German dealer might have followed him, but the man was dining with a second man, evidently a valued customer. Shannon averted his head and strode past.

On the doorstep of the hotel he shook hands with Baker. "You'll be hearing from me," he said. "And don't let me down."

"Don't worry, Cat. You can trust me," said Baker. He turned and hurried off down the street.

"In a pig's ear I can," muttered Shannon and went back into the hotel.

On the way up to his room the face of the man he had seen dining with the German arms merchant stayed in his memory. He had seen the face somewhere but could not place it. As he was falling asleep it came to him. The man was the chief of staff of Provisional IRA.

The next morning, Wednesday, he flew back to London. It was the start of Day Nine.

13

Martin Thorpe stepped into Sir James Manson's office about the time Cat Shannon was taking off from Hamburg.

"Lady Macallister," he said by way of introduction, and Sir James waved him to a seat.

"I've been into her with a fine-tooth comb," Thorpe went on. "As I suspected, she has twice been approached by people interested in buying her thirty-percent holding in Bormac Trading. It would seem each person used the wrong approach and got turned down. She's eighty-six, halfway senile, and very tetchy. At least, that's her reputation. She's also broad Scottish and has all her affairs handled by a solicitor up in Dundee. Here's my full report on her."

He handed Sir James a buff folder, and the head of Manson Consolidated read it within a few minutes. He grunted several times and muttered, "Bloody hell," once. When he had finished, he looked up. "I still want those three hundred thousand shares in Bormac," he said. "You say the others went about it the wrong way. Why?"

"She would appear to have one obsession in life, and it's not money. She's rich in her own right. When she married, she was the daughter of a Scottish laird with more land than ready cash. The marriage was no doubt arranged between the families. After her old man died she inherited the lot, mile after mile of desolate moorland. But over the past twenty years the fishing and hunting rights have brought in a small fortune from city-dwelling sportsmen, and parcels of land sold off for industry have made even more. It's been shrewdly invested by her broker, or whatever they call them up there. She has a nice income to live on. I suspect the other bidders offered a lot of money but nothing else. That would not interest her."

"Then what the hell would?" asked Sir James.

"Look at paragraph two on the second page, Sir James. See what I mean? The notices in *The Times* every anniversary, the attempt to have a statue erected, which was refused by the London County Council. The memorial she had put up in his home town. I think that's her obsession—the memory of the old slave-driver she married."

"Yes, yes, you may be right. So what do you propose?"

Thorpe outlined his idea, and Manson listened thoughtfully.

"It might work," he said eventually. "Stranger things have happened. The trouble is, if you try it and she still refuses, you can hardly go back again with another offer couched in a different vein. But then, I suppose a pure cash offer would in any case get the same reaction the previous two proposals met. All right, play it your way. Just get her to sell those shares."

With that, Thorpe was on his way.

Shannon was back in his London flat shortly after twelve. Lying on the mat was a cable from Langarotti in Marseilles. It was signed simply "Jean" and addressed to Keith Brown. Its message was an address, a hotel in a street a little way out of the center of the town, where the Corsican had checked in under the name of Lavallon. Shannon approved the precaution. Checking into a French hotel requires the filling out of a form which is later collected by the police. They might have wondered why their old friend Langarotti was staying so far out of town from his usual haunts.

Shannon spent ten minutes extracting the number of the hotel from Continental, Directory Enquiries, and placed a call. When he asked the hotel for M. Lavallon, he was told the monsieur was out. He left a message asking M. Lavallon to call M. Brown in London on his return. He had already given each of the four his own telephone number and made them commit it to memory.

Still using the telephone, he sent a telegram to the *poste restante* address of Endean under the name of Walter Harris, advising the project manager that he was back in London and would like to discuss something. Another telegram went to Janni Dupree at his flat, instructing him to report to Shannon as soon as he received the cable.

He rang his own Swiss bank and learned that of the salary for himself of £10,000, half that amount had been transferred to him, the credit having come from an unnamed account-holder at the Handelsbank. This he knew to be Endean. He shrugged. It was normal for half the salary only to be paid at this early date. He was confident, from the sheer size of ManCon and its evident eagerness to see Kimba fall from power, that the other £5000 would be his as the operation progressed.

Through the afternoon he typed out a full report of his Luxembourg and Hamburg trip, excluding the names of the firm of accountants in Luxembourg and the two arms dealers. To these sheets he attached a full statement of expenditure.

It was past four when he finished, and he had not eaten since the midmorning snack provided by Lufthansa on the flight from Hamburg. He found half a dozen eggs in the refrigerator, made a complete mess of an omelet, threw it away, and had a nap.

The arrival of Janni Dupree at the door just after six woke him, and five minutes later the phone rang. It was Endean, who had picked up the telegram in the post office.

Endean soon noticed that Shannon was not in a position to talk freely. "Is there someone with you?" he asked.

"Yes."

"Is it connected with business?"

"Yes."

"Do you want to meet?"

"I think we ought," said Shannon. "What about tomorrow morning?"

"Okay. About eleven suit you?"

"Sure," said Shannon.

"Your place?"

"Suits me fine."

"I'll be there at eleven," said Endean and hung up.

Shannon turned to the South African. "How are you getting on, Janni?" he asked.

Dupree had made a little progress in the three days he had been working. The hundred pairs of socks, T-shirts, and underpants were on order and would be ready for collection by Friday. He had found a supplier for the fifty combat tunics and had placed the order. The same firm could have provided trousers to match, but, according to his orders, Dupree was seeking another firm to supply the trousers, so that no one supplier would realize he was providing complete sets of uniforms. Dupree mentioned that no one seemed suspicious in any case, but Shannon decided nevertheless to stick to the original idea.

Janni said he had tried several footwear stores but had not found the canvas boots he was looking for. He would go on trying for the rest of the week and start searching for berets, haversacks, knapsacks, a variety of webbing, and sleeping bags next week. Shannon advised him to contact his first export agent and get the first consignment of underwear and tunics off to Marseilles as soon as possible. He promised Dupree to get from Langarotti the name and address of a consignee agent in Marseilles within the next forty-eight hours.

Before the South African left, Shannon typed out a

letter to Langarotti and addressed it to him under his real name at the main post office of Marseilles. In the letter he reminded the Corsican of a conversation they had had six months earlier beneath the palm trees, when the talk had turned to the buying of arms. The Corsican had mentioned that he knew a man in Paris who could get End User Certificates from a diplomat in one of the Paris embassies of an African republic. Shannon needed to know the name of the man and where he could be contacted.

When he had finished he gave Dupree the letter and ordered him to post it, express rate, that same evening from Trafalgar Square. He explained he would have done it himself, but he had to wait in the flat for Langarotti to call from Marseilles.

He was getting very hungry by eight, when Langarotti finally called, his voice crackling over a telephone line that must have been created personally by the inventor of that antique masterpiece the French telephone network.

Shannon asked him, in guarded terms, how he had been getting on. Before any of the mercenaries had left him, he had warned them all that under no circumstances was a telephone line to be used to talk openly about what they were doing.

"I checked into a hotel and sent you a telegram with my address on it," said Langarotti.

"I know. I got it," shouted Shannon.

"I hired a scooter and toured all the shops that deal in the kind of merchandise we are looking for," came the voice. "There are three manufacturers in each category. I got the addresses and names of the three boat-makers and wrote off to each for their brochures. I should get them in a week or so. Then I can order the best-suited from the local dealers, quoting the maker's name and brand name of the article," said Langarotti.

"Good idea," said Shannon. "What about the second articles?"

"They depend on the kind we pick from the brochures I shall get. One depends on the other. But don't worry. On the second thing we need, there are thousands of every kind and description in the shops along this coast. With spring coming, every shop in every port is stocking up with the latest models."

"Okay. Fine," Shannon shouted. "Now listen. I need the name of a good export agent for shipping. I need it earlier than I thought. There will be a few crates to be sent from here in the near future, and another from Hamburg."

"I can get that easy enough," said Langarotti from the other end. "But I think it will be better in Toulon. You can guess why."

Shannon could guess. Langarotti could use another name at his hotel, but for exporting goods from the port on a small freighter he would have to show his identity card. Moreover, in the past year or so Marseilles police had tightened up considerably in their watch on the port and a new customs chief had been drafted in, who was believed to be a holy terror. The aim of both operations was to clamp down on the heroin traffic that made Marseilles the start of the French connection with New York, but a search of a boat for drugs could just as easily turn up arms instead. It would be the worst irony to be caught because of something one was not even involved in.

"Fair enough, you know that area best," said Shannon. "Cable me the name and address as soon as you have them. There is one other thing. I have sent a letter by express rate tonight, to you personally at the main post office in Marseilles. You'll see what I want when you read it. Cable me the man's name at once when you get the letter, which should be Friday morning."

"Okay," said Langarotti. "Is that all?"

"Yes, for the moment. Send me those brochures as soon as you get them, with your own comments and the prices. We must stay in budget."

"Right. By-by," called Langarotti, and Shannon hung up. He had dinner alone at the Bois de St. Jean and slept early.

Endean arrived at eleven the next morning and spent an hour reading the report and accounts and discussing both with Shannon.

"Fair enough," he said at length. "How are things going?"

"Well," said Shannon, "it's early days yet, of course. I've only been on the job for ten days, but a lot of ground has been covered. I want to get all the orders placed by Day Twenty, which will leave forty days for them to be fulfilled. After that there must be an allowance of twenty days to collect all the component parts and get them safely and discreetly aboard the ship. Sailing date should be Day Eighty, if we are to strike on schedule. By the way, I shall need more money soon."

"You have three and a half thousand in London, and seven thousand in Belgium," objected Endean.

"Yes, I know. But there is going to be a spate of payments soon."

He explained he would have to pay Johann, the Hamburg arms dealer, the outstanding $26,000 within twelve days to allow him forty days to get the consignment through the formalities in Madrid and ready for shipment; then there would be $4800, also to Johann, for the ancillary gear he needed for the attack. When he had the End User Certificate in Paris, he would have to send it to Alan, along with a credit transfer for $7200, 50 per cent of the Yugoslav arms price.

"It all mounts up," he said. "The big payments, of course, are the arms and the boat. They form over half the total budget."

"All right," said Endean. "I'll consult and prepare a draft to your Belgian account for another twenty thousand pounds. Then the transfer can be made on a telephone call from me to Switzerland. In that way it will only take a matter of hours, when you need it." He rose to go. "Anything else?"

"No," said Shannon. "I'll have to go away again at the weekend for another trip. I should be away most of next week. I want to check on the search for the boat, the choice of dinghies and outboards in Marseilles, and the submachine guns in Belgium."

"Cable me at the usual address when you leave and when you get back," said Endean.

The drawing room in the sprawling apartment above Cottesmore Gardens, not far from Kensington High Street, was gloomy in the extreme, with heavy drapes across the windows to shut out the spring sunshine. A gap a few inches wide between them allowed a little daylight to filter in through thick net curtains. Between the four formally placed and overstuffed chairs, each of them late-Victorian pieces, myriad small tables bore assorted bric-à-brac. There were buttons from long-punctured uniforms, medals won in long-past skirmishes with long-liquidated heathen tribes. Glass paperweights nudged Dresden china dolls, cameos of once demure Highland beauties, and fans that had cooled faces at balls whose music was no longer played.

Around the walls of discolored brocade hung portraits of ancestors, Montroses and Monteagles, Farquhars and Frazers, Murrays and Mintoes. Surely such a gathering could not be the ancestors of one old woman? Still, you never knew, with the Scots.

Bigger than them all, in a vast frame above the fire that clearly was never lit, stood a man in a kilt, a painting evidently much more recent than the other blackened antiques, but still discolored by age. The face, framed by two bristling ginger muttonchop whiskers, glared down into the room as if its owner had just spotted a coolie impudently collapsing from overwork at the other end of the plantation. "Sir Ian Macallister, K.B.E.," read the plate beneath the portrait.

Martin Thorpe dragged his eyes back to Lady Macallister, who was slumped in a chair, fiddling as she constantly did with the hearing aid that hung on her chest. He tried to make out from the mumblings and ramblings, sudden digressions, and difficult accent, what she was saying.

"People have come before, Mr. Martin," she was saying; she insisted on calling him Mr. Martin, although he had introduced himself twice. "But I don't see why I should sell. It was my husband's company, don't you see. He founded all these estates that they make their money from. It was all his work. Now people come and say they want to take the company away and do other things with it—build houses and play around with other things. I don't understand it all, not at all, and I will not sell—"

"But Lady Macallister—"

She went on as if she had not heard him, which indeed she had not, for her hearing aid was up to its usual tricks because of her constant fiddling with it. Thorpe began to understand why other suitors had eventually gone elsewhere for their shell companies.

"You see, my dear husband, God rest his poor soul, was not able to leave me very much, Mr. Martin. When those dreadful Chinese killed him, I was in Scotland on furlough, and I never went back. I was advised not to go. But they told me the estates belonged to the company, and he had left me a large part of the company. So that was his legacy to me, don't you see. I could not sell his own legacy to me . . ."

Thorpe was about to point out that the company was worthless, but realized that would not be the right thing to say. "Lady Macallister—" he began again.

"You'll have to speak directly into the hearing aid. She's deaf as a post," said Lady Macallister's companion.

Thorpe nodded his thanks at her and really noticed her for the first time. In her late sixties, she had the careworn look of those who once had their own independence but who, through the strange turns of fortune, have fallen on harder times and to survive have to put themselves in bond to others, often to cantankerous, troublesome, exhausting employers whose money enables them to hire others to serve them.

Thorpe rose and approached the senile old woman in the armchair. He spoke closer to the hearing aid.

"Lady Macallister, the people I represent do not want to change the company. On the contrary, they want to put a lot of money into it and make it rich and famous again. We want to start up the Macallister estates, just like when your husband ran them. . . ."

For the first time since the interview had started an hour before, something like a glimmer of light awoke in the old woman's eyes. "Like when my husband ran them?" she queried.

"Yes, Lady Macallister," bawled Thorpe. He pointed up at the figure of the tyrant on the wall. "We want to create all his life's work again, just the way he would have wanted it, and make the Macallister estates a memorial to him and his work."

But she was gone again. "They never put up a memorial to him," she quavered. "I tried, you know. I wrote to the authorities. I said I would pay for the statute, but they said there was no room. No room. They put up lots of statutes, but not to my Ian."

"They will put up a memorial to him if the estates and the company become rich again," Thorpe shouted into the hearing aid. "They'll have to. If the company was rich, it could insist on a memorial. It could found a scholarship, or a foundation, called the Sir Ian Macallister Trust, so that people would remember him."

He had already tried that ploy once, but no doubt she had not heard him or had not grasped what he was saying. But she heard him this time.

"It would cost a lot of money," she quavered. "I am not a rich woman." She was in fact extremely rich, but probably unaware of it.

"You don't have to pay for it, Lady Macallister," he said. "The company would pay for it. But the company would have to expand again. And that means money. The money would be put into the company by my friends."

"I don't know, I don't know," she wailed and began to sniff, reaching for a cambric handkerchief in her sleeve. "I don't understand these things. If only my dear Ian were here. Or Mr. Dalgleish. I always ask him what would be for the best. He always signs the papers for me. Mrs. Barton, I'd like to go back to my room."

"It's time enough," said the housekeeper-companion brusquely. "Now come along, it's time for your nap. And your medicine."

She helped the old woman to her feet and assisted her out of the sitting room and down the corridor. Through the open door Thorpe could hear her businesslike voice commanding her charge to get onto the bed, and the old woman's protests as she took the medicine.

After a while Mrs. Barton came back to the sitting room. "She's on the bed, she'll rest for a while," she said.

Thorpe smiled his most rueful smile. "It looks as if I've failed," he said sadly. "And yet, you know, the stock she holds is quite valueless unless the company is rejuvenated with fresh management and some hard cash, quite a lot of it, which my partners would be prepared to put in." He turned to the door. "I'm sorry if I put you to inconvenience," he said.

"I'm quite used to inconvenience," said Mrs. Barton, but her face softened. It had been a long time since anyone had apologized for putting her to trouble. "Would you care for a cup of tea? I usually make one at this hour."

Some instinct at the back of Thorpe's mind prompted him to accept. As they sat over a pot of tea in the back kitchen, which was the housekeeper-companion's domain, Martin Thorpe felt almost at home. His mother's kitchen in Battersea had not been dissimilar. Mrs. Barton told him about Lady Macallister, her whining and tantrums, her obstinacy and the constant strain of competing with her all-too-convenient deafness.

"She can't see all your fine arguments, Mr. Thorpe, not even when you offered to put up a memorial to that old ogre in the sitting room."

Thorpe was surprised. Evidently the tart Mrs. Barton had a mind of her own when her employer was not listening. "She does what you tell her," he said.

"Would you like another cup of tea?" she asked. As she poured it, she said quietly, "Oh, yes, she does what I tell her. She depends on me, and she knows it. If I went, she'd never get another companion. You can't nowadays. People aren't prepared to put up with that sort of thing these days."

"It can't be much of a life for you, Mrs. Barton."

"It's not," she said shortly, "but I have a roof over my head, and food and some clothes. I get by. It's the price one pays."

"For being a widow?" asked Thorpe gently.

"Yes."

There was a picture of a young man in the uniform of a pilot of the Royal Air Force propped on the mantelpiece next to the clock. He wore a sheepskin jacket, a polka-dotted scarf, and a broad grin. Seen from one angle, he looked not unlike Martin Thorpe.

"Your son?" said the financier, with a nod.

Mrs. Barton gazed at the picture. "Yes. Shot down over France in nineteen-forty-three."

"I'm sorry."

"It was a long time ago. One becomes accustomed."

"So he won't be able to look after you when she's dead and gone."

"No."

"Then who will?"

"I'll get by. She'll no doubt leave me something in her will. I've looked after her for sixteen years."

"Yes, of course she will. She'll see you all right—no doubt of it."

He spent another hour in the back kitchen, and when he left he was a much happier man. It was nearly closing time for shops and offices, but from a corner phone booth he made a call to the head office of Man-Con, and within ten minutes Endean had done what his colleague asked.

In the West End an insurance broker agreed to stay late in his office that night and receive Mr. Thorpe at ten the next morning.

That Thursday evening Johann Schlinker flew into London from Hamburg. He had arranged his appointment by telephone from Hamburg the same morning, phoning his contact at his home rather than at the office.

He met the diplomat from the Iraqi embassy for dinner at nine. It was an expensive dinner, even more so when the German arms dealer handed over an envelope containing the equivalent in German marks of £1000. In return he took an envelope from the Arab and checked the contents. They took the form of a letter on crested embassy notepaper. The letter was addressed to whom it might concern and stated that the undersigned, being a diplomat on the staff of the London embassy of the Republic of Iraq, had been required and requested by the Interior and Police Ministry of his country to authorize Herr Johann Schlinker to negotiate the purchase of 400,000 rounds of standard 9mm. ball for shipment to Iraq to replenish the stocks of the police forces of the country. It was signed by the diplomat and bore the stamp and seal of the Republic of Iraq, which would normally be on the desk of the Ambassador. The letter further stated that the purchase would be wholly and exclusively for the use of the Republic of Iraq and would under no circumstances be passed, in whole or in part, to any other party. It was an End User Certificate.

When they parted, it was too late for the German to return home, so he spent the night in London and left the following morning.

At eleven on Friday morning, Cat Shannon phoned Marc Vlaminck at his flat above the bar in Ostend.

"Did you find that man I asked you to trace?" he inquired after introducing himself. He had already warned the Belgian to talk very carefully on the telephone.

"Yes, I found him," replied Tiny Marc. He was sitting up in bed, while Anna snored gently beside him. The bar usually closed between three and four in the morning, so midday was the habitual rising time for both of them.

"Is he prepared to talk business about the merchandise?" asked Shannon.

"I think so," said Vlaminck. "I haven't raised the matter with him yet, but a business friend here says he will normally do business after a suitable introduction through a mutual acquaintance."

"He still has the goods I mentioned to you at our last meeting?"

"Yes," said the voice from Belgium, "he still has them."

"Fine," said Shannon. "Get a meeting and introduction with him yourself first, and tell him you have a customer who has approached you and would like to talk business. Ask him to be available for a meeting next weekend with the customer. Tell him the customer is good and reliable and is an Englishman called Brown. You know what to say. Just get him interested in a business deal. Tell him the customer would wish to examine one example of the goods at the meeting, and if it is up to standard, discuss terms and delivery. I'll ring you toward the weekend and let you know where I am and when I could come to see you and him together. Understand?"

"Sure," said Marc. "I'll get on with it over the next couple of days and set the meeting up for some time to be confirmed later, but during next weekend."

They exchanged the usual good wishes and hung up.

At half past two a cable from Marseilles arrived at the flat. It bore the name of a Frenchman and an address. Langarotti said he would telephone the man and introduce Shannon with a personal recommendation. The cable concluded by saying inquiries regarding the shipping agent were under way, and he expected to be able to give Shannon a name and address within five days.

Shannon picked up the phone and called the offices of UTA airlines in Piccadilly to get himself a seat on the flight of the following Sunday midnight to Africa from Le Bourget, Paris. From BEA he reserved a ticket to Paris on the first flight the next morning, Saturday.

He put £2000 of the money he had brought back from Germany into an envelope and slipped it into the lining at the bottom of his handgrip, for London airport representatives of the Treasury by and large disapprove of British citizens strolling out of the country with more than the permitted £25 in cash and £300 in travelers' checks.

Just after lunch Sir James Manson summoned Simon Endean to his office. He had finished reading Shannon's report and was agreeably surprised at the speed with which the mercenary's proposed plan of twelve days earlier was being carried out. He had checked the accounts and approved the expenditures. What pleased him even more was the long telephone call he had had from Martin Thorpe, who had spent half the night and most of the morning with an insurance broker.

"You say Shannon will be abroad for most of next week," he told Endean when his aide entered the office.

"Yes, Sir James."

"Good. There's a job that has to be done sooner or later, and it might as well be now. Get one of our standard contracts of employment, the kind we use for the engagement of African representatives. Paste over the name of ManCon with a strip of white paper and fill in the name of Bormac in its place. Make it out for a one-year engagement for the services as West African representative of Antoine Bobi at a salary of five hundred pounds a month. When you've got it done, show it to me."

"Bobi?" queried Endean. "You mean Colonel Bobi?"

"That's the one. I don't want the future president of Zangaro running off anywhere. Next week, starting Monday, you are going down to Cotonou to interview the colonel and persuade him that Bormac Trading

Company, whose representative you are, has been so impressed by his mental and business acumen that it would like to engage his services as a West African consultant. Don't worry, he'll never check to see who or what Bormac is, or that you are its representative. If I know anything about these lads, the hefty salary will be what interests him. If he's short of the ready, it ought to be manna from heaven.

"You are to tell him his duties will be communicated to him later, but the sole condition of employment for the moment is that he remain where he is at his house in Dahomey for the next three months or until you visit him again. Persuade him there will be a bonus in salary if he waits where he is. Tell him the money will be transferred to his local account in Dahomean francs. On no account is he to receive any hard currency. He might vamoose. One last thing. When the contract is ready, have it photocopied to hide the traces of the change of name of the employing company, and only take with you photocopies. As for the date on it, make sure the last figure for the year is blurred. Smudge it yourself."

Endean absorbed the instructions and left to begin setting up the employment under false pretenses of Colonel Antoine Bobi.

That Friday afternoon, just after four, Thorpe emerged from the gloomy Kensington apartment with the four share-transfer deeds he needed, duly signed by Lady Macallister and witnessed by Mrs. Barton. He also bore a letter of authority signed by the old woman, instructing Mr. Dalgleish, her attorney in Dundee, to hand over to Mr. Thorpe the share certificates upon presentation of the letter and proof of identity and the necessary check.

The name of the recipient of the shares had been left blank on the transfer deeds, but Lady Macallister had not noticed. She had been too distraught at the thought of Mrs. Barton packing her bags and leaving. Before nightfall the name of the Zwingli Bank's nominee company acting on behalf of Messrs. Adams, Ball, Carter, and Davies would be written into the vacant space. After a visit to Zurich the following Monday, the bank stamp and countersignature of Dr. Steinhofer would complete the form, and four certified checks, one drawn against the account of each of the four nominees buying 7.5 per cent of the stock of Bormac, would be brought back from Switzerland.

It had cost Sir James Manson 2 shillings to buy each of the 300,000 shares, then quoted at 1 shilling and 1 penny on the Stock Exchange, or a total of £30,000. It had also cost him another £30,000, shunted that morning through three bank accounts, withdrawn once in cash and repaid into a fresh account an hour later, to purchase a life annuity which would assure a comfortable and worry-free end to her days for an elderly housekeeper-companion.

All in all, Thorpe reckoned it was cheap at the price. Even more important, it was untraceable. Thorpe's name appeared nowhere on any document; the annuity had been paid for by a solicitor, and solicitors are paid to keep their mouths shut. Thorpe was confident Mrs. Barton would have enough sense to do the same. And to cap it all, it was even legal.

14

Benoit Lambert, known to friends and police as Benny, was a small-fry member of the underworld and self-styled mercenary. In point of fact, his sole appearance in the mercenary-soldier field had occurred when, with the police looking for him in the Paris area, he had taken a plane for Africa and signed on in the Sixth Commando in the Congo under the leadership of Denard.

For some strange reason the mercenary leader had taken a liking to the timorous little man and had given him a job at headquarters, which kept him well away from combat. He had been useful in his job, because it enabled him to exercise to good effect the one talent he really did possess. He was a wizard at obtaining things. He seemed to be able to conjure up eggs where there were no chickens and whisky where there was no still. In the headquarters of any military unit, such a man is always useful, and most units have one. He had stayed with the Sixth Commando for nearly a year, until May 1967, when he spotted trouble brewing in the form of a pending revolt by Schramme's Tenth Commando against the Congolese government. He felt—rightly, as it turned out—that Denard and the Sixth might be drawn into this fracas and there would be an opportunity for all, including headquarters staff, to see some real combat. For Benny Lambert this was the moment to move briskly in the other direction.

To his surprise, he had been allowed to go.

Back in France, he had cultivated the notion of himself as a mercenary and later had called himself an arms dealer. The first he certainly was not, but as for arms, with his variety of contacts he had occasionally been able to provide an item of weaponry here and there, usually hand guns for the underworld, occasionally a case of rifles. He had also come to know an African diplomat who was prepared, for a price, to provide a moderately serviceable End User Certificate in the form of a letter from the Ambassador's personal desk, complete with embassy stamp. Eighteen months earlier he had mentioned this in a bar to a Corsican called Langarotti.

Nevertheless, he was surprised on Friday evening to hear the Corsican on the phone, calling long distance to tell him he would be visited at his home the next day or Sunday by Cat Shannon. He had heard of Shannon, but, even more, he was aware of the vitriolic hatred Charles Roux bore for the Irish mercenary, and he had long since heard on the grapevine that circulated among the mercenaries of Paris that Roux was prepared to pay money to anyone who would tip him off as to Shannon's whereabouts, should the Irishman ever turn up in Paris. After consideration, Lambert agreed to be at home to see Shannon.

"Yes, I think I can get that certificate," he said when Shannon had finished explaining what he wanted. "My contact is still in Paris. I deal with him fairly frequently, you know."

It was a lie, for his dealings were very infrequent, but he was sure he could swing the deal.

"How much?" asked Shannon shortly.

"Fifteen thousand francs," said Benny Lambert.

"*Merde*," said Shannon. "I'll pay you a thousand pounds, and that's over the rate."

Lambert calculated. The sum was just over eleven

thousand francs at the current rate. "Okay," he said.

"You let out one word of this, and I'll slit your gizzard like a chicken," said Shannon. "Even better, I'll get the Corsican to do it, and he'll start at the knee."

"Not a word, honest," protested Benny. "A thousand pounds, and I'll get you the letter in four days. And not a word to anyone."

Shannon put down five hundred pounds. "You'll take it in sterling," he said. "Half now, half when I pick it up."

Lambert was about to protest but realized it would do no good. The Irishman did not trust him.

"I'll call you here on Wednesday," said Shannon. "Have the letter here, and I'll hand over the other five hundred."

When he had gone, Benny Lambert thought over what he would do. Finally he decided to get the letter, collect the remainder of his fee, and tell Roux later.

The following evening Shannon flew to Africa on the midnight flight and arrived at dawn on Monday morning.

It was a long drive upcountry. The taxi was hot and rattled abominably. It was still the height of the dry season, and the sky above the oil-palm plantations was robin's-egg blue, without a cloud. Shannon did not mind. It was good to be back in Africa again for a day and a half, even after a six-hour flight without sleep.

It was familiar to him, more so than the cities of Western Europe. Familiar were the sounds and the smells, the villagers walking along the edge of the road to market, columns of women in Indian file, their gourds and bundles of wares balanced on their heads, unwaveringly steady.

At each village they passed, the usual morning market was set out beneath the shade of the palm-thatch roofs of the rickety stalls, the villagers bargaining and chattering, buying and selling, the women tending the stalls while the men sat in the shade and talked of important matters that only they could understand, and the naked brown children scampering through the dust between the legs of their parents and the stalls.

Shannon had both windows open. He sat back and sniffed the moisture and the palms, the woodsmoke and the brown, stagnant rivers they crossed. From the airport he had already telephoned the number the writer had given him and knew he was expected. He arrived at the villa set back from the road in a private, if small, park just before noon.

The guards checked him at the gate, frisking him from ankles to armpits, before letting him pay off the taxi and enter the gate. Inside, he recognized a face, one of the personal attendants of the man he had come to see. The servant grinned broadly and bobbed his head. He led Shannon to one of the three houses in the grounds of the park and ushered him into an empty sitting room. Shannon waited alone for half an hour.

He was staring out of the windows, feeling the cool of the air-conditioner dry out his clothes, when he heard the creak of a door and the soft sound of a sandal on tiles behind him. He turned around.

The general was much the same as when they had last met on the darkened airstrip, the same luxuriant beard, the same deep bass voice.

"Well, Major Shannon, so soon. Couldn't you stay away?"

He was bantering, as he usually did. Shannon grinned as they shook hands.

"I've come down because I need something, sir. And because there is something I think we ought to talk over. An idea in the back of my head."

"There's not much that an impoverished exile can offer you," said the general, "but I'll always listen to your ideas. If I remember rightly, you used to have some fairly good ones."

Shannon said, "There's one thing you have, even in exile, that I could use. You still have your people's loyalty. And what I need is men."

The two men talked through the lunch hour and through the afternoon. They were still discussing when darkness fell, Shannon's freshly drawn diagrams spread out on the table. He had brought nothing with him but clean white paper and a variety of colored felt-tipped pens, just in case of a skin search at customs.

They reached agreement on the basic points by sundown and elaborated the plan through the night. Only at three in the morning was the car summoned to drive Shannon back to the coast and the airport for take-off on the dawn plane to Paris.

As they parted on the terrace above the waiting car and its sleepy chauffeur, they shook hands again.

"I'll be in touch, sir," said Shannon.

"And I'll have to send my emissaries immediately," replied the general. "But in sixty days the men will be there."

Shannon was dead tired. The strain of the constant traveling was beginning to tell; the nights without sleep, the endless succession of airports and hotels, negotiations and meetings, had left him drained. In the car driving to the south he slept for the first time in two days, and dozed again on the plane trip back to Paris. The flight stopped too many times to allow a real sleep: an hour at Ouagadougou, another at a godforsaken strip in Mauretania, and again at Marseilles. He reached Le Bourget just before six in the evening. It was the end of Day Fifteen.

While he was landing in Paris, Martin Thorpe was boarding the overnight sleeper train to Glasgow, Stirling, and Perth. From there he could take a connecting train to Dundee, where were situated the old-established offices of Dalgleish and Dalgleish, attorneys-at-law. He carried in his briefcase the document signed before the weekend by Lady Macallister and witnessed by Mrs. Barton, along with the checks issued by the Zwingli Bank of Zurich, four of them, each in the sum of £7500 and each enough to purchase 75,000 of Lady Macallister's shares in Bormac.

Twenty-four hours, he thought as he drew down the blinds of his first-class sleeping compartment, blotting out the sight of the scurrying on the platform of King's Cross station. Twenty-four hours should see it through, and they would be home and dry; and three weeks later a new director on the board, a nominee responding to the strings pulled by him and Sir James Manson. Settling himself on the bunk, his briefcase under the pillow, Martin Thorpe gazed up at the ceiling and enjoyed the feeling.

Later that Tuesday evening Shannon was settled into a hotel not far from the Madeleine in the heart of Paris's 8th arrondissement. He had had to forsake his regular Montmartre hideout, where he was known as Carlo Shannon, because he was now using the name of Keith Brown. But the Plaza-Surène was a good substitute. He had bathed and shaved and was about to go out for dinner. He had telephoned to reserve a table at his favorite eating place in the quarter, the Restaurant Mazagran, and Madame Michèle had promised him a filet mignon the way he liked it, with a tossed-lettuce salad by the side and a Pot de Chirouble to wash it down.

The two person-to-person calls he had put in came through almost together. First on the line was a certain M. Lavallon from Marseilles.

"Do you have that shipping agent yet?" asked Shannon when they had exchanged greetings.

"Yes," said the Corsican. "It's in Toulon. A very good one, very respectable and efficient. They have their own bonded warehouse on the harbor."

"Spell it out," said Shannon. He had pencil and paper ready.

"Agence Maritime Duphot," spelled Langarotti and dictated the address. "Send the consignments to the agency, clearly marked as the property of Monsieur Langarotti."

Shannon hung up, and the hotel operator came on the line immediately to say a Mr. Dupree was calling from London.

Shannon dictated the name and address of the Toulon agent to him, letter by letter.

"Fine," Janni said at length. "I've got the first of the four crates ready and bonded here. I'll tell the London agents to get the stuff on its way as soon as possible. Oh, by the way, I've found the boots."

"Good," said Shannon, "well done."

He placed one more call, this time to a bar in Ostend. There was a fifteen-minute delay before Marc's voice came through.

"I'm in Paris," said Shannon. "That man with the samples of merchandise I wanted to examine . . ."

"Yes," said Marc. "I've been in touch. He's prepared to meet you and discuss prices and terms."

"Good. I'll be in Belgium Thursday night or Friday morning. Tell him I propose Friday morning over breakfast in my room at the Holiday Inn near the airport."

"I know it," said Marc. "All right, I'll put it to him and call you back."

"Call me tomorrow between ten and eleven," said Shannon and hung up.

Only then did he slip on his jacket and head for a long-awaited dinner to be followed by a long-desired full night's sleep.

While Shannon slept, Simon Endean also was winging his way southward to Africa on the overnight flight. He had arrived in Paris by the first flight on Monday and taken a taxi immediately to the embassy of Dahomey in the Avenue Victor Hugo. Here he had filled out a lengthy pink form requesting a six-day tourist visa. It was ready for collection just before the closing of the consular office on the Tuesday afternoon, and he had caught the midnight flight to Cotonou via Niamey. Shannon would not have been particularly surprised to know that Endean was going to Africa, for he assumed the exiled Colonel Bobi had to play a part in Sir James Manson's scheme of things and that the former commander of the Zangaran army was cooling his heels somewhere along the mangrove coast. But if Endean had known Shannon had just returned from a secret visit to the general in the same area of Africa, it would have quite ruined his sleep aboard the UTA DC-8 that night, despite the pill he had taken to ensure an uninterrupted slumber.

Marc Vlaminck called Shannon at his hotel at ten-fifteen the next day. "He agrees to the meeting, and he'll bring the sample," said the Belgian. "Do you want me to come too?"

"Certainly," said Shannon. "When you get to the hotel, ask at reception for the room of Mr. Brown. One other thing. Have you bought that truck I asked you to get?"

"Yes, why?"

"Has this gentleman seen it yet?"

There was a pause while Vlaminck thought. "No."

"Then don't bring it to Brussels. Hire a car and drive yourself. Pick him up on the way. Understand?"

"Yes," said Vlaminck, still perplexed. "Anything you say."

Shannon, who was still in bed but feeling a sight better, rang for breakfast and had his habitual five minutes under the shower, four of them in steaming hot water and sixty seconds under a stream of ice-cold.

The coffee and rolls were on the side table when he emerged. He placed two calls from the bedside phone, to Benny Lambert in Paris and Mr. Stein of Lang and Stein in Luxembourg.

"Have you got that letter for me?" he asked Lambert.

The little crook's voice sounded strained. "Yes. I got it yesterday. Luckily my contact was on duty on Monday, and I saw him that night. He produced the letter of introduction yesterday evening. When do you want it?"

"This afternoon," said Shannon.

"All right. Have you got my fee?"

"Don't worry, I've got it right here."

"Then come to my place about three," said Lambert.

Shannon thought for a moment. "No, I'll meet you here," he said and gave Lambert the name of his hotel. He preferred to meet the little man in a public place. Rather to his surprise, Lambert agreed to come to the hotel with what sounded like elation in his voice. There was something not quite right about this deal, but Shannon could not put his finger on it. He did not realize that he had given the Paris crook the information he would later sell to Roux.

Mr. Stein was engaged on the other phone when the call came, so, rather than wait, Shannon said he would ring back. This he did an hour later.

"About the meeting to launch my holding company, Tyrone Holdings," he began.

"Ah yes, Mr. Brown," said Stein's voice. "Everything is in order. When would you suggest?"

"Tomorrow afternoon," replied Shannon. It was agreed the meeting would be in Stein's office at three. Shannon got the hotel to reserve a seat on the express from Paris to Luxembourg just after nine the next morning.

"I must say, I find it all very strange, very strange indeed."

Mr. Duncan Dalgleish, Senior, in appearance and manner matched his office, and his office looked as if it had been the scene for the reading of the will of Sir Walter Scott.

He examined the four share-transfer deeds signed by Lady Macallister and witnessed by Mrs. Barton carefully and at length. He had muttered, "Aye," in sorrowful tones several times, and the glances he shot at the younger man from London were disapproving. He was evidently quite unused to handling certified checks from a bank in Zurich, and he had held them between forefinger and thumb as he read them. He was examining the four deeds again as he spoke.

"Ye'll understand, Lady Macallister has been approached before concerning the sale of these shares. In the past she has always seen fit to consult the firm of Dalgleish, and I have always seen fit to advise her against selling the stock," he went on.

Thorpe thought privately that no doubt other clients of Mr. Duncan Dalgleish were holding on to piles of valueless stock on the basis of his advice, but he kept his face polite.

"Mr. Dalgleish, you must agree the gentlemen whom I represent have paid Lady Macallister close to twice the face value of the stock. She, for her part, has freely signed the deeds and empowered me to collect the shares on presentation of check or checks totaling thirty thousand pounds. Which you now hold in your hand."

The old man sighed again. "It's just so strange that she should not have consulted me first," he said sadly. "I usually advise her on all her financial matters. For this I hold her general power of attorney."

"But her own signature is still perfectly valid," insisted Thorpe.

"Yes, yes, my power of attorney in no way invalidates her own power to sign on her behalf."

"Then I would be grateful if you would let me have the share certificates so that I can return to London," said Thorpe.

The old man rose slowly. "Would you excuse me, Mr. Thorpe?" he said with dignity and withdrew into an inner sanctum. Thorpe knew he was going to telephone London and prayed Lady Macallister's hearing aid would make it necessary for Mrs. Barton to interpret for the pair of them on the telephone. It was half an hour before the old attorney came back. He held a large wad of old and discolored share certificates in his hand.

"Lady Macallister has confirmed what you say, Mr. Thorpe. Not, of course, that I doubted your word, ye understand. I felt obliged to speak with my client before completing such a large transaction."

"Of course," said Thorpe, rose, and held out his hand. Dalgleish parted with the shares as if they had been his own.

An hour later Thorpe was in his train, rolling through the springlit countryside of Angus County on his way back to London.

Six thousand miles away from the heather-clad hills of Scotland, Simon Endean was seated with the hulking form of Colonel Bobi in a small rented villa in the residential district of Cotonou. He had arrived on the morning plane and checked into the Hotel du Port, whose Israeli manager had helped him trace the house where the Zangaran army officer lived in the straitened circumstances of exile.

Bobi was a lumbering giant of a man with a face of brooding brutishness and massive hands. The combination pleased Endean. It was of no consequence to him with what disastrous effects Bobi might rule Zangaro in succession to the equally disastrous Jean Kimba. What he had come to find was a man who would sign away the mineral rights of the Crystal Mountain range to Bormac Trading Company for a pittance and a hefty bribe to his personal account. He had found what he sought.

In exchange for a salary of £500 a month the colonel would be delighted to accept the post of West African consultant to Bormac. He had pretended to study the contract Endean had brought, but the Englishman noted with pleasure that when he turned to the second page, which Endean had stapled upside down between the first and third pages, Bobi's expression did not flicker. He was illiterate, or the next thing to it.

Endean explained the terms of the contract slowly in the mishmash of language they had been using, a mixture of basic French and Coast-pidgin English. Bobi nodded soberly, his small eyes, much flecked with bloodshot vessels around the whites, studying the contract intently. Endean stressed that Bobi was to remain in his villa or near it for the next two to three months, and that Endean would return to see him again in that time.

The Englishman elicited that Bobi still had a valid Zangaran diplomatic passport, a legacy of a visit he had once made outside Zangaro at the side of the Defense Minister, Kimba's cousin.

Shortly before sundown he scrawled what could pass for a signature on the bottom of the Bormac document. Not that a signature really mattered. Only later would Bobi be told that Bormac was putting him back into power in exchange for mining rights. Endean surmised that, if the price was right, Bobi would not quibble.

The following morning at dawn Endean was on another plane, heading back to Paris and London.

The meeting with Benny Lambert took place, as agreed, in the hotel. It was short and to the point. Lambert handed over an envelope, which Shannon flicked open. From it he took two pieces of paper, both identical and both bearing the printed crest and letterhead of the stationery of the Ambassador in Paris of the Republic of Togo.

One of the sheets was blank, except for a signature on the bottom and an embassy seal. The other sheet was a letter in which the writer stated that he had been authorized by his government to engage the services of ———— to apply to the government of ———— for the purchase of the military weapons listed on the attached sheet. The letter concluded with the usual assurance that the weapons were intended solely for use by the armed forces of the Republic of Togo and would not be given or sold to any third party. This too was signed and decorated with the seal of the republic.

Shannon nodded. He was confident Alan Baker would be able to insert his own name as the authorized agent and the Federal Republic of Yugoslavia as the vender government in such a way as to leave no trace of the insertion. He handed to Lambert the £500 he owed him, and the latter left.

Like most weak men, Lambert was indecisive. He had for three days been on the verge of calling Charles Roux and telling him that Shannon was in town and seeking an End User Certificate. He knew the French mercenary would be more than interested in the news, but he did not know why. He assumed it was because Roux regarded Paris and its resident mercenaries as his private preserve. He would not take kindly to a foreigner coming there to set up an operation in either arms or men without cutting Roux in on the deal as equal partner or, more desirable, as the *patron,* the boss of the project. It would never occur to Roux that no one would want to finance him to set up an operation because he had blown far too many already, taken too many bribes to kill a project, and cheated too many men of their salary.

But Lambert was afraid of Roux and felt he ought to tell him. He had been on the verge of doing so that afternoon, and would have if Shannon had not had the balance of £500 with him. But to have warned Roux in those circumstances would have cost the little crook that £500, and he was sure Roux would not have made up such a large sum to him simply for a tip-off. What Lambert did not know was that Roux had placed a killing contract on the Irishman. So in his state of ignorance he worked out another idea.

He could collect his full £1000 from Shannon and tell Roux the Irishman had approached him with a request for an End User Certificate, which he had promptly refused. There was just one snag. He had heard enough of Shannon to be afraid of him also, and he feared that if Roux was in contact with the Irishman too soon after Lambert's own meeting at the hotel, Shannon would guess from whom the tip-off came. He decided to wait until the following morning.

When he finally gave Roux the tip-off, it was too late. Roux telephoned the hotel at once under another name and asked if a Mr. Shannon was staying there. The chief desk clerk replied quite truthfully that there was no one of that name at the hotel.

Cross-examined, a thoroughly frightened Lambert claimed he had not actually visited the hotel but had simply received a call from Shannon, who had given that hotel as the place where he was staying.

Shortly after nine Roux's man Henri Alain was at the reception desk of the Plaza-Surène and established that the only Englishman or Irishman who had stayed in the hotel the previous night exactly corresponded in description to Cat Shannon, that his name and passport had been those of Keith Brown, and that he had reserved through the reception desk a ticket on the 9:00 a.m. express train to Luxembourg. Henri Alain learned two more things: of a meeting that M. Brown had had in the residents' lounge the previous afternoon, and a description of the Frenchman with whom he had been seen speaking. All this he reported back to Roux at midday.

In the French mercenary leader's flat, Roux, Henri Alain, and Raymond Thomard held a conference of war. Roux made the final decision.

"Henri, we've missed him this time, but the chances are that he still knows nothing about it. So he may well return to that hotel next time he has to overnight in Paris. I want you to get friendly, real friendly, with someone on the staff there. The next time that man checks in there, I want to know, but at once. Understand?"

Alain nodded. "Sure, *patron*. I'll have it staked out from the inside, and if he even calls to make a reservation, we'll know."

Roux turned to Thomard. "When he comes again, Raymond, you take the bastard. In the meantime, there's one other little job. That shit Lambert lied his head off. He could have tipped me off last night, and we'd have been finished with this affair. So he probably took money off Shannon, then tried to take some more off me for out-of-date information. Just make sure Benny Lambert doesn't do any walking for the next six months."

The floating of the company to be known as Tyrone Holdings was shorter than Shannon could have thought possible. It was so quick it was over almost before it had begun. He was invited into Mr. Stein's private office, where Mr. Lang and a junior partner were already seated. Along one wall were three secretaries—as it turned out, the secretaries of the three accountants present. With the required seven stockholders on hand, Mr. Stein set up the company within five minutes. Shannon handed over the balance of £500, and the thousand shares were issued. Each person present received one and signed for it, then passed it to Mr. Stein, who agreed to keep it in the company safe. Shannon received 994 shares in a block constituted by one sheet of paper, and signed for them. His own shares he pocketed. The articles and memorandum of association were signed by the chairman and company secretary, and copies of each would later be filed with the Registrar of Companies for the Archduchy of Luxembourg. The three secretaries were then sent back to their duties, the board of three directors met and approved the aims of the company, the minutes were noted on one sheet of paper, read out by the secretary, and signed by the chairman. That was it. Tyrone Holdings SA existed in law.

The other two directors shook hands with Shannon, calling him Mr. Brown as they did so, and left. Mr. Stein escorted him to the door.

"When you and your associates wish to buy a company in the chosen field of operations, to be owned by Tyrone Holdings," he told Shannon, "you will then need to come here, present us with a check for the appropriate amount, and buy the new issue at one pound per share. The formalities you can leave to us."

Shannon understood. Any inquiries would stop at

Mr. Stein as company chairman. Two hours later he caught the evening plane for Brussels, and he checked into the Holiday Inn just before eight.

The man who accompanied Tiny Marc Vlaminck when they knocked at Shannon's door the following morning just after ten was introduced as M. Boucher. The pair of them, standing on the threshold when he opened the door, looked like a comic turn. Marc was bulky, towering over his companion, and he was beefy in every place. The other man was fat, extremely fat —the sort of fatness associated with fairground sideshows. He seemed almost circular, balanced like one of those children's spherical plastic toys that cannot be overturned. Only on closer examination was it apparent there were two tiny feet in brilliantly polished shoes beneath the mass, and that the bulk constituting the lower half was divided into two legs. In repose, the man looked like one single unit.

M. Boucher's head appeared to be the only object to mar the contours of the otherwise uniformly globular mass. It was small at the top and flowed downward to engulf his collar and hide it from view, the flesh of the jowls resting thankfully on the shoulders. After several seconds Shannon conceded that he also had arms, one on each side, and that one held a sleek document case some five inches thick.

"Please come in," said Shannon and stepped back.

Boucher entered first, turning slightly sideways to slip through the door, like a large ball of gray worsted fabric on castors. Marc followed, giving Shannon a wink as he caught his eye. They all shook hands. Shannon gestured to an armchair, but Boucher chose the edge of the bed. He was wise and experienced. He might never have got out of the armchair.

Shannon poured them all coffee and went straight to business. Tiny Marc sat and stayed silent.

"Monsieur Boucher, my associate and friend may have told you that my name is Brown, I am English by nationality, and I am here representing a group of friends who would be interested in acquiring a quantity of submachine carbines or machine pistols. Monsieur Vlaminck kindly mentioned to me that he was in a position to introduce me to someone who might have a quantity of machine pistols for sale. I understand from him that these are Schmeisser nine-mm. machine pistols, of wartime manufacture but never used. I also understand and accept that there can be no question of obtaining an export license for them, but this is accepted by my people, and they are prepared to take all responsibility in this regard. Is that a fair assessment?"

Boucher nodded slowly. He could not nod fast. "I am in a position to make available a quantity of these pieces," he said carefully. "You are right about the impossibility of an export license. For that reason the identity of my own people has to be protected. Any business arrangement we might come to would have to be on a cash basis, and with security arrangements for my own people."

He's lying, thought Shannon. There are no people behind Boucher. He is the owner of this stuff and works alone.

In fact M. Boucher in his younger and slimmer days had been a Belgian SS man and had worked as a cook in the SS barracks at Namur. His obsession with food had taken him into cooking, and before the war he had lost several jobs because he tasted more than he served through the hatch. In the starving conditions of wartime Belgium he had opted for the cookhouse of the Belgian SS unit, one of the several local SS groups the Nazis recruited in the occupied countries. In the SS, surmised the young Boucher, one could eat. In 1944, when the Germans pulled back from Namur toward the frontier, a truckload of unused Schmeissers from the armory had been on its way east when the truck broke down. There was no time to repair it, so the cargo was shifted into a nearby bunker and the entrance dynamited. Boucher watched it happen. Years later he had returned, shoveled away the rubble, and removed the thousand weapons.

Since then they had reposed beneath a trapdoor built into the floor of the garage of his country cottage, a building left him by his parents, who died in the mid-1950s. He had sold job lots of Schmeissers at various times and had "unloaded" half of his reserve.

"If these guns are in good working order, I would be interested in buying a hundred of them," said Shannon. "Of course, payment would be by cash, in any currency. All reasonable conditions imposed by you would be adhered to in the handing over of the cargo. We also would expect complete discretion."

"As for the condition, monsieur, they are all brand new. Still in their maker's grease and each still wrapped in its sachet of greaseproof paper with seals unbroken. As they came from the factory thirty years ago and, despite their age, still possibly the finest machine pistol ever made."

Shannon needed no lectures about the Schmeisser 9mm. Personally he would have said the Israeli Uzi was better, but it was heavy. The Schmeisser was much better than the Sten, and certainly as good as the much more modern British Sterling. He thought nothing of the American grease-gun and the Soviet and Chinese burp-guns. However, Uzis and Sterlings are almost unobtainable and never in mint condition.

"May I see?" he asked.

Wheezing heavily, Boucher pulled the black case he carried onto his knees and flicked open the catches after twirling the wheels of the combination lock. He lifted the lid and held the case forward without attempting to get up.

Shannon rose, crossed the room, and took the case from him. He laid it on the bedside table and lifted out the Schmeisser.

It was a beautiful piece of weaponry. Shannon slid his hands over the smooth blue-black metal, gripped the pistol grip, and felt the lightness of it. He pulled back and locked the folding stock and operated the breech mechanism several times and squinted down the barrel from the foresight end. The inside was untouched, unmarked.

"That is the sample model," wheezed Boucher. "Of course it has had the maker's grease removed and carries only a light film of oil. But the others are identical. Unused."

Shannon put it down.

"It takes standard nine-mm. ammunition, which is easy to come by," said Boucher helpfully.

"Thank you, I know," said Shannon. "What about magazines? They can't be picked up just anywhere, you know."

"I can supply five with each weapon," said Boucher.

"Five?" Shannon asked in feigned amazement. "I need more than five. Ten at least."

The bargaining had begun, Shannon complaining about the arms dealer's inability to provide enough magazines, the Belgian protesting that was the limit he could provide for each weapon without beggaring himself. Shannon proposed $75 for each Schmeisser on a deal for 100 guns; Boucher claimed he could allow that price only for a deal of not less than 250 weapons, and that for 100 he would have to demand $125 each. Two hours later they settled for 100 Schmeissers at $100 each. They fixed time and place for the following Wednesday evening after dark, and agreed on the method for the handover. Shannon offered Boucher a lift back in Vlaminck's car to where he had come from, but the fat man chose to call a taxi and be taken to Brussels city center to make his own way home. He was not prepared to assume that the Irishman, who he was certain was from the IRA, would not take him somewhere quiet and work on him until he had learned the location of the secret hoard. Boucher was quite right. Trust is silly and superfluous weakness in the black-market arms business.

Vlaminck escorted the fat man with his lethal briefcase down to the lobby and saw him away in his taxi. When he returned, Shannon was packing.

"Do you see what I mean about the truck you bought?" he asked Tiny.

"No," said the other.

"We will have to use that truck for the pick-up on Wednesday," Shannon pointed out. "I saw no reason why Boucher should see the real number plates. Have a spare set ready for Wednesday night, will you? It's only for an hour, but if Boucher does want to tip off anyone, they'll have the wrong truck."

"Okay, Cat, I'll be ready. I got the lock-up garage two days ago. And the other stuff is on order. Is there anywhere I can take you? I have the hired car for the rest of the day."

Shannon had Vlaminck drive him westward to Brugge and wait in a café while Shannon went to the bank. Mr. Goossens was at lunch, so the pair ate their own lunch in the small restaurant on the main square and Shannon returned to the bank at two-thirty.

There was still £7000 in the Keith Brown account, but a debit of £2000 for the four mercenaries' salaries was due in nine days. He drew a banker's check in favor of Johann Schlinker and placed it in an envelope containing a letter from him to Schlinker that he had written in his hotel room late the previous night. It informed Schlinker that the enclosed check for $4800 was in full payment for the assorted marine and life-saving articles he had ordered a week earlier, and gave the German the name and address of the Toulon shipping agent to whom the entire consignment should be sent in bond for export, for collection by M. Jean-Baptiste Langarotti. Last, he informed Schlinker that he would be telephoning him the coming week to inquire if the End User Certificate for the ordered 9mm. ammunition was in order.

The other letter was to Alan Baker, addressed to his home in Hamburg. The check it contained was in Baker's name for $7200, and Shannon's letter stated that the sum was in full settlement of the required 50-per-cent advance for the purchase of the goods they had discussed over dinner at the Atlantic a week earlier. He included the End User Certificate from the government of Togo and the spare sheet from the same source.

Last, he instructed Baker to get right on with the purchase and promised to be in touch by phone regularly to check on progress. Both letters were mailed from Brugge post office, express rate and registered.

Shannon had Vlaminck drive him from Brugge to Ostend, had a couple of beers with the Belgian in a local bar near the seaport, and bought himself a single ticket on the evening ferry to Dover.

The boat train deposited him at Victoria Station at midnight, and he was in bed and asleep by one in the morning of that Saturday. The last thing he did before sleeping was to send a telegram to Endean's *poste restante* address to say he was back and he felt they ought to meet.

The Saturday morning mail brought a letter mailed at express rate from Malaga in the south of Spain. It was addressed to Keith Brown but began "Dear Cat." It came from Kurt Semmler and stated briefly that he had found a boat, a converted motor fishing vessel built twenty years earlier in a British shipyard, owned by a British citizen, and registered in London. It flew a British flag, was 90 feet overall and 80 tons deadweight, with a large central hold amidships and a smaller one aft. It was classed as a private yacht but could be reregistered as a coaster.

Semmler went on to say the vessel was for sale at a price of £20,000 and that two of the crew would be worth engaging under the new management. He was certain he could find good replacements for the other two crew members.

He finished by saying he was staying at the Malaga Palacio Hotel and asked Shannon to contact him there with his own date of arrival to inspect the boat. Shannon cabled him he would arrive on Monday.

The boat was called the MV *Albatross*.

Endean phoned Shannon that afternoon after checking his mail and receiving the telegram. They met around dinnertime that evening at the flat, and Shannon presented Endean with his third lengthy progress report and statement of accounts and expenditures.

"You'll have to make further transfers of money if we are to move ahead in the forthcoming weeks," Shannon told him. "We are entering the areas of major expenditure now—the arms and the ship."

"How much do you need at once?" Endean asked.

Shannon said, "Two thousand for salaries, four thousand for boats and engines, four thousand for submachine guns, and over ten thousand for nine-mm. ammunition. That's over twenty thousand. Better make it thirty thousand, or I'll be back next week."

Endean shook his head. "I'll make it twenty thousand," he said. "You can always contact me if you need more. By the way, I would like to see some of this stuff. That will be fifty thousand you'll have gone through inside a month."

"You can't," said Shannon. "The ammunition is not yet bought, nor the boats, engines, and so forth. Nor are the mortars and bazookas, nor the submachine pistols. All these deals have to be put through cash on the barrelhead or in advance. I explained that in my first report to your associates."

Endean eyed him coldly. "There had better be some purchases being made with all this money," he grated.

Shannon stared him out. "Don't threaten me, Harris. A lot of people have tried it; it costs a fortune in flowers. By the way, what about the boat?"

Endean rose. "Let me know which boat and from whom it is being bought. I'll make the credit transfer direct from my Swiss account."

"Please yourself," said Shannon.

He dined alone and well that evening and had an early night. Sunday would be a free day, and he had found Julie Manson was already at home with her parents in Gloucestershire. Over his brandy and coffee he was lost in thought, planning the weeks ahead and trying to visualize the attack on the palace of Zangaro.

It was in the middle of Sunday morning that Julie

Manson decided to call her new lover's flat in London and see if he was there. Outside, the spring rain fell in a steady curtain on the Gloucestershire countryside. She had hoped to be able to saddle up the handsome new gelding her father had given her a month earlier and gallop through the parkland surrounding the family mansion. She had hoped the ride would be a tonic to the feelings that flooded through her when she thought of the man she had fallen for. But the rain had washed out the idea of riding. Instead she was confined to wandering around the old house, listening to her mother's chitchat about charity bazaars and orphan-relief committees, or staring at the rain falling on the garden.

Her father had been working in his study, but she had seen him go out to the stables to talk to the chauffeur a few minutes earlier. As her mother was within earshot of the telephone in the hallway, she decided to use the extension in the study.

She had lifted the telephone beside the desk in the empty room when her eye caught the sprawl of papers lying across the blotter. On top of them was a single folder. She noted the title and idly lifted the cover to glance at the first page. A name on it caused her to freeze, the telephone still buzzing furiously in her ear. The name was Shannon.

Like most young girls, she had had her fantasies, seeing herself as she lay in the darkness of the dormitory at boarding school in the role of heroine of a hundred hazardous exploits, usually saving the man she loved from a terrible fate, to be rewarded by his undying devotion. Unlike most girls, she had never completely grown up. From Shannon's persistent questioning about her father she had already half managed to translate herself into the role of a girl agent on her lover's behalf. The trouble was, most of what she knew about her father was either personal, in his role of indulgent daddy, or very boring. Of his business affairs she knew nothing. And then here, on a rainy Sunday morning, lay her chance.

She flicked her eyes down the first page of the folder

and understood nothing. There were figures, costings, a second reference to the name Shannon, a mention of several banks by name, and two references to a man called Clarence. She got no further. The turning of the door handle interrupted her.

With a start she dropped the cover of the folder, stood back a yard, and began to babble into the unhearing telephone. Her father stood in the doorway.

"All right, Christine, that will be marvelous, darling. I'll see you on Monday, then. 'By now," she chattered into the telephone and hung up.

Her father's set expression had softened as he saw the person in the room was his daughter, and he walked across the carpet to sit behind his desk. "Now what are you up to?" he said with mock gruffness.

For answer she twined her soft arms around his neck from behind and kissed him on the cheek. "Just phoning a friend in London, Daddy," she said in her small, little-girl voice. "Mummy was fussing about in the hall, so I came in here."

"Humph. Well, you've got a phone in your own room, so please use that for private calls."

"All right, Daddikins." She cast her glance over the papers lying under the folder on the desk, but the print was too small to read and was mostly columns of figures. She could make out the headings only. They concerned mining prices. Then her father turned to look up.

"Why don't you stop all this boring old work and come and help me saddle up Tamerlane?" she asked him. "The rain will stop soon, and I can go riding."

He smiled up at the girl who was the apple of his eye. "Because this boring old work happens to be what keeps us all clothed and fed," he said. "But I will, anyway. Give me a few more minutes, and I'll join you in the stable."

Outside the door, Julie Manson stopped and breathed deeply. Mata Hari, she was sure, could not have done better.

15

The Spanish authorities are far more tolerant to tourists than is generally thought. Bearing in mind the millions of Scandinavians, Germans, French, and British who pour into Spain each spring and summer, and since the law of averages must provide that a certain percentage of them are up to no good, the authorities have quite a lot to put up with. Irrelevant breaches of regulations such as importing two cartons of cigarettes rather than the permitted one carton, which would be pounced on at London airport, are shrugged off in Spain.

The attitude of the Spanish authorities has always tended to be that a tourist really has to work at it to get into trouble in Spain, but once he has made the effort, the Spaniards will oblige and make it extremely unpleasant for him. The four items they object to finding in passenger luggage are arms and/or explosives, drugs, pornography, and Communist propaganda. Other countries may object to two bottles of duty-free brandy but permit *Penthouse* magazine. Not Spain. Other countries have different priorities, but, as any Spaniard will cheerfully admit, Spain is different.

The customs officer at Malaga airport that brilliant Monday afternoon cast a casual eye over the bundle of £1000 in used £20 notes he found in Shannon's travel bag and shrugged. If he was aware that, to get it to Malaga, Shannon must have carried it with him through London airport customs, which is forbidden, he gave no sign. In any case, that was London's problem. He found no copies of *Sexy Girls* or *Soviet News* and waved the traveler on.

Kurt Semmler looked fit and tanned from his three weeks orbiting the Mediterranean looking for ships for sale. He was still rake-thin and chain-smoked nervously, a habit that belied his cold nerve when in action. But the suntan gave him an air of health and set off with startling clarity his close-cropped pale hair and icy blue eyes.

As they rode from the airport into Malaga, Semmler told Shannon he had been in Naples, Genoa, Valletta, Marseilles, Barcelona, and Gibraltar, looking up old contacts in the world of small ships, checking the lists of perfectly respectable shipping brokers and agents for ships for sale, and looking some of them over as they lay at anchor. He had seen a score, but none of them suitable. He had heard of another dozen in ports he had not visited, and had rejected them because he knew from the names of their skippers they must have suspect backgrounds. From all his inquiries he had drawn up a list of seven, and the *Albatross* was the third. Of her qualities, all he would say was that she looked right.

He had reserved Shannon a room in the Malaga Palacio in the name of Brown, and Shannon checked in there first. It was just after four when they strolled through the wide gates of the south face of the Acera de la Marina square and onto the docks.

The *Albatross* was drawn up alongside a quay at the far end of the port. She was as Semmler had described her, and her white paint glistened in the sun and heat. They went aboard, and Semmler introduced Shannon to the owner and captain, George Allen, who showed him over the vessel. Before very long Shannon had come to the conclusion that it was too small for his purposes. There were a master cabin to sleep two, a pair of single cabins, and a saloon where mattresses and sleeping bags could be laid on the floor.

The after hold could, at a pinch, be converted into a sleeping area for another six men, but with the crew of four and Shannon's five, they would be cramped. He cursed himself for not warning Semmler there were six more men expected who would also have to be fitted in.

Shannon checked the ship's papers, which appeared to be in order. She was registered in Britain, and her Board of Trade papers confirmed it. Shannon spent an hour with Captain Allen, discussing methods of payment, examining invoices and receipts showing the amount of work that had been done on the *Albatross* over recent months, and checking the ship's log. He left with Semmler just before six and strolled back to the hotel, deep in thought.

"What's the matter?" asked Semmler. "She's clean."

"It's not that," said Shannon. "She's too small. She's registered as a private yacht. She doesn't belong to a shipping company. The thing that bugs me is that she might not be accepted by the exporting authorities as a fit vessel to take on board a load of arms."

It was too late back at the hotel to make the calls he wanted to make, so they waited till the following morning. Shortly after nine Shannon called Lloyds of London and asked for a check of the Yacht List. The *Albatross* was there all right, listed as an auxiliary ketch of 74 tons NRT, with her home port given as Milford and port of residence as Hooe, both of them in Britain.

Then what the hell's she doing here? he wondered, and then recalled the method of payment that had been demanded. His second call, to Hamburg, clinched it.

"*Nein,* not a private yacht, please," said Johann Schlinker. "There would be too great a possibility she would not be accepted to carry freight on a commercial basis."

"Okay. When do you need to know the name of the ship?" asked Shannon.

"As soon as possible. By the way, I have received

your credit transfer for the articles you ordered in my office. These will now be crated and sent in bond to the address in France you supplied. Secondly, I have the paperwork necessary for the other consignment, and as soon as I receive the balance of the money owing, I will go ahead and place the order."

"When is the latest you need to know the name of the carrying vessel?" Shannon bawled into the phone.

There was a pause while Schlinker thought. "If I receive your check within five days, I can make immediate application for permission to buy. The ship's name is needed for the export license. In about fifteen days after that."

"You will have it," said Shannon and replaced the receiver. He turned to Semmler and explained what had happened.

"Sorry, Kurt. It has to be a registered company in the maritime freighting business, and it has to be a licensed freighter, not a private yacht. You'll have to keep on searching. But I want the name within twelve days and no later. I have to provide the man in Hamburg with the ship's name in twenty days or less."

The two men parted that evening at the airport, Shannon to return to London and Semmler to fly to Madrid and thence to Rome and Genoa, his next port of call.

It was late when Shannon reached his flat again. Before turning in, he called BEA and booked a flight on the noon plane to Brussels. Then he called Marc Vlaminck and asked him to be present at the airport to pick him up on arrival, to take him first to Brugge for a visit to the bank and then to the rendezvous with Boucher for the handover of the equipment.

It was the end of Day Twenty-two.

Mr. Harold Roberts was a useful man. Born sixty-two years earlier of a British father and a Swiss mother, he had been brought up in Switzerland after the premature death of his father, and retained dual nationality. After entering banking at an early age, he had spent twenty years in the Zurich head office of one of Switzerland's largest banks before being sent to their London branch as an assistant manager.

That had been just after the war, and over the second twenty-year period of his career he had risen to become the manager of the investment accounts section and later overall manager of the London branch, before retiring at the age of sixty. By then he had decided to take his retirement and his pension in Swiss francs in Britain.

Since retirement he had been available for several delicate tasks on behalf not only of his former employers but also of other Swiss banks. He was engaged on such a task that Wednesday afternoon.

It had taken a formal letter from the Zwingli Bank to the chairman and the secretary of Bormac to achieve the introduction to them of Mr. Roberts, and he had been able to present letters corroborating his engagement as agent of the Zwingli Bank in London.

Two further meetings had taken place between Mr. Roberts and the secretary of the company, the second one attended by the chairman, Major Luton, younger brother of the deceased under manager for Sir Ian Macallister in the Far East.

The extraordinary board meeting had been agreed on, and was called in the City offices of the secretary of Bormac. Apart from the solicitor and Major Luton, one other director had agreed to come to London for the meeting and was present. Although two directors made up a working board, three gave an outright majority. They considered the resolution put by the company secretary and the documents he placed before them. The four unseen shareholders whose interests were being looked after by the Zwingli Bank undoubtedly did now own between them 30 per cent of the stock of the company. They certainly had empowered the Zwingli Bank to act on their behalf, and the bank had incontrovertibly appointed Mr. Roberts to represent it.

The argument that clinched the discussion was the simple one that if a consortium of businessmen had

agreed together to buy up such a large amount of Bormac stock, they could be believed when their bank said
on their behalf that their intention was to inject fresh
capital into the company and rejuvenate it. Such a
course of action could not be had for the share price,
and all three directors were shareholders. The resolution was proposed, seconded, and passed. Mr. Roberts
was taken onto the board as a nominee director representing the interests of the Zwingli Bank. No one
bothered to change the company rule stipulating that
two directors constituted a quorum with power to pass
resolutions, although there were now six and no longer
five directors.

Mr. Keith Brown was becoming a fairly regular visitor to Brugge and a valued customer at the Kredietbank. He was received with the usual friendliness by
Mr. Goossens, and the latter confirmed that a credit of
£20,000 had arrived that morning from Switzerland.
Shannon drew $10,000 in cash and a certified bank
check for $26,000 in the name of Johann Schlinker of
Hamburg.

From the nearby post office he mailed the check to
Schlinker by registered mail, accompanied by a letter
from himself asking the arms dealer to go ahead with
the Spanish purchase.

He and Marc Vlaminck had nearly four hours to kill
before the rendezvous with Boucher, and they spent
two of them taking a leisurely pot of tea in a café in
Brugge before setting off just before dusk.

There is a lonely stretch of road between Brugge and
Ghent, which lies 44 kilometers to the east. Because the
road twists and winds through flat farmland, most mo-
torists prefer to take the new motorway E5, which
also links the two Flemish towns as it runs from Ostend
to Brussels. Halfway along the old road the two mercenaries found the abandoned farm that Boucher had
described, or rather they found the faded notice board
pointing down the track to the farm, which was
hidden from view by a clump of trees.

Shannon drove on past the spot and parked, while Marc got out and went to check the farm over. He came back twenty minutes later to confirm the farm was indeed deserted and there were no signs that anyone had been there for quite a time. Nor were there any preparations in progress to provide an unpleasant reception for the two buyers.

"Anyone in the house or outbuildings?" asked Shannon.

"The house is locked front and back. No signs of interference. I checked out the barns and stables. No one there."

Shannon glanced at his watch. It was dark already, and there was still an hour to go. "Get back there and keep a watch from cover," he ordered. "I'll watch the front entrance from here."

When Marc had gone, Shannon checked the truck once again. It was old and rattled, but it was serviceable and the engine had been looked over by a good mechanic. Shannon took the two false number plates from the facia and whipped them onto the real number plates with sticky insulating tape. They could be ripped off easily enough once the truck was well away from the farm. On each side of the truck was a large publicity sticker that gave the vehicle a distinctive air but which could also come off in a hurry. In the back were the six large sacks of potatoes he had ordered Vlaminck to bring with him, and the broad wooden board sawn to make an internal tailgate when slotted into place. Satisfied, he resumed his vigil by the roadside.

The truck he was expecting turned up at five to eight. As it slowed and swung down the track to the farm, Shannon could make out the form of the driver hunched over the wheel and beside him the blob surmounted by a pimple of a head that could only be M. Boucher. The red taillights of the vehicle disappeared down the track and went out of sight behind the trees. Apparently Boucher was playing it straight.

Shannon gave him three minutes; then he too pulled his truck off the hard road and onto the track. When he got to the farmyard, Boucher's truck was standing with sidelights on the center. He cut his engine and climbed down, leaving his own sidelights on, the nose of his truck parked ten feet from the rear of Boucher's.

"Monsieur Boucher," he called into the gloom. He stood in darkness himself, well to one side of the glow of his own lights.

"Monsieur Brown," he heard Boucher wheeze, and the fat man waddled into view. He had evidently brought his "helper" along with him, a big, beefy-looking type whom Shannon assessed as being good at lifting things but slow-moving. Marc, he knew, could move like a ballet dancer when he wished. He saw no problem if it came to trouble.

"You have the money?" asked Boucher as he came close.

Shannon gestured to the driving seat of the truck. "In there. You have the Schmeissers?"

Boucher waved a pudgy hand at his own truck. "In the back."

"I suggest we get both our consignments out onto the ground between the trucks," said Shannon. Boucher turned and said something to his helper in Flemish, which Shannon could not follow. The man moved to the back of his own truck and opened it. Shannon tensed. If there were to be any surprises, they would come when the doors opened. There were none. The dull glimmer from his own truck's lights showed ten flat, square crates and an open-topped carton.

"Your friend is not here?" asked Boucher.

Shannon whistled. Tiny Marc joined them from behind a nearby barn.

There was silence. Shannon cleared his throat. "Let's get the handover done," he said. He reached into the driving compartment and pulled out the fat brown envelope. "Cash, as you asked for. Twenty-dollar bills. Bundles of fifty. Ten bundles."

He stayed close to Boucher as the fat man flicked through each bundle, counting with surprising speed for such plump hands, and stuffing the bundles into his side pockets. When he had reached the last he pulled all the bundles back out and selected a note at random from each. By the light of a pencil flashlight he scanned them closely, the samples, checking for forgeries. There were none. At last he nodded.

"All in order," he said and called something to his helper. The man moved aside from the truck doors. Shannon nodded at Marc, who went to the truck and heaved the first crate onto the grass. From his pocket he produced a wrench and prised up the lid. By the light of his own flashlight he checked the ten Schmeissers lying side by side in the crate. One of them he took out and checked for firing-mechanism pin and breech movement. He replaced the machine pistol and smacked the loose lid back down tight.

It took him twenty minutes to check all ten cases. While he did so the big helper brought by M. Boucher stood nearby. Shannon stood at Boucher's elbow, twelve feet away. Finally Marc looked into the open-topped crate. It contained five hundred magazines for the Schmeissers. He tested one sample magazine to ensure it fitted and that the magazines were not for a different model of pistol. Then he turned to Shannon and nodded.

"All in order," he said.

"Would you ask your friend to help mine load them up?" asked Shannon of Boucher. The fat man passed the instruction to his assistant. Before loading, the two beefy Flemings removed the potato sacks, and Shannon heard them discussing something in Flemish. Then Boucher's helper laughed. Within another five minutes the ten flat crates and the carton of magazines were loaded in Marc's truck.

When the crates of arms were loaded, Marc placed the board in position as a tailgate which came halfway up the back of the truck. Taking a knife, he slit the first sack, hefted it onto his shoulder, and emptied the contents into the back of the van. The loose potatoes rolled about furiously, finding the cracks between the edges of the crates and the sides of the van and filling them up. With a laugh, the other Belgian started to help him. The quantity of potatoes they had brought more than covered every trace of the ten crates of guns and the carton of magazines. Anyone looking in the back would be confronted with a sea of loose potatoes. The sacks were thrown into the hedge.

When they were finished, both men came around from the back of the truck together.

"Okay, let's go," said Marc.

"If you don't mind, we'll leave first," said Shannon to Boucher. "After all, we now have the incriminating evidence."

He waited till Marc had started the engine and turned the truck around so that it was facing the drive back to the road before he left Boucher's side and leaped aboard. Halfway down the track there was a particularly deep pothole, over which the truck had to move with great care and very slowly. At this point Shannon muttered something to Marc, borrowed his knife, and jumped from the truck to hide in the bushes by the side of the lane.

Two minutes later, Boucher's truck came along. It too slowed almost to a halt to negotiate the pothole. Shannon slipped from the bushes as the truck went past, caught up, stooped low, and jammed the knife point into the rear offside tire. He heard it hiss madly as it deflated; then he was back in the bushes. He rejoined Tiny Marc on the main road, where the Belgian had just ripped the stickers from the sides of their vehicle and the false number plates off front and back. Shannon had nothing against Boucher; he just wanted a clear half-hour's start.

By ten-thirty the pair was back in Ostend, the truck loaded with spring potatoes was garaged in the lock-up Vlaminck had hired on Shannon's instructions, and the two were in Marc's bar on Kleinstraat, toasting each other in foaming steins of ale while Anna prepared a meal. It was the first time Shannon had met the well-built woman who was his friend's mistress, and, as is the tradition with mercenaries when meeting each other's womenfolk, he treated her with elaborate courtesy.

Vlaminck had reserved a room for him at a hotel in the town center, but they drank until late, talking about old battles and skirmishes, recalling incidents and people, fights and narrow escapes, alternately laughing at the things that seemed hilarious in retrospect and nodding glumly at the memories that still rankled. The bar stayed open as long as Tiny Marc drank, and the lesser mortals sat around and listened.

It was almost dawn when they got to bed.

Tiny Marc called for him at his hotel in the middle of the morning, and they had a late breakfast together. He explained to the Belgian that he wanted the Schmeissers packaged in such a way that they could be smuggled over the Belgian border into France for loading onto the ship in a southern French port.

"We could send them in crates of spring potatoes," suggested Marc.

Shannon shook his head. "Potatoes are in sacks, not crates," he said. "The last thing we need is for a crate to be tipped over in transit or loading, so that the whole lot falls out. I've got a better idea." For half an hour he told Vlaminck what he wanted done with the submachine pistols.

The Belgian nodded. "All right," he said when he understood exactly what was wanted. "I can work mornings in the garage before the bar opens. When do we run them south?"

"About May fifteenth," said Shannon. "We'll use the champagne route. I'll bring Jean-Baptiste up here to help, and we'll change to a French-registered truck at Paris. I want you to have everything packed and ready for shipment by May fifteenth."

Marc accompanied him down to the car ferry to Dover, for the truck would not be used again until it made its last run from Ostend to Paris with its cargo of illegal arms. Shannon was back in London by early evening.

He spent what remained of the day writing a full

report for Endean, omitting to mention from whom he had bought the guns or where they were stored. He attached to the report a statement of expenditure and a tally of what was left in the Brugge account.

The first morning mail of that Friday brought a large packet from Jean-Baptiste Langarotti. It contained a sheaf of brochures from three European firms that manufactured the rubberized inflatable semi-rigid boats of the kind he wanted. They were variously advertised as being capable of use as sea-rescue launches, power boats, speed craft for towing water-skiers, pleasure boats, launching vessels for sub-aqua diving, runabouts, and fast tenders for yachts and suchlike. No mention was made of the fact that they all had been developed from an original design produced to give marine commandos a fast and maneuverable type of assault craft.

Shannon read each brochure with interest. Of the three firms, one was Italian, one British, and one French. The Italian firm, with six stockists along the Côte d'Azur, seemed to be the best suited for Shannon's purpose and to have the best delivery capability. Of their largest model, an 18-foot launch, there were two available for immediate delivery. One was in Marseilles and the other in Cannes. The brochure from the French manufacturer showed a picture of their largest example, a 16-foot craft, speeding through a blue sea, tail down, nose up.

Langarotti said in his letter there was one of these available at a shop for marine equipment in Nice. He added that all the British-made models needed to be ordered specially and, last, that although there were several more of each type available in brilliant orange color, he was concerning himself only with those in black. He added that each could be powered by any outboard engine above 50 horsepower, and that there were seven different makes of engine available locally and immediately which would suit.

Shannon replied with a long letter instructing Langarotti to buy the two models made by the Italian firm that were available for immediate delivery, and the

third of French manufacture. He stressed that on receipt of the letter the Corsican should ring the stockists at once and place a firm order, sending each shop-
keeper a 10-per cent deposit by registered mail. He
should also buy three engines of the best make, but
at separate shops.

He noted the prices of each item and that the total
came to just over £4000. This meant he would over-
run on his estimated budget of £5000 for ancillary
equipment, but he was not worried by that. He would
be under budget on the arms and, he hoped, the ship.
He told Langarotti he was transferring to the Corsican's
account the equivalent of £4500, and with the balance
he should buy a serviceable second-hand 20-hundred-
weight truck, making sure it was licensed and insured.

With this he should drive along the coast and buy his
three crated inflatable assault craft and his three outboard engines, delivering them himself to his freight
agent in Toulon to be bonded for export. The whole
consignment had to be in the warehouse and ready for
shipment by May 15. On the morning of that day
Langarotti was to rendezvous with Shannon in Paris
at the hotel Shannon usually used. He was to bring
the truck with him.

The mercenary leader sent another letter that day.
It was to the Kredietbank in Brugge, requiring the
transfer of £4500 in French francs to the account of
M. Jean-Baptiste Langarotti at the head office of the
Société Général bank in Marseilles.

When he got back to his flat, Cat Shannon lay on
his bed and stared at the ceiling. He felt tired and
drained; the strain of the past thirty days was taking its
toll. On the credit side, things seemed to be going
according to plan. Alan Baker should be setting up the
purchase of the mortars and bazookas from Yugoslavia
for pick-up during the early days of June; Schlinker
should be in Madrid buying enough 9mm. ammunition
to keep the Schmeissers firing for a year. The only reason he had ordered such an excessive amount of rounds
was to make the purchase plausible to the Spanish

authorities. Clearance for their export should be obtained for mid to late June, provided he could let the German have the name of the carrier by the middle of May, and provided the ship and its company were acceptable to the officials in Madrid.

Vlaminck should already have the machine pistols stowed for transporting across Belgium and France to Marseilles, to be loaded by June 1. The assault craft and engines should be loaded at the same time in Toulon, along with the other ancillary gear he had ordered from Schlinker.

Apart from smuggling the Schmeissers, everything was legal and aboveboard. That did not mean things could not still go wrong. Perhaps one of the two governments would make problems by taking overlong or refusing to sell on the basis of the provided documentation.

Then there were the uniforms, which Dupree was presumably still buying in London. They too should be in a warehouse in Toulon by the end of May at the latest.

But the big problem still to be solved was the ship. Semmler had to find the right ship, and he had been searching in vain for almost a month.

Shannon rolled off his bed and telephoned a telegram to Dupree's flat in Bayswater, ordering him to check in. As he put the phone down, it rang again.

"Hi, it's me."

"Hello, Julie," he said.

"Where have you been, Cat?"

"Away. Abroad."

"Are you going to be in town this weekend?" she asked.

"Yes. Should be." In fact there was nothing more he could do and nowhere he could go until Semmler contacted him with news of a ship for sale. He did not even know where the German was by this time.

"Good," said the girl on the phone. "Let's spend the weekend doing things."

It must be the tiredness. He was getting slow on the uptake. "What things?" he asked.

She began to tell him in precise and clinical detail until he interrupted her and told her to come straight around and prove it.

Although she had been bubbling with it a week earlier, in the thrill of seeing her lover again Julie had forgotten the news she had for him. It was not until nearly midnight that she remembered. She bent her head low over the half-asleep mercenary and said, "Oh, by the way, I saw your name the other day."

Shannon grunted.

"On a piece of paper," she insisted. Still he showed no interest, his face buried in the pillow beneath crossed forearms.

"Shall I tell you where?"

His reaction was disappointing. He grunted again.

"In a folder on my daddy's desk."

If she had meant to surprise him, she succeeded. He came off the sheet in one movement and faced her, gripping both her upper arms hard. There was an intensity about his stare that frightened her.

"You're hurting me," she said irrelevantly.

"What folder on your father's desk?"

"A folder." She sniffed, on the verge of tears. "I only wanted to help you."

He relaxed visibly, and his expression softened. "Why did you go looking?" he asked.

"Well, you're always asking about him, and when I saw this folder, I just sort of looked. Then I saw your name."

"Tell me about it from the beginning," he said gently.

When she had finished she reached forward and coiled her arms around his neck. "I love you, Mr. Cat," she whispered. "I only did it for that. Was it wrong?"

Shannon thought for a moment. She already knew far too much, and there were only two ways of ensuring her silence. "Do you really love me?" he asked.

"Yes. Really."

"Would you want anything bad to happen to me because of something you did or said?"

She pulled herself back from him, staring deep into his face. This was much more like the scenes in her schoolgirl dreams. "Never," she said soulfully. "I'd never talk. Whatever they did to me."

Shannon blinked several times in amazement. "Nobody's going to do anything to you," he said. "Just don't tell your father that you know me or went through his papers. You see, he employs me to gather information for him about the prospects of mining in Africa. If he learned we knew each other, he'd fire me. Then I'd have to find another job. There is one that's been offered to me, miles away in Africa. So you see, I'd have to go and leave you if he ever found out about us."

That struck home, hard. She did not want him to go. Privately he knew one day soon he would have to go, but there was no need to tell her yet.

"I won't say anything," she promised.

"A couple of points," said Shannon. "You said you saw the title on the sheets with mineral prices on them. What was the title?"

She furrowed her brow, trying to recall the words. "That stuff they put in fountain pens. They mention it in the ads for the expensive ones."

"Ink?" asked Shannon.

"Platium," she said.

"Platinum," he corrected, his eyes pensive. "Lastly, what was the title on the folder?"

"Oh, I remember that," she said happily. "Like something out of a fairy tale. The Crystal Mountain."

Shannon sighed deeply. "Go and make me some coffee, there's a love."

When he heard her clattering cups in the kitchen he leaned back against the bedhead and stared out over London. "You cunning bastard," he breathed. "But it won't be that cheap, Sir James, not that cheap at all."

Then he laughed into the darkness.

That same Saturday night Benny Lambert was ambling home toward his lodgings after an evening drinking with friends in one of his favorite cafés. He had been buying a lot of rounds for his cronies, using the money, now changed into francs, that Shannon had paid him. It made him feel good to be able to talk of the "big deal" he had just pulled off and buy the admiring bar girls champagne. He had had enough, more than enough, himself, and took no notice of the car that cruised slowly behind him, two hundred yards back. Nor did he think much of it when the car swept up to him as he came abreast of a vacant lot half a mile short of his home.

By the time he took notice and started to protest, the giant figure that had emerged from the car was hustling him across the lot and behind a hoarding that stood ten yards from the road.

His protests were silenced when the figure spun him around and, still holding him by the scruff, slammed a fist into his solar plexus. Benny Lambert sagged and, when the grip on his collar was removed, slumped to the ground. Standing above him, face shadowed in the obscurity behind the hoarding, the figure drew a two-foot iron bar from his belt. Stooping down, the big man grabbed the writhing Lambert by the left thigh and jerked it upward. The iron bar made a dull *whumph* as it crashed down with all the assailant's force onto the exposed kneecap, shattering it instantly. Lambert screamed once, shrilly, like a skewered rat, and fainted. He never felt the second kneecap being broken at all.

Twenty minutes later, Thomard was phoning his employer from the booth in a late-night café a mile away.

At the other end, Roux listened and nodded. "Good," he said. "Now I have some news for you. The hotel where Shannon usually stays. Henri Alain has just informed me they have received a letter from Mr. Keith Brown. It reserves a room for him on the night of the fifteenth. Got it?"

"The fifteenth," Thomard said. "Yes. He will be there then."

"And so will you," said the voice on the phone. "Henri will keep in touch with his contact inside the hotel, and you will remain on standby, not far from the hotel, from noon of that day onward."

"Until when?" asked Thomard.

"Until he comes out, alone," said Roux. "And then you will take him. For five thousand dollars."

Thomard was smiling slightly when he came out of the booth. As he stood at the bar sipping his beer, he could feel the pressure of the gun under his left armpit. It made him smile even more. In a few days it would earn him a tidy sum. He was quite sure of it. It would, he told himself, be simple and straightforward to take a man, even Cat Shannon, who had never even seen him and did not know he was there.

It was in the middle of a Sunday morning that Kurt Semmler phoned. Shannon was lying naked on his back on the bed while Julie puttered around the kitchen making breakfast.

"Mr. Keith Brown?" asked the operator.

"Yes. Speaking."

"I have a personal call for you from a Mr. Semolina in Genoa."

Shannon swung himself off the bed and crouched on the edge, the telephone up to his ear. "Put him on the line," he ordered.

The German's voice was faint, but reception was reasonably clear. "Carlo?"

"Yes. Kurt?"

"I'm in Genoa."

"I know. What news?"

"I have it. This time I am sure. She is just what you wanted. But there is someone else would like to buy her also. We may have to outbid them if we want the boat. But she is good. For us, very good. Can you come out and see her?"

"You're quite sure, Kurt?"

"Yes. Quite sure. Registered freighter, property of a Genoa-based shipping company. Made to order."

Shannon considered. "I'll come tomorrow. What hotel are you staying at?"

Semmler told him.

"I'll be there on the first available plane. I don't know when that will be. Stay at the hotel in the afternoon, and I'll contact you when I get there. Book me a room."

A few minutes later he was booked on the Alitalia flight to Milan at 0905 the following morning, to make a connection from Milan to Genoa and arrive at the port just after one in the afternoon.

He was grinning when Julie returned with the coffee. If the ship was the right one, he could conclude the deal over the next twelve days and be in Paris on the fifteenth for his rendezvous with Langarotti, secure in the knowledge that Semmler would have the ship ready for sea, with a good crew and fully fueled and supplied, by June 1.

"Who was that?" asked the girl.

"A friend."

"Which friend?"

"A business friend."

"What did he want?"

"I have to go and see him."

"When?"

"Tomorrow morning. In Italy."

"How long will you be gone?"

"I don't know. Two weeks. Maybe more."

She pouted over her coffee cup. "So what am I supposed to do all that time?" she asked.

Shannon grinned. "You'll find something. There's a lot of it about."

"You're a shit," she said conversationally. "But if you have to go, I suppose you must. It only leaves us till tomorrow morning, so I, my dear Tomcat, am going to make the best of it."

As his coffee was spilled over the pillow, Shannon reflected that the fight for Kimba's palace was going to be a holiday compared with trying to satisfy Sir James Manson's sweet little daughter.

16

The port of Genoa was bathed in late-afternoon sunshine when Cat Shannon and Kurt Semmler paid off their taxi and the German led his employer along the quays to where the motor vessel *Toscana* was moored. The old coaster was dwarfed by the two 3000-ton freighters that lay on either side of her, but that was no problem. To Shannon's eye she was big enough for her purposes.

There was a tiny forepeak and a four-foot drop to the main deck, in the center of which was the large square hatch to the only cargo hold set amidships. Aft was the tiny bridge, and below it evidently were the crew quarters and captain's cabin. She had a short, stubby mast, to which a single loading derrick was attached, rigged almost vertical. Right aft, above the stern, the ship's single lifeboat was slung.

She was rusty, her paint blistered by the sun in many places, flayed off by salt spray in others. Small and old and dowdy, she had the quality Shannon looked for—she was anonymous. There are thousands of such small freighters plying the coastal inshore trade from Haifa to Gibraltar, Tangier to Dakar, Monrovia to Simonstown. They all look much the same, attract no attention, and are seldom suspected of being up to anything beyond carrying small cargoes from port to port.

Semmler took Shannon on board. They found their way aft to where a companionway led down into the darkness of the crew quarters, and Semmler called. Then they went on down. They were met at the bottom by a muscular, hard-faced man in his mid-forties who nodded at Semmler and stared at Shannon.

Semmler shook hands with him and introduced him to Shannon. "Carl Waldenberg, the first mate."

Waldenberg nodded abruptly and shook hands. "You have come to look her over, our old *Toscana?*" he asked.

Shannon was pleased to note he spoke good, if accented, English and looked as if he might be prepared to run a cargo that did not appear on the manifest, if the price was right. He could understand the German seaman's interest in him. Semmler had already briefed him on the background, and he had told the crew his employer would be coming to look the ship over, with a view to buying. For the first mate, the new owner was an interesting person. Apart from anything else, Waldenberg had to be concerned about his own future.

The Yugoslav engineer was ashore somewhere, but they met the deckhand, a teenage Italian boy reading a girlie magazine on his bunk. Without waiting for the Italian captain's return, the first mate showed them both over the *Toscana*.

Shannon was interested in three things: the ability of the boat to accommodate another twelve men somewhere, even if they had to sleep out on deck in the open; the main hold and the possibility of secreting a few crates below the flooring down in the bilges; and the trustworthiness of the engines to get them as far as, say, South Africa.

Waldenberg's eyes narrowed slightly as Shannon asked his questions, but he answered them civilly. He could work out for himself that no fare-paying passengers were coming on board the *Toscana* for the privilege of sleeping wrapped in blankets on the hold-cover under the summer stars; nor was the *Toscana* going to pick up much freight for a run to the other end of Africa. Cargo sent that distance will be shipped in a bigger vessel. The advantage of a small coaster is that she can often load a cargo at very short notice and deliver it two days later a couple of hundred miles away. Big ships spend longer in port while turning around. But on a long run like that from the Mediterranean to South Africa, a bigger ship makes up in extra speed what she spent in port before setting out. For the exporter, the *Toscanas* of the sea have little attraction for trips of more than 500 miles.

After seeing the boat they went topside, and Waldenberg offered them bottles of beer, which they drank in the shade of the canvas awning set up behind the bridge. That was when the negotiations really started. The two Germans rattled away in their own language, the seaman evidently putting the questions and Semmler answering.

At last Waldenberg looked keenly at Shannon, looked back at Semmler, and nodded slowly. "Possibly," he said in English.

Semmler turned to Shannon and explained. "Waldenberg is interested why a man like yourself, who evidently does not know the charter cargo business, wants to buy a freighter for general cargo. I said you were a businessman and not a seaman. He feels the general cargo business is too risky for a rich man to want to hazard money on it, unless he has something specific in mind."

Shannon nodded. "Fair enough. Kurt, I want a word with you alone."

They went aft and leaned over the rail while Waldenberg drank his beer.

"How do you reckon this guy?" muttered Shannon.

"He's good," said Semmler without hesitation. "The captain is the owner also, and he is an old man and wants to retire. For this he has to sell the boat and retire on the money. That leaves a place vacant as captain.

I think Waldenberg would like it, and I agree with that. He has his master's license, and he knows this boat inside out. He also knows the sea. That leaves the question of whether he would run a cargo with a risk attached. I think he would, if the price is right."

"He suspects something already?" asked Shannon.

"Sure. Actually he thinks you are in the business of running illegal immigrants into Britain. He would not want to get arrested, but if the price is right, I think he would take the risk."

"Surely the first thing is to buy the ship. He can decide whether to stay on later. If he wants to quit, we can find another captain."

Semmler shook his head. "No. For one thing, we would have to tell him enough beforehand for him to know roughly what the job was. If he quit then, it would be a breach of security."

"If he learns what the job is and then quits, he only goes out one way," said Shannon and pointed his forefinger down at the oil-slicked water beneath the stern.

"There's one other point, Cat. It would be an advantage to have him on our side. He knows the ship, and if he decides to stay on he will try to persuade the captain to let us have the *Toscana,* rather than the local shipping company that is sniffing around. His opinion counts with the captain, because the old boy wants the *Toscana* to be in good hands, and he trusts Waldenberg."

Shannon considered the logic. It appealed to him. Time was running short, and he wanted the *Toscana.* The first mate might help him get it and could certainly run it. He could also recruit his own first mate and make sure he was a kindred spirit. Apart from that, there is one useful precept about bribing people: Never try to bribe them all; just buy the man who controls his own subordinates, and let him keep the rest in line. Shannon decided to make an ally of Waldenberg if he could. They strolled back to the awning.

"I'll be straight with you, mister," he told the German. "It's true if I bought the *Toscana* she would not be used for carrying peanuts. It's also true that there would be a slight element of risk as the cargo went on board. There would be no risk as the cargo went ashore, because the ship would be outside territorial waters. I need a good skipper, and Kurt Semmler tells me you're good. So let's get down to basics. If I get the *Toscana* I'll offer you the post of captain. You get a six-month guaranteed salary double your present one, plus a five-thousand-dollar bonus for the first shipment, which is due ten weeks from now."

Waldenberg listened without saying a word. Then he grinned and uncoiled himself from where he sat. He held out his hand. "Mister, you just got yourself a captain."

"Fine," said Shannon. "Except the first thing is to buy the boat."

"No problem," said Waldenberg. "How much would you spend for her?"

"What's she worth?" countered Shannon.

"What the market will take," answered Waldenberg. "The opposition has fixed its own ceiling at twenty-five thousand pounds and not a penny more."

"I'll go to twenty-six," said Shannon. "Will the captain take that?"

"Sure. Do you speak Italian?"

"No."

"Spinetti speaks no English. So let me interpret for you. I'll fix it with the old man. With that price, and me as captain, he'll let you have her. When can you meet him?"

"Tomorrow morning?" asked Shannon.

"Right. Tomorrow at ten, here on board."

They shook hands again, and the two mercenaries left.

Tiny Marc Vlaminck was contentedly at work in the garage he had rented, while the locked truck stood outside the door in the alley. Marc had closed and locked the garage door also, so he would not be disturbed while he worked. It was his second afternoon alone in the garage, and he had almost finished the first part of the job.

Along the rear wall of the garage he had erected a workbench of solid timber balks and equipped it with what he needed, the tools bought with Shannon's £500, as the truck and the rest of the necessary items had also been. Along one wall stood five large drums. They were bright green and bore the trading mark of the Castrol oil company. They were empty, which was the way Marc had bought them, quite cheap, from one of the big shipping firms in the port, and they had once contained heavy lubricating oil, as was plainly marked on each barrel.

From the first in the line, Marc had cut a circular disk out of the bottom, and the barrel stood up-ended, with the gaping hole showing upward and the screw cap at the top of the barrel on the floor. Around the hole was a 1½-inch flange, all that was left of the original base of the drum.

From the truck Marc had taken two crates of Schmeissers, and the twenty machine pistols were almost ready to enter their new hiding place. Each gun had been carefully mummified from end to end in sticky masking tape, and each had five magazines taped to the weapon itself. Following the wrapping process, each machine pistol had been slipped into a stout polyethylene envelope, which Marc had then sucked empty of air and tied securely at the neck with twine. After that, each had gone into a second, outer envelope of polyethylene, which was again tied at the neck. Such wrapping, he reckoned, should keep each weapon dry until it was next brought out into the air.

He took the twenty stubby packages and with two stout webbing straps rolled them all into one large bundle. This he inserted into the hole at the top of the drum and lowered it to the bottom. The drums were the usual 44-gallon or 200-liter type, and there was enough room in each for twenty Schmeissers and their accompanying magazines, with a little room to spare around the walls.

When the first bundle was secreted, Marc began the process of resealing the barrel. He had had fresh tinplate disks cut at a machine-shop in the port, and the first of these he fitted onto the top of the opened drum. It took half an hour of filing and rasping before the disk finally settled tight and neatly onto the drumhead, running right up to the rim in all places and nicely covering the 1½-inch overlap that remained of the previous end of the drum. Turning on his steam jet, powered by a gas bottle and burner, and taking a stick of soft solder, he began to "sweat" the tinplate to tinplate.

Metàl can be welded to metal and, to get the hardest join, it usually is. But a barrel that has once contained oil or ignitable fuel always retains a residue of film on the inner surface of the metal. When heated, as it must be by welding, the film turns to fumes and can easily explode very dangerously. "Sweating" a piece of tinplate onto another piece does not give the same strength of join but can be done with steam heat at a lower temperature. Provided the drums were not laid on their sides and juggled about, which would produce a powerful surge inside, they would hold together against a fair amount of handling.

When he had finished, Marc packed any remaining crevices with solder and, when all was cool, spray-painted the whole area with a color the exact replica of the color of Castrol oil drums the whole world over. After leaving the paint to dry, he eased the drum gently onto its new base, removed the screw cap at the top, took one of several large jerrycans standing ready, and began to pour in the lubricating oil.

The emerald-green liquid, thick, sticky, viscous, flowed into the open aperture and gurgled its way to the bottom of the drum. Slowly it filled up the air spaces between the sides of the drum and the bundle of machine pistols inside, slid noiselessly into every nook and cranny between the individual weapons, and impregnated the webbing and twine. Despite Marc's sucking before twisting the ends of each polyethylene bag tight shut, there were still bubbles of air inside the bags, trapped in magazines, barrels, and breeches. These offset the weight of the metal so that, as the barrel filled, the cumbersome bundle of guns became almost weightless, bobbing in the heavy oil like a body on the tide, and finally sinking slowly below the surface.

The Belgian used two jerrycans, and when the drum was full to the brim he estimated seven-tenths of the interior was taken up by the bundle, three-tenths by oil. He had poured 60 liters into the 200-liter drum. Finally he took a pencil flashlight and scanned the surface of the liquid. It gleamed back at him in the light, slick and green, with hints of gold. Of what lay at the bottom of the drum there was not a sign. He waited another hour before he checked around the base. Nothing had leaked; the new base of the barrel was sealed tight.

There was a jauntiness to him as he rolled open the garage doors and ran the truck back inside. He still had the wood of two flat crates with German markings to destroy, and a disk of now useless tinplate to throw away. The latter would go into the harbor, the former onto a bonfire. He knew now that the system worked and that he could convert one barrel every two days. He would be ready for Shannon by May 15, as promised. It was good to be back at work.

Dr. Ivanov was incensed, not for the first time and doubtless not for the last.

"The bureaucracy," he snapped at his wife across the breakfast table, "the sheer, incompetent, stultifying bureaucracy in this country is bloody unbelievable."

"I'm sure you're right, Mikhail Mikhailovich," his wife said soothingly as she poured two more cups of tea, strong, dark, and bitter as she knew her husband liked it. A placid and contented woman, she wished her volatile scientist husband would be careful with his outbursts, or at least confine them to the house.

"If the capitalist world knew how long it takes to

get a couple of nuts and bolts in this country, they'd die laughing."

"Shush, dear," she told him, stirring in the sugar for herself. "You must be patient."

It had been weeks since the director had summoned him to the pine-paneled office in the heart of the vast complex of laboratories and living quarters that made up the institute in the heart of the Siberian New Lands, to inform him that he would be in charge of a survey team being sent to West Africa and that he should take charge of the details himself.

It had meant forsaking a project that interested him deeply, and asking two of his junior colleagues to do the same. He had put in for the necessary equipment for an African climate, sending off his requirements to the half-dozen different supply directorates concerned, answering the petty queries as politely as he could, and waiting, always waiting, for the equipment to arrive and be crated. He knew from having been on a survey team in Ghana what working in the deep bush could entail.

"Give me the snow any time," he had told his team leader at the time. "I'm a cold-weather man."

But he had done it, on orders and on time. His team was ready, his equipment prepared and crated, down to the last water-purification tablet and camp bed. With luck, he had thought, he could be there, do the survey, and be back with his rock samples before the brief and glorious days of the Siberian summer had been eaten by the bitter autumn. The letter in his hand told him it was not to be.

It came from his director personally, and he bore the man no animosity, for he knew he was only passing on instructions from Moscow. Unfortunately the Transport Directorate there had ruled that the confidential nature of the survey forbade the use of public transport, but the Foreign Ministry did not feel able to instruct Aeroflot to put an airliner at the team's disposal. In view of continuing Middle East developments, neither would it be possible to use one of the military's Antonov freighters.

In consequence, ran the instructions from Moscow, it had been felt advisable, in view of the volume of equipment necessary for the survey, and the even greater volumes of samples that would have to be brought back from West Africa, to use maritime transport. It was decided that the team could be best transported by a Soviet freighter heading past the coast of West Africa toward the Far East. On its return, it would simply notify Ambassador Dobrovolsky that it had completed the survey, and, on instructions from him, a freighter heading back toward home would divert to take the three-man team and its crates of samples on board. Notification would be made in due course of the date and port of departure, and vouchers authorizing the use of state transport to the port of embarkation would be provided.

"The whole summer," shouted Ivanov as his wife helped him into his fur-collared coat and fur hat. "I'm going to miss the whole damned summer. And it'll be the rainy season down there."

Cat Shannon and Kurt Semmler were at the ship again the following morning and met Captain Alessandro Spinetti for the first time. He was a gnarled old man with a face like a walnut, a T-shirt over what was still a barrel of a chest, and a white-topped peaked cap aslant on his head.

The negotiating started then and there, before they adjourned to the office of the captain's lawyer, a certain Giulio Ponti, who ran his practice from one of the narrow side streets that lead backward and upward from the brawling, riotous Via Gramschi. To be fair to the signor, he was at least at the better end of the Via Gramschi, and the prostitutes in the bars they passed became progressively more presentable and expensive as they neared the lawyer's office.

Nothing to do with the business of the law moves faster than a snail's pace in Italy—and usually the pace of an arthritic snail.

The terms had been agreed on already. With Carl

Waldenberg translating, Captain Spinetti had accepted the package deal Shannon offered: £26,000 cash for the ship, to be paid in any currency or country the captain cared to name; his own first mate to be offered a minimum six-month contract as the new skipper, at a salary double that he had received as first mate; the chance for the other two men, the engineer and the deckhand, to stay on for six months at existing salary, or part company with severance pay of £500 for the deckhand and £1000 for the engineer.

Privately Shannon had already decided to persuade the deckhand to leave but to do all he could to keep the engineer, a surly Serbian who Waldenberg said could coax those engines to hell and back, who said nothing and asked less, and, best of all, whose papers were probably not in order and who therefore needed the job.

For tax reasons, the captain had long ago invested £100 in forming a small private company, Spinetti Maritimo Shipping Company. It had one hundred ordinary shares, of which he held ninety-nine and his lawyer, Signor Ponti, held one plus the position of company secretary. The sale of the MV *Toscana*, the company's only asset, was therefore linked to the sale of the shipping company, Spinetti Maritimo, which suited Shannon perfectly.

What did not suit him so well was that it took five days of meetings with the lawyer before the details were in order. And that was only for the first stage.

It was a week into May, and Day Thirty-One of Shannon's private calendar of a hundred days, before Ponti could start drawing up the contracts. As the deal was going through in Italy, and the *Toscana* was an Italian-registered and -resident vessel, the contract had to comply with Italian law, which is complicated. There were three contracts, that for the sale of Spinetti Maritimo and all her assets to Tyrone Holdings of Luxembourg, that which contracted Tyrone Holdings to offer Carl Waldenberg the job of captain for six months at the agreed salary, and the third guaranteeing the two other crewmen their existing salaries or severance pay. This process took four days, and Ponti's attitude was evidently that he was breaking all speed records, although all participant parties were anxious to complete the sale as soon as possible.

Big Janni Dupree was content with life that bright May morning when he emerged from the camping-goods store, having placed the last of his orders. He had put down a deposit for the required number of haversacks and sleeping bags. Delivery had been promised for the next day, and that same afternoon he intended to pick up two large cardboard boxes full of military-style knapsacks and berets from a warehouse in East London.

Three bulky consignments of miscellaneous equipment were already on their way to Toulon. The first should have arrived, he estimated, and the other two should be in transit. The fourth would be crated and put in the hands of the shipping agent the following afternoon, which left him a week ahead of time. The day before, he had received a letter from Shannon, telling him to vacate his London flatlet and fly to Marseilles on May 15. He was to check into a given hotel in the French port and wait there to be contacted. He liked precise instructions; they left little room for errors, and if anything did go wrong, it could not be his fault. He had bought his ticket and was eager for the remaining week to pass so that he could be off. It was good to be going into action again.

When Signor Ponti had finally drawn up the necessary papers, Cat Shannon dispatched a series of letters from his Genoa hotel. The first was to Johann Schlinker to tell him that the ship that would be engaged to carry the ammunition from Spain would be the MV *Toscana*, owned by Spinetti Maritimo Shipping Company of Genoa. He himself would need from

Schlinker details of where the arms shipment was supposed to be heading, so that the captain could draw up the appropriate manifest.

He included in his letter full details of the *Toscana* and had already checked with Lloyds Shipping List, to make sure the *Toscana* was listed there. He told Schlinker he would be contacting him within the next fifteen days.

Another letter went to Alan Baker, so that he could inform the Yugoslav authorities of the name and details of the carrying vessel, so the export license could be granted. Shannon already knew what the manifest would have to read. It would say the vessel was proceeding with her cargo from the Yugoslav port of embarkation to Lome, the capital of Togo.

He wrote a long letter to Mr. Stein as chairman of Tyrone Holdings, instructing him to prepare the papers for a board meeting of the company in his office four days hence, with two resolutions on the agenda. One would be for the company to buy Spinetti Maritimo and all its assets for £26,000 and the other would be to issue a further 26,000 bearer shares of £1 each to Mr. Keith Brown in exchange for a certified check for £26,000.

He dashed off a line to Marc Vlaminck, telling him the pick-up of the cargo in Ostend would have to be delayed until May 20, and another to Langarotti, putting back the Paris rendezvous to May 19.

Last, he sent Simon Endean a letter in London, asking him to meet Shannon in Luxembourg four days hence and to have at his disposal funds amounting to £26,000 for the purchase of the ship to carry the whole operation to the target area.

The evening of May 13 was soft and cool, and several hundred miles along the same coastline Jean-Baptiste Langarotti was driving his truck westward from Hyères on the last stretch into Toulon. He had the window down and sniffed the smell of conifer and *maquis* coming off the hills to his right. Like Dupree in London, who was preparing that evening to fly to Marseilles, like Vlaminck in Ostend, who was putting the final touches to his fifth and last oil drum of guns, Langarotti was content with life.

He had in the back of the truck the last two outboard engines, bought for cash and equipped with underwater exhaust attachments for silent running. He was on his way back to Toulon to deliver them to the bonded warehouse. Already in the warehouse of Maritime Duphot were three inflatable black dinghies, each crated and unopened, and the third engine. Also there were four large crates of assorted clothing that had arrived over the past two weeks from London in his own name. He too would be ready on time.

It was a pity he had had to move from his hotel. A chance encounter with an old underworld friend as he left the doorway three days ago had forced him to make a quick excuse and move out the following morning. He was now in a new hotel and would have informed Shannon of this, except he did not know where Shannon was. It made no difference. In forty-eight hours, on May 15, he would keep his rendezvous with his chief at the Plaza-Surène hotel in Paris.

The meeting in Luxembourg on May 14 was surprisingly short. Shannon was not present. That morning he had taken delivery from Endean of the £26,000 purchase price for the ship. Just before the board meeting he had met Mr. Stein in his office and handed over to him the documents for the sale of the Spinetti Maritimo Shipping Company and its vessel, the *Toscana*, along with a certified check for £26,000, payable to Tyrone Holdings SA.

Thirty minutes later, Mr. Stein emerged from the board meeting and handed Shannon 26,000 ordinary bearer shares in Tyrone Holdings. He also showed him an envelope which contained the documents concerning the sale of the ship to Tyrone, and Tyrone Holdings' check in the name of Signor Alessandro Spinetti. He sealed the envelope, which was addressed to Signor

Giulio Ponti at his Genoa office, and gave it to Shannon. The last document he handed over was a board decision to appoint Herr Kurt Semmler managing director of Spinetti Maritimo Shipping Company.

Two days later, in the Italian lawyer's office, the deal was finished. The check for the purchase of the *Toscana* had been cleared, and Tyrone Holdings legally owned 100 per cent of Spinetti Maritimo. In respect of this, Signor Ponti dispatched by registered mail the 100 ordinary shares in Spinetti Maritimo to the company office of Tyrone in Luxembourg. As a separate matter, Signor Ponti accepted a package from Shannon and locked it in his vault for safekeeping. He took two sample signatures from Shannon, in the name of Keith Brown, to be able later to certify the authenticity of any letter from Shannon regarding disposal of the package. Unknown to Ponti, the package contained the 26,994 controlling shares of Tyrone.

Carl Waldenberg received his captaincy and his six-month contract, and the Serbian engineer was kept on. One month's salary was paid to each man in cash, and the remaining five months' pay for each was placed in escrow in the hands of Signor Ponti.

The Italian deckhand was persuaded without difficulty to take his £500 severance pay, plus a bonus of £100, and left the crew. Semmler was installed as managing director.

Shannon had had a further £5000 transferred from Brugge to his credit in Genoa, and with this he had covered the two salaries of the crewmen who were remaining with the *Toscana*. Before he left Genoa on May 18, he handed the rest over to Semmler and gave him his briefing.

"How about the two replacements for the crew?"

"Waldenberg is seeing to it already," Semmler told him. "He reckons this port is crawling with men available for recruitment. He knows the place inside out. He also knows what we need. Good hard men, the kind who ask no questions and do what they are told, particularly if they know there is a bonus at the end of it. Don't worry, he'll have a good pair before the end of the week."

"Right. Fine. This is what I want. Get the *Toscana* ready for sea. A complete engine overhaul and servicing. Port dues paid up, papers in order with the new captain's name. Manifest prepared for Toulon to pick up general cargo for Morocco. Get her fueled and supplied. Take on enough stores for the crew plus a further dozen men. Extra fresh water, beer, wine, cigarettes. When she's ready, take her to Toulon. You have to be there by June first, at the latest. I'll be there with Marc, Jean-Baptiste, and Janni. Contact me through the shipping agent, Agence Maritime Duphot. They're in the port area. I'll see you then. Good luck."

17

Jean-Baptiste Langarotti was alive, in part, at least, because of his ability to sense danger before it came looking for him. The first day he reported to the Paris hotel, he just sat quietly at the appointed hour in the residents' lounge and read a magazine. He gave Shannon two hours, but the mercenary leader did not show up.

On the off chance, the Corsican inquired at the reception desk, for although Shannon had said nothing about staying the night, it might be he had arrived early and taken a room. The reception clerk checked the register and informed Langarotti there was no Monsieur Brown from London in the hotel. Langarotti assumed Shannon had been delayed and would make the rendezvous at the same hour on the next day.

So the Corsican was there, sitting in the residents' lounge, at the same hour on May 16. There was still no Shannon, but there was something else. Twice the same staff member of the hotel peeked into the room and vanished as soon as Langarotti looked up. After another two hours, Shannon still not having come, he left the hotel again. As he passed down the street he had a glimpse of a man in the corner doorway showing a bizarre interest in the window into which he was staring with such fixed intensity. The shop window was full of women's corsets. Langarotti had the feeling the man was one component that did not fit into the pattern of that quiet back street on a spring morning.

Over the next twenty-four hours the Corsican began to sniff the wind in the bars of Paris where mercenaries forgather, using his old contacts of the Corsican Union in the Paris underworld. He continued to go to the hotel each morning, and on the fifth morning, that of May 19, Shannon was there.

He had arrived the previous evening by plane from Genoa and Milan, and had stayed the night at the hotel. He seemed in good spirits and told his colleague over coffee in the lounge that he had bought a ship for their operation.

"No problems?" asked Langarotti.

Shannon shook his head. "No problems."

"But here in Paris we have a problem."

Unable to strop his knife in such a public place, the small Corsican sat with his hands idle in his lap. Shannon put down his coffee cup. He knew if Langarotti referred to problems, that meant trouble.

"Such as?" he asked softly.

"There's a contract on you," said Langarotti.

The two men sat in silence for a while, as Shannon considered the news. His friend did not interrupt. He usually answered questions only when they were asked.

"Do you know who placed it?" asked Shannon.

"No. Nor who has taken it up. But it's high, about five thousand dollars."

"Recently?"

"The word is, the contract was placed some time in the past six weeks. It seems uncertain whether the contractor, who must be Paris-based, is the one who placed it, or whether he is acting for someone behind the scenes. The word is, only a good hit-man would take a contract on you, or a stupid one. But someone has taken it. Inquiries are being made about you."

Shannon cursed silently. He had little doubt the Corsican was right. He was too careful a man to go bandying unchecked information like that around. He tried to think back to any incident that might have given rise to the placing of a contract on his head. The trouble was, there were so many possible reasons, some of which he knew he could not even guess.

Methodically he began to go over the possibilities he could envisage. Either the contract stemmed from something to do with the present operation, or it came from a motive that lay further back. He considered the first option first.

Had there been a leak? Had some government agency received a whiff of intelligence that he was mounting a coup in Africa and decided to stop it permanently by snuffing out the operations commander? The thought even crossed his mind that Sir James Manson had learned of his ewe lamb's multiple ravishing —if that was the word for such an experienced Lolita. He rejected all three possibilities. It could be that he had offended someone in the murky world of the black-market arms dealers, who had decided to settle the score the hard way while remaining in the background. But such a move would have been preceded by an argument over a deal, a squabble over money, a stand-up row, or threats. There had been none.

He turned his memory further back, to the wars and the fights gone by. The trouble was, one never knew if one might at some time have angered a big organization without meaning to. Perhaps one of the men he had gunned down had secretly been an agent of the CIA or the KGB. Both organizations bore long grudges and, being peopled by the world's most savagely unprincipled men, insisted on settling scores even when there was no pragmatic motive, but simply for revenge. He was aware the CIA still had an open-ended hit contract out on Bruce Rossiter, who had shot an American in a bar in Léopoldville because the man was staring at him. The American, it had later turned out, was one of the horde of local CIA men, though Rossiter had not known this. His ignorance did not help him. The contract still went out, and Rossiter was still running.

The KGB was as bad. It sent assassins across the world to liquidate fugitives, foreign agents who had hurt the KGB and had been blown for all to see, and were thus unprotectable by their own former employers; and the Russians needed no practical motive, like the information in the man's head that he had not yet spilled. They did it just for revenge.

That left the French SDECE and the British SIS. The French could have taken him a hundred times over the past two years and made sure it happened in the jungles of Africa. Moreover, they would not place the deal with a Paris contractor and risk a leak. They had their own men, good ones, on the staff. The British were even less likely. Legalistic to the end, they would have to get permission from almost Cabinet level for a hit and used the method only in the direst emergency, to prevent a vital leak, to create a nasty example to encourage others to have confidence in the Service, or occasionally to even a score where one of their own men had been knowingly knocked over by an identifiable killer. Shannon was sure he had never hit a white-carded Britisher, and that left the motive of preventing an embarrassment. The Russians and French would kill for that reason, but not the British. They had left Stephen Ward alive to stand trial and nearly ruin the Macmillan government; they had left Philby alive after he was blown, and Blake too; in France or Russia both traitors would have entered the road-accident statistics.

That left a private firm. The Corsican Union? No, Langarotti could not have stuck by him if it had been the Union. So far as he knew, he had never upset the Mafia in Italy or the Syndicate in America. That took the matter back to a private individual with a private grudge. If it was not a government agency and not a big private firm, it had to be an individual. But who, for God's sake?

Langarotti was still watching him, waiting for his reaction. Shannon kept his face still, his air bored.

"Do they know I'm here in Paris?"

"I think so. I believe they know about this hotel. You always stay here. It's a mistake. I was here four days ago, as you had said—"

"Didn't you get my letter, putting the meeting back to today?"

"No. I had to move from my Marseilles hotel a week ago."

"Oh. Go on."

"There was someone watching the hotel the second time I came. I had already asked for you by the name of Brown. So I think the leak came from inside this hotel. The man was watching yesterday and today."

"So I change hotels," said Shannon.

"You might shake him. You might not. Someone knows the name of Keith Brown. They could find you elsewhere. How much do you have to be in Paris over the next few weeks?"

"Quite a bit," admitted Shannon. "I have to go through several times, and we have to bring Marc's stuff down from Belgium to Toulon through Paris in two days."

Langarotti shrugged. "They might not find you. We don't know how good they are, or how many of them. Or who. But they might find you a second time. Then there would be problems, perhaps with the police."

"I can't afford that. Not now. Not with Marc's consignment sitting in the truck," said Shannon.

He was a reasonable man and would much prefer to have negotiated with the one who had placed the contract on him. But whoever it was had chosen to do it the other way.

Shannon would still have tried to talk to the man, but first he had to identify him. There was only one man who could do that for him: the man who had taken the contract to kill him. He put this to the Corsican, who nodded somberly.

"Yes, *mon ami,* I think you're right. We have to take the hit-man. But first he must be lured out."

"Will you help me, Jean-Baptiste?"

"Of course," said Langarotti. "Whoever it is, it is not the Union. It is not my people, so I am your man."

They spent close to an hour with a street map of Paris on the table in front of them. Then Langarotti left.

During the day he parked his Marseilles-registered truck at an agreed prearranged spot. In the late afternoon Shannon went to the reception desk and asked the way to a well-known restaurant a mile away. He was within earshot of the hotel clerk who had been described to him by Langarotti. The chief receptionist told him where the restaurant was.

"Within walking distance?" asked Shannon.

"But certainly, m'sieur. About fifteen minutes, maybe twenty."

Shannon thanked him and used the desk telephone to make a reservation in the name of Brown for ten o'clock that night. He did not leave the hotel all day.

At nine-forty exactly, carrying his overnight bag in one hand and a light raincoat over the other arm, he left the hotel and turned up the street in the direction for the restaurant. The route he took was not direct. It led down two streets even smaller than the one in which the hotel was situated. As he walked, he left the other pedestrians behind and entered streets in the first arrondissement which were dimly lit and where no passers-by came his way. He dawdled, passing the time staring into lighted shop windows, killing time until the hour of his restaurant reservation was long past. He never looked back. Sometimes, in the quiet, he thought he could hear the soft slap of a moccasin somewhere up the dim-lit streets behind him. Whoever was there, it was not Langarotti. The Corsican could move without disturbing the dust.

It was past eleven when he reached the dark, black alley he had been told was there. It led to his left and had no lights in it at all. The far end was blocked by a row of bollards, making it into a cul-de-sac. On each side the walls were blank and tall. Any light that might have entered the alley from the other end was muted by the bulk of the French truck that stood parked there, empty but with its rear doors open. Shannon walked toward the truck's gaping back and, when he reached it, turned.

Like most fighting men, he always preferred to face danger rather than knowing it was somewhere behind. He knew from past experience that, even when moving backward, it is safer always to face the danger source. At least, then, you can watch it. Moving up the alley with his back to the entrance, he had felt the hairs on his neck prickling. If the psychology was wrong, he could be very dead. But the psychology had been right. Keeping to empty streets, the man behind him had stayed well back, hoping for just such an opportunity as now presented itself.

Shannon tossed his bag and raincoat to the ground and stared at the hulking shadow that blocked the vertical streak of lamplight from the end of the alley. He waited patiently. He hoped there would be no sound, not in the center of Paris. The shadow paused, assessed the situation, and evidently checked Shannon for a gun. But the sight of the open truck reassured the hit-man. He assumed Shannon had simply parked it there for discretion's sake and had been all this time returning to it.

The shadow in the alley moved softly forward. Shannon could make out the right arm, out of the raincoat pocket now, held forward, holding something. The face was in shadow, the whole man was a silhouette, but he was big. His form stood dead center in the cobbled cul-de-sac, stopped now, raising his gun. He paused for several seconds as he aimed, then slowly lowered it again, straight-armed, down to his side. It was almost as if he had changed his mind.

Still staring at Shannon from the shadow-black face, the man slowly leaned forward and went onto his knees. Some shots do this to steady themselves. The gunman cleared his throat, leaned forward again, and placed both his hands, knuckles down, on the cobbles in front of him. The metal of the Colt .45 clattered on the stones. Slowly, like a Moslem facing Mecca at the hour of prayer, the gunman bowed his head, staring for the first time in twenty seconds not at Shannon but at the cobbles. There was a light splashing sound, as of a liquid running fast onto cobbles, and finally the man's arms and thighs gave out. He slumped forward into the puddle of his own aortic blood and went to sleep, quite gently, like a child.

Shannon was still standing against the doors of the truck. With the man down, a shaft of lamplight came from the lit end of the alley. It glistened on the polished black sheen of the four-inch bone knife-handle that protruded upward from the mackintoshed back of the man on the pavement, slightly left of center, between the fourth and fifth ribs.

The Cat looked up. There was another figure against the lamplight, small, spare, motionless, still standing fifteen yards from the body at the point where it had made its throw. Shannon hissed, and Langarotti padded noiselessly down the cobbles.

"I thought you'd left it too late," said Shannon.

"Non. Never too late. He could not have squeezed the trigger of that Colt at any time since you emerged from the hotel."

The rear of the truck was already laid with a large sheet of tough industrial plastic over a canvas tarpaulin. The tarpaulin had loopholes all around the edge for easy lashing into a bundle, and plenty of cord and bricks were stacked at the far end. Each taking an arm and a leg, the two men swung the body up and inward. Langarotti climbed in to retrieve his knife, while Shannon shut the doors. He heard them securely locked from the inside.

Langarotti climbed into the front seat and started up. Slowly he backed out, down the alley and into the street. As he swung the truck around before driving off, Shannon approached the driver's window.

"Have you had a good look at him?"

"Sure."

"You know him?"

"Yes. Name of Thomard, Raymond. In the Congo once for a short period, more of a city type. Professional hit-man. But not quality. Not the sort one of the big contractors would use. More likely to work for his own boss."

"Who's that?" asked Shannon.

"Roux," said Langarotti. "Charles Roux."

Shannon swore quietly and viciously. "That bastard, that stupid, ignorant, incompetent fool. He could have fouled up a whole operation just because he wasn't invited to come in on it."

He fell silent and thought for a while. Roux had to be discouraged, but in a way that would keep him out of the Zangaro affair once and for all.

"Hurry up," said the Corsican, the engine still running. "I want to get this customer put to bed before anyone comes along."

Shannon made up his mind and spoke urgently and rapidly for several seconds.

Langarotti nodded. "All right. Actually, I like it. It should fix that bugger for a long time. But it will cost extra. Five thousand francs."

"Done," said Shannon. "Get moving, and meet me outside the Porte de la Chapelle métro station in three hours."

They met Marc Vlaminck for lunch in the small South Belgian town of Dinant by agreement. Shannon had called him the previous day and given him the instructions and the rendezvous. Tiny Marc had kissed Anna good-by that morning, and she had given him his lovingly packed suitcase of clothes and his snack box with half a loaf, some butter, and a hunk of cheese for midmorning break. As usual, she had told him to take care of himself.

He had driven the truck, carrying in the back five 200-liter drums of engine oil by Castrol, across Belgium without being stopped. There was no reason why he should be. His license was in order, as were the permit for the truck and the insurance.

As the three men sat over lunch at a main-street café, Shannon asked the Belgian, "When do we go over?"

"Tomorrow morning, just before sun-up. It's the quietest time. Did you two sleep last night?"

"Nope."

"You'd better get some rest," said Marc. "I'll watch over both trucks. You can have till midnight."

Charles Roux was another one who was tired that day. All the previous evening, since he had received the telephone call from Henri Alain about Shannon walking to his restaurant meal, he had waited for news. There had been none by midnight, when there should have been a call from Thomard to say it was all over. There had been none by three in the morning and none by sunrise.

Roux was unshaven and puzzled. He knew Thomard was no match for Shannon on equal terms, but he was sure the Irishman would be taken in the back as he walked through one of the quieter streets on his way to the evening meal.

At midmorning, as Langarotti and Shannon in their empty truck were passing without trouble into Belgium north of Valenciennes, Roux finally slipped on a pair of trousers and a shirt and took the elevator five floors down to the lobby to check his mailbox.

There did not seem to be anything wrong with the lock of his mailbox, a container some twelve inches tall, nine wide, and nine deep, screwed to the wall of the lobby along with a score more for the other tenants. There was no indication that it had been opened, but of course a clever burglar would have picked the lock.

Roux used his personal key to unlock the door and swung it open.

He stood for about ten seconds without moving. Nothing changed about him except the normal ruddy color of his face, which slid into a chalky gray. Still staring, mesmerized, he began to mutter, *"Mon Dieu, O mon Dieu . . ."* over and over again like an incantation. His stomach turned over; he felt as he had at the moment in the Congo when he had heard the Congolese soldiers questioning his identity as he lay inside the bandages on a stretcher while John Peters smuggled him out from certain death. He felt he wanted to urinate, run, but could only sweat with fear. With an air of almost sleepy sadness, eyes half closed, lips gummed together, the head of Raymond Thomard gazed back at him from inside the mailbox.

Roux was not squeamish, but he was no lionheart either. He closed the box, went back to his flat, and started on the brandy bottle, for medicinal purposes only. He needed a lot of medicine.

Alan Baker emerged from the office of the Yugoslav state arms company into the bright sunshine of Belgrade, feeling well pleased with the way things were going. On receiving Shannon's down payment of $7200 and the End User Certificate, he had gone to a licensed arms dealer for whom he had occasionally done work in the past on a subcontractual level. As in the case of Schlinker, the man had felt the amount of weaponry and money involved in the proposed deal to be derisory, but he had yielded to Baker's argument that if the buyers were satisfied with the first consignment they might well return for more, a lot more.

So he had given Baker his fiat to fly to Belgrade and make application for the purchase, using the certificate from Togo, duly filled out with the appropriate names, and with a letter of authority from the dealer appointing Baker his representative.

It meant Baker would lose a part of his cut, but it was the only way he could be received in Belgrade, and for such a small deal he had in any case allowed a mark-up of 100 per cent on the buying price of the arms.

His five days of talks with Mr. Pavlovič had been

fruitful and had included a visit to the state warehouse, in which he had selected the two mortar tubes and two bazookas. The ammunition for both was standard and supplied in crates of twenty bazooka rockets and ten mortar bombs.

The Yugoslavs had accepted the Togolese End User Certificate without demur, and although Baker, the licensed dealer, and probably Mr. Pavlovič, must be aware the certificate was just a piece of paper, the air was maintained that the government of Togo was eagerly awaiting the chance to buy Yugoslavia's weaponry for testing. Mr. Pavlovič had also required full payment in advance, and Baker had had to pay over what remained of the $7200 Shannon had given him, after his travel costs, plus $1000 of his own. He was confident Shannon's balance of another $7200 would reimburse him and, even after the licensed dealer had taken his cut, leave $4000 for Baker's pocket.

His morning's talks had confirmed that the goods would be granted an export license and sent by army lorries to a bonded warehouse at the port of Ploce in the northwest, close to the holiday resorts of Dubrovnik and Split.

It was here that the *Toscana* should dock to take the shipment aboard, any time after June 10. With a light heart, Baker took the next flight for Munich and Hamburg.

Johann Schlinker was in Madrid that morning, May 20. He had Telexed the full details of the deal in 9mm. ammunition that he wanted to put through to his Madrid partner, a Spanish national, a full month earlier, and had later flown to the Spanish capital himself with his Iraqi End User Certificate, as soon as he had received Shannon's $26,000 in full payment.

The Spanish formalities were more complicated than those Alan Baker had discovered in Belgrade. Two applications were necessary, the first to buy the hardware, the second to export it. The application to buy had been made three weeks earlier and over the past twenty days had been vetted by the three departments of state in Madrid who concern themselves with such matters. First the Finance Ministry had been needed to confirm that the full purchase price of $18,000 had been received into the appropriate bank in hard currency. A few years earlier, only United States dollars had been acceptable, but more recently Madrid was more than happy to take German marks.

The second department was the Foreign Ministry. Its job had been to confirm that the buyer country was not a state to which Spain was opposed. There was no problem with Iraq, since the great bulk of Spanish arms exports habitually go to the Arabs, with whom Spain has always maintained close and friendly relations. The Foreign Ministry had no hesitation in confirming its approval of Iraq as a recipient of Spanish 9mm. ball ammunition.

Last, the Defense Ministry had been required to confirm that nothing in the proposed sale was on the secret list or among the categories of arms not for export. With simple small-arms ammunition, this too had been no problem.

Although there had been no sticky problems with such a consignment, it had taken eighteen days for the papers to pass through the three departments, accumulating more paperwork as they went, until the final dossier emerged with the stamp of approval. At this point the crates of ammunition were taken from the CETME factory and stored in a warehouse of the Spanish army on the outskirts of Madrid. From this point the Army Ministry took over, and notably the head of its arms-export section, Colonel Antonio Salazar.

Schlinker had come to Madrid to present personally the application for an export license. He had been in possession of the full details of the MV *Toscana* on his arrival, and the seven-page questionnaire had been filled out and presented. Back in his room in the Hotel Mindanao, the German expected no problems here either. The *Toscana* was a clean ship, small but belonging to a registered shipping company, Spinetti Maritimo, as Lloyds Shipping List confirmed. According to the application form, she would wish to berth in Valencia between June 16 and June 20, take the shipment on board, and proceed straight to Latakia on the coast of Syria, where the consignment would be handed over to the Iraqis for trucking to Baghdad. The export license should take no longer than another two weeks, and then application would be made for a movement order, permitting the crates to be taken from the army warehouse and detailing an army officer to mount escort with ten soldiers as far as Valencia quayside. The latter precaution, brought into force over the previous three years, was to prevent any risk of hijacking by the Basque terrorists. The last thing the government of El Caudillo wanted was to see Madrid's bullets being used against the Guardia Civil in Coruna.

As Schlinker prepared to leave for Hamburg, he reflected that his Madrid partner was perfectly capable of ensuring that the liaison with the Army Ministry remained at a cordial level and that the crates would be waiting in Valencia for the arrival of the *Toscana* on time.

In London a third and seemingly unconnected meeting took place. Over the past three weeks Mr. Harold Roberts, the nominee director of Bormac Trading Company, controlling 30 per cent of the company stock, had been cultivating the chairman, Major Luton. He had several times taken him to lunch and once visited him at his Guildford home. They had become quite friendly.

Throughout their talks, Roberts had made it clear that if the company were to get off the ground and go back into business, whether in rubber or in some other area of trading, a large injection of fresh capital would be needed. Major Luton could well see that. When the time was ripe, Mr. Roberts proposed to the chairman that the company should make a new one-for-two issue of shares—a total, therefore, of half a million of new stock.

At first the major was aghast at the boldness of the move, but Mr. Roberts assured him that the bank whose nominee he was would find the necessary fresh finance. Mr. Roberts added that in the event that any of the new shares were not taken up by existing shareholders or new shareholders, the Zwingli Bank would take up the rest at full value on behalf of its customers.

The clinching argument was that when news of the fresh share issue broke on the market, the price of Bormac ordinaries would be bound to rise, perhaps by as much again as their present value, which then stood at one shilling and threepence. Major Luton thought of his own hundred thousand shares and agreed. As is so often the case when a man has once weakened, he then went along with Mr. Roberts's proposal without further demur.

The new director pointed out that the pair of them could form a quorum and hold a directors' meeting able to pass a resolution binding on the company. At the major's insistence, a letter was still sent to the other four directors, simply stating that it was intended to hold a board meeting to discuss company business, including the possibility of making a share issue.

In the event, only the company secretary, the City solicitor, turned up. The resolution was passed and the announcement of the new share issue posted. There was no need for a meeting of shareholders, as in the long-distant past an increase in capital had been authorized but never carried out.

Existing shareholders were given first choice to buy the stock and were sent allotment letters for the appropriate number of new shares. They were also given the right to apply for any shares not subscribed by those to whom they were originally offered.

Within a week, papers and checks signed by Messrs. Adams, Ball, Carter, and Davies, forwarded by the Zwingli Bank, were in the company secretary's hands.

Each man opted to buy fifty thousand of the new shares, including those originally allotted to him because of his existent holdings.

The shares had to be issued at par, which was four shillings each, and, with the existing shares standing at less than a third of that price, it was an unattractive offer. Two City speculators noticed the press announcement and tried to offer to underwrite the issue, assuming there had to be something in the wind. They would have succeeded but for Mr. Roberts. His own bid on behalf of the Zwingli Bank was already in, wishing to buy any shares remaining at the closing of the offer that had not been bought by existing shareholders or Bormac.

Some idiot in Wales agreed to buy a thousand shares, even at the too high price, and another three thousand were bought by eighteen other shareholders scattered around the country, who apparently could not do basic arithmetic or were clairvoyant. Mr. Roberts, as a nominee director, was not in a position to buy for himself, since he owned no stock. But at three in the afternoon of May 20, the closing date of the offer, he subscribed for all the 296,000 remaining unsold shares in the name of the Zwingli Bank, which in turn was buying these on behalf of two of its customers. Their names happened to be Edwards and Frost. Again the bank used designated accounts of its nominee company.

In no case were the rules of the Companies Act regarding disclosure broken. Messrs. Adams, Ball, Carter, and Davies each owned 75,000 of the shares from their first purchase and 50,000 from their second. But as the number of shares now in circulation had risen from 1 million to 1.5 million, each man held less than 10 per cent and was able to remain anonymous. Messrs. Edwards and Frost each owned 148,000 shares, just under the 10-per-cent limit.

What did not appear in public, or even to the directors, was that Sir James Manson owned 796,000 shares in Bormac, an overwhelming majority. He controlled, through Martin Thorpe, the six nonexistent shareholders who had bought so heavily. They could, through Martin Thorpe, direct the Zwingli Bank in its dealings with the company, and the bank controlled his contracted servant, Mr. Roberts. Using their proxies, the six invisible men behind the Zwingli Bank, operating through Harold Roberts, could make the company do anything they wished.

It had cost Sir James Manson £60,000 to buy the original shares, and £100,000 to buy up the bulk of the new issue of half a million. But when the shares reached the predicted £100 each, which he was sure they would do after the chance "discovery" of the Crystal Mountain in the heart of Bormac's Zangaran franchise, he stood to make £80 million.

Mr. Roberts was a contented man when he left the Bormac offices after hearing how many shares his six Swiss-based stockholders had been allotted. He knew that when he placed the share certificates in the hands of Dr. Martin Steinhofer, there would be a handsome bonus for him. Although he was not a poor man, he was relieved to know his retirement in comfort was secured.

In Dinant, Shannon and Langarotti woke from their slumbers shortly after dark had fallen, to find Marc shaking them. Both were stretched out in the back of the empty French truck.

"Time to be going," said the Belgian.

Shannon looked at his watch. "I thought you said before sunrise," he grumbled.

"That's when we go over," said Marc. "We ought to get these trucks out of town before they become too noticeable. We can park by the roadside for the rest of the night."

They did park, but none of the men slept any more. Instead they smoked and played cards with the pack Vlaminck kept in the glove compartment of his truck. Sitting under the trees by the Belgian roadside in the darkness, waiting for the dawn, feeling the night air on their faces, each could almost think he was back in the African bush again, about to go into action, except for the flashing lights through the trees where cars headed south on the road to France.

As they sat through the wee small hours, tired of playing cards, too tensed to sleep, each fell back into his old habits. Tiny Marc munched the remnants of the bread and cheese his girl, Anna, had made for him. Langarotti stropped his knife blade a little sharper. Shannon gazed at the stars and whistled softly.

18

There is no great technical difficulty in running an illegal consignment across the Belgian-French border in either direction, and that includes a quantity of black-market arms.

Between the sea at La Panne and the junction with Luxembourg near Longwy, this border sprawls for miles, and most of it in the southeast corner is through heavily wooded hunting country. Here the border is crossed by scores of side roads and tracks through the forest, and by no means all of them are manned.

Both governments seek to establish some kind of control, using what they call *douanes volantes,* or flying customs. These are units of customs men who pick a track or side road at random and set up a border post. At the existing customs points, one may reasonably assume that one vehicle in ten is likely to be stopped and examined. On the unmanned roads, if the flying customs on either side happen to be sitting there for the day, every vehicle going through gets a check. One can take one's choice.

The third alternative is to pick a road where there is definitely no customs post set up, and drive straight through. This method of running cargoes through the frontier is particularly favored by the smugglers of French champagne, who see no reason why this drink connected with mirth and gaiety should receive the attentions of the very unhumorous Belgian import duty. As a bar-owner, Marc Vlaminck knew about this route. It is called the champagne run.

Running south from Namur, the old fortress town of Belgium, following the line of the river Meuse, one comes first to Dinant, and from here the road runs almost due south over the border to the French town called Givet. Along this road there is a finger of French territory that juts upward into Belgium's underbelly, and this corridor of France is surrounded on three sides by Belgian territory. It is also a hunting forest and intersected by scores of tracks and paths. The main road from Dinant to Givet has a customs post on it—in fact, one Belgian post and one French, set four hundred yards apart but in sight of each other.

Shortly before dawn, Marc got out his maps and briefed Shannon and Jean-Baptiste on what he needed to be sure of getting across the border unspotted. When both men understood exactly what was required, they set off in convoy, the Belgian truck in front, driven by Marc, the other two in the French truck, two hundred yards behind.

South from Dinant the road is fairly well built up, with a series of villages whose outskirts almost connect with each other. In the predawn darkness these hamlets were quiet and obscure. At kilometer six, south of Dinant, there is a side road leading to the right, and this Marc took. It was the last they saw of the river Meuse. For four and a half kilometers they ran through undulating country of even-sized, rounded hills, thickly wooded and covered in the lush leafage of late May. The run was parallel to the border and into the heart of hunting country. Without warning, Vlaminck swung his truck off to the left, heading again toward the frontier, and after three to four hundred yards he pulled to the side. He climbed down and walked back to the French truck.

"Make it snappy," he said. "I don't want to wait here for long. It's too obvious where I'm heading for, with Ostend number plates." He pointed down the road.

"The border is down there at one and a half kilometers exactly. I'll give you twenty minutes while I pretend to change a tire. Then I get back to Dinant and we meet at the café."

The Corsican nodded and let in the clutch. The drill is, if either the Belgian or French customs men have set up a flying barricade, the first vehicle stops and allows itself to be searched. Being clean, it then proceeds south to rejoin the main road, heads into Givet, turns north, and returns via the fixed customs post to Dinant. If either customs post is in operation, it cannot return back up the road within twenty minutes.

At kilometer one and a half, Shannon and Langarotti saw the Belgian post. At each side of the road a vertical steel upright had been placed, embedded in concrete. Beside the right-hand one was a small glass-and-wood booth, where the customs men could shelter while drivers passed their papers through the window. If it was occupied, there would be a red-and-white striped pole, supported by both uprights, blocking the road. There was none.

Langarotti cruised slowly past, while Shannon scanned the booth. Not a sign. The French side was trickier. For half a kilometer the road wound between the flanks of the hills, lost to sight from the Belgian posts. Then came the French border. No posts, no booth. Just a parking area on the left, where the French customs car always parks. There was nothing there. They had been gone five minutes. Shannon gestured to the Corsican to go around two more corners, but there was nothing in sight. A glimmer of light showed in the east over the trees.

"Turn her around," snapped Shannon. "*Allez.*"

Langarotti pulled the truck into a tight turn, almost made it, backed up, and was off toward Belgium like a cork from a bottle of the very best champagne. From then on, time was precious. They shot past the French parking space, through the Belgian posts, and less than a mile later saw the bulk of Marc's waiting truck. Langarotti flashed his lights, two short, one long, and Marc gunned his engine into life. A second later he was past them, racing through to France.

Jean-Baptiste turned around more leisurely and followed. If Marc drove fast, he could be through the danger area within four minutes, even heavily laden with a ton of cargo. If any customs men hove in sight during the vital five minutes, it was bad luck. Marc would try to bluff it out, say he had got lost, hope the oil barrels stood up to a thorough checking.

There were no officials there, even on the second run. South of the French parking space is a five-kilometer stretch with no turnings. Even here the French *gendarmerie* sometimes patrols, but there was nothing that morning. Langarotti caught up with the Belgian truck and followed it at six hundred feet. After three miles Marc turned off to the right at another parking area, and for three more miles wended his way through more back roads until he finally emerged onto a sizable main road. There was a signpost by the roadside. Shannon saw Marc Vlaminck wave his arm out of the window and point to it. The sign said GIVET in the direction from which they had come, and pointed the way they were going with the word REIMS. A muted cheer came wafting back from the truck in front.

They did the change-over on a hard concrete parking lot next to a truckers' café just south of Soissons. The two trucks, open-doored, were backed up tight against each other, and Marc eased the five barrels from the Belgian truck to the French one. It would have taken Shannon and Langarotti together all their strength, the more so as the loaded truck was squashed on its springs, so the floors of the two vehicles were not at the same height. There was a 6-inch step-up to get into the empty truck. Marc managed it on his own, gripping each barrel at the top in huge hands and swinging it in arcs while balancing it on its lower rim.

Jean-Baptiste went to the café and returned with a breakfast of long, crisp baguette loaves, cheese, fruit, and coffee. Shannon had no knife, so they all used Marc's. Langarotti would never use his knife for eating. He had his finer feelings. It would dishonor the knife to use it on orange peel.

Just after ten they set off again. The drill was different. The Belgian truck, being old and slow, was soon driven into a gravel pit and abandoned, the license plates and windshield sticker being taken off and thrown into a stream. The truck had originally been of French make anyway. After that, the three proceeded together. Langarotti drove. It was legally his truck. He was licensed. If stopped, he would say he was driving five barrels of lubricating oil south to his friend who owned a farm and three tractors outside Toulon. The other two were hitchhikers he had picked up.

They left the A1 autoroute, took the peripheral road around Paris, and picked up the A6 south to Lyon, Avignon, Aix, and Toulon.

Just south of Paris they saw the sign to the right pointing to Orly Airport. Shannon climbed out, and they shook hands.

"You know what to do?" he asked.

They both nodded.

"Keep her under cover and safe till you get to Toulon."

"Don't worry, no one will find this little baby when I've hidden her," said Langarotti.

"The *Toscana* is due in by June first at the latest, maybe before. I'll be with you before then. You know the rendezvous? Then good luck."

He hefted his bag and walked away as the truck headed south. At the nearby garage he used the telephone, called a cab from the airport, and was driven there an hour later. Paying cash, he bought his single ticket to London and was home in St. John's Wood by sundown. Of his hundred days, he had used up forty-six.

Although he sent Endean a telegram on his arrival home, it was a Sunday, and twenty-four hours went by before Endean called him at the flat. They agreed to meet on Tuesday morning.

It took him an hour to explain to Endean all that had happened since they last met. He also explained that he had used up all the money both in the cash sum he had retained in London and in the Belgian account.

"What's the next stage?" asked Endean.

"I have to return to France within five days at the latest and supervise the loading of the first section of the cargo onto the *Toscana*," said Shannon. "Everything about the shipment is legal except what's in those oil barrels. The four separate crates of assorted uniforms and webbing should pass without any problem on board, even if examined by customs. The same goes for the nonmilitary stuff bought in Hamburg. Everything in that section is the sort of stuff a ship might normally take on as ship's stores: distress flares, night glasses, and so on.

"The inflatable dinghies and outboard engines are for shipping to Morocco—at least, that's what the manifest will say. Again, it's perfectly legal. The five oil drums have to go aboard as ship's stores. The quantity is rather excessive, but there shouldn't be any problem despite that."

"And if there is?" asked Endean. "If Toulon customs men examine those barrels too closely?"

"We're busted," said Shannon simply. "The ship impounded, unless the captain can show he hasn't a clue what was going on. The exporter arrested. The operation wrecked."

"Bloody expensively," observed Endean.

"What do you expect? The guns have got to go on board somehow. The oil barrels are about the best possible way. There was always that risk involved."

"You could have bought the submachine guns legally, through Spain," said Endean.

"I could," Shannon conceded, "but there would then have been a good chance the order would have been refused. The guns and the ammo together make a matching pair. That would have looked like a special

order to outfit one company of men—in other words,
a small operation. Madrid might have turned it down
on those grounds, or examined the End User Certificate too thoroughly. I could have ordered the guns from
Spain and bought the ammunition on the black. Then
I would have had to smuggle the ammo on board, and
it would have been a much bigger consignment. Either
way, there has to be an element of smuggling, and hence
of risk. So if it all goes wrong, it'll be me and my
men who go down, not you. You're protected by a
series of cut-outs."

"I still don't like it," snapped Endean.

"What's the matter?" Shannon mocked. "Losing your
nerve?"

"No."

"So cool it. All you have to lose is a bit of money."

Endean was on the verge of telling Shannon just how
much he and his employer stood to lose, but thought
better of it. Logic dictated that if the mercenary was
going to face prison, he would be as careful as possible.

They talked finance for another hour. Shannon explained that the payment to Johann Schlinker in full,
and half to Alan Baker, along with the mercenaries'
second months' salary, the £5000 he had transferred
to Genoa to fit out the *Toscana,* and his own traveling, had emptied the Brugge account.

"Also," he added, "I want the second half of my
salary."

"Why now?" asked Endean.

"Because the risks of arrest start next Monday, and
I shall not be returning to London after that. If the
ship is loaded without fuss, she sails for Brindisi while
I arrange the pick-up of the Yugoslav arms. After that,
Valencia and the Spanish ammunition. Then we head
for the target. If I'm ahead of schedule, I'd prefer to
kill the extra time on the high seas rather than wait
in a port. From the moment that ship has hardware
on board, I want her in port as little as possible."

Endean digested the argument. "I'll put it to my associates," he said.

"I want the stuff in my Swiss account before the weekend," countered Shannon, "and the rest of the agreed budget transferred to Brugge."

They worked out that, with Shannon's salary paid in full, there would be £20,000 of the original money left in Switzerland. Shannon explained why he needed it all.

"From now on I need a wad of big-denomination travelers' checks in United States dollars on me all the time. If anything goes wrong from now, it can only be of a nature where a fat bribe on the spot might sort out the problem. I want to tidy up all the remaining traces, so that, if we all get the chop, there are no clues left. Also, I may need to make cash bonuses on the spot to the ship's crewmen to persuade them to go ahead when they find out what the job really is, as they must when we are at sea. With the last half-payment for the Yugoslav arms still to come, I could need up to twenty thousand."

Endean agreed to report all this to "his associates" and let Shannon know.

The following day he rang back to say that both transfers of the money had been authorized and the letter instructing the Swiss bank had been sent.

Shannon reserved his ticket from London to Brussels for the following Friday, and a Saturday morning flight from Brussels to Paris to Marseilles.

He spent that night with Julie, and Thursday as well, and Thursday night. Then he packed his bags, mailed the flat keys with an explanatory letter to the agents, and left. Julie drove him to the airport in her red MGB.

"When are you coming back?" she asked him as they stood outside the "Departing Passengers Only" entrance to the customs area of Number Two Building.

"I won't be coming back," he said and gave her a kiss.

"Then let me come with you."

"No."

"You will come back. I haven't asked where you

are going, but I know it has to be dangerous. It's not just business, not ordinary business. But you will come back. You must."

"I won't be coming back," he said quietly. "Go find someone else, Julie."

She began to sniffle. "I don't want anybody else. I love you. You don't love me. That's why you're saying you won't see me again. You've got another woman, that's what it is. You're going to see another woman—"

"There's no other woman," he said, stroking her hair. An airport policeman looked discreetly away. Tears in the departure lounge are not uncommon anywhere. There would be, Shannon knew, no other woman in his arms. Just a gun, the cool, comforting caress of the blued steel against his chest in the night. She was still crying when he kissed her on the forehead and walked through into Passport Control.

Thirty minutes later the Sabena jet made its last turn over South London and headed for its home in Brussels. Below the starboard wing, the country of Kent was spread out in the sunshine. Weatherwise, it had been a beautiful month of May. From the portholes one could see the acres of blossom where the apple, pear, and cherry orchards covered the land in pink and white.

Along the lanes that trickle through the heart of the Weald, the Maythorn would be out, the horse-chestnut trees glowing with green and white, the pigeons clattering among the oaks. He knew the country well from the time years ago when he had been stationed at Chatham and had bought an old motorcycle to explore the ancient country pubs between Lamberhurst and Smarden. Good country, good country to settle down in, if you were the settling type.

Ten minutes later, one of the passengers farther back summoned the stewardess to complain that someone up front was whistling a monotonous little tune.

It took Cat Shannon two hours on Friday afternoon to withdraw the money transferred from Switzerland

and close his account. He took two certified bank checks, each for £5000, which could be converted into a bank account somewhere else, and from that into more travelers' checks; and the other £10,000 in fifty $500 checks that needed only countersignature to be used as cash.

He spent that night in Brussels and flew the next morning to Paris and Marseilles.

A taxi from the airport brought him to the small hotel in the outskirts where Langarotti had once lived under the name of Lavallon, and where Janni Dupree, still following orders, was in residence. He was out at the time, so Shannon waited until he returned that evening, and together they drove, in a hired car Shannon had engaged, to Toulon. It was the end of Day Fifty-two, and the sprawling French naval port was bathed in warm sunshine.

On Sunday the shipping agent's office was not open, but it did not matter. The rendezvous spot was the pavement in front of it, and here Shannon and Dupree met Marc Vlaminck and Langarotti on the dot of nine o'clock. It was the first time they had been together for weeks, and only Semmler was missing. He should be a hundred miles or so along the coast, steaming offshore in the *Toscana* toward Toulon.

At Shannon's suggestion, Langarotti telephoned the harbormaster's office from a nearby café and ascertained that the *Toscana*'s agents in Genoa had cabled that she was due in on Monday morning and that her berth was reserved.

There was nothing more to do that day, so they went in Shannon's car along the coast road toward Marseilles and spent the day at the cobbled fishing port of Sanary. Despite the heat and the holiday atmosphere of the picturesque little town, Shannon could not relax. Only Dupree bought himself a pair of swimming trunks and dived off the end of the jetty of the yacht harbor. He said later the water was still damn cold. It would warm up later, through June and July, when the tourists began to pour south from Paris. By then they would all be preparing to strike at another harbor town, not much larger and many miles away.

Shannon sat for most of the day with the Belgian and Corsican on the terrace of Charley's bar, the Pot d'Etain, soaking up the sunshine and thinking of the next morning. The Yugoslav or the Spanish shipment might not turn up, or might be late, or might be blocked for some as yet unknown bureaucratic reason, but there would be no reason for them to be arrested in Yugoslavia or Spain. They might be held for a few days while the boat was searched, but that would be all. The following morning was different. If anyone insisted on peering deep into those oil barrels, there would be months, maybe years, spent sweating in Les Baumettes, the great forbidding fortress prison he had passed on Saturday as he drove from Marseilles to Toulon.

The waiting was always the worst, he reflected as he settled the bill and called his three colleagues to the car.

It turned out to be smoother than they thought. Toulon is known as an enormous navy base, and the skyline at the harbor is dominated by the superstructures of the French navy warships lying at anchor. The center of attraction for the tourists and the strollers of Toulon that Monday was the battle cruiser *Jean Bart,* home from a voyage to the French Caribbean territories, full of sailors with back pay to spend and looking for girls.

Along the broad sweep of esplanade fronting the harbor, the cafés were full of people indulging in the favorite pastime of every Mediterranean country— watching life go by. They sat in brightly colored hordes, gazing from the shaded awnings across the half-mile of bobbing yachts—from little outboard-powered runabouts to the sleek sea greyhounds of the very rich.

Up against the eastward quay were the dozen fishing boats that had elected not to go to sea, and behind these were the long, low customs sheds, warehouses, and harbor offices.

It was beyond these, in the small and hardly observed commercial port, that the *Toscana* slipped into her berth just before noon.

Shannon waited till she was tied up, and from his seat on a bollard 150 feet away he could see Semmler and Waldenberg moving about the decks. There was no sign of the Serbian engineer, who was probably still in his beloved engine room, but two other figures were also on deck, making fast and coiling ropes. These had to be the two new crewmen recruited by Waldenberg.

A small Renault buzzed along the quay and came to a halt by the gangway. A rotund Frenchman in a dark suit emerged and went aboard the *Toscana*. The representative of Agence Maritime Duphot. Before long he came back down, followed by Waldenberg, and the two strolled over to the customs shed. It was nearly an hour before the two men emerged, the shipping agent to return to his car and drive away into town, the German captain to get back to his ship.

Shannon gave them another thirty minutes, then he too strolled up the gangway and onto the *Toscana*. Semmler beckoned him into the companionway that led down to the crew's saloon.

"So, what's been going on?" Shannon asked when he and Semmler were seated below.

Semmler grinned. "All smooth and easy," he said. "I got the papers changed to show the new captain, had a complete engine service done, bought an unnecessarily large amount of blankets and a dozen foam-rubber mattresses. No one asked any questions, and the captain still thinks we are going to run immigrants into Britain.

"I used the *Toscana*'s usual shipping agent in Genoa to book us in here, and the manifest says we are taking on a mixed cargo of sporting goods and leisure equipment for a holiday camp on the coast of Morocco."

"What about the engine-lubricating oil?"

Semmler grinned. "It was all ordered; then I called

up and canceled it. When it didn't arrive, Waldenberg wanted to delay for a day and wait for it. I vetoed that and said we would get it here in Toulon."

"Fine," said Shannon. "Don't let Waldenberg order it. Tell him you've done it yourself. Then when it arrives, he'll be expecting it. That man who came on board . . ."

"The shipping agent. He has all the stuff still in bond, and the papers prepared. He's sending it down this afternoon in a couple of trucks. The crates are so small we can load them ourselves with the derrick."

"Good. Let him and Waldenberg sort out the paperwork. An hour after the stuff is all aboard, the fuel-company truck will arrive with the oil. Driven by Langarotti. You have enough money left to pay for it?"

"Yes."

"Then pay for it in full, cash, and get a signed receipt. Just make sure no one bangs it about too hard as it goes aboard. The last thing we need is for the bottom of one of the barrels to fall out. The quay will be waist-deep in Schmeissers."

"When do the men come aboard?"

"Tonight after dark. One by one. Just Marc and Janni. I'm leaving Jean-Baptiste here for a while. He has the truck, and there's one more job to be done at this end. When can you sail?"

"Any time. Tonight. I can fix it. Actually, it's rather nice being the managing director."

"Don't get too accustomed to it. It's only a front."

"Okay, Cat. Incidentally, where are we going when we leave?"

"Brindisi. Know it?"

"Sure I know it. I've run more cigarettes into Italy from Yugoslavia than you've had hot dinners. What do we pick up there?"

"Nothing. You wait for my telegram. I'll be in Germany. I'll cable you through the port office at Brindisi with the next destination and the day you have to arrive. Then you must get a local agent to cable the

Yugoslav port in question and reserve a berth. Are you okay to go to Yugoslavia?"

"I think so. Anyway, I won't get off the ship. We pick up more arms?"

"Yes. At least, that's the plan. I just have to hope my arms dealer and the Yugoslav officials have not cocked it up. Do you have all the charts you need?"

"Yes, I bought them all in Genoa as you told me. You know, Waldenberg will have to realize what we are taking on board in Yugoslavia. Then he'll know we aren't running illegal immigrants. He accepts the speedboats and the engines, the walkie-talkies and the clothing as quite normal, but arms are something else again."

"I know," said Shannon. "It will cost a bit of money. But I think he'll get the message. There'll be you and me, Janni and Marc on board. Besides, by then we can tell him what's in the oil drums. He'll be so far in by then, he'll have to go along. What are the two new crewmen like?"

Semmler nodded and stubbed out his fifth cigarette. The air was a blue haze in the small saloon. "Good. Two Italians. Hard boys, but obedient. I think they're both wanted by the *carabinieri* for something. They were so pleased to get on board and under cover. They couldn't wait to get to sea."

"Fine. Then they won't want to be put ashore in a foreign country. That would mean they'd be picked up without papers and repatriated, straight into the hands of their own police."

Waldenberg had done well. Shannon met both men briefly, and short nods were exchanged. Semmler simply introduced him as a man from the head office, and Waldenberg translated. The men, Norbiatto, the first mate, and Cipriani, the deckhand, evinced no further interest. Shannon exchanged a few instructions with Waldenberg and left.

In midafternoon the two vans from Agence Maritime Duphot rolled to a stop by the *Toscana,* accompanied by the same man who had appeared that morning. A

French customs officer, clipboard in hand, emerged from the customs house and stood by as the crates were swung inboard by the ship's derrick: four crates of assorted rough clothing, belts, boots, and caps, for the Moroccan workers at the holiday village; three crated large-size inflatable dinghies for sporting and leisure purposes; three outboard engines for same; two crates assorted flares, binoculars, ship's gas-powered foghorn, radio parts, and magnetic compasses. The last crates were listed under ship's stores.

The customs officer ticked them off as they went aboard, and confirmed with the shipping agent that they were either bonded for re-export, having arrived from Germany or Britain, or they were locally bought and carried no export duty. The customs man did not even look inside the crates. He knew the agency well, dealing with them every day.

When all was aboard, the customs man stamped the ship's cargo manifest. Waldenberg said something to Semmler in German, and the latter translated. He explained to the agency man that Waldenberg needed lubricating oil for his engines. It had been ordered in Genoa but had not been delivered in time.

The agency man noted in his book. "How much do you need?"

"Five drums," said Semmler. Waldenberg did not understand the French.

"That's a lot," said the agent.

Semmler laughed. "This old bucket uses as much oil as Diesel. Besides, we might as well get it here and have enough for a long time to come."

"When do you need it?" asked the agent.

"Five o'clock this afternoon be all right?" asked Semmler.

"Make it six," said the agency man, noting the type and quantity in his notebook, along with the hour of delivery. He looked up at the customs man. The official nodded. He was uninterested and strolled away. Shortly after, the agency man left in his car, followed by the two trucks.

At five o'clock Semmler left the *Toscana,* went to a phone in a café on the waterfront, rang the agency, and canceled the oil order. The skipper, he said, had discovered a full barrel at the rear of the stores locker and would not be needing any more for several weeks. The agency man was disgruntled but agreed.

At six a truck drove carefully along the quay and stopped opposite the *Toscana.* It was driven by Jean-Baptiste Langarotti in a bright green overall suit with the word Castrol on the back.

After opening the back of the truck, he carefully rolled five large oil drums down the plank he had fitted to the rear step. From the window of the customs house the duty officer peered out.

Waldenberg caught his eye and waved. He pointed to the barrels and back to his ship.

"Okay?" he called, adding with a thick accent, *"Ça va?"*

From the window the customs man nodded and withdrew to make a note on his clipboard. At Waldenberg's orders, the two Italian crewmen slipped cradles under the barrels and, one by one, winched them aboard. Semmler was uncommonly eager to help, steadying the drums as they swung over the ship's rail, shouting in German to Waldenberg on the winch to let them down easily. They slid out of sight into the dark, cool hold of the *Toscana,* and soon the hatch was back in place and clamped down.

Langarotti, having made his dispatch, had long since left in his truck. A few minutes later the overall suit was at the bottom of a waste bin in the heart of town. From his bollard at the other end of the quay, Shannon had watched the loading with bated breath. He would have preferred to be involved, like Semmler, for the waiting was almost physically painful, worse than going into action.

When it was over, things quieted down on the *Toscana.* The captain and his three men were below decks, the engineer having taken one turn of the ship to sniff the salt air and then having gone back to his

Diesel fumes. Semmler gave them half an hour, then slipped down to the quay and came to join Shannon. They met around three corners and out of sight of the harbor.

Semmler was grinning. "I told you. No problems."

Shannon nodded and grinned back with relief. He knew better than Semmler what was at stake, and, unlike the German, he was not familiar with port procedures.

"When can you take the men aboard?"

"The customs office closes at nine. They should come between twelve and one in the morning. We sail at five. It's fixed."

"Good," said Shannon. "Let's go and find them and have a drink. I want you back there quickly in case there are any inquiries still to come."

"There won't be."

"Never mind. We'll play safe. I want you to watch that cargo like a mother hen. Don't let anyone near those barrels till I say so, and that will be in a harbor in Yugoslavia. Then we tell Waldenberg what he's carrying."

They met the other three mercenaries at a prearranged café and had several beers to cool down. The sun was setting, and the sea within the vast bowl of land that forms the anchorage and roads of Toulon was ruffled by only a slight breeze. A few sailboats pirouetted like ballerinas far out on the stage as their crews brought them about to catch the next gust.

Semmler left them at eight and returned to the *Toscana*.

Janni Dupree and Marc Vlaminck slipped quietly aboard between midnight and one, and at five, watched from the quay by Shannon and Langarotti, the *Toscana* slipped back to the sea.

Langarotti ran Shannon to the airport in midmorning to catch his plane. Over breakfast Shannon had given the Corsican his last set of instructions and enough money to carry them out.

"I'd prefer to be going with you," Jean-Baptiste said, "or with the ship."

"I know," said Shannon. "But I need someone good to do this part of it. It's vital. Without it we can't go through. I need someone reliable, and you have the added advantage of being French. Besides, you know two of the men well, and one speaks a smattering of French. Janni couldn't go in there with a South African passport. Marc I need to intimidate the crew if they cut up rough. I know you're better with a knife than he is with his hands, but I don't want a fight, just enough to persuade the crew to do what they're told. And I need Kurt to check the navigation, in case Waldenberg chickens out. In fact, if the worst comes to the worst and Waldenberg goes over the side, Kurt has to skipper the ship. So it has to be you."

Langarotti agreed to go on the mission. "They're good boys," he said with a little more enthusiasm. "It will be good to see them again."

When they parted at the airport, Shannon reminded him, "It can all fall through if we get there and we have no back-up force. So it depends on you to do it right. It's all set up. Just do what I said and cope with the small problems as they arise. I'll see you in a month."

He left the Corsican, walked through customs, and boarded his plane for Paris and Hamburg.

19

"My information is that you can pick up the mortars and bazookas any time after June tenth, and that was reconfirmed yesterday by Telex," Alan Baker told Shannon the day after his arrival in Hamburg.

"What port?" asked Shannon.

"Ploce."

"Where?"

"Ploce. Spelled P-L-O-C-E, pronounced Plochay. It's a small port almost exactly halfway between Split and Dubrovnik."

Shannon thought. He had ordered Semmler while in Genoa to pick up the necessary sea charts to cover the whole Yugoslav coast, but he had supposed the pick-up would be at one of the larger ports. He hoped the German had a chart covering the sea approaches to Ploce, or could get one at Brindisi.

"How small?"

"Quite small. Very discreet. Half a dozen wharves and two large warehouses. The Yugoslavs usually use it for their arms exports. The last shipment out of Yugoslavia I did by plane, but I was told at that time if it was to be by sea, it would be from Ploce. It's better if it's a small port. There's usually a berth, and loading facilities are quicker. Moreover, the customs there must be a very small unit, probably with one lowly man in charge, and if he gets his present, he'll see everything on board within a few hours."

"Okay, Ploce. On June eleventh," said Shannon.

Baker noted the date. "The *Toscana* is okay?" he asked. He decided to bear the *Toscana* in mind for later use. Shannon, he was sure, would have little use for her after whatever operation he was mounting was finished, and Baker was always on the lookout for a good boat for running his cargoes into deserted coves.

"She's fine," said Shannon. "She's running for an Italian port now, where I have to let her know by Telex or letter where to head for. Any problems at your end?"

Baker shifted slightly. "One," he said. "The price."

"What about it?"

"I know I quoted you fixed prices, totaling fourteen thousand, four hundred dollars. But the system inside Yugoslavia has changed over the past six months. To get the paperwork through on time, I had to engage a Yugoslav partner. At least, that's what he is called, though in fact he's another middleman."

"So?" asked Shannon.

"So he has to get a fee or salary for getting the paperwork through the Belgrade office. On balance, I supposed it was worth it to you to have the shipment ready on time and no bureaucratic hang-ups. So I agreed to engage him. He's the brother-in-law of the official in the Trade Ministry. It's another way of taking a kickback. But what can you expect these days? The Balkans are still the Balkans, and they've got wised up."

"How much extra will he cost?"

"A thousand pounds sterling."

"In dinars or dollars?"

"In dollars."

Shannon thought it over. It might be the truth, or it might be that Baker was trying to squeeze a bit more out of him. If it was the truth, refusing to pay would simply force Baker to pay the Yugoslav out of his own cut. That would reduce Baker's margin to such a small amount he might lose interest in the deal, not caring whether it went through or not. And he still needed Baker, and would need him until he saw the white wake of the *Toscana* heading out of Ploce harbor on her way to Spain.

"All right," he said. "Who is this partner?"

"Fellow called Ziljak. He's out there now, taking care of the shipment right up to Ploce and into the warehouse there. When the ship comes in, he'll get the stuff from the warehouse through customs and onto the boat."

"I thought that was your job."

"It is, but now I have to engage a Yugoslav as partner. Honestly, Cat, they left me no alternative."

"Then I'll pay him personally, in travelers' checks."

"I wouldn't," said Baker.

"Why not?"

"The buyers of this shipment are supposed to be the government of Togo, right? Black men. Another white turns up, obviously the paymaster, and they might begin to smell a rat. We can go to Ploce, if you like, or I can go alone. But if you want to come with me, you'll have to come ostensibly as my assistant. Besides, travelers' checks have to be cashed at a bank, and in Yugoslavia that means they take the man's name and identity-card number. If someone cashing them is a Yugoslav, there are questions asked. It would be better if Ziljak got cash, as he has asked."

"All right, I'll cash some checks here in Hamburg, and I'll pay him in dollar bills," said Shannon. "But you get yours in checks. I'm not carrying vast sums of dollars in cash around. Not to Yugoslavia. They get sensitive about that sort of thing. Security gets interested. They think you're funding a spy operation. So we go as tourists with travelers' checks."

"Fine by me," said Baker. "When do you want to go?"

Shannon glanced at his watch. The next day would be June 1.

"Day after tomorrow," he said. "We'll fly to Dubrovnik and have a week in the sun. I could do with a rest anyway. Or you can join me on the eighth or ninth, but not a day later. I'll hire a car, and we can drive up the coast to Ploce on the tenth. I'll have the *Toscana* come in that night or early on the morning of the eleventh."

"You go on alone," said Baker. "I have work to do in Hamburg. I'll join you on the eighth."

"Without fail," said Shannon. "If you don't turn up, I'll come looking. And I'll be hopping mad."

"I'll come," said Baker. "I still want the balance of my money, don't forget. So far, I'm out of pocket on this deal. I want it to go through just as much as you."

That was the way Shannon wanted him to feel.

"You do have the money, I suppose?" asked Baker, fingering a lump of sugar.

Shannon flicked through a booklet of large-denomination dollar checks under Baker's nose. The arms dealer smiled.

They left the table and on the way out used the restaurant telephone to call a Hamburg charter company specializing in package tours for the thousands of Germans who vacation along the Adriatic coast. From this company they learned the names of the three best hotels in the Yugoslav resort. Baker was told he would find Shannon in one of them under the name of Keith Brown.

Johann Schlinker was as confident as Baker that he could fulfill his arms deal, though he had no idea that Baker was also doing business with Shannon. No doubt the men knew of each other, might even be acquainted, but there would not be a question of discussing each other's business together.

"The port should be Valencia, though this has yet to be fixed and is in any case the choice of the Spanish authorities," he told Shannon. "Madrid tells me the dates have to be between the sixteenth and twentieth of June."

"I'd prefer the twentieth for loading," said Shannon.

"The *Toscana* should be permitted to berth on or during the night of the nineteenth and load in the morning."

"Good," said Schlinker. "I'll inform my Madrid partner. He habitually handles the transporting and loading side of things, and employs a first-class freight agent in Valencia who knows all the customs personnel very well. There should be no problem."

"There must be no problem," growled Shannon. "The ship has been delayed already once, and by loading on the twentieth I have enough sailing time but no margin to fulfill my own contract."

It was not true, but he saw no reason why Schlinker should not believe it was true.

"I shall want to watch the loading also," he told the arms dealer.

Schlinker pursed his lips. "You may watch it from afar, of course," he said. "I cannot stop you. But as the customers are supposed to be an Arab government, you cannot propose yourself as the buyer of the merchandise."

"I also want to board the ship at Valencia," said Shannon.

"That will be even harder. The whole port is sealed off inside a chain-link fence. Entry is by authority only. To board the ship you would have to go through passport control. Also, as she will be carrying ammunition, there will be a Guardia Civil at the bottom of the gangplank."

"Supposing the captain needed another crewman. Could he engage a seaman locally?"

Schlinker thought it over. "I suppose so. Are you connected with the company owning the vessel?"

"Not on paper," said Shannon.

"If the captain informed the agent on arrival that he had permitted one of his crewmen to leave the vessel at its last port of call to fly home and attend his mother's funeral, and that the crewman would be rejoining the vessel at Valencia, I suppose there would be no objection. But you would need a merchant seaman's card to prove you were a seaman. And in the same name as yourself, Mr. Brown."

Shannon thought for a few minutes. "Okay. I'll fix it."

Schlinker consulted his diary. "As it happens, I shall be in Madrid on the nineteenth and twentieth," he said. "I have another business deal to attend to. I shall be at the Mindanao Hotel. If you want to contact me, you can find me there. If loading is for the twentieth, the chances are the convoy and escort from the Spanish army will run the shipment down to the coast during the night of the nineteenth to arrive at crack of dawn. If you are going to board the ship at all, I think you should do so before the military convoy arrives at the docks."

"I could be in Madrid on the nineteenth," said Shannon. "Then I could check with you that the convoy had indeed left on time. By driving fast to Valencia, I could be there ahead of it, and board the *Toscana* as the rejoining seaman before the convoy arrives."

"That is entirely up to you," said Schlinker. "For my part, I will have my agents arrange the freighting, transportation, and loading, according to all the normal procedures, for dawn of the twentieth. That is what I contracted to do. If there is any risk attached to your boarding the vessel in harbor, that must be your affair. I cannot take the responsibility for that. I can only point out that ships carrying arms out of Spain are subjected to scrutiny by the army and customs authorities. If anything goes wrong with the loading and clearance of the ship to sail, because of you, that is not my responsibility. One other thing. After loading arms a ship must leave a Spanish port within six hours, and may not re-enter Spanish waters until the cargo has been offloaded. Also, the manifest must be in perfect order."

"It will be," said Shannon. "I'll be with you in Madrid on the morning of the nineteenth."

Before leaving Toulon, Kurt Semmler had given Shannon a letter to mail. It was from Semmler to the *Toscana*'s shipping agents in Genoa. It informed them there had been a slight change of plan, and that the *Toscana* would be proceeding from Toulon not directly to Morocco but first to Brindisi to pick up further cargo. The order, Semmler informed the agents, had been secured locally by him in Toulon and was lucrative, since it was a rush order, whereas the consignment of mixed cargo from Toulon to Morocco was in no hurry. As managing director of Spinetti Maritimo, Semmler's instructions were those of the boss. He required the Genoa agents to cable Brindisi reserving a berth for June 7 and 8, and to instruct the port office to hold any mail addressed to the *Toscana* for collection when she berthed.

Such a letter was what Shannon wrote and dispatched from Hamburg. It was to Signor Kurt Semmler, MV *Toscana,* c/o the Port Office, Brindisi, Italy.

In it he told Semmler that from Brindisi he should proceed to Ploce on the Adriatic coast of Yugoslavia, and that if he had no charts to negotiate the tricky straits north of Korcula Island, he should get them locally. He had to get the *Toscana* there on the evening of June 10, and his berth would be reserved. There was no need to inform the agents in Genoa of the extra leg from Brindisi to Ploce.

His last instruction to Semmler was important. He told the German ex-smuggler he wanted him to acquire a merchant seaman's card for a deckhand called Keith Brown, stamped and up to date, and issued by the Italian authorities. The second thing the ship would need was a cargo manifest showing the *Toscana* had proceeded straight from Brindisi to Valencia without a halt, and would be heading from Valencia to Latakia, Syria, after taking cargo aboard in Valencia. Semmler would have to use his old Brindisi contacts to obtain these documents.

Before he left Hamburg for Yugoslavia, Shannon's

last letter was to Simon Endean in London. It required Endean to meet Shannon at a rendezvous in Rome on June 16, and to bring certain maritime charts with him.

About the same time, the MV *Toscana* was chugging steadily through the Bight of Bonifacio, the narrow channel of limpid blue water that separates the southern tip of Corsica from the northern end of Sardinia. The sun was blistering, but mellowed by a light wind. Marc Vlaminck was stretched out, stripped to the waist, on the hatch cover of the main hold, a wet towel beneath him, his torso like a pink hippopotamus covered in suntan oil. Janni Dupree, who always turned brick red in the sun, was propped up against the wall of the after structure, under the awning, swigging from his tenth bottle of beer of the morning. Cipriani, the deckhand, was painting part of the rail around the forepeak white, and the first mate, Norbiatto, was snoozing on his bunk below after taking the night watch.

Also down below, in the stinking heat of the engine room, was the engineer, Grubič, oiling some piece of machinery that only he could understand but which no doubt was vital to keep the *Toscana* steady on her eight knots through the Mediterranean. In the wheelhouse Kurt Semmler and Carl Waldenberg were sipping cold beer and exchanging reminiscences of their respective careers.

Jean-Baptiste Langarotti would have liked to be there. From the port rail he could have watched the gray-white sunbleached coast of his homeland slipping past barely four miles across the water. But he was many miles away, in West Africa, where the rainy season had already begun and where, despite the fever heat, the clouds were leaden gray.

Alan Baker came into Shannon's hotel in Dubrovnik just as the mercenary was returning from the beach on the evening of June 8. He looked tired and dusty.

Cat Shannon, by contrast, was looking and feeling

better. He had spent his week in the Yugoslav holiday resort behaving like any other tourist, sunbathing and swimming several miles each day. He looked thinner, but fit and tanned. He was also optimistic.

After settling into his hotel, he had sent Semmler a cable at Brindisi requesting confirmation of the arrival of the vessel and receipt of the waiting letter mailed from Hamburg. That morning he had got Semmler's telegraphed reply. The *Toscana* had arrived safely in Brindisi, the letter had been received and acted on, and they would depart on the morning of June 9 to make destination by midnight of the tenth.

Over drinks on the terrace of their hotel, where Shannon had reserved Baker a room for the night, he told the dealer from Hamburg the news.

Baker nodded and smiled. "Fine. I got a cable forty-eight hours ago from Ziljak in Belgrade. The crates have arrived in Ploce and are in the government warehouse near the quay, under guard."

They spent the night in Dubrovnik and the following morning hired a taxi to take them the hundred kilometers up the coast to Ploce. It was a boneshaker of a car that appeared to have square wheels and cast-iron suspension, but the drive along the coast road was agreeable, mile upon mile of unspoiled coastline, with the small town of Slano at the halfway mark, where they stopped for a cup of coffee and to stretch their limbs.

They were established in a Ploce hotel by lunchtime and waited in the shade of the terrace until the port office opened again at four in the afternoon.

The port was set on a broad sweep of deep blue water, shielded to its seaward side by a long peninsula of land called Peliesac, which curved out of the main coast to the south of Ploce and ran northward parallel to the coast. Up to the north the gap between the tip of the peninsula and the coast was almost blocked by the rocky island of Hvar, and only a narrow gap gave access to the sea lagoon on which Ploce stood. This lagoon, nearly thirty miles long, surrounded on nine-tenths of its perimeter by land, was a paradise for swimming, fishing, and sailing.

As they approached the port office, a small and battered Volkswagen squealed to a halt a few yards away and hooted noisily. Shannon froze. His first instinct said trouble, something he had been fearing all along, some slip-up in the paperwork, a sudden block put on the whole deal by the authorities, and an extended stay under questioning in the local police station.

The man who climbed out of the small car and waved cheerily might have been a policeman, except that police in most totalitarian states of East or West seemed to be banned from smiling by standing orders. Shannon glanced at Baker and saw his shoulders sag in relief.

"Ziljak," Baker muttered through closed mouth and went to meet the Yugoslav. The latter was a big shaggy man, like an amiable black-haired bear, and he embraced Baker with both arms. When he was introduced, his first name turned out to be Kemal, and Shannon supposed there was more than a touch of Turk in the man. That suited Shannon fine; he liked the type, normally good fighters and comrades with a healthy dislike of bureaucracy.

"My assistant," said Baker, and Ziljak shook hands and muttered something in what Shannon assumed to be Serbo-Croat. Baker and Ziljak communicated in German, which many Yugoslavians speak a little. He spoke no English.

With Ziljak's assistance, they roused the head of the customs office and were taken off to inspect the warehouse. The customs man jabbered a few words at the guard on the door, and in the corner of the building they found the crates. There were thirteen of them; one apparently contained the two bazookas, and each of two others contained one mortar, including the baseplates and sighting mechanisms in each. The rest were of ammunition, four of them with ten bazooka rockets in each, and the other six containing the ordered three hundred mortar bombs. The crates were in new timber, unmarked with any description of contents, but stenciled with serial numbers and the word *Toscana.*

Ziljak and the customs chief babbled away in their own dialect—and it appeared they were using the same one, which was helpful, because there are dozens in Yugoslavia, including seven major languages, and difficulties have been known to occur.

Eventually Ziljak turned to Baker and said several sentences in his halting German. Baker replied, and Ziljak translated for the customs man. He smiled, and they all shook hands and parted. Outside, the sunshine struck like a sledgehammer.

"What was all that about?" asked Shannon.

"Kemal was asked by the customs man if there was a little present in it for him," explained Baker. "Kemal told him there would be a nice one if the paperwork could be kept trouble-free and the ship was loaded on time tomorrow morning."

Shannon had already given Baker the first half of Ziljak's £1000 bonus for helping the deal go through, and Baker drew the Yugoslav to one side to slip it to him. The man's all-embracing bonhomie became even more embracing for both of them, and they adjourned to the hotel to celebrate with a little slivovitz. A little was the word Baker used. Ziljak may have used the same word. He did not mean it. Happy Yugoslavs never drink a little slivovitz. With £500 under his belt, Ziljak ordered a bottle of the fiery plum liquor and bowl after bowl of almonds and olives. As the sun went down and the Adriatic evening slipped through the streets, he relived again his years in the war, hunting and hiding in the Bosnian hills to the north with Tito's partisans.

Baker was hard put to it to translate as the exuberant Kemal related his forays behind Dubrovnik in Montenegro, in the mountains behind where they sat, on the coast of Herzegovina, and among the cooler, richer, wooded countryside north of Split in Bosnia. He relished the thought that he would once have been shot out of hand for venturing into any of the towns where he now drove on behalf of his brother-in-law who was in the government. Shannon asked if he was a committed Communist, having been a partisan, and Ziljak listened while Baker translated, using the word "good" for "committed."

Ziljak thumped his chest with his fist. *"Guter Kommunist,"* he exclaimed, eyes wide, pointing at himself. Then he ruined the effect by giving a broad wink, throwing back his head, and roaring with laughter as he tossed another glass of slivovitz down the hatch. The folded notes of his first £500 bonus made a bulge under his waistband, and Shannon laughed too and wished the giant was coming along to Zangaro with them. He was that kind of man.

They had no supper but at midnight wandered unsteadily back to the quay to watch the *Toscana* come in. She was rounding the harbor wall and an hour later was tied up alongside the single quay of hewn local stone. From the forepeak Semmler looked down in the half-light cast by the dock lamps. Each nodded slowly at the other, and Waldenberg stood at the top of the gangplank, consulting with his first mate. He had already been instructed, following Shannon's letter, that he should leave the talking to Semmler.

After Baker had headed back to the hotel with Ziljak, Shannon slipped up the gangplank and into the captain's tiny cabin. No one on the quay took any notice. Semmler brought Waldenberg in, and they locked the door.

Slowly and carefully Shannon told Waldenberg what he had really brought the *Toscana* to Ploce to take on board. The German captain took it well. He kept his face expressionless until Shannon had finished.

"I never carried arms before," he said. "You say this cargo is legal. How legal?"

"Perfectly legal," said Shannon. "It has been bought in Belgrade, trucked up here, and the authorities are of course aware what the crates contain. Otherwise there would be no export license. The license has not been forged, nor has anyone been bribed. It's a perfectly legal shipment under the laws of Yugoslavia."

"And the laws of the country it's going to?" asked Waldenberg.

"The *Toscana* never enters the waters of the country where these arms are due to be used," said Shannon. "After Ploce, there are two more ports of call. In each case only to take on board cargoes. You know ships are never searched for what they are carrying when they arrive in a port to take on more cargo only, unless the authorities have been tipped off."

"It has happened, all the same," said Waldenberg. "If I have these things on board and the manifest doesn't mention them, and there is a search and they are discovered, the ship gets impounded and I get imprisoned. I didn't bargain on arms. With the Black September and the IRA about these days, everyone's looking for arms shipments."

"Not at the port of embarkation of fresh cargo," said Shannon.

"I didn't bargain for arms," repeated Waldenberg.

"You bargained for illegal immigrants to Britain," Shannon pointed out.

"They're not illegal until their feet touch British soil," the captain said. "And the *Toscana* would be outside territorial waters. They could go inshore in fast boats. Arms are different. They are illegal on this ship if the manifest says there aren't any. Why not put it on the manifest? Just say these arms are being legally transported from Ploce to Togo. No one can prove we later deviate from course."

"Because if there are arms already on board, the Spanish authorities will not allow the ship to stay in Valencia or any other Spanish port. Even in transit. Certainly not to take on more arms. So they have to remain unmentioned on the manifest."

"So where did we come from to reach Spain?" asked Waldenberg.

"From Brindisi," replied Shannon. "We went there

to take on cargo, but it was not ready in time. Then the owners ordered you to Valencia to pick up a new cargo for Latakia. Of course you obeyed."

"Supposing the Spanish police search the boat?"

"There's not the slightest reason why they should," said Shannon. "But if they do, the crates have to be below decks in the bilges."

"If they find them there, there's not a hope for us," Waldenberg pointed out. "They'd think we were bringing the stuff to the Basque territories. We'd be inside forever."

The talk went on till three in the morning. It cost Shannon a flat bonus of £5000, half before loading and half after sailing from Valencia. There was no extra charge for the stopover in the African port. That would present no problem.

"You'll take care of the crew?" Shannon asked.

"I'll take care of the crew," said Waldenberg with finality. Shannon knew he would, too.

Back in his hotel, Shannon paid Baker the third quarter of his bill for the arms, $3600, and tried to get some sleep. It was not easy. The sweat rolled off him in the heat of the night, and he had an image of the *Toscana* lying down there in the port, the arms in the customs shed, and prayed there would be no problems. He felt he was so close now, just three short ceremonies away from the point where no one could stop him, whatever was tried.

The loading started at seven, and the sun was already well up. With a customs man, armed with a rifle, walking beside the crates, they were wheeled on trolleys down to the dockside, and the *Toscana* hoisted them aboard with her own jumbo derrick. None of the crates was very large, and down in the hold Vlaminck and Cipriani swung them easily into position before they were roped down across the floor of the hold. By nine in the morning it was over, and the hatches went on.

Waldenberg had ordered the engineer to stand by for casting off, and the latter needed no second bidding. Shannon learned later he had suddenly become very voluble when he learned three hours out from Brindisi that they were heading for his native country. Apparently he was wanted there for something or other. He stayed well hidden in his engine room, and no one went looking for him.

As he watched the *Toscana* chugging out of the port, Shannon slipped Baker the remaining $3600 and the second £500 for Ziljak. Unbeknownst to either, he had had Vlaminck quietly prise up the lids on five of the crates, taken at random, as they came aboard. Vlaminck had verified the contents, waved up to Semmler on the deck above him, and Semmler had blown his nose, the signal Shannon wanted. Just in case the crates contained scrap iron. It has been known to happen, quite frequently, in the arms world.

Baker, having received his money, gave the £500 to Ziljak as if it came from himself, and the Yugoslav saw the customs chief did not go without supper. Then Alan Baker and his British "assistant" quietly left town.

On Shannon's calendar of a hundred days, given him by Sir James Manson to bring off his coup, it was Day Sixty-seven.

No sooner was the *Toscana* out to sea than Captain Waldenberg began to organize his ship. One by one, the three other crewmen were brought into his cabin for a quiet interview. Although none of them knew it, had they refused to continue to serve aboard the *Toscana,* there would have been some unfortunate accidents on board. Few places are quite as well suited for a complete disappearing act as a ship on a dark night at sea, and Vlaminck and Dupree between them could have pitched anyone else on board a long way from the ship's side before he touched the water. Perhaps their presence did the trick. In any case, no one objected.

Waldenberg dispensed £1000 of the £2500 he had received in travelers' checks from Shannon. The Yugoslav engineer, delighted to be back out of his own country, took his £250, stuffed it into his pocket, and went back to his engines. He made no comment one way or the other. The first mate, Norbiatto, became quite excited at the thought of a Spanish jail, but pocketed his £600 in dollars and thought of the difference that could make to his chances of owning his own ship one day. The crewman, Cipriani, seemed almost happy at the prospect of being on a vessel full of contraband, took his £150, said an ecstatic thank you, and left, muttering, "This is the life." He had little imagination and knew nothing about Spanish jails.

With this done, the crates were broken open, and all afternoon the contents were examined, wrapped in polyethylene, and stowed deep in the bilges, below the floor of the hold and inside the curvature of the ship's hull. The planks which had been removed to make this possible were replaced and covered with the innocent cargo of clothing, dinghies, and outboard engines.

Finally Semmler told Waldenberg he had better put the Castrol oil drums at the back of the stores locker, and when he told his fellow countryman why, Waldenberg finally did lose his composure. He lost his temper as well and used some expressions that could best be described as regrettable.

Semmler calmed him down, and they sat having beer as the *Toscana* plowed her way south for the Otranto Channel and the Ionian Sea.

Finally Waldenberg began to laugh. "Schmeissers," he said. "Bloody Schmeissers. *Mensch,* it's a long time since they've been heard in the world."

"Well, they're going to be heard again," said Semmler.

Waldenberg looked wistful. "You know," he said at length, "I wish I was going ashore with you."

20

When Shannon arrived, Simon Endean was reading a copy of *The Times* bought that morning in London before he left for Rome. The lounge of the Excelsior Hotel was almost empty, for most of those taking late-morning coffee were on the outside terrace watching the chaotic traffic of Rome inch past and trying to make themselves heard above the noise.

Shannon had picked the place only because it was in easy reach of Dubrovnik to the east and in line with Madrid to the west. It was the first time he had ever been to Rome, and he wondered what the ecstatic guide books were talking about. There were at least seven separate strikes in progress, one of them being among the garbage workers, and the city stank in the sun from the uncleared fruit and other rubbish on the pavements and down every back alley.

He eased himself into a seat beside the man from London and savored the cool of the inner room after the heat and frustration of the taxi in which he had been stuck for the past hour.

Endean eyed him. "You've been out of touch a long time," he said coldly. "My associates were beginning to think you had run out. That was unwise."

"There was no point in my making contact until I had something to say. That ship doesn't exactly fly across the water. It takes time to get her from Toulon to Yugoslavia, and during that time there was nothing to report," said Shannon. "By the way, did you bring the charts?"

"Of course." Endean pointed to the bulging attaché case beside his chair. On receiving Shannon's letter from Hamburg, he had spent several days visiting three of the top maritime-chart companies in Leadenhall Street, London, and in separate lots had acquired inshore charts for the entire African coast from Casablanca to Cape Town. "Why the hell do you need so many?" he asked in annoyance. "One or two would suffice."

"Security," said Shannon briefly. "If you or I were searched at customs, or if the ship were boarded and searched in port, one single chart showing the area of the ship's destination would be a giveaway. As it is, no one, including the captain and crew, can discover which section of the coast really interests me. Until the last moment, when I have to tell them. Then it's too late. Do you have the slides as well?"

"Yes, of course."

Another of Endean's jobs had been to make up slides of all the photographs Shannon had brought back from Zangaro, along with others of the maps and sketches of Clarence and the rest of Zangaro's coastline.

Shannon himself had already sent a slide projector, bought duty-free at London airport, onto the *Toscana* in Toulon.

He gave Endean a complete progress report from the moment he had left London, mentioning the stay in Brussels, the loading of the Schmeissers and other equipment onto the *Toscana* in Toulon, the talks with Schlinker and Baker in Hamburg, and the Yugoslav shipment a few days earlier in Ploce.

Endean listened in silence, making a few notes for the report he would later have to give to Sir James Manson. "Where's the *Toscana* now?" he asked at length.

"She should be south and slightly west of Sardinia, en route for Valencia."

Shannon went on to tell him what was planned in three days' time: the loading of the 400,000 rounds of 9mm. ammunition for the machine pistols in Valencia, and then departure for the target. He made no mention of the fact that one of his men was already in Africa.

"Now there's something I need to know from you," he told Endean. "What happens after the attack? What happens at dawn? We can't hold on for very long before some kind of new regime takes over, establishes itself in the palace, and broadcasts news of the coup and the new government."

"That's all been thought of," said Endean smoothly. "In fact, the new government is the whole point of the exercise."

From his briefcase he withdrew three sheets of paper covered with close typing. "These are your instructions, starting the moment you have possession of the palace and the army and guards have been destroyed or scattered. Read, memorize, and destroy these sheets before we part company, here in Rome. You have to carry it all in your head."

Shannon ran his eyes quickly over the first page. There were few surprises for him. He had already suspected the man Manson was boosting into the presidency had to be Colonel Bobi, and although the new president was referred to simply as X, he did not doubt Bobi was the man in question. The rest of the plan was simple from his point of view.

He glanced up at Endean. "Where will you be?" he asked.

"A hundred miles north of you," said Endean.

Shannon knew Endean meant he would be waiting in the capital of the republic next door to Zangaro on its northern side, the one with a road route straight along the coast to the border and thence to Clarence.

"Are you sure you'll pick up my message?" he asked.

"I shall have a portable radio set of considerable

range and power. The Braun, the best they make. It will pick up anything within that range, provided it's broadcast on the right channel and frequency. A ship's radio should be powerful enough to send in clear over at least twice that distance."

Shannon nodded and read on. When he had finished, he put the sheets on the table. "Sounds all right," he said. "But let's get one thing clear. I'll broadcast on that frequency at those hours from the *Toscana,* and she'll be hove to somewhere off the coast, probably at five or six miles. But if you don't hear me, if there's too much static, I can't be responsible for that. It's up to you to hear me."

"It's up to you to broadcast," said Endean. "The frequency is one that has been tested before by practical use. From the *Toscana*'s radio it must be picked up by my radio set at a hundred miles. Not first time, perhaps, but if you repeat for thirty minutes, I have to hear it."

"All right," said Shannon. "One last thing. The news of what has happened in Clarence should not have reached the Zangaran border post. That means it'll be manned by Vindu. It's your business to get past them. After the border, and particularly nearer Clarence, there may be scattered Vindu on the roads, running for the bush but still dangerous. Supposing you don't get through?"

"We'll get through," said Endean. "We'll have help."

Shannon supposed, rightly, that this would be provided by the small operation in mining that he knew Manson had going for him in that republic. For a senior company executive it could provide a truck or jeep and maybe a couple of repeater hunting rifles. For the first time he supposed Endean might have some guts to back up his nastiness.

Shannon memorized the code words and the radio frequency he needed and burned the sheets with Endean in the men's room. They parted an hour later. There was nothing else to say.

Five floors above the streets of Madrid, Colonel Antonio Almela, head of the exporting office of the Spanish Army Ministry (Foreign Arms Sales), sat at his desk and perused the file of papers in front of him. He was a gray-haired, grizzled man, a simple man whose loyalties were uncomplicated and uncompromising. His fidelity was to Spain, his beloved Spain, and for him all that was right and proper, all that was truly Spanish, was embodied in one man, the short and aged generalissimo who sat in El Pardo. Antonio Almela was a Falangist to his boot-heels.

Two years from retirement at the age of fifty-eight, he had been one of those who stepped ashore on the sand of Fuengirola with Francisco Franco many years ago when El Caudillo of modern Spain had been a rebel and outcast, returning against orders to launch war against the Republican government in Madrid. They had been few then, and condemned to death by Madrid, and they had nearly died.

Sergeant Almela was a good soldier. He carried out his orders, whatever they were, went to mass between the battles and the executions, and believed, deeply, in God, the Virgin, Spain, and Franco.

In another army, at another time, he would have retired as a sergeant-major. He emerged from the civil war a full captain, one of the ultras, the inner circle. His background was solid peasant, his education next to nil. But he had made full colonel, and he was grateful. He was also trusted with one of the jobs that in Spain is unmentionable and top secret. No Spaniard ever, under any circumstances, learns that Spain exports arms in large quantities to almost all comers. Publicly, Spain regrets the international arms trade as unethical and conducive to further warfare in a world already torn by war. Privately, she makes a lot of money out of it. Antonio Almela could be trusted to check the paperwork, decide whether to grant or refuse permission for export licenses, and keep his mouth shut.

The dossier in front of him had been in his hands for four weeks. Individual papers from the dossier had been checked out by the Defense Ministry, which had confirmed, without knowing why the question was being asked, that 9mm. bullets were not on the secret list; by the Foreign Ministry, which had confirmed simply that a sum of money in dollars, paid into a certain account in the Banco Popular, had been received and cleared.

The top paper on the file was an application for a movement order to shift a quantity of crates from Madrid to Valencia and export them on a vessel called the MV *Toscana*. Beneath this sheet was the export license, granted by his own signature.

He glanced up at the civil servant in front of him. "Why the change?" he asked.

"Colonel, it is simply that there is no berth available in Valencia port for two weeks. The place is crowded to capacity."

Colonel Almela grunted. The explanation was plausible. In the summer months Valencia was always crowded, with millions of oranges from the nearby Gancia area being exported. But he did not like changes. He liked to play things by the book. Nor did he like this order. It was small, too small, for an entire national police force. Target practice alone for a thousand policemen would use it up in an hour. Nor did he trust Schlinker, whom he knew well and who had slipped the order through his Ministry with a batch of other orders, including more than ten thousand artillery shells for Syria.

He glanced through the papers again. Outside, a church bell struck the hour of one, the hour of lunch. There was still nothing wrong with the papers, including the End User Certificate. Everything bore the right stamp. If only he could find one discrepancy, in the certificate, in the carrying ship of the company that owned it. But everything was clean. Making a final decision, he scrawled his signature across the bottom of the movement order and handed the file back to the civil servant.

"All right," he growled. "Castellón."

"We've had to change the port of embarkation from Valencia to Castellón," said Johann Schlinker two nights later. "There was no choice if the loading date of the twentieth was to be adhered to. Valencia was full for weeks."

Cat Shannon was sitting on the bed in the German arms dealer's room in the Mindanao Hotel. "Where's Castellón?" he asked.

"Forty miles up the coast. It's a smaller port, and quieter. Probably better than Valencia for you. The turn-around of your ship is likely to be quicker. The cargo agent in Valencia has been informed and will personally go north to Castellón to supervise the loading. As soon as the *Toscana* checks in with Valencia harbor authorities by radio, she will be advised of the change of port. She will only have a couple of hours' extra steaming if she diverts at once."

"What about my going aboard?"

"Well, that's your business," said Schlinker. "However, I have informed the agent that a seaman from the *Toscana* who was left behind ten days ago in Brindisi is due to rejoin, and given him the name of Keith Brown. How are your papers?"

"Fine," said Shannon. "They're in order, passport and merchant seaman's card."

"You'll find the agent at the customs office in Castellón as soon as it opens on the morning of the twentieth," Schlinker told him. "His name is Señor Moscar."

"What about the Madrid end of things?"

"The movement order provides for the truck to be loaded under army supervision between eight and midnight on the nineteenth, tomorrow. It will set off with escort at midnight, timing its arrival at Castellón harbor gates for six a.m., the hour they open. If the *Toscana* is on time, she should have docked during the night. The truck carrying the crates is a civilian one, from the same freight firm I always employ. They're very good and very experienced. I have given the transport manager instructions to see the convoy depart from the warehouse and to phone me here immediately."

Shannon nodded. There was nothing he could think of that might go wrong. "I'll be here," he said, and left.

That afternoon he hired a powerful Mercedes from one of the internationally known car agencies that have offices in Madrid.

At half past ten the following evening he was back in the Mindanao with Schlinker while they waited for the telephone call. Both men were nervous, as men must be when a carefully laid plan rests for its success or catastrophic failure in the hands of others. Schlinker was as concerned as Shannon but for different reasons. He knew that, if anything went badly wrong, a complete investigation into the End User Certificate he had supplied could be ordered, and that certificate would not stand up to a complete investigation, which must include a check with the Interior Ministry in Baghdad. If he were exposed on that one, other, and for him far more lucrative, deals with Madrid would be forfeit. Not for the first time he wished he had not taken the order in the first place, but, like most arms dealers, he was a man so greedy that no offer of money could be turned down. It would almost be physical pain to do it.

Midnight came, and still there was no call. Then half past midnight. Shannon paced the room, snarling his anger and frustration at the fat German, who sat drinking whisky. At twelve-forty the phone rang. Schlinker leaped at it. He spoke several words in Spanish and waited.

"What is it?" snapped Shannon.

"Moment," replied Schlinker and waved his hand for silence. Then someone else came on the phone and there was more Spanish, which Shannon could not understand. Finally Schlinker grinned and said, *"Gracias,"* into the phone several times.

"It's on its way," he said when he put the phone down. "The convoy left the depot fifteen minutes ago under escort for Castellón."

But Shannon was gone.

The Mercedes was more than a match for the convoy, even though on the long motorway from Madrid to Valencia the convoy could keep up a steady 60 miles per hour. It took Shannon forty minutes to find his way out of the sprawling suburbs of Madrid, and he supposed the convoy would know the way much better. But on the motorway he could take the Mercedes to 100 mph. He kept a careful eye open as he sped past hundreds of trucks roaring through the night toward the coast, and found what he was looking for just past the town of Requena, forty miles west of Valencia.

His lights picked up the army jeep keeping station to a covered 8-ton truck, and as he swept past he noted the name on the truck's side. It was the name of the trucking company Schlinker had given him. Driving ahead of the truck was another army vehicle, a four-door sedan, evidently with an officer sitting alone in the back. Shannon touched the accelerator, and the Mercedes sped past toward the coast.

At Valencia he took the ring road around the sleeping city, following the signs to the E26 highway to Barcelona. The motorway ran out just north of Valencia, and he was back to crawling behind orange trucks and early farm vehicles, past the miraculous Roman fortress of Sagunto, hacked by the legionaries out of the living rock and later converted by the Moors into a citadel of Islam. He drove into Castellón just after four and followed the signs labelled PUERTO.

The port of Castellón lies three miles from the main town, down a narrow, arrow-straight road that leads from the city to the sea. At the end of the road it is impossible to miss the port and harbor, for there is nothing else there.

As usual with Mediterranean ports, there are three separate harbors, one for freighters, one for yachts and pleasure craft, and one for fishing vessels. In Castellón the commercial port lies to the left as one faces the sea, and like all Spanish ports is ringed by a fence, and the gates are manned day and night by armed Guardia Civil. In the center lies the harbormaster's office, and beside it the splendid yacht club, with a dining room looking out over the commercial port on one side and the yacht basin and fishing harbor on the other. Landward of the harbor office is a row of warehouses.

Shannon turned to the left and parked the car by the roadside, climbed out, and started walking. Halfway around the perimeter fence of the port area he found the main gate, with a sentry dozing in a box beside it. The gate was locked. Farther on, he peered through the chain-links and with a surge of relief spotted the *Toscana* berthed against the far side of the basin. He settled to wait till six o'clock.

He was at the main gate at quarter to six, smiled and nodded at the Guardia Civil sentry, who stared coldly back. In the rising sunlight he could see the army staff car, truck, and jeep, with seven or eight soldiers milling around them, parked a hundred yards away. At 6:10 a civilian car arrived, parked next to the gate, and sounded its horn. A small, dapper Spaniard climbed out. Shannon approached him.

"Señor Moscar?"

"*Sí.*"

"My name's Brown. I'm the seaman who's got to join his ship here."

The Spaniard puckered his brows. "*Por favor? Que?*"

"Brown," insisted Shannon. "*Toscana.*"

The Spaniard's face lightened. "*Ah, sí. El marinero.* Come, please."

The gate had been opened, and Moscar showed his pass. He babbled for several seconds at the guard and the customs man who had opened the gate, and pointed at Shannon. Cat caught the word *marinero* several times, and his passport and merchant seaman's card were examined. Then he followed Moscar to the customs office. An hour later he was on board the *Toscana.*

The search started at nine. There was no warning. The captain's manifest had been presented and checked out. It was perfectly in order. Down on the quay the truck from Madrid was parked, along with the car and the jeep. The army escort captain, a thin, sallow man with a face like a Moor's and a lipless mouth, consulted with two customs officers. Then the latter came aboard. Moscar followed. They checked the cargo to make sure it was what the manifest said and no more. They peered into nooks and crannies, but not under the floorboards of the main hold. They looked in the stores locker, gazed at the tangle of chains, oil drums, and paint cans, and closed the door. It took an hour. The main thing that interested them was why Captain Waldenberg needed seven men on such a small ship. It was explained that Dupree and Vlaminck were company employees who had missed their ship in Brindisi and were being dropped off at Malta on the way to Latakia. They had no seamen's cards with them because they had left their gear on board their own ship. Asked for a name, Waldenberg gave them the name of a ship he had seen in Brindisi harbor. There was silence from the Spaniards, who looked at their chief for advice. He glanced down at the army captain, shrugged, and left the ship. Twenty minutes later, loading began.

At half past noon the *Toscana* slipped out of Castellón harbor and turned her helm south to Cape San Antonio. Cat Shannon, feeling sick now that it was all over, knowing that from then on he was virtually unstoppable, was leaning against the after rail, watching the flat green orange groves south of Castellón slip away as they headed for the sea.

Carl Waldenberg came up behind him. "That's the last stop?" he asked.

"The last where we have to open our hatches," said Shannon. "We have to pick up some men on the coast of Africa, but we'll moor in the roads. The men will come out by launch. Deck cargo native workers. At least, that's what they'll be shipped as."

"I've only got charts as far as the Strait of Gibraltar," objected Waldenberg.

Shannon reached into his zip-up windbreaker and pulled out a sheaf of charts, half of the number Endean had handed him in Rome. "These," he said, handing them to the skipper, "will get you as far as Freetown, Sierra Leone. That's where we anchor and pick up the men. Please give me an arrival time at noon on July second. That is the rendezvous."

As the captain left to return to his cabin and start to plot his course and speed, Shannon was left alone at the rail. Seagulls wheeled around the stern, seeking morsels dropped from the galley, where Cipriani was preparing lunch, squealing and cawing as they dipped toward the foaming wake to snatch up a scrap of bread or vegetable.

Anyone listening would have heard another sound amid their screaming, the sound of a man whistling "Spanish Harlem."

Far away to the north, another ship slipped her moorings and under the guidance of a port pilot eased her way out of the harbor of Archangel. The motor vessel *Komarov* was only ten years old and something over five thousand tons.

Inside her bridge, the atmosphere was warm and cosy. The captain and the pilot stood side by side, staring forward as the quays and warehouses slipped past to her port side, and watching the channel ahead to the open sea. Each man held a cup of steaming coffee. The helmsman kept the vessel on the heading given him by the pilot, and to his left the radar screen gleamed and died endlessly, its iridescent sweep arm picking up on each turn the dotted ocean ahead and beyond it the fringe of the ice that would never melt, even in high summer.

In the stern two men leaned over the rail beneath the flag with the hammer-and-sickle emblem and watched the Russian Arctic port slip past. Dr. Ivanov

clipped the crushed cardboard filter of his black cigarette between his teeth and sniffed the crisp, salt-caked
air. Both men were wrapped against the cold, for even
in June the wind off the White Sea is no invitation to
shirtsleeves. By his side, one of his technicians,
younger, eager for his first trip abroad, turned to him.

"Comrade Doctor," he began.

Ivanov took the stump of the Papiross from his
teeth and flicked it into the foaming wake. "My friend,"
he said, "I think, as we are now aboard, you can call
me Mikhail Mikhailovich."

"But at the institute—"

"We are not at the institute. We are on board a
ship. And we will be in fairly close confinement either
here or in the jungle for months to come."

"I see," said the younger man, but he was not to be
repressed. "Have you ever been to Zangaro before?"

"No," said his superior.

"But to Africa," insisted the younger man.

"To Ghana, yes."

"What is it like?"

"Full of jungle, swamps, mosquitoes, snakes, and
people who don't understand a damn thing you say."

"But they understand English," said the assistant.
"We both speak English."

"Not in Zangaro, they don't."

"Oh." The junior technician had read all he could
find, which was not much, in the encyclopaedia borrowed from the vast library at the institute, about
Zangaro.

"The captain told me if we make good time we
should arrive at Clarence in twenty-two days. That will
be their Independence Day."

"Bully for them," said Ivanov and walked away.

Past Cape Spartel, nosing her way from the Mediterranean into the Atlantic, the MV *Toscana* radioed a
ship-to-shore telegram to Gibraltar for onpassing to
London. It was to Mr. Walter Harris at a London

address. It said simply: "Pleased announce your brother completely recovered." It was the sign meaning the *Toscana* was on her way and on schedule. Slight variations of the message about Mr. Harris's brother's health could have meant she was on course but late, or in some kind of trouble. No telegram of any kind meant she had not been cleared from Spanish territorial waters.

That afternoon there was a conference in Sir James Manson's office.

"Good," said the tycoon when Endean broke the news. "How much time has she got to reach target?"

"Twenty-two days, Sir James. It is now Day Seventy-eight of the hundred estimated for the project. Shannon had allowed Day Eighty for his departure from Europe, and that would have left him twenty days. He estimated the time at sea between sixteen and eighteen days, allowing for adverse weather or a two-day breakdown. He had four days in hand, even on his own estimate."

"Will he strike early?"

"No, sir. Strike Day is still Day One Hundred. He'll kill time hove-to at sea if he has to."

Sir James Manson paced up and down his office. "How about the rented villa?" he asked.

"It has been arranged, Sir James."

"Then I don't see any point in your waiting around London any longer. Get over to Paris again, get a visa for Cotonou, fly down there, and get our new employee, Colonel Bobi, to accompany you to this place next to Zangaro. If he seems shifty, offer him more money.

"Get settled in, get the truck and the hunting guns ready, and when you receive Shannon's signal that he is going in for the attack that evening, break the news to Bobi. Get him to sign that mining concession as President Bobi, date it one month later, and send all three copies by registered post in three different envelopes to me here.

"Keep Bobi virtually under lock and key until

Shannon's second signal to say he has succeeded. Then in you go. By the way, that bodyguard you are taking with you—is he ready?"

"Yes, Sir James. For the kind of money he's getting, he's good and ready."

"What's he like?"

"As nasty as they come. Which is what I was looking for."

"You could still have problems, you know. Shannon will have all his men round him, at least those who survive the battle. He could prove troublesome."

Endean grinned. "Shannon's men will follow Shannon," he said. "And I can handle him. Like all mercenaries, he's got his price. I'll just offer it to him—but in Switzerland and out of Zangaro."

When he had gone, Sir James Manson stared down at the City below him and wondered if any man did not have his price. "They can all be bought, and if they can't, they can be broken," one of his mentors had once said to him. And after years as a tycoon, watching politicians, generals, journalists, editors, businessmen, ministers, entrepreneurs and aristocrats, workers and union leaders, blacks and whites, at work and play, he was still of that view.

Many years ago a Spanish seafarer, looking from the sea toward the land, had seen a mountain which, with the sun behind it in the east, appeared to him to have the shape of a lion's head. He called the land Lion Mountain and passed on. The name stuck, and the country became known as Sierra Leone. Later another man, seeing the same mountain in a different light, or through different eyes, called it Mount Aureole. That name also stuck. Even later, and in a more whimsical bout of fantasy, a white man named the town founded in its shadow Freetown, and it still bears the name today. It was just after noon on July 2, Day Eighty-eight in Shannon's private calendar, that the motor vessel *Toscana* dropped anchor a third of a mile out from the shore, off Freetown, Sierra Leone.

On the voyage from Spain, Shannon had insisted that the cargo remain just where it was, untouched and unopened. This was just in case there was a search at Freetown, although since they had nothing to discharge and no cargo to take on board, that would have been most unusual. The ammunition crates had been scrubbed clean of their Spanish markings and sanded down with a disk sander to the bright white wood. Stenciled markings showing that the crates contained drilling bits for the oil rigs off the Cameroon coast had been painted on.

Only one job had he allowed to be done on the way south. The bundles of mixed clothing had been sorted, and the one containing the haversacks and webbing had been opened. With canvas needle and palm, Cipriani, Vlaminck, and Dupree had passed the days cutting the haversacks to pieces and transforming them into backpacks fitted with a score of long, narrow pouches, each capable of taking one bazooka rocket. These now shapeless and inexplicable bundles were stored in the paint locker among the cleaning rags.

The smaller knapsacks had also been altered. The packs had been cut away so that only the shoulder straps remained, with braces across the chest and around the waist. Dog-clips had been fastened atop each shoulder strap, and others at the belt, and later these frames would accommodate an entire crate of mortar bombs, enabling up to twenty to be carried at one time.

The *Toscana* had announced her presence while six miles offshore to the harbormaster's office of Freetown, and had been given permission to enter port and anchor out in the bay. As she had no cargo to load or unload, there was no need for her to take up room at the port's precious Queen Elizabeth II Quay. She had come only to take on deck crew.

Freetown is one of the favorite ports along the West African coast for taking aboard these brawny laborers who, trained in the use of tackle and winches, are used by the tramp steamers frequenting the smaller timber ports along the coast. They board at Freetown on the outward voyage and are discharged with their pay on the way back. In a hundred coves and creeks along the coast, where cranes and jetties are at a premium, ships have to use their own jumbo derricks to load cargo. It is grindingly hard work, as one sweats in the tropical fever heat, and white seamen are paid to be seamen, not stevedores. Locally recruited labor might not be available and probably would not know how to handle cargo, so Sierra Leonians are brought along. They sleep in the open on the ship's deck for the voyage, brewing up their own food and performing their ablutions over the stern. It caused no surprise in Freetown when the *Toscana* gave this as her reason for calling.

When the anchor cable rattled down, Shannon scanned the shoreline right around the bay, almost all of it taken up by the outer shantytown of the country's capital.

The sky was overcast, no rain fell, but beneath the clouds the heat was like a greenhouse, and he felt the sweat clamping his shirt to his torso. It would be like this from here on. His eyes riveted on the central area of the city's waterfront, where a large hotel stood looking out over the bay. If anywhere, this was where Langarotti would be waiting, staring out to sea. Perhaps he had not arrived yet. But they could not wait forever. If he was not there by sundown, they would have to invent a reason for staying on—like a broken refrigerator. It would be unthinkable to sail without the cold store working. He took his eyes away from the hotel and watched the tenders plying around the big Elder Dempster ship tied up at the quay.

On shore, the Corsican had already seen the *Toscana* before she dropped anchor, and was heading back into the town. He had been there for a week and had all the men Shannon wanted. They were not the same tribal group as the Leonians, but no one minded. A mixture of tribes was available as stevedores and deck cargo.

Just after two, a small pinnace came out from the customs house with a uniformed man standing in the back. He was the assistant chief customs officer, white socks agleam, khaki shorts and tunic pressed, epaulettes sparkling, and stiff peaked cap set dead straight. Among the regalia a pair of ebony knees and a beaming face could be distinguished. When he came aboard, Shannon met him, introduced himself as the owner's representative, shook hands profusely, and led the customs man to the captain's cabin.

The three bottles of whisky and two cartons of cigarettes were waiting. The officer fanned himself, sighed gustily with pleasure at the cool of the air-conditioning, and sipped his beer. He cast an incurious eye over the new manifest, which said the *Toscana* had picked up machine parts at Brindisi and was taking them to the AGIP oil company's offshore concessions near the Cameroon coast. There was no mention of Yugoslavia or Spain. Other cargo was listed as power boats (inflatable), engines (outboard), and tropical clothing (assorted), also for the oil drillers. On the way back she would wish to load cocoa and some coffee at San Pedro, Ivory Coast, and return to Europe. He exhaled on his official stamp to moisten it, and placed his approval on the manifest. An hour later he was gone, his presents in his tucker bag.

Just after six, as the evening cooled, Shannon made out the longshore boat moving away from the beach. Amidships the two local men who ran passengers out to the waiting vessels in the bay heaved at their oars. Aft sat seven other Africans, clutching bundles on their knees. In the prow sat a lone European. As the craft swung expertly in to the side of the *Toscana,* Jean-Baptiste Langarotti came nimbly up the ladder that hung to the water.

One by one the bundles were heaved from the bobbing rowboat up to the rail of the freighter; then the seven Africans followed. Although it was indiscreet to do so in sight of land, Vlaminck, Dupree, and Semmler started to clap them on the back and shake hands.

The Africans, grinning from ear to ear, seemed as
happy as the mercenaries. Waldenberg and his mate
looked on in surprise. Shannon signed to the captain
to take the *Toscana* back to sea.

After dark, sitting in groups on the main deck,
taking with gratitude the cooling breeze off the sea as
the *Toscana* rolled on to the south, Shannon introduced his recruits to Waldenberg. The mercenaries
knew them all, as they did the mercenaries. Six of the
Africans were young men, called Johnny, Patrick, Jinja
(nicknamed Ginger), Sunday, Bartholomew, and Timothy.

Each of them had fought with the mercenaries before; each of them had been personally trained by one
of the European soldiers; each of them had been tried
and tested in battle many times and would stick it out
however hard the firefight. And each of them was
loyal to his leader. The seventh was an older man, who
smiled less, bore himself with a confident dignity, and
was addressed by Shannon as "Doctor." He too was
loyal to his leader and his people.

"How are things at home?" Shannon asked him.

Dr. Okoye shook his head sadly. "Not well," he
said.

"Tomorrow we start work," Shannon told him.
"We start preparing tomorrow."

PART THREE
The Big Killing

21

For the remainder of the sea voyage, Cat Shannon worked his men without pause. Only the middle-aged African whom he called "Doctor" was exempt. The rest were divided into parties, each with a separate job to do.

Marc Vlaminck and Kurt Semmler broke open the five green Castrol oil drums by hammering off the false bottoms, and from each plucked the bulky package of twenty Schmeissers and a hundred magazines that was inside. The superfluous lubricating oil was poured into smaller containers and saved for the ship's use.

Aided by the six African soldiers, the pair stripped the masking tape from each of the hundred submachine guns, which were then individually wiped clean of oil and grease. By the time they had finished, the six Africans had already learned the operating mechanisms of the Schmeisser in a way that was as good if not better than any weapons-familiarization course that they could have undergone.

After breaking open the first ten boxes of 9mm. ammunition, the eight of them sat around the decks slotting the shells into the magazines, thirty to each, until the first fifteen thousand rounds from their store had gone into the five hundred magazines at their disposal. Eighty of the Schmeissers were then set aside while Jean-Baptiste Langarotti prepared sets of uniforms from the bales stored in the hold. These sets consisted of two T-shirts, two pairs of shorts, two pairs of socks, one pair of boots, one set of trousers, one beret, one combat blouse, and one sleeping bag. When these were ready, the bundle was wrapped up, one Schmeisser and five full magazines were wrapped in an oily cloth and slipped into a polyethylene bag, and the whole lot was stuffed into the sleeping bag. Tied at the top and ready for handling like a sack, each sleeping bag contained the necessary clothing and weaponry for one future soldier.

Twenty sets of uniforms and twenty Schmeissers with five magazines per carbine were set aside. These were for the attack force itself, although the force numbered only eleven, with spares for the crew if necessary. Langarotti, who had learned while in the army and in prison to handle a needle and thread, altered and sewed eleven sets of uniforms for the members of the attack party until each man was fitted out.

Dupree and Cipriani, the deckhand, who turned out to be a useful carpenter, stripped down several of the packing crates that had once contained ammunition, and turned their attention to the outboard engines. All three were Johnson 60-horsepower units. The two men built a wooden box to fit neatly over the top of each engine, and lined the boxes with foam rubber from the mattresses that had been brought along. With the exhaust noise of the engines muffled by the underwater exhausts, the mechanical noise emanating from the engine casings could also be reduced to a low murmur by the muffling boxes.

When Vlaminck and Dupree had finished these tasks, each turned his attention to the weapon he would be using on the night of the strike. Dupree uncrated his two mortar tubes and familiarized himself with the aiming mechanisms. He had not used the Yugoslav model of mortar before, but was relieved to see it was simple. He prepared seventy mortar bombs, checking and arming the primers in the nose-cone of each bomb.

Having repacked the prepared bombs into their boxes, he clipped two boxes, one above the other, to the webbing harness that had already been prepared from the army-style knapsacks he had bought in London two months earlier.

Vlaminck concentrated on his two bazookas, of which only one would be used on the night of the attack. Again, the main limitation to what he could take with him was the weight factor. Everything had to be carried on a human back. Standing on the forepeak, using the tip of the flagpole sticking above the stern as a fixed point, his aiming disk slotted to the end of the bazooka, he carefully adjusted the sights to the weapon until he was certain he could take a barrel at two hundred yards with no more than two shots. He had already picked Patrick as his back-up man, for they had been together before and knew each other well enough to make a good team. With his backpack, the African would be carrying ten bazooka rockets as well as his own Schmeisser. Vlaminck added another two rockets as his personal load, and Cipriani sewed him two pouches to hang from his belt, which could contain the extra rockets.

Shannon concentrated on the ancillary gear, examining the magnesium-flare rockets and explaining to Dupree how they worked. He distributed one compass to each mercenary, tested the gas-powered foghorn, and checked the portable radio sets.

Having time, Shannon had the *Toscana* heave to for two days well out at sea in an area where the ship's radar told them there was no other shipping within twenty miles. As the ship lay almost stationary, heaving slightly on the swell, each man tested his personal Schmeisser. The whites had no problems; they had each in their time used half a dozen different submachine guns, and these weapons vary but slightly. The Africans took longer to get used to them, for most of their experience had been with bolt-action 7.92mm. Mausers or the standard 7.62 NATO self-loading rifle. One of the German carbines jammed repeatedly, so Shannon threw it overboard and gave the man another. Each African fired off nine hundred rounds, until he was accustomed to the feel of the Schmeisser in his hands, and each man had been cured of the annoying habit African soldiers tend to adopt, of closing their eyes while they fire. There was no point in testing the mortars, since they have no moving parts—the bombs do the work—and they cannot be fired with accuracy anyway from the deck of a ship at sea.

The five empty and open-topped oil barrels had been stored for later use, and these were now streamed astern of the *Toscana* for bazooka practice. At a hundred yards all of the men, black and white, could riddle a barrel before they had ceased their practice. Four barrels were destroyed and sunk in this manner, and the fifth was used by Marc Vlaminck. He let it stream to two hundred yards, then planted himself in the stern of the *Toscana,* feet apart and braced, the bazooka across his right shoulder, right eye applied to the sight. Judging the gentle heave of the deck, he waited until he was sure and fired off his first rocket. It screamed over the top of the barrel and exploded with a spout of spray into the ocean. His second rocket took the barrel in the center. There was a crash, and the boom of the explosion echoed back over the water to the watching mercenaries and crew. Fragments of tinplate spattered the water close to where the barrel had been, and a cheer came from the watchers. Grinning widely, Vlaminck turned to Shannon, ripped off the glasses he had used to protect his eyes, and wiped the specks of smut from his face.

"You said you wanted a door taken off, Cat?"

"That's right, a bloody great wooden gate, Tiny."

"I'll give it to you in matchsticks, and that's a promise," said the Belgian.

Because of the noise they had made, Shannon ordered the *Toscana* to move on the next day, and two days later he called his second halt. In the period under way, the men had hauled out the three assault craft and inflated them. They lay side by side along the main deck. Each, despite being a deep, dark gray in color, had a brilliant orange nose and the name of the manufacturer in the same luminous color down each side. These were painted out with black paint from the ship's store.

When they were hove-to for the second time, they tested all three. Without the muffling boxes placed over the top of each engine, the Johnsons made an audible mutter even when four hundred yards away from the *Toscana*. With the boxes in place and the engines throttled back to less than quarter-power, there was hardly a sound at thirty yards. They tended to overheat after twenty minutes at half-power, but this could be stretched to thirty minutes if power was reduced. Shannon took one of the craft out for two hours, checking throttle settings for speed against noise, to get the best combination. As the powerful outboards gave him a large reserve, he elected never to push them beyond one-third of full power, and advised his men to close down to less than quarter-power for the last two hundred yards as they approached the landing beaches of the target area.

The walkie-talkies were also tested at up to four miles, and despite the heavy atmospherics and the hint of thunder in the stifling air, messages could still be heard if read over clearly and slowly. To get them used to the notion, the Africans were also given trips in the power craft, at a varying range of speeds, in daylight and at night. The night exercises were the most important.

For one of them Shannon took the other four whites and the six Africans three miles out from the *Toscana,* which burned one small light at her masthead. On the journey away from the ship, the ten men had their eyes bandaged. When the masks were taken off, each was given ten minutes to accustom his vision to the blackness of the sky and the ocean, before the move back to the boat began. With the engine throttled down and dead silence maintained aboard, the assault craft moved quietly back toward the light that represented the *Toscana*. Sitting with the tiller bar in his hand, holding the power setting steady at one-third, then cutting back to less than a quarter for the final run-in, Shannon could feel the tension of the men in front of him. They knew this was what it would be like when they struck, and there would be no second chances.

Back on board, Carl Waldenberg came up to Shannon as the two men watched the crew winch the vessel inboard by torchlight.

"I hardly heard a sound," he said. "Not until you were a couple of hundred meters away, and I was listening hard. Unless they have very alert guards posted, you should be able to make the beach, wherever you are going. Incidentally, where are you going? I need more charts if I have to proceed much farther."

"I think you'd all better know," said Shannon. "We'll spend the rest of the night going through the briefing."

Until dawn, the crew (with the exception of the engineer, who still slept with his engines), the seven Africans, and the four mercenaries listened to Shannon in the main saloon while he went through the entire plan of attack. He had prepared and set up his projector and slide transparencies, some of which were pictures he had obtained of Zangaro, others of which were the maps and charts he had bought or drawn for himself.

When he had finished, there was dead silence in the stifling cabin, the blue wreaths of cigarette smoke trickling out through the open portholes into the equally clammy night outside.

Finally Waldenberg said, *"Gott in Himmel."* Then they all started. It took an hour before the questions were answered. Waldenberg wanted reassurance that if anything went wrong the survivors would be back on board and the *Toscana* well over the horizon before sunrise. Shannon gave it to him.

"We have only your word for it they have no navy, no gunboats," Waldenberg said.

"Then my word will have to do," said Shannon. "They have none."

"Just because you did not see any—"

"They have none," snapped Shannon. "I spent hours talking with people who have been there for years. There are no gunboats, no navy."

The six Africans had no questions. Each would stick close to the mercenary who would lead him and trust that he knew what he was doing. The seventh, the doctor, asked briefly where he would be, and accepted that he would remain on board the *Toscana*. The four mercenaries had a few purely technical questions, which Shannon answered in technical terms.

When they came back up on deck, the Africans stretched themselves out on their sleeping bags and went to sleep. Shannon had often envied their ability to sleep at any time, in any place, in almost any circumstances. The doctor retired to his cabin, as did Norbiatto, who would take the next watch. Waldenberg went into his wheelhouse, and the *Toscana* began to move again toward her destination, just three days away.

The five mercenaries grouped themselves on the afterdeck behind the crew quarters and talked until the sun was high. They all approved of the plan of attack and accepted that Shannon's reconnaissance had been accurate and precise. If anything had changed since then, if there had been an unforeseen addition to the town's defenses or improvements to the palace, they knew they could all die. They would be very few, dangerously few, for such a job, and there was no margin for things going wrong. But they accepted that either they had to win within twenty minutes or they would have to get back to their boats and leave in a hurry—those that could leave. They knew that no one was going to come looking for wounded, and that anyone finding one of his colleagues badly hurt and unmovable would be expected to give him one mercenary's last gift to another, the quick, clean way out, preferable to capture and the slow death. It was part of the rules, and they had all had to do it before.

Just before noon they parted company and turned in.

They all woke early on the morning of Day Ninety-nine. Shannon had been up half the night, watching beside Waldenberg as the coastline loomed out of the perimeter of the tiny radar screen at the rear of the wheelhouse.

"I want you to come within visual range of the coast to the south of the capital," he had told the captain, "and spend the morning steaming northwards, parallel to the shore, so that at noon we are off the coast here."

His finger jabbed the sea off the coast of Manandi. During the twenty days at sea he had come to trust the German captain. Waldenberg, having taken his money in Ploce port, had stuck by his side of the bargain, giving himself completely to making the operation as successful as he could. Shannon was confident the seaman would hold his ship at readiness four miles off the coast, a bit to the south of Clarence, while the firefight went on, and if the distress call came over the walkie-talkie, that he would wait until the men who had managed to escape rejoined the *Toscana* in their speedboats, before making at full power for the open sea. There was no spare man Shannon could leave behind to ensure this, so he had to trust Waldenberg.

He had already found the frequency on the ship's radio on which Endean wanted him to transmit his first message, and this was timed for noon.

The morning passed slowly. Through the ship's telescope Shannon watched the estuary of the Zangaro River move past, a long, low line of mangrove trees along the horizon. At midmorning he could make out the break in the green line where the town of Clarence lay, and passed the telescope to Vlaminck, Langarotti, Dupree, and Semmler. Each studied the off-white blur in silence and handed the glass to the next man. They smoked more than usual and mooched around the deck, tense and bored with the waiting, wishing, now they were so close, that they could go straight into action.

At noon Shannon began to transmit his message. He read it clear into the radio speaker. It was just one word, "Plantain." He gave it every ten seconds for five minutes, then broke for five minutes, then gave it again. Three times within thirty minutes, each time over a five-minute period, he broadcast the word and hoped that Endean would hear it somewhere on the mainland. It meant simply that Shannon and his men were on time and in position, and that they would strike Clarence and Kimba's palace in the small hours of the following morning.

Twenty-two miles away across the water, Simon Endean heard the word on his Braun transistor radio, folded the long wasp-antenna, left the hotel balcony, and withdrew into the bedroom. Then he began slowly and carefully to explain to the former colonel of the Zangaran army that within twenty-four hours he, Antoine Bobi, would be President of Zangaro. At four in the afternoon the colonel, grinning and chuckling at the thought of the reprisals he would take against those who had assisted in his ousting, struck his deal with Endean. He signed the document granting Bormac Trading Company a ten-year exclusive mining concession in the Crystal Mountains for a flat annual fee, a tiny profits-participation by the Zangaran government, and watched Endean place in an envelope and seal a check certified by a Swiss bank for half a million dollars in the name of Antoine Bobi.

In Clarence preparations went ahead through the afternoon for the following day's independence celebrations. Six prisoners, lying badly beaten in the cells

beneath the former colonial police station, listened to
the cries of the Kimba Patriotic Youth marching
through the streets above them, and knew that they
would be battered to death in the main square as part
of the celebrations Kimba had prepared. Photographs
of the President were prominently hung on every public building, and the diplomatic wives prepared their
migraines so they would be excused attendance at
the ceremonies.

In the shuttered palace, surrounded by his guards,
President Jean Kimba sat alone at his desk, contem-
plating the advent of his sixth year of office.

During the afternoon the *Toscana* and her lethal
cargo put about and began to cruise slowly back down
the coast from the north.

In the wheelhouse Shannon sipped his coffee and
explained to Waldenberg how he wanted the *Toscana*
placed.

"Hold her just north of the border until sundown,"
he told his captain. "After nine p.m., start her up
again and move diagonally toward the coast. Between
sundown and nine, we will have streamed the three
assault craft astern of the ship, each loaded with its
complement. That will have to be done by flashlight,
but well away from the land, at least ten miles out.

"When you start to move, around nine, keep her
really slow, so you end up here, four miles out from
the shore and one mile north of the peninsula at two
a.m. You'll be out of sight of the city in that position.
With all lights doused, no one should see you. So far
as I know, there's no radar on the peninsula, unless a
ship is in port."

"Even if there is, she should not have a radar on,"
growled Waldenberg. He was bent over his inshore
chart of the coast, measuring his distances with compasses and set-square. "When does the first craft set
free and move inshore?"

"At two. That will be Dupree and his mortar crew.

The other two boats cast adrift and head for the beach one hour later. Okay?"

"Okay," said Waldenberg. "I'll have you there."

"It has to be accurate," insisted Shannon. "We'll see no lights in Clarence, even if there are any, until we round the headland. So we'll be on compass heading only, calculating by speed and heading, until we see the outline of the shore, which might be no more than a hundred meters. It depends on the sky; cloud, moon, and stars."

Waldenberg nodded. He knew the rest. After he heard the firefight begin, he was to ease the *Toscana* across the mouth of the harbor four miles out, and heave to again two miles to the south of Clarence, four miles out from the tip of the peninsula. From then on he would listen on his walkie-talkie. If all went well, he would stay where he was until sunup. If things went badly, he would turn on the lights at the masthead, the forepeak, and the stern, to guide the returning force back to the *Toscana*.

Darkness that evening came early, for the sky was overcast and the moon would not rise until the small hours of the morning. The rains had already started, and twice in the previous three days the men had weathered drenching downpours as the skies opened. The weather report from Monrovia, listened to avidly on the radio, indicated there would be scattered squalls along the coast that night, but no tornadoes, and they could only pray there would be no torrential rains while the men were in their open boats or while the battle for the palace was on.

Before sundown the tarpaulins were hauled off the equipment piled in rows along the main deck, and when darkness fell Shannon and Norbiatto began organizing the departure of the assault craft. The first over the side was the one Dupree would use. There was no point in using the derrick; the sea was only eight feet beneath the deck at the lowest point. The men lowered the fully inflated craft into the water manually, and Semmler and Dupree went down into it as it bobbed against the *Toscana*'s side in the slow swell.

The two of them hoisted the heavy outboard engine into place over the stern and screwed it tight to the backboard. Before placing the muffler on top of it, Semmler started the Johnson up and ran her for two minutes. The Serbian engineer had already given all three engines a thorough check-over, and it ran like a sewing machine. With the muffling box on top, the noise died to a low hum.

Semmler climbed out, and the equipment was lowered to Dupree's waiting hands. There were the baseplates and sighting gear for both mortars, then the two mortar tubes. Dupree was taking forty mortar bombs for the palace and twelve for the barracks. To be on the safe side, he took sixty bombs, all primed and fused for detonation on impact.

He also took both flare-launching rockets and the ten flares, one of the gas-powered foghorns, one walkie-talkie, and his night glasses. Slung over his shoulder he had his personal Schmeisser, and tucked in his belt were five full magazines. The two Africans who were going with him, Timothy and Sunday, were the last into the assault craft.

When it was ready, Shannon stared down at the three faces that looked back up at him in the dim glow from the flashlight. "Good luck," he called softly.

For answer Dupree raised one thumb and nodded. Holding the painter of the assault craft, Semmler moved back along the rail while Dupree fended off from down below. When the craft was streamed astern of the *Toscana* in complete darkness, Semmler tied her painter to the after rail, leaving the three men to bob up and down on the swell.

The second boat took less time to get into the water, for the men had got the hang of it. Marc Vlaminck went down with Semmler to set the outboard engine in position, for this was their boat. Vlaminck was taking one bazooka and twelve rockets, two on his own body, the other ten carried by his back-up man, who was Patrick. Semmler had his Schmeisser and five magazines in easy-extraction pouches hung around his belt. He had a set of night glasses around his neck and the second walkie-talkie strapped to one thigh. As he was the only man who could speak German, French, and reasonable English, he would double as the main attack party's radio operator. When the two whites were ensconced in their craft, Patrick and Jinja, who would be Semmler's back-up man, slid down the Jacob's ladder from the *Toscana* and took their places.

The boat was streamed astern of the ship, and Dupree's painter was passed to Semmler, who made it fast to his own assault craft. The two inflatable vessels bobbed behind the *Toscana* in line astern, separated by the length of rope, but none of their occupants said a word.

Langarotti and Shannon took the third and last boat. They were accompanied by Bartholomew and Johnny, the latter a big, grinning fighter who had been promoted at Shannon's insistence when they last fought together, but who had refused to take his own company, as his new rank entitled him to, preferring to stick close to Shannon and look after him.

Just before Shannon, who was the last man into the boats, descended the ladder, Captain Waldenberg appeared from the direction of the bridge and tugged at his sleeve. The German pulled the mercenary to one side and muttered quietly, "We may have a problem."

Shannon was immobile, frozen by the thought that something had gone seriously wrong. "What is it?" he asked.

"There's a ship. Lying off Clarence, farther out than we are."

"How long since you saw it?"

"Some time," said Waldenberg, "but I thought it must be cruising south down the coast, like us, or moving northward. But it's not; it's riding to."

"You're sure? There's no doubt about it?"

"None at all. When we came down the coast we

were moving so slowly that if the other had been steaming in the same direction, she'd be well away by now. If northward, she'd have passed us by now. She's immobile."

"Any indication of what she is, who she belongs to?"

The German shook his head. "The size of a freighter. No indication who she is, unless we contact her."

Shannon thought for several minutes. "If she were a freighter bringing cargo to Zangaro, would she anchor till morning before entering harbor?" he asked.

Waldenberg nodded. "Quite possible. Entry by night is frequently not allowed in some of the smaller ports along this coast. She's probably riding out until the morning before asking permission to enter port."

"If you've seen her, presumably she's seen you?" Shannon suggested.

"Bound to," said Waldenberg. "We're on her radar all right."

"Could her radar pick up the dinghies?"

"Unlikely," said the captain. "Too low in the water, most probably."

"We go ahead," said Shannon. "It's too late now. We have to assume she's just a freighter waiting out the night."

"She's bound to hear the firefight," said Waldenberg.

"What can she do about it?"

The German grinned. "Not much. If you fail, and we're not out of here before sunrise, she'll recognize the *Toscana* through binoculars."

"We mustn't fail, then. Carry on as ordered."

Waldenberg went back to his bridge. The middle-aged African doctor, who had watched the proceedings in silence, stepped forward.

"Good luck, Major," he said in perfectly modulated English. "God go with you."

Shannon felt like saying that he would have preferred a Wombat recoilless rifle, but held his tongue.

He knew these people took religion very seriously. He nodded, said, "Sure," and went over the side.

Out in the darkness, as he looked up at the dim blob of the *Toscana*'s stern above him, there was complete silence but for the slap of the water against the rubberized hulls of the boats. Occasionally it gurgled behind the ship's rudder. From the landward side there was not a sound, for they were well out of earshot of the shore, and by the time they came close enough to hear shouts and laughter it would be well past midnight and, with luck, everyone would be asleep. Not that there was much laughter in Clarence, but Shannon was aware how far a single, sharp sound can travel over water at night, and everyone in his party, in the boats and on the *Toscana,* was sworn to silence and no smoking.

He glanced at his watch. It was quarter to nine. He sat back to wait.

At nine the hull of the *Toscana* emitted a low rumble, and the water beneath her stern began to churn and bubble, the phosphorescent white wake running back to slap against the snub nose of Shannon's assault craft. Then they were under way, and by dipping his fingers over the side he could feel the caress of the passing water. Five hours to cover twenty-eight nautical miles.

The sky was still overcast, and the air was like that inside an old greenhouse, but a hole in the cloud cover let a little dim starlight through. Astern he could make out the craft of Vlaminck and Semmler at the end of twenty feet of rope, and somewhere behind them Janni Dupree was moving along in the wake of the *Toscana.*

The five hours went by like a nightmare. Nothing to do but watch and listen, nothing to see but the darkness and the glitter of the sea, nothing to hear but the low thump of the *Toscana*'s old pistons moving inside her rusted hull. No one could sleep, despite the mesmeric rocking of the light craft, for the tensions were building up in every man in the operation.

But the hours did pass, somehow. Shannon's watch said five past two when the noise of the *Toscana*'s engines died and she slowed to idle in the water. From above the after rail a low whistle came through the darkness—Waldenberg, letting him know they were in position for cast-off. Shannon turned his head to signal Semmler, but Dupree must have heard the whistle, for a few seconds later they heard his engine cough into life and begin to move away toward the shore. They never saw him go, just heard the low buzz of the engine under its muffler vanishing into the darkness.

At the helm of his assault craft big Janni checked his power setting on the twist-grip he held in his right hand, and held his left arm with the compass as steady as he could under his eyes. He knew he should have four and a half miles to cover, angling in toward the coast, trying to make landfall on the outer side of the northern arm that curved around the harbor of Clarence. At that power setting, on that course, he should make it in thirty minutes. At twenty-five minutes he would shut the engine almost off and try to make out his landfall by eyesight. If the others gave him one hour to set up his mortars and flare-rockets, they should move past the tip of the point toward their own beach landing just about the time he was ready. But for that hour he and his two Africans would be the only ones on the shore of Zangaro. That was all the more reason why they should be completely silent as they set up their battery.

Twenty-two minutes after he left the *Toscana*, Dupree heard a low *psst* from the bow of his dinghy. It was Timothy, whom he had posted as a lookout. Dupree glanced up from his compass, and what he saw caused him to throttle back quickly. They were already close to a shoreline, little more than three hundred yards away, and the dim starlight from the hole in the clouds above them showed a line of deeper darkness right ahead. Dupree squinted hard, easing the craft another two hundred yards inshore. It was mangrove; he could hear the water chuckling among the roots. Far out to his right he could discern the line of vegetation ending and the single line of the horizon between sea and night sky running away to the end of vision. He had made landfall three miles along the northern coast of the peninsula.

He brought his boat about, still keeping the throttle very low and virtually silent, and headed back out to sea. He set the tiller to keep the shoreline of the peninsula in vision at half a mile until he reached the limit of the strip of land at whose end the town of Clarence stood, then again headed slowly inshore. At two hundred yards he could make out the long, low spit of gravel that he was seeking, and in the thirty-eighth minute after leaving the *Toscana* he cut the engine and let the assault craft drift on its own momentum toward the spit. It grounded with a soft grating of fabric on gravel.

Dupree stepped lightly down the boat, avoiding the piles of equipment, swung a leg over the prow, and dropped onto the sand. He felt for the painter and kept it in his hand to prevent the boat from drifting away. For five minutes all three men remained immobile, listening for the slightest sound from the town they knew lay over the low hummock of gravel and scrub in front of them, and four hundred yards to the left. But there was no sound. They had arrived without causing any alarm.

When he was certain, Dupree slipped a marlin spike out of his belt, rammed it deep into the shingle of the shore, and tied the painter securely to it. Then he rose to a crouch and ran lightly up the hummock ahead of him. It was barely fifteen feet above sea level at its top, and covered in knee-high scrub that rustled against his boots. The rustling was no problem; it was drowned by the slap of the sea on the shingle and far too soft to be heard away in the town. Crouching at the spine of the strip of land that formed one arm of the harbor, Dupree looked over the top. To his left he could make out the spit running away into the darkness, and straight ahead lay more water, the flat mirror-calm of the protected harbor. The end of the spit of gravel was ten yards to his right.

Returning to the assault craft, he whispered to the two Africans to begin unloading the equipment in complete silence. As the bundles came onto the shore he picked them up and carried them one by one up to the top of the rise. Each metallic piece was covered in sacking to prevent noise if two should knock together.

When the whole of his weaponry was assembled, Dupree began to set it up. He worked fast and quietly. At the far end of the spit, where Shannon had told him there was a round, flat area, he set up his main mortar. He knew, if Shannon's measurements were accurate— and he trusted they would be—that the range from the tip of the land to the center of the palace courtyard was 781 yards. Using his compass, he pointed the mortar on the exact compass bearing Shannon had given him from the point he stood to the presidential palace, and carefully adjusted his mortar's elevation to drop his first range-finding bomb as near to the center of the palace courtyard as possible.

He knew that when the flares went up he would see not the whole palace but just the top story, so he could not watch the bomb hit the ground. But he would see the upward flash of the explosion over the brow of the ground behind the warehouse at the other end of the harbor, and that would be enough.

When he was finished with the first mortar, he set up the second. This was pointed at the barracks, and he put the baseplate ten yards away from the first, down the spine of the land on which he stood. He knew both range and bearing from this mortar to the barracks, and that the accuracy of the second mortar was not vital, since its purpose was to drop bombs at random into the acreage of the former police lines and scatter the Zangaran army men through panic. Timothy, who had been his sergeant on mortars the last time they fought, would handle the second mortar on his own.

He established a pile of a dozen mortar bombs next to the second tube, settled Timothy beside it, and whispered a few last instructions into his ear.

Between the two mortars he established the two flare-launching rockets and jammed one rocket down each launcher, leaving the other eight lying handy. Each flare was reputed to have a life of twenty seconds, so if he was to operate both his own mortar and the illuminations, he knew he would have to work fast and skillfully. He needed Sunday to pass him his mortar bombs from the stack he had built beside the emplacement.

When he was finished, he looked at his watch. Three twenty-two in the morning. Shannon and the other two boats must be off the shore somewhere, heading for the harbor. He took his walkie-talkie, extended the aerial to its full length, switched on, and waited the prescribed thirty seconds for it to warm up. From then on, it would not be switched off again. When he was ready, he pressed the blip button three times at one-second intervals.

A mile off the shore, Shannon was at the helm of the leading assault craft, eyes straining into the darkness ahead. To his left side, Semmler kept the second craft in formation order, and it was he who heard the three buzzes from the walkie-talkie on his knee. He steered his boat softly into the side of Shannon's, so the two rounded sides scuffed each other. Shannon looked toward the other boat. Semmler hissed and pulled his boat away again to maintain station at 2 yards. Shannon was relieved. He knew Semmler had heard Dupree's signal across the water, and that the rangy Afrikaner was set up and waiting for them. Two minutes later, 1000 yards off the shore, Shannon caught the quick flash from Dupree's flashlight, heavily masked and blinkered to a pinpoint of light. It was off to his right, so he knew that he was heading too far north. In unison, the two craft swung to starboard, Shannon trying to recall the exact point from which the light had come and to head for a point 100 yards to the right of it. That would be the harbor entrance. The light came again when Dupree caught the low buzz of the two outboard engines as they were 300 yards from the tip of the point. Shannon spotted the light and changed course a few degrees.

Two minutes later, shut down to less than quarter-power and making no noise louder than a bumblebee, the two assault craft went by the tip of the spit where Dupree was crouching, fifty yards out. The South African caught the glitter of the wake, the bubbles from the exhausts rising to the surface; then they were gone into the harbor entrance and across the still water toward the warehouse on the other side.

There was still no sound from the shore when Shannon's straining eyes made out the bulk of the warehouse against the marginally lighter skyline, steered to the right, and grounded on the shingle of the fishing beach among the natives' dugout canoes and hanging fishnets.

Semmler brought his own boat to the shore a few feet away, and both engines died together. Like Dupree, all the men remained motionless for several minutes, waiting for an alarm to be called. They tried to make out the difference between the humped backs of the fishing canoes and the shape of a waiting ambush party. There was no ambush. Shannon and Semmler stepped over the side; each jabbed a marlin spike into the sand and tethered the boats to it. The rest followed. With a low, muttered "Come on, let's go," Shannon led the way across the beach and up the sloping incline to the 200-yard-wide plateau between the harbor and the silent palace of President Jean Kimba.

22

The eight men ran in a low crouch, up through the
scrubland of the hillside and out onto the plain at the
top. It was after half past three, and no lights were
burning in the palace. Shannon knew that halfway
between the top of the rise and the palace 200 yards
away they would meet the coast road, and standing
at the junction would be at least two palace guards.
He expected he would not be able to take them both
silently, and that after the firing started the party would
have to crawl the last hundred yards to the palace wall.
He was right.

Out across the water, in his lonely vigil, big Janni
Dupree waited for the shot that would send him into
action. He had been briefed that whoever fired the
shot, or however many there were, the first one would
be his signal. He crouched close to the flare-launching
rockets, waiting to let the first one go. In his spare
hand was his first mortar bomb.

Shannon and Langarotti were out ahead of the
other six when they made the road junction in front of
the palace, and already both were wet with sweat.
Their faces, darkened with sepia dye, were streaked
by the running perspiration. The rent in the clouds
above them was larger, and more stars showed through,
so that, although the moon was still hidden, there

was a dim light across the open area in front of the palace. At 100 yards Shannon could make out the line of the roof against the sky, though he missed the guards until he stumbled over one. The man was seated on the ground, snoozing.

Shannon was too slow and clumsy with the commando knife in his right hand. After stumbling, he recovered, but the Vindu guard rose with equal speed and emitted a brief yell of surprise. The call attracted his partner, also hidden in the uncut grass a few feet away. The second man rose, gurgled once as the Corsican's knife opened his throat from carotid artery to jugular vein, and went back down again, choking out his last seconds. Shannon's man took the swipe with the Bowie knife in the shoulder, let out another scream, and ran.

A hundred yards in front, close to the palace gate, there was a second cry, and the sound of a bolt operating in the breech of a rifle. It was never quite certain who fired first. The wild shot from the palace gate and the snarling rip of Shannon's half-second burst that sliced the running man almost in two blended with each other. From far behind them came a whoosh and a scream in the sky; two seconds later the sky above them exploded in blistering white light. Shannon caught a brief impression of the palace in front of him, two figures in front of its gate, and the feeling that his other six men were fanning out to right and left of him. Then the eight of them were face down in the grass and crawling forward.

Janni Dupree stepped away from the rocket-launcher the instant he had torn the lanyard off the first rocket, and was slipping his mortar bomb down the tube as the rocket screamed upward. The *smack-thump* of the mortar bomb departing on its parabola toward the palace blended with the crash of the magnesium flare exploding away toward the land, over the spot he hoped his colleagues would have reached. He took his second bomb and, squinting into the light from the palace, waited to watch the first one fall. He had given himself four sighting shots, on an estimate of fifteen seconds for each bomb in flight. After that he knew he could keep up a fire rate of one every two seconds, with Sunday feeding him the ammunition singly but fast and in rhythm.

His first sighting bomb hit the front right-hand cornice of the palace roof, high enough for him to see the impact. It did not penetrate but blew tiles off the roof just above the gutter. Stooping, he twirled the traverse knob of the directional aiming mechanism a few mils to the left and slipped in his second bomb just as the flare fizzled out. He had stepped across the other rocket-launcher, ripped off the firing lanyard of the rocket, sent it on its way, and stuffed a fresh pair into the two launchers before he needed to look up again. The second flare burst into light above the palace, and four seconds later the second bomb landed. It was dead center, but short, for it fell onto the tiles directly above the main door.

Dupree was also pouring with sweat, and the grub-screw was slick between his fingers. He brought the angle of elevation slightly down, lowering the nose of the mortar a whisker toward the ground for extra range. Working the opposite way from artillery, mortars have to be lowered for extra range. Dupree's third mortar bomb was on its way before the flare fizzled out, and he had a full fifteen seconds to send up the third flare, trot down the spit a short way to actuate the foghorn, and be back in time to watch the mortar explode. It went clean over the palace roof and into the courtyard behind. He saw the red glow for a split second; then it was gone. Not that it mattered. He knew he had got his range and direction exactly right. There would be no shortfalls to endanger his own men in front of the palace.

Shannon and his men were face down in the grass as the three flares lit up the scene around them and Janni's ranging shots went in. No one was prepared to raise his head until the Afrikaner was sending the hardware over the top of the palace and into the rear courtyard.

Between the second and third explosions Shannon risked putting his head up. He knew he had fifteen seconds until the third mortar went home. He saw the palace in the glare of the third magnesium flare, and two lights had gone on in the upper rooms. After the reverberations of the second mortar bomb died away, he heard a variety of screams and shouts from inside the fortress. These were the first and last sounds the defenders made before the roar of explosives blotted out all else.

Within five seconds the foghorn had gone on, the long, maniacal scream howling across the water from the harbor spit, filling the African night with a wail like a thousand released banshees. The crash of the mortar going into the palace courtyard was almost drowned out, and he heard no more screams. When he raised his head again he could see no further damage to the front of the palace and assumed Janni had dropped the bomb over the top. By agreement, Janni would use no more testing shots after his first on target, but go straight into the faster rhythm. From the sea behind him, Shannon heard the thud of mortars begin, steady, pulsing like a heartbeat in the ears, backed by the now monotonous wail of the foghorn, which had a life of seventy seconds on its gas canister.

To get rid of forty bombs, Janni would need eighty seconds, and it was agreed that, if there were a ten-second pause at any point after halfway, he would cease the bombardment so his colleagues would not run forward and be blown apart by a latecomer. Shannon had few worries that Janni would muff it.

When the main barrage began to hit the palace fifteen seconds after the thumps of their firing were heard, the eight men in the grass had a grandstand view. There was no more need for flares; the roaring crash of the mortar bombs going into the flagstone-covered courtyard behind the palace threw up gobbets of red light every two seconds. Only Tiny Marc Vlaminck had anything to do.

He was out to the left of the line of men, almost exactly in front of the main gate. Standing foursquare to the palace, he took careful aim and sent off his first rocket. A twenty-foot-long tongue of flame whirled out of the rear of the bazooka, and the pineapple-sized warhead sped for the main gate. It exploded high on the right-hand edge of the double doors, ripping a hinge out of the masonry and leaving a yard-square hole in the woodwork.

Kneeling by his side, Patrick slipped the rockets out of his backpack spread on the ground, and passed them upward. The second shot began to topple in mid-air and exploded against the stonework of the arch above the door. The third hit the center lock. Both doors seemed to erupt upward under the impact; then they sagged on the twisted hinges, fell apart, and swung inward.

Janni Dupree was halfway through his barrage, and the red glare from behind the roof of the palace had become constant. Something was burning in the court-yard, and Shannon supposed it was the guardhouses. When the doors swung open, the men crouching in the grass could see the red glare through the archway, and two figures swayed in front of it and fell down before they could emerge.

Marc sent four more rockets straight through the open gate into the furnace beyond the archway, which apparently was a through passage to the courtyard behind. It was Shannon's first glimpse of what lay beyond the gate.

The mercenary leader screamed to Vlaminck to stop firing, for he had used seven of his dozen rockets, and for all Shannon knew there might be an armored vehicle somewhere in the town, despite what Gomez had said. But the Belgian was enjoying himself. He sent another four rockets through the front wall of the palace at ground level and on the second floor, finally standing exultantly waving both his bazooka and his last rocket at the palace in front, while Dupree's mortar bombs caromed overhead.

At that moment the foghorn whined away to a whisper and died. Ignoring Vlaminck, Shannon shouted to the others to move forward, and he, Semmler, and Langarotti began to run at a crouch through the grass, Schmeissers held forward, safety catches off, fingers tense on the triggers. They were followed by Johnny, Jinja, Bartholomew, and Patrick, who, having no more bazooka rockets to carry, unslung his submachine gun and joined the others.

At twenty yards, Shannon stopped and waited for Dupree's last bombs to fall. He had lost count of how many were still to come, but the sudden silence after the last bomb fell told him they were over. For a second or two the silence itself was deafening. After the foghorn and the mortars, the roar and crash of Tiny's bazooka rockets, the absence of sound was uncanny. So much so that it was almost impossible to realize the entire operation had lasted less than five minutes.

Shannon wondered for a second if Timothy had sent off his dozen mortar bombs to the army barracks, if the soldiers had scattered as he surmised they would, and what the other citizens of the town had thought of the inferno that must have nearly deafened them. He was jerked into wakefulness when the next two magnesium flares exploded over him, one after the other, and without waiting longer he leaped to his feet, screamed, "Come on," and ran the last twenty yards to the smoldering main gate.

He was firing as he went through, sensing more than seeing the figure of Jean-Baptiste Langarotti to his left and Kurt Semmler closing up on his right. Through the gate and inside the archway the scene was enough to stop anybody in his tracks. The arch went straight through the main building and into the courtyard. Above the courtyard the flares still burned with a stark brilliance that lit the scene behind the palace like something from the *Inferno*.

Kimba's guards had been caught asleep by the first sighting shots, which had brought them out of their lean-to barrack huts and into the center of the paved area. That was where the third shot and the succeeding forty quick-succession bombs had found them. Up one wall ran a ladder, and four mangled men hung from its rungs, caught in the back as they tried to run to the top of the enclosing wall. The rest had taken the full force of the mortars, which had exploded on stone flags and scattered lethal shards of steel in all directions.

There were piles of bodies, some still half alive, most very dead. Two army trucks and three civilian vehicles, one the presidential Mercedes, were standing shredded from end to end against the rear wall. Several palace servants about to flee the horror in the rear had apparently been grouped behind the main gate when Vlaminck's mortars came through. They were strewn all over the undercover area beneath the archway.

To right and left were further arches, each leading to what seemed to be a set of stairs to the upper floors. Without waiting to be asked, Semmler took the right-hand set, Langarotti the left. Soon there were bursts of submachine-carbine fire from each side as the two mercenaries laundered the upper floor.

Just beyond the stairs to the upper floors were doors at ground level, two on each side. Shouting to make himself heard above the screams of the maimed Vindu and the chattering of Semmler's Schmeisser upstairs, Shannon ordered the four Africans to take the ground floor. He did not have to tell them to shoot everything that moved. They were waiting to go, eyes rolling, chests heaving.

Slowly, cautiously, Shannon moved through the archway into the threshold to the courtyard at the rear. If there was any opposition left in the palace guards, it would come from there. As he stepped outside, a figure with a rifle ran screaming at him from his left. It could be that a panic-stricken Vindu was making a break for safety, but there was no time to find out. Shannon whirled and fired; the man jackknifed and blew a froth of blood from an already dead mouth onto Shannon's blouse front. The whole area and palace smelled of blood and fear, sweat and death, and over it all was the greatest intoxicant smell in the world for mercenaries, the reek of cordite.

He sensed rather than heard the scuff of footsteps in the archway behind him and swung around. From one of the side doors, into which Johnny had run to start mopping up the remaining Vindu alive inside the palace, a man had emerged. What happened when he reached the center of the flagstones under the arch, Shannon could recall later only as a kaleidoscope of images. The man saw Shannon the same time Shannon saw him, and snapped off a shot from the gun he clenched in his right hand at hip level.

Shannon felt the slug blow softly on his cheek as it passed. He fired half a second later, but the man was agile. After firing he went to the ground, rolled, and came up in the fire position a second time. Shannon's Schmeisser had let off five shots, but they went above the gunman's body as he went to the flagstones; then the magazine ran out. Before the man in the hallway could take another shot, Shannon stepped aside and out of sight behind a stone pillar, snapped out the old magazine, and slapped in a new one. Then he came around the corner, firing. The man was gone.

It was only then he became fully conscious that the gunman, stripped to the waist and barefoot, had not been an African. The skin of his torso, even in the dim light beneath the arch, had been white, and the hair dark and straight.

Shannon swore and ran back toward the embers of the gate on their hinges. He was too late.

As the gunman ran out of the shattered palace, Tiny Marc Vlaminck was walking toward the archway.

He had his bazooka cradled in both hands across his chest, the last rocket fitted into the end. The gunman never even stopped. Still running flat out, he loosed off two fast shots that emptied his magazine. They found the gun later in the long grass. It was a Makarov 9mm., and it was empty.

The Belgian took both shots in the chest, one of them in the lungs. Then the gunman was past him, dashing across the grass for safety beyond the reach of the light cast by the flares Dupree was still sending up. Shannon watched as Vlaminck, moving in a kind of slow motion, turned to face the running man, raised his bazooka and slotted it carefully across his right shoulder, took steady aim, and fired.

Not often does one see a bazooka the size of the warhead on the Yugoslav RPG-7 hit a man in the small of the back. Afterward, they could not even find more than a few pieces of cloth from his trousers.

Shannon had to throw himself flat again to avoid being broiled in the backlash of flame from the Belgian's last shot. He was still on the ground, eight yards away, when Tiny Marc dropped his weapon and crashed forward, arms outspread, across the hard earth before the gateway. Then the last of the flares went out.

Big Janni Dupree straightened up after sending off the last of his ten magnesium flares and yelled, "Sunday."

He had to shout three times before the African standing ten yards away could hear him. All three men were partly deaf from the pounding their ears had taken from the mortar and the foghorn. He shouted to Sunday to stay behind and keep watch over the mortars and the boat, then, signaling to Timothy to follow him, he began to jog-trot through the scrub and bushes along the spit of land toward the mainland. Although he had loosed off more firepower than the other four mercenaries put together, he saw no reason why he should be denied all the action.

Besides, his job was still to silence the army barracks, and he knew, from his memory of the maps on board the *Toscana,* roughly where it was. It took the pair of them ten minutes to reach the road that ran across the end of the peninsula from side to side, and, instead of turning right toward the palace, Dupree led the way left, toward the barracks. Janni and Timothy had slowed to a walk, one on each side of the laterite road, their Schmeissers pointing forward, ready to fire the moment trouble showed itself.

The trouble was around the first bend in the road. Scattered twenty minutes earlier by the first of the mortar bombs dispatched by Timothy, which fell between the hutments that made up the barracks line, the two hundred encamped men of Kimba's army had fled into the night. But about a dozen of them had regrouped in the darkness and were standing at the edge of the road, muttering in low whispers among themselves. If they had not been so deaf, Dupree and Timothy would have heard them sooner. As it was, they were almost on the group before they saw them, shadows in the shadows of the palm trees. Ten of the men were naked, having been roused from sleep. The other two had been on guard duty and were clothed and armed.

The previous night's torrential rain had left the ground so soft that most of Timothy's dozen mortar bombs had embedded themselves too deeply in the earth to have their full intended impact. The Vindu soldiers Dupree and Timothy found waiting around that corner still had something of their wits about them. One of them also had a hand grenade.

It was the sudden movement of the soldiers when they saw the white gleam of Dupree's face, from which the dye had long since run away with his sweat, that alerted the South African. He screamed, "Fire," and opened up at the group. Four of them were cut apart by the stream of slugs from the Schmeisser. The other eight ran, two more falling as Dupree's fire pursued them into the trees. One of them, as he ran, turned and hurled the thing he carried in his hand. He had never used one before and never seen one used. But it was his pride and joy, and he had always hoped to use it one day.

The grenade went high in the air, out of sight, and when it fell, it hit Timothy full in the chest. In instinctive reaction, the African veteran clutched at the object as he went over backward and, sitting on the ground, recognized it for what it was. He also saw that the fool who had thrown it had forgotten to take the pin out. Timothy had seen a mercenary catch a grenade once. He had watched as the man hurled it straight back at the enemy. Rising to his feet, Timothy whipped the pin out of the grenade and threw it as far as he could after the retreating Vindu soldiers.

It went high into the air a second time, but this time it hit a tree. There was a dull clunk, and the grenade fell short of where it was intended to go. At that moment Janni Dupree started in pursuit, a fresh magazine in his carbine. Timothy shouted a warning, but Dupree must have thought it was a scream of elation. He ran eight paces forward into the trees, still firing from the hip, and was two yards from the grenade when it exploded.

He did not remember much more. He remembered the flash and the boom, the sensation of being picked up and tossed aside like a rag doll. Then he must have passed out. He came to, lying out on the laterite road, and there was someone kneeling in the road beside him, cradling his head. He could feel that his throat was very warm, as it had been the time he had had fever as a boy—a comfortable, drowsy feeling of being half awake and half asleep. He could hear a voice talking to him, saying something repeatedly and urgently, but he could not make out the words. "Sorry, Janni, so sorry, sorry . . ."

He could understand his own name, but that was all. This language was different, not his own language, but something else. He swiveled his eyes around to the person who was holding him and made out a dark face in the half-light beneath the trees. He smiled and said quite clearly in Afrikaans, "Hallo Pieter."

He was staring up at the gap between the palm fronds when finally the clouds shifted to one side and the moon came out. It looked enormous, as it always does in Africa, brilliant white and shining. He could smell the rain in the vegetation beside the road and see the moon sitting up there glistening like a giant pearl, like the Paarl Rock after the rain. It was good to be back home again, he thought. Janni Dupree was quite content when he closed his eyes again and died.

It was half past five when enough natural daylight filtered over the horizon for the men at the palace to be able to switch off their flashlights. Not that the daylight made the scene in the courtyard look any better. But the job was done.

They had brought Vlaminck's body inside and laid it out straight in one of the side rooms off the ground-floor hallway. Beside him lay Janni Dupree, brought up from the seashore road by three of the Africans. Johnny was also dead, evidently surprised and shot by the white bodyguard who had seconds later stopped Vlaminck's last bazooka rocket. The three of them were side by side.

Semmler had summoned Shannon to the main bedroom on the second floor and showed him by flashlight the figure he had gunned down as it tried to clamber out of the window.

"That's him," said Shannon.

There were six survivors from among the dead President's domestic staff. They had been found cowering in one of the cellars, which they had found, more by instinct than by logic, to be the best security from the rain of fire from the skies. These were being used as forced labor to tidy up. Every room in the main part of the palace was examined, and the bodies of all the other friends of Kimba and palace servants that had been lying around the rooms were carried down and dumped in the courtyard at the back. The remnants of the door could not be replaced, so a large carpet taken from one of the state rooms was hung over the entrance to mask the view inside.

At five o'clock Semmler had gone back to the *Toscana* in one of the speedboats, towing the other two behind him. Before leaving, he had contacted the *Toscana* on his walkie-talkie to give the code word meaning all was in order.

He was back by six-thirty with the African doctor and the same three boats, this time loaded with stores, the remaining mortar bombs, the eighty bundles containing the remaining Schmeissers, and nearly a ton of 9mm. ammunition.

At six, according to a letter of instruction Shannon had sent to Captain Waldenberg, the *Toscana* had begun to broadcast three words on the frequency to which Endean was listening. The words, *paw-paw, cassave,* and *mango,* meant respectively: The operation went ahead as planned, it was completely successful, and Kimba is dead.

When the African doctor had viewed the scene of carnage at the palace, he sighed and said, "I suppose it was necessary."

"It was necessary," affirmed Shannon and asked the older man to set about the task he had been brought to do.

By nine, nothing had stirred in the town and the clearing-up process was almost complete. The burial of the Vindu would have to be done later, when there was more manpower available. Two of the speedboats were back at the *Toscana,* slung aboard and stowed below, while the third was hidden in a creek not far from the harbor. All traces of the mortars on the point had been removed, the tubes and baseplates brought inside, the rocket-launchers and packing crates dropped out at sea. Everything and everyone else had been brought inside the palace, which, although battered to hell from the inside, bore only two areas of shattered tiles, three broken windows in the front, and the destroyed door to indicate from the outside that it had taken a beating.

At ten, Semmler and Langarotti joined Shannon in the main dining room, where the mercenary leader was finishing off some jam and bread that he had found in the presidential kitchen. Both men reported on the results of their searches. Semmler told Shannon the radio room was intact, apart from several bullet holes in the wall, and the transmitter would still send. Kimba's private cellar in the basement had yielded at last to the persuasion of several magazines of ammunition. The national treasury was apparently in a safe at the rear of the cellar, and the national armory was stacked around the walls—enough guns and ammunition to keep an army of two or three hundred men going for several months in action.

"So what now?" asked Semmler when Shannon had heard him out.

"So now we wait," said Shannon.

"Wait for what?"

Shannon picked his teeth with a spent match. He thought of Janni Dupree and Tiny Marc lying below on the floor, and of Johnny, who would not liberate another farmer's goat for his evening supper. Langarotti was slowly stropping his knife on the leather band around his left fist.

"We wait for the new government," said Shannon.

The American-built 1-ton truck carrying Simon Endean arrived just after one in the afternoon. There was another European at the wheel, and Endean sat beside him, clutching a large-bore hunting rifle. Shannon heard the growl of the engine as the truck left the shore road and came slowly up to the front entrance of the palace, where the carpet hung lifeless in the humid air, covering the gaping hole where the main gate had been.

He watched from an upper window as Endean

climbed suspiciously down, looked at the carpet and the other pockmarks on the front of the building, and examined the eight black guards at attention before the gate.

Endean's trip had not been completely without incident. After the *Toscana*'s radio call that morning, it had taken him two hours to persuade Colonel Bobi that he was actually going back into his own country within hours of the coup. The man had evidently not won his colonelcy by personal courage.

They had set off from the neighboring capital by road at nine-thirty on the hundred-mile drive to Clarence. In Europe that distance may take two hours; in Africa it takes more. They arrived at the border in midmorning and began the haggle to bribe their way past the Vindu guards, who had still not heard of the night's coup in the capital. Colonel Bobi, hiding behind a pair of large and very dark glasses and dressed in a white flowing robe like a nightshirt, posed as their car-boy, a personal servant who, in Africa, never requires papers to cross a border. Endean's papers were in order, like those of the man he brought with him, a hulking strong-arm from London's East End, who had been recommended to Endean as one of the most feared protectors in Whitechapel and a former enforcer for the Kray Gang. Ernie Locke was being paid a very handsome fee to keep Endean alive and well and was carrying a gun under his shirt, acquired locally through the offices of ManCon's mining enterprise in the republic. Tempted by the money offered, he had already made the mistake of thinking, like Endean, that a good hatchet man in the East End will automatically make a good hatchet man in Africa.

After crossing the frontier, the truck had made good time until it blew a tire ten miles short of Clarence. With Endean mounting guard with his rifle, Locke had changed the tire while Bobi cowered under the canvas in the back. That was when the trouble started. A handful of Vindu troops, fleeing from Clarence, had spotted them and loosed off half a dozen shots. They all went wide except one, which hit the tire Locke had just replaced. The journey was finished in first gear on a flat tire.

Shannon leaned out the window and called down to Endean.

The latter looked up. "Everything okay?" he called.

"Sure," said Shannon. "But get out of sight. No one seems to have moved yet, but someone is bound to start snooping soon."

Endean led Colonel Bobi and Locke through the curtain, and they mounted to the second floor, where Shannon was waiting. When they were seated in the presidential dining room, Endean asked for a full report on the previous night's battle. Shannon gave it to him.

"Kimba's palace guard?" asked Endean.

For answer Shannon led him to the rear window, whose shutters were closed, pushed one open, and pointed down into the courtyard, from which a ferocious buzzing of flies mounted.

Endean looked out and drew back. "The lot?" he asked.

"The lot," said Shannon. "Wiped out."

"And the army?"

"Twenty dead, the rest scattered. All left their arms behind except perhaps a couple of dozen bolt-action Mausers. No problem. The arms have been gathered up and brought inside."

"The presidential armory?"

"In the cellar, under our control."

"And the national radio transmitter?"

"Downstairs on the ground floor. Intact. We haven't tried the electricity circuits yet, but the radio seems to have a separate Diesel-powered generator."

Endean nodded, satisfied. "Then there's nothing for it but for the new President to announce the success of his coup last night, the formation of a new government, and to take over control," he said.

"What about security?" asked Shannon. "There's no

army left intact until they filter back, and not all of the Vindu may want to serve under the new man."

Endean grinned. "They'll come back when the word spreads that the new man has taken over, and they'll serve under him just so long as they know who is in charge. And they will. In the meantime, this group you seem to have recruited will suffice. After all, they're black, and no European diplomats here are likely to recognize the difference between one black and another."

"Do you?" asked Shannon.

Endean shrugged. "No," he said, "but it doesn't matter. By the way, let me introduce the new President of Zangaro."

He gestured toward the Zangaran colonel, who had been surveying the room he already knew well, a broad grin on his face.

"Former commander of the Zangaran army, successful operator of a coup d'état as far as the world knows, and new president of Zangaro. Colonel Antoine Bobi."

Shannon rose, faced the colonel, and bowed. Bobi's grin grew even wider.

Shannon walked to the door at the end of the dining room. "Perhaps the President would like to examine the presidential office," he said. Endean translated.

Bobi nodded and lumbered across the tiled floor and through the door, followed by Shannon. It closed behind them. Five seconds later came the crash of a single shot.

After Shannon reappeared, Endean sat for a moment staring at him. "What was that?" he asked unnecessarily.

"A shot," said Shannon.

Endean was on his feet, across the room, and standing in the open doorway to the study. He turned around, ashen-faced, hardly able to speak.

"You shot him," he whispered. "All this bloody way, and you shot him. You're mad, Shannon, you're fucking crazy."

His voice rose with his rage and bafflement. "You don't know what you've done, you stupid, blundering maniac, you bloody mercenary idiot."

Shannon sat back in the armchair behind the dining table, gazing at Endean with scant interest. From the corner of his eye he saw the bodyguard's hand move under his floppy shirt.

The second crash seemed louder to Endean, for it was nearer. Ernie Locke went back out of his chair in a complete somersault and sprawled across the tiles, varying the pattern of the old colonial marquetry with a thin filament of blood that came from his midriff. He was quite dead, for the soft bullet had gone through to shatter his spine.

Shannon brought his hand out from under the oak table and laid the Makarov 9mm. automatic on the table. A wisp of blue smoke wriggled out of the end of the barrel.

Endean seemed to sag at the shoulders, as if the knowledge of the certain loss of his personal fortune, promised by Sir James Manson when Bobi was installed, had suddenly been compounded by the realization that Shannon was the most completely dangerous man he had ever met. But it was a bit late for that.

Semmler appeared in the doorway of the study, behind Endean, and Langarotti slipped quietly through the dining-room door from the corridor. Both held Schmeissers, catch off, very steady, pointing at Endean.

Shannon rose. "Come on," he said, "I'll drive you back to the border. From there you can walk."

The single unpunctured tire from the two Zangaran trucks in the courtyard had been fitted to the vehicle that had brought Endean into the country. The canvas behind the cab had been taken away, and three African soldiers crouched in the back with submachine carbines. Another twenty, fully uniformed and equipped, were being marshaled into a line outside the palace.

In the hallway, close to the shattered door, they met a middle-aged African in civilian clothes. Shannon nodded to him and exchanged a few words.

"Everything okay, Doctor?"

"Yes, so far. I have arranged with my people to send a hundred volunteer workers to clean up. Also another fifty will be here this afternoon for fitting out and equipping. Seven of the Zangaran men on the list of notables have been contacted at their homes and have agreed to serve. They will meet this evening."

"Good. Perhaps you had better take time off to draft the first bulletin from the new government. It should be broadcast as soon as possible. Ask Mr. Semmler to try to get the radio working. If it can't be done, we'll use the ship."

"I have just spoken to Mr. Semmler," said the African. "He has been in touch with the *Toscana* by walkie-talkie. Captain Waldenberg reports there is another ship out there trying to raise Clarence port authorities with a request for permission to enter port. No one is replying, but Captain Waldenberg can hear her on the radio."

"Any identification?" asked Shannon.

"Mr. Semmler says she identifies herself as the Russian ship *Komarov*, a freighter."

"Tell Mr. Semmler to man the port radio before going to work on the palace transmitter. Tell him to make to *Komarov*: 'Permission refused. Permanently.' Thank you, Doctor."

They parted, and Shannon took Endean back to his truck. He took the wheel himself and swung the truck back on the road to the hinterland and the border.

"Who was that?" asked Endean sourly as the truck sped along the peninsula, past the shantytown of the immigrant workers, where all seemed to be bustle and activity. With amazement Endean noticed that each crossroads had an armed soldier with a submachine carbine standing on point duty.

"The man in the hallway?" asked Shannon.

"Yes."

"That was Doctor Okoye."

"A witch doctor, I suppose."

"Actually he's an Oxford Ph.D."

"Friend of yours?"

"Yes."

There was no more conversation until they were on the highway toward the north.

"All right," said Endean at last, "I know what you've done. You've ruined one of the biggest and richest coups that has ever been attempted. You don't know that, of course. You're too bloody thick. What I'd like to know is, why? In God's name, why?"

Shannon thought for a moment, keeping the truck steady on the bumpy road, which had deteriorated to a dirt track.

"You made two mistakes, Endean," he said carefully. Endean started at the sound of his real name.

"You assumed that because I'm a mercenary, I'm automatically stupid. It never seemed to occur to you that we are both mercenaries, along with Sir James Manson and most of the people who have power in this world. The second mistake was that you assumed all black people were the same, because to you they look the same."

"I don't follow you."

"You did a lot of research on Zangaro; you even found out about the tens of thousands of immigrant workers who virtually keep this place running. It never occurred to you that those workers form a community of their own. They're a third tribe, the most intelligent and hard-working one in the country. Given half a chance, they can play a part in the political life of the country. What's more, you failed to recognize that the new army of Zangaro, and therefore the power in the country, might be recruited from among that third community. In fact, it just has been. Those soldiers you saw were neither Vindu nor Caja. There were fifty in uniform and armed when you were in the palace, and by tonight there'll be another fifty. In five days there will be over four hundred new soldiers in

Clarence—untrained, of course, but looking efficient enough to keep law and order. They'll be the real power in this country from now on. There was a coup d'état last night, all right, but it wasn't conducted for or on behalf of Colonel Bobi."

"For whom, then?"

"For the general."

"Which general?"

Shannon told him the name.

Endean faced him, mouth open in horror. "Not him. He was defeated, exiled."

"For the moment, yes. Not necessarily forever. Those immigrant workers are his people. They call them the Jews of Africa. There are one and a half million of them scattered over this continent. In many areas they do most of the work and have most of the brains. Here in Zangaro they live in the shantytown behind Clarence."

"That stupid great idealistic bastard—"

"Careful," warned Shannon.

"Why?"

Shannon jerked his head over his shoulder. "They're the general's soldiers too."

Endean turned and looked at the three impassive faces above the three Schmeisser barrels.

"They don't speak English all that well, do they?"

"The one in the middle," said Shannon mildly, "was a chemist once. Then he became a soldier; then his wife and four children were wiped out by a Saladin armored car. They're made by Alvis in Coventry, you know. He doesn't like the people who were behind that."

Endean was silent for a few more miles. "What happens now?" he asked.

"The Committee of National Reconciliation takes over," said Shannon. "Four Vindu members, four Caja, and two from the immigrant community. But the army will be made up of the people behind you. And this country will be used as a base and a headquarters. From here the newly trained men will go back one day to avenge what was done to them. Maybe the general will come and set up residence here—in effect, to rule."

"You expect to get away with that?"

"You expected to impose that slobbering ape Bobi and get away with it. At least the new government will be moderately fair. That mineral deposit, or whatever it was, that you were after—I don't know where or what it is, but I can deduce that there has to be something here to interest Sir James Manson. No doubt the new government will find it, eventually. And no doubt it will be exploited. But if you want it, you will have to pay for it. A fair price, a market price. Tell Sir James that when you get back home."

Around the corner they came within view of the border post. News travels fast in Africa, even without telephone, and the Vindu soldiers on the border post were gone.

Shannon stopped the truck and pointed ahead. "You can walk the rest," he said.

Endean climbed down. He looked back at Shannon with undiluted hatred. "You still haven't explained why," he said. "You've explained what and how, but not why."

Shannon stared ahead up the road. "For nearly two years," he said musingly, "I watched between half a million and a million small kids starved to death because of people like you and Manson. It was done basically so that you and your kind could make bigger profits through a vicious and totally corrupt dictatorship, and it was done in the name of law and order, of legality and constitutional justification. I may be a fighter, I may be a killer, but I am not a bloody sadist. I worked out for myself how it was done and why it was done, and who were the men behind it. Visible up front were a bunch of politicians and Foreign Office men, but they are just a cage full of posturing apes, neither seeing nor caring past their interdepartmental squabbles and their re-election. Invisible behind them were profiteers like your precious James Manson.

That's why I did it. Tell Manson when you get back home. I'd like him to know. Personally. From me. Now get walking."

Ten yards on, Endean turned around. "Don't ever come back to London, Shannon," he called. "We can deal with people like you there."

"I won't," yelled Shannon. Under his breath he murmured, "I won't ever have to." Then he turned the truck around and headed for the peninsula and Clarence.

get and the Corsican went back to Europe. The
last news of Langarotti he had, he was in Vienna,
recruiting Hussein men who had fled there, preparing
to mount another operation on [...]

EPILOGUE

The new government was duly installed, and at the last
count was ruling humanely and well. There was hardly
a mention of the coup in the European newspapers,
just a brief piece in *Le Monde* to say that dissident
units of the Zangaran army had toppled the President
on the eve of Independence Day and that a governing
council had taken over the administration pending national elections. But there was nothing in the newspaper to report that one of the council's first acts was
to inform Ambassador Dobrovolsky that the Soviet
mining survey team would not be received, and new
arrangements for surveying the area would be made
in due course.

Big Janni Dupree and Tiny Marc Vlaminck were
buried down on the point, beneath the palm trees,
where the wind blows off the gulf. The graves were left
unmarked at Shannon's request. The body of Johnny
was taken by his own people, who keened over him
and buried him according to their own ways.

Simon Endean and Sir James Manson kept quiet
about their parts in the affair. There was really nothing
they could say publicly.

Shannon gave Jean-Baptiste Langarotti the £5000
remaining in his money belt from the operations bud-

get, and the Corsican went back to Europe. He was last heard of heading for Burundi, where he wanted to train the Hutu partisans who were trying to oppose the Tutsi-dominated dictatorship of Micombero. As he told Shannon when they parted on the shore, "It's not really the money. It was never for the money."

Shannon wrote out letters to Signor Ponti in Genoa in the name of Keith Brown, ordering him to hand over the bearer shares controlling the ownership of the *Toscana* in equal parts to Captain Waldenberg and Kurt Semmler. A year later Semmler sold out his share to Waldenberg, who raised a mortgage to pay for it. Then Semmler went off to another war. He died in South Sudan, when he, Ron Gregory, and Rip Kirby were laying a mine to knock out a Sudanese Saladin armored car. The mine went off, killing Kirby instantly and badly injuring Semmler and Gregory. Gregory got home via the British Embassy in Ethiopia, but Semmler died in the bush.

The last thing Shannon did was to send letters to his bank in Switzerland through Langarotti, ordering the bank to make a credit transfer of £5000 to the parents of Janni Dupree in Paarl, Cape Province, and another in the same sum to a woman called Anna who ran a bar in the Kleinstraat in Ostend's red-light district.

He died a month after the coup, the way he had told Julie he wanted to go, with a gun in his hand and blood in his mouth and a bullet in the chest. But it was his own gun and his own bullet. It was not the risks or the danger or the fighting that destroyed him, but the trivial black mole on the back of his neck. That was what he had learned from Dr. Dunois in the Paris surgery. Up to a year if he took things easy, less than six months if he pushed himself, and the last month would be bad. So he went out alone when he judged the time had come, and walked into the jungle with his gun and a fat envelope full of typescript, which was sent to a friend in London some weeks later.

The natives who saw him walking alone, and later brought him back to the town for burial, said he was whistling when he went. Being simple peasants, growers of yams and cassava, they did not know what the whistling was. It was a tune called "Spanish Harlem."

ABOUT THE AUTHOR

FREDERICK FORSYTH was born in Ashford, England, in 1938 and educated at Tonbridge School. He has been an RAF fighter pilot, newspaperman, foreign correspondent and a BBC radio and television reporter. Mr. Forsyth has traveled to more than forty countries in Europe, the Middle East, North and West Africa, and speaks several languages including French, German and Russian. His first book, *The Biafra Story*, was published in 1969, followed later by his bestsellers *The Day of the Jackal* and *The Odessa File*, both of which were made into motion pictures.

RELAX!
SIT DOWN
and Catch Up On Your Reading!

☐ THE PLANTATION by George McNeill (2232—$1.7·

☐ THE BELL JAR by Sylvia Plath (6400—$1.7·

☐ THE REINCARNATION OF PETER PROUD by Max Ehrlich (6444—$1.7·

☐ HER by Anonymous (6669—$1.5·

☐ THE EXORCIST by William Peter Blatty (7200—$1.7·

☐ THE DAY OF THE JACKAL by Frederick Forsyth (7377—$1.7·

☐ THE ODESSA FILE by Frederick Forsyth (7744—$1.7·

☐ THE HARRAD EXPERIMENT by Robert Rimmer (7950—$1.5·

☐ THE LOVE MACHINE by Jacqueline Susann (7970—$1.7·

☐ ONCE IS NOT ENOUGH by Jacqueline Susann (8000—$1.9·

☐ THE MANNINGS by Fred Mustard Stewart (8400—$1.9·

☐ BURR by Gore Vidal (8484—$1.95

☐ JAWS by Peter Benchley (8500—$1.95

☐ THE BEGGARS ARE COMING by Mary Loos (8540—$1.7·

☐ THE FAN CLUB by Irving Wallace (8727—$1.95

☐ TINKER, TAILOR, SOLDIER, SPY by John Le Carré (8844—$1.9·

☐ THE DOGS OF WAR by Frederick Forsyth (8884—$1.95

Buy them at your local bookstore or use this handy coupon for ordering